GW01377188

THE OTHER SIDE OF SILENCE

THE OTHER SIDE OF SILENCE

Helen Reno

The Book Guild Ltd
Sussex, England

First published in Great Britain in 2002 by
The Book Guild Ltd
25 High Street
Lewes, East Sussex
BN7 2LU

Copyright © Helen Reno 2002

The right of Helen Reno to be identified as the author of this work has been asserted by her in accordance with the Copyright, Designs and Patents Act 1988.

All rights reserved. No part of this publication may be reproduced, transmitted, or stored in a retrieval system, in any form, or by any means, without permission in writing from the publishers, nor be otherwise circulated in any form of binding or cover other than that in which it is published and without a similar condition being imposed on the subsequent purchaser.

All characters in this publication are fictitious and any resemblance to real people, alive or dead, is purely coincidental.

Typesetting in Baskerville by
SetSystems Ltd, Saffron Walden, Essex

Printed in Great Britain by
Antony Rowe Ltd, Chippenham, Wiltshire

A catalogue record for this book is
available from the British Library

ISBN 1 85776 651 2

1

Tick, tick, tick went the noise in Sylvia's head, like a metronome. It had been there since she boarded the plane and was driving her crazy. She tried to concentrate on the cabin sounds. There was the hissing of air vents, the occasional tinkle of the service bell, desultory conversations petering out. The engine drone was lulling people to sleep. To her, it was as irritating as the buzz of a giant mosquito which had the added disadvantage that, out of habit, she instinctively expected a silence to signify the dive. *Don't be silly.*

Her head throbbed on: tick, tick, tick. Dilating, pulsing blood vessels causing migraine from all the stress, no doubt. It had begun at Manchester Airport.

She had meant to say goodbye to her husband but couldn't work out how. It should have been simple. Put her arms around him and kiss him. But Ian rubbed his hands nervously, scolded the kids for fidgeting, looked at his watch, edged her towards Passport Control and pushed the hand luggage she had put down in order to take her leave, to the point of no return. No need for panic. There was plenty of time. She knew that, yet the pressure built up, her breathing quickened with needless anxiety and she had to exercise restraint not to stand on tiptoe and box his ears for relief. A few years back she would have laughed all this off and given him a hug and a kiss, all the same. She wouldn't even have minded his blush and the look over his shoulder to see if anyone had noticed such un-English behaviour. In time, her natural effusiveness withered and she felt like soliciting a stranger.

She made up by fussing over the children and went through Passport Control after a last look at her departing family: Ian, his lanky frame slightly stooped, a sign of tensed stomach muscles, the usual way he manifested stress; her ten-year-old son, Peter, trying to match Ian's long strides; her eight-year-old daughter, Diana, little legs tripping over each other to keep up, brown curls bouncing, catching the fluorescent light from the ceiling, sparkling. Peter's lighter head, almost as blond as his father's, turned for a last secretive smile. 'Come back soon,' he mouthed. Sylvia smiled back, crossing her heart.

By the time she boarded the plane, her enthusiasm for the trip had evaporated. But then, it had always been so: dreaming of being somewhere else, and every time she found herself in a car or boat or train or aeroplane that could get her there, the doubts would begin. Worse still, such doubts were always vindicated, but she didn't give up searching until she became a mother. Lately, she had let Ian pressurise her to seek a job because the children were old enough. It coincided with an advertisement in the journal for a conference in her own speciality.

'Fate,' she said tongue in cheek, and applied.

'Do you have to go all the way to Brazil to renew your contacts and kick-start your career, as you call it? Wouldn't anywhere nearer do?' had been Ian's refrain for weeks.

He ought to have known, she didn't do anything by halves. Still, should she have left the children even for such a short time? She hadn't prepared them for it. The longest she had been separated from them was a rare evening out when they slept at her mother-in-law's house just a couple of streets away from their home. Their school friends were more hardened, adapted to single parenting or working mothers, sometimes both, like she had been at their age. Routine, security, what people called normality, were not things she knew much about, nor did she value them, yet she insisted the children had everything she had not. Once they grew up, she would be free to do as she wanted, and they could reject conventions if they so wished. It would be their choice, not hers.

Even on the odd occasion she worked, Sylvia made sure she was there to take them to school and pick them up. It meant accepting jobs menial for her qualifications, mentally unchallenging, poorly remunerating, which left her at the mercy of Ian's economic tyranny. She didn't feel an unliberated woman, however contradictory it appeared. Freedom meant having a choice and being prepared to pay the price. All Ian wanted was extra wages and very little extra responsibility.

'How about sharing child care?' she asked time and time again.

'Why not?' Ian answered just as often. But if a baby cried at night, he turned the other way and said it would expand its lungs. If they hurt, it would harden them up and so forth. She was not going to let the children suffer to prove to herself, or anyone else, she was liberated.

Tick, tick, tick . . . like a clock in her head measuring time. She'd soon be back.

The smell of food wafted through the cabin. People woke up. There was a surge of mild excitement. No doubt, the expectation couldn't stand up to the reality of plastic food, but Sylvia, too, was looking forward to it. Something to relieve the tedium. It might silence the ticking that reverberated in her skull, echoing her heartbeat.

Next to her, a desiccated lady, weighted down with gold jewellery the size of slave fetters, and her dapper little husband beamed at her, not for the first time. They had been haunting her since they saw her in the transit lounge of Miami Airport. They had tried to catch her eye, open up conversation. Small talk wasn't Sylvia's thing. It embarrassed her. She never knew what to say, and in the end she would spurt out any old stupid thing that would make her cringe for hours afterwards. To keep them at bay, she had fussed with her file, rereading her notes until the flight was announced, and then she dashed away, leaving the file behind. Thankfully, somebody handed it back to her. *Oh, yes!* No matter how much in a hurry she had been, she noticed. One doesn't see it that often: perfection. And boy, was he aware of it! So much so, she pretended not to have seen him at all. She hurried to board, only to find that the couple she was trying to avoid came to sit next to her. It might have been paranoia, but she suspected that they had contrived it, somehow.

She ignored their overtures again and shrugged out of her jacket without unfastening her seat belt, then bent awkwardly to rummage in her handbag at her feet. A cigarette would keep her occupied as well as calm her and ease the noise in her head. She sighed. It was a no-smoking flight. Better replace the cigarettes and lighter in her pocket to save herself the discomfort of bending down again. She could undo the belt, of course, but maybe not. It shouldn't be long now. Where were they? The window was two seats beyond her, and she craned her neck to peer through it.

The man, who sat by the window, rose immediately. 'You could have my seat if . . .'

'Don't undo your seat belt!' Sylvia said before she could check herself.

The man laughed and pointed, first overhead to show that there was no sign indicating fastening of seat belts, and then at his wife, who also had her belt undone.

Stupid! Sylvia was not sure if she thought they were stupid for undoing their belts or she for being so jumpy, but nothing would make her undo hers or move from where she was meant to sit. 'I can see well enough from here,' she said.

'It's not all that exciting a view, anyway,' the man said and added, 'from up here,' before buzzing for the stewardess. 'What you need, little lady,' he continued, oblivious to Sylvia's grimace at the 'little', 'is a stiff drink. It works in cases like this. My wife and I noticed.' He tapped his nose. 'In Miami my wife said you must be nervous of flying. Not good to be alone. So . . .'

Nervous of flying? Certainly not. She was nervous of heights, yes. She couldn't stand six feet above ground level without the impression that her stomach hit the soles of her feet and her joints loosened as if her limbs wanted to weigh anchor and go their own way. But in an aeroplane, she normally felt safe, even on the flight from Nigeria where the cabin crew had screamed 'Women and children first!' – and that was for boarding the plane. After she had fought for a spare seat, she found the belt was not working and a side arm was missing, yet she found it amusing. What made the difference was the sense of being enclosed. The wall of metal between her and space.

The man was still talking and stretched over to pat Sylvia's hand which unconsciously gripped the arm of her seat. Sylvia snatched it away. It was not just that his fingers reminded her of slugs, she abhorred being touched by strangers as much as she welcomed it from loved ones, and she was meant to be frustrated in both. But he meant well and there was no need for rudeness. Better say something to make up for it. From his accent and looks, he was obviously of Latin extraction. The question would be superfluous, but then the function of politeness was not information but to smooth contact between people.

'From Brazil?' she said, looking from the husband to the wife and trying to smile.

He sat down again, obviously unoffended. 'Yes, Manaus. You meeting somebody there?'

'No.'

He exchanged words with his wife in Portuguese and then back to Sylvia. 'You must come and see us. Can't have such a charming little lady,' he winked playfully at her, 'on holiday alone.'

'I'm attending a Medicinal Plant Conference,' Sylvia said and her irritation resurfaced, both at his surprise that she should travel for anything other than pleasure, which he was now communicating to his wife, and that she had felt obliged to justify herself.

The wife showed her approval for Sylvia's unsuspected talents by throwing her arms around her, gold bangles jingling and showered her in Portuguese.

'We can still take care of you. Show you around . . .' the husband was translating while Sylvia extricated herself from the woman's tentacles with a sigh. It was not the first time that people thought her unable to look after herself.

The food trolley had by now reached them and interrupted the conversation. Afterwards, the couple succumbed to food and wine and fell asleep. The plane tipped to one side as it made a turn, and Sylvia glimpsed the view below. The Brazilian had been right about it being uninspiring. The vast Pointillist canvas, each dot a variation on the green theme, was broken by a glimmer of pink snaking through it. A tributary of the Amazon, no doubt. But she had a fair idea of what that camouflage concealed from previous experience in the African jungle, and was as keen as any addict to rediscover its thrills.

She longed to feel its moist breath over her skin; to hear its twitters, gurgles, screeches and cackles; to smell the earthiness all around as it regenerated itself through endless decomposition and recycling; to experience the shock of a brilliant bloom, absent yesterday and invisible tomorrow, leaping out of a sea of green; to taste the fear when it frowned in the mysterious depth of its shadows, relieved only by the unexpected smile of a sunlit clearing; to bear the weight of its enormity like a lover's body.

In such an embrace, she could forget everything even this nerve-racking journey. Funny enough, just thinking about it had helped. There was silence in her head. Her eyelids grew heavy. *That's right. Relax.* She took a deep breath and . . .

She came to, adrenalin pumping furiously through her, every sense alert, every nerve tinkling. *Oh my God!* How could she not have realised what she had been listening to all the time? She opened her mouth to scream a warning.

Her throat was constricted. The shriek exploded in her head, or maybe it came from the plane, which lurched sideways like a startled animal. Whatever its source, it seemed to have generated a wave of compressed air that surged in the enclosed space of the cabin, slammed her against the back rest and smashed into the nearby window. The glass burst outwards into millions of tiny suns. With the sudden decompression, released energy exploded through the gap, ripping the metal frame into giant jaws. The row of seats in front of Sylvia shivered in the vacuum left behind, it convulsed with increasing violence, shook itself off its moorings, hovered for an instant before being sucked into the gaping mouth, snagged on the teeth, a hand appeared above the back of the seat like that of a drowning man, and it was gone.

After the initial numbness, different parts of Sylvia reclaimed their shape in her consciousness in a biased inventory. Her ears, lips, hands and feet swelled and rounded and throbbed into life with a prominence unmerited by their share in her anatomy. The wind tore at her clothes. Her hair whipped her face. She had glimpses of mouths opened on distorted faces as they were pelted with bags, boxes, bottles, coats, disgorged from the overhead compartments of the aircraft's cabin now steadily tilting forward, their contents trailing horizontally in a frontal assault. She could even detect the ammoniacal odour of urine and cold sweat.

The Brazilians next to her fought to hold on to their seats. They were losing their battle against the syphoning force of the wind. The wife levitated first. Her husband followed. Sylvia released her grip on the arm rests to grab them. The woman's dress tore off instantly. She disappeared into the steel-toothed void, together with cups, bottles, clothes and papers passing in a constant stream inches from Sylvia's nose. The man was beyond her reach, but he managed to get hold of the jagged edge. The pull was too strong, or the pain in his hands grasping the sharp metal too much, or both. Sylvia's last glimpse of him resembled a frequent nightmare: a rag doll tumbling through space in a chaotic semblance of flight. All that was left to remind her this was real, were the warm spots on her face from the blood trailing after him.

Sylvia repented her ingratitude to the pair's friendly approach, but she convinced herself she would rejoin them soon. That she hadn't so far she owed to her seat belt. If only they had listened to her. Now she prayed that the pain from the seat belt cutting into her would continue. Just in case, she held onto the arm rests with renewed vigour, her knuckles turning white, the fingers frozen in place. Instinctive and futile. It had not prevented the Brazilian couple going overboard or most of the passengers piling with trolleys and baggage at the front end of the plane as it kept its inexorable nosedive.

Some people hung on the backs of seats still bolted to the floor, in spite of the vibration, or to the shelves above. Bizarre branches caught in a hurricane, a matter of time when they would be torn off by the savage energy.

Sylvia reverted to her childhood trick in times of agony, terror or despair: reciting verses while she tried to imagine how wonderful it would be when the ordeal was over.

'He then swooped down on the waves like a seagull . . .'

The warmth that would engulf her; the tranquillity that would follow; the luxuriant feel of safety; the certainty that, no matter what, life was sweet!

'. . . drenching its thickly feathered wings with spray as it hunts the fish . . .'

That this nightmare would end sometime, there was no doubt. It was too irrational and she would admit it to nobody, but at times like this, she had a perverse conviction that fate, luck, whatever, was on her side.

'. . . down the fearful gulfs . . .'

She had been in danger before, not as dire but serious enough, and something had intervened to save her. Always.

She felt a crunch immediately beneath her independent of the shuddering of the plane as a whole. The vibration transmitted from the base of her spine to her skull. It became progressively violent, threatening to dislodge her head from the rest of her.

The recitation speeded up: '... about the cave grew a thick wood: alders, aspens and fragrant cypresses.'

The man holding on to the back of the chair vacated by the Brazilian was thrown off.

'In it roosted wide winged birds ...'

His eyes bulged with terror. He grabbed at the shelf above Sylvia.

'... horned owls and falcons ...'

He jerked his legs. A boot caught her on the jaw. Her brain rattled. The cocoon of silence that had enveloped her since the explosion shattered. Out spilled waves of demented shrieks, mechanical crunches, bangs and rattles and the maniacal whistle of the wind that swept her into a vortex of panic. Mind-shattering. Dehumanising. Primitive. Thrashing to escape her bonds. Her throat raw from screaming. Something should make it stop. Death or madness, she didn't care. It had to stop.

Then she was floating on a warm cushion of air, bathed in blinding light. She felt diaphanous, insubstantial. Peace all around. Bliss. Out-of-life experience or out-of-mind? No time to decide as her limbs changed from gossamer to lead. She was going down. Everything else reversed direction: her skirt, a tent above her lap; her hair pulled by the roots straight up as if she sat on top of a powerful air vent; her inner organs headed for her mouth; her worst nightmare, a terrible reality.

2

Mark walked along the beach, his feet sinking into the sand. When a stray ball zoomed by, he instinctively plucked it out of the air. He was about to tuck it under his arm and burst into a run, the kind that used to draw howls from the crowds in the stands back home not a million years ago, but restrained himself. With a rueful smile he lobbed it over to the young people playing volleyball. They had to run a lot to catch it. His throw was not as gentle as he intended.

Mark didn't like travelling abroad. One could find anything one wanted in the States if one bothered to travel around, so why bother? And how many places could compete with the setting of San Francisco, for instance? He was not sure anymore. São Sebastião do Rio de Janeiro, as the guidebook called this place, sprawling in the sun with her golden hems trailing in the sea and her shoulders cloaked in emerald, could compete quite successfully. He ought to be grateful to Paul for forcing him to come. In stages. First it was just Miami.

'You need the break,' Paul had said.
'Why Miami?'
Paul draped himself across the seat from Mark, a bourbon in his hand. For once, someone else piloted his private jet. 'It's no trick,' he said. 'I have to pick up some geological reports, that's all. You don't think I will lease a chunk of

jungle with nothing in it but trees?' He swirled the crushed ice in his glass. There was hardly any bourbon left to give it colour. 'A mineral company needs minerals.' He took a swig, screwed his features and decided to add the missing colour to his ice. 'It won't take long. By the time you finish a couple of drinks in the VIP lounge, I will be back. Then off to sunny Rio.'

'What about my work?'

There was a blue glint from behind Paul's dark fringe. 'Your rich clients can have their haemorrhoids or ingrown toenails taken care of without your help. That's what staff is for. I, on the other hand,' and here he revealed the perfect state of his teeth, 'couldn't do without your sparkling repartee.'

Mark nursed his beer like he had done for the last half-hour. He did not indulge in alcohol or even coffee. People, albeit rich ones as Paul had just reminded him, put their lives in his hands. The least he could do was to keep them steady. Angry as he felt at the accusation of selling out to Mammon – he didn't give shit about the sarcasm for social inadequacy – he was not going to defend himself. There was no defence. But he should say something, or Paul would realise he had found the target. Not that anybody could accuse Paul of ever missing it. Two sentences, two bull's eyes.

'You don't have to go, either,' he said. 'Your lawyers could negotiate the takeover of a tinpot company in the back of beyond.'

'See what a bit of relaxation does? You strung two sentences consecutively.' Paul laughed at Mark's grunt. 'The lawyers will be there, too,' he continued. 'They will deal with the facts, but what about instinct?'

'For Latino bimbos?'

It was Paul's turn to ignore the insult. 'If I felt for one moment that something wasn't right with the transaction, I could abort the whole thing like that,' and he snapped his fingers.

Mark was unconvinced. He had allowed Paul to drag him

into his glamorous world before, and ended up married to Nicol.

That was unfair. It wasn't Paul's fault he was dazzled or Nicol's for dazzling him, and Paul had a point. In new surroundings, he could look at things more objectively.

'You may be right,' he said.

'Am I not always?'

Paul had chosen the Super Deluxe Hotel Meridien-Rio, right at the beginning of the Copacabana beach, for the panoramic view from the rooftop restaurant, he said and, of course, its business centre. It was a lot of bull. He never made the rooftop restaurant last night, and Mark would be surprised if he did so tonight. There were always better attractions on offer, and as for the business facilities, there he was on the beach in his swimming trunks with government representatives. They had arrived as scantily clad, carrying briefcases. Obviously, it was a custom here.

It wasn't just business that took place on the beach, it seemed, but all of Rio's life. Around Paul's improvised meeting, besides the guards supplied by the hotel together with the cabanas, umbrellas, chairs and towels, there were maids attending children; sunbathing mothers; vendors creating havoc with whistles, shouts, songs, banging tins or drums; urchins on the lookout for unattended possessions; youths exhibiting their pectorals, thrown in relief as they played football or volleyball or took attitudes while flirting with girls in bikinis. Acres of them.

He remembered a popular song from his youth, 'The Girl from Ipanema'. Ipanema was round the corner, but any one of these girls could have inspired the song and every one of them sent a longing glance towards Paul.

Mark stretched on the sand and through half-closed eyes watched a great fleece of a cloud in the distance glide on the ocean breeze, unthreatening and lazy. He ignored the women. Sure, some of them had eyed him, but that was a ploy to get nearer to Paul. And even if they were not and he was unattached, temporarily, and not quite the monk Paul accused him of being, minisculely clad, seriously pleasure-seeking women reminded him too much of his wife. He was here to get away from her.

He would much rather talk to someone like the lady who had ignored Paul at Miami airport.

Mark had looked at the crowds. 'There must be an inconspicuous way for VIPs . . .' he began.

'Not all of us are hermits,' Paul threw over his shoulder and hurried to put distance between himself and Mark. Hands in the pockets of his Armani suit, he cut a path like Moses through the dividing waters of the Red Sea. Female heads, and some male too, swivelled around to follow his progress.

Why did Paul insist on walking either ahead or behind him but never by his side? He couldn't possibly fear comparison with a great big hulk like himself, dressed in faded jeans and white cotton shirt. True, Mark had the advantage of a few inches on Paul, not that Paul at six feet was particularly small, but that was where any advantage began and ended.

Maybe it was better this way. On the rare occasions people saw them together, they drew unjustifiable conclusions, to Paul's amusement. Mark could do without that.

Paul was about to pass perhaps the only lady unaware of his presence. She was preoccupied with the announcement of the Manaus flight and gathered her things in a hurry. She left a folder behind on the seat. Paul scooped it up in one flowing motion, beating a middle-aged couple to it. Probably her parents. All three had the same dark colouring, though the younger woman was cast from a more delicate mould. Quietly dressed compared to her mother, too. A softly flowing grey dress with a matching, close-fitting jacket on top and the glimpse of a purple scarf to break the monotony. No jewellery at all except for the ring on the third finger. Not the woman to draw attention to herself, and yet she drew his, who only noticed women in his professional capacity or if they accosted him and he needed to react. It might have been the novelty of a woman so immune to Paul's presence. Whatever! She certainly was not the sort of woman to be stared at like that, as if she were one of Paul's bimbos.

'A colleague of yours,' Paul said later. 'She doesn't like aeroplanes.'

Mark knew she hadn't spoken a word and that none of her attributes would make Paul remember her this long. It must have been at least ten minutes.

'I saw the label on the file,' Paul responded to Mark raising an inquiring eyebrow. 'Dr Sylvia something Peters from the UK going to a conference in Manaus. She was so flustered, she didn't even acknowledge my existence.'

That, of course, should have made her memorable.

It might have had something to do with his staring at the cloud that her image appeared to Mark in soft focus as if surrounded by the opalescent aura of a pearl. Unlike the women in his life so far, she looked precious.

He couldn't help his regret of never talking to her. He wouldn't, of course, have any idea of what to say, but she looked like someone you could talk to, not just jump in bed with. He couldn't imagine her throwing things and using foul language. He certainly wouldn't dare as much as frown at her. She would be somebody to treasure. He had never had anybody to treasure.

Paul kicked sand at him. 'Hey! All these glorious women circle you like bees round a honey pot, and all you do is look at clouds!'

Mark started but was pleased to be rescued from self-pity. He sat up. 'Finished business?' he said noticing that Paul was now alone.

Paul was unwilling to be diverted from his favourite topic. 'What do women have to do to draw your attention?'

'Bull! You know they are all after you.'

'Only because you ignore them. Check this, for instance.' He motioned with his chin at a flamingo of a brunette who, once sure she had drawn their attention, tossed her hair. Red highlights caught the sun. 'It's the third time she found an excuse to walk by, twice before I arrived. Don't you find her attractive?'

'Very beautiful,' said Mark, thinking of his wife and what it took to make her like that. Hours and hours of grooming like a cat, diets, liposuction, a nose job, breast enlargement, astronomical hairdresser's bills. Beautiful, but not attractive. Not like the lady in grey. Her dark hair shone with cleanliness and health, not highlights. He was sure it shone. Everything about her did. At least in the picture in his mind.

He made himself look at Paul to stop daydreaming, and indicated the brunette. 'What could I talk to her about?'

'Talk!' Paul stretched out his arms in despair. 'Since when were you interested in talking and with a woman at that?'

'Two-thirds of my patients are women, and nearly all the nurses.'

'And you look at them just as patients or employees and nothing more, of course.' The way Paul looked at him from behind the fringe infuriated Mark.

'Yes!'

And that mocking half-smile on Paul's lips made it worse. 'Even though at least half of the patients invent symptoms just to have the opportunity to come anywhere near you?' Paul ignored Mark's disgusted look and pulled his fingers through his hair, brushing the fringe away from his face. 'Tell me, honestly, that you have never been propositioned by a patient, to say nothing of nurses.'

'An occupational hazard.'

Paul stared at the horizon as if deep in thought, then turned back to Mark. 'Do you talk to Nicol?'

'Exactly,' Mark said, more fiercely than he meant to. Nicol was busy taking care of her looks, or she was drunk.

He wanted to make love to a woman he could converse with.

Suddenly he felt deflated. He couldn't imagine himself making love to the little lady in grey. Talk, maybe. After all, they were both scientists. They should find something to talk about. But make love? It just didn't seem right. He would feel all clumsy. He had always made love to tough women like Nicol or the brunette, who was on her way back with studied indifference. All these toned muscles, long legs entwined around one . . .

For a moment he felt sexual desire. She passed him, and the lust subsided in proportion to the distance between them. That was it. These women left nothing in their wake. One wouldn't remember them after just one glance. It wasn't much more than that. One long glance and this hopeless wish to see her again.

Paul sighed in resignation. 'I have to meet another bunch of people in the Barracuda. Fancy coming?'

'I was thinking of taking a taxi and doing the rounds of the city. Visit the favelas or whatever.'

'Great! I offer him luncheon at an exclusive restaurant and he wants to visit the slums.'

But Paul did not sound all that disappointed, not with a pair of dark eyes flashing at him from over a suntanned shoulder. He vaguely waved at Mark and made straight for the owner of the eyes, who also possessed a tight butt unobscured by anything more than a black thong. It wiggled seductively from side to side, with just a slight tremor on the gluteus maximus with every step.

It was the last Mark saw of Paul until evening.

As he had expected, Mark dined alone at the rooftop restaurant that night. The city sported garlands of lights among buildings and trees, right up to the mountains. Enchanting, but how long would it keep him occupied? He had already seen Botafogo, the Sugar Loaf, the Christ statue, and travelled along the Flamengo Beach right back to Copacabana but not the favelas, now that he realised they were slums. It would have been in bad taste for someone staying in the Meridien-Rio.

But was it that he had exhausted the charms of the city, or Paul's promise to visit Manaus that made him so impatient?

'We could take a tourist flight, for a change,' Paul had said in their shared suite while getting ready for his evening rendezvous. 'Mix with the hoi polloi. From there we could take a boat to the piece of jungle in question while the experts tease out details.' A last look in the mirror and a flick on the hair to create the careless fringe. 'There is nothing there to see but trees, I'm told. A lot more exploration is necessary before there would be any felling or digging, but what the heck!'

Mark's heart accelerated now, as it had when Paul first mentioned Manaus. Suppose they bumped into that lady . . .

Was he acting like a teenager or what? He didn't know the woman. He just compared what he knew of women in general with what he imagined she would be like, and he was not a good judge of female character, to say the least. There was nothing more, not even the likelihood he would meet her. Manaus was a big place. But . . .

3

A bird of prey on the lookout, was the first thought that struck Paul when he entered the Rio Negro Hotel lobby.

Mark glared at everyone going into the conference hall from the shadows of his brow. Paul couldn't guess from his expression what preoccupied him but, on second thoughts, preying was wishful thinking. Mark did not approach any scientist, male or female. He just read a book and watched, as if the mere proximity of people with similar qualifications to himself were preferable to the company of anybody else in the world.

The waiter approached instantly he sat next to Mark.

'Bourbon,' Paul said and pointed at Mark for his order.

Mark shook his head.

There was no helping the bastard. He insisted on wallowing in the mess created by his indecision or some perverse desire for martyrdom.

'Look,' he said unable to hide his impatience. 'You should have the odd fling then go back to Nicol refreshed and tell her to hop it.' Mark's raised eyebrows made Paul go on the defensive. 'Well, somebody had to tell you.'

'None of your business.'

Mark's voice sounded rusty from disuse. After all, he had hardly spoken since they left Manaus, and before Paul coaxed him away from Los Angeles, God knows for how long. Maybe he should have minded his own business, but Mark was the only person that had been there for him, years ago, before he knew his name was Paul Alexander Jr.

*

Paul had sent George, the butler-cum-chauffeur, into a shop. The moment he was out of view, Paul jumped out of the car and made a run for it.

Public transport was a piece of cake, considering his inexperience. He smiled in self-congratulation which turned to hilariousness when he imagined the surprise on George's usually inexpressive face that he had misplaced his passenger. Nanny would give him Hell. Well, he deserved it. He had refused point blank to even consider driving Paul through downtown Los Angeles. It wasn't as if there was anything to shock him. He had seen it often enough on the screen, either in newsreels or films.

He could be as cool a dude as the kids ahead of him. He imitated their walk: legs apart, swinging from the hips. Just right. Nobody had paid any attention, which proved his point. The kids hadn't even turned their heads once to look at him.

When they stopped, he nearly bumped into them. They turned around, showing no surprise as if they knew all along.

One looked at him nose to nose. 'What you doin' here, rich kid?'

They had no way of knowing. He didn't have it stamped on his forehead.

'I am not!' he said.

It was not that funny that they should be holding their sides and rolling around with laughter.

The kid who had addressed him fingered his jacket. 'Found this on the sidewalk?'

'It's mine,' a second boy said while the rest split their sides with forced laughter. 'I put it down to tie my Nike sneakers.'

Before Paul could do anything, he was pushed around from one boy to the other, each claiming different articles of his clothing until he was dropped to the ground crying with humiliation and impotent fury, in nothing more than his undershorts.

'Wan' your mama, kid?'

Paul knew how to look after himself but they were too many. All he could do was to make himself into a ball to protect his face and stomach from their kicks.

In films, that's when rescue came: the cavalry, the Lone Ranger, the Superhero. So he was not surprised when he heard a shout and the kicks stopped.

He looked up in gratitude. The older boy loomed over him. The others stood back out of respect or fear. Paul was about to pick himself up with the remnants of his dignity when the newcomer's face cracked open to expose two rows of teeth like enormous seeds, all the more white for being set in the fleshy pod of the mouth, framed by overripe sleek skin.

'Well, well, well. What's a pretty lil' thing like you doin' in a place like this?' and he undid his trousers slowly, while the rest went crazy. 'Looking for this?' He waved it about to everyone's delight.

Screaming, crazy faces whirled above Paul. Fear's huge, icy tongue licked him, turning him into a clammy statue. This was the primordial fear Nanny communicated to him by so many sudden interventions whenever any male friend of his parents tried to be friendly, just smiled at him or, worse still, extended a hand to touch him. He heard her once whisper to George that they were all perverts, trying to corrupt him. He looked up the word, only to find out that it was something that would turn him infected and rotten. His panic was rendered more sinister for lack of detail. He had a vague idea about men doing terrible things to young boys, but he lacked specifics. Especially how one could tell a pervert and how he would turn him rotten like his pet cat that disappeared for weeks and then was found under a bush at the bottom of the garden, with maggots crawling all over it and smelling awful. It made him seek out feminine company that was the more comforting the further away Nanny was. Everyone seemed to be afraid of her, except Paul, of course. But where was she, or anyone else, to protect him now?

When he was roughly pushed onto his knees, any vestige

of hope disappeared, refusing to return even when another shout quietened down the pandemonium.

The boy with the open flies left the ground and flew over Paul's head. The rest of the gang scattered but not out of sight. The show was not over yet. That was when Paul got a glimpse of his very own urban Lone Ranger, and even in his panic and confusion, he seemed familiar.

It wasn't until he was driven away in a police car, still wearing Mark's football jersey that came down to his knees, he remembered where he had seen him before. On television! Beckermann, the hero of college football, destined, according to everyone in the know, for stardom.

Mark had saved him, and by doing so, instead of a football hero, he became a successful doctor and a failed husband.

Now it was Paul's turn to help. His fortune wouldn't be enough if Mark killed that bitch, no matter what the provocation. Not with his record. One death could be put down to accident. Two was pushing it a bit. That was why Paul had to remove him from harm's way and put up with this shit.

'My business isn't any better,' he said. 'No guide is willing to take us that deep into the bush.' He impersonated a Brazilian with a heavy accent. 'It's too far, senhor! Not on tourist circuit, senhor! Needs too much planning, senhor.' Then, reverting to his normal speech, 'We are fucking stuck.'

Mark had resumed his vigil. 'Didn't offer enough money?'

'Nothing happens just like that here. Even with a bribe, one has to negotiate and wait. Especially wait. I am not going to hang around for much longer. A few decades back, it might have been different.'

Manaus wasn't the paradise in the jungle Paul had expected. The rubber boom before 1912, the fall from grace and the so-called regeneration of the city since 1966, were represented in an architectural jumble. The ostentatious opera and Victorian mansions were drowned in skyscrapers, shacks, suburban homes and prefabricated warehouses. This hotel wasn't bad. It had a reasonable restaurant, a disco and a view over the Rio Negro, but still Paul missed the buzz of nightlife and, even more importantly, the beach life of Rio.

'Oh, yes,' said Mark, his eyes still on the delegates, 'the good old days!' And he launched into a lecture: 'Rubber barons who could afford palaces and fountains of champagne on money made by enslaving rubber tappers through debts they could never repay. Indians, worked to death under the lash, or left to die slowly and miserably from infected wounds. Indian women raped as a matter of routine and their unproductive kids killed by smashing their brains against tree trunks. What fun!'

A talkative Mark was not such a good idea, especially when he indulged in subversive literature under the guise of a travel book.

'Well, a lot of unpleasant things happened in history,' Paul said. 'If you mean it as a warning, I have no intention to enslave anybody, let alone rape. Not even the forest. It's all in the contract.' He tapped the table as if the contract was spread open for all to see. 'Provide jobs on reasonable pay and make good the damage.'

'By reforestation with monoculture that survives a couple of years.'

'Fuck you!' Mark was obviously taking revenge for the invasion of his privacy.

Mark deigned to look at Paul, probably because all the delegates had gone in for a lecture. 'No reforestation scheme ever succeeded in Brazil in anything other than theory.'

'I don't see why not. We will use indigenous trees.'

'They usually grow mixed up in all sorts of different species, avoiding the spread of disease which is not true for monoculture.'

Mark could be such a bore. 'Whatever. If the fact is known, we will take it into account. Mix them up.'

'Only nature has found the right mix.'

'Look at it this way,' Paul stood up and banged his empty glass on the table. 'If I don't do it, somebody else will, with less intention to make anything good. I mean to try and avoid obvious disasters from the past. Anyway, what I came to say was that I decided to hire a small plane and fly over my property myself.' He made for the door. 'Coming? Or are you unable to drag yourself from scientist-spotting?'

'What do you mean?' Mark sounded so confused, Paul turned back alerted.

The bastard must have found some glamorous scientist, if such a thing existed, among the female delegates, after all! That explained this obsession with the conference, which reminded him of something.

'Do you remember the woman who was so nervous about flying to Manaus for the conference?' Now why should Mark jump like that at such an innocent remark?

'You saw her?' Mark asked after regaining his composure. The man made no sense at all. 'Hardly.'

'Then what made you remember her? Not your type, is she?'

Completely round the bend. He was jealous at the mention of a total stranger. 'Damn right not my type, but she was absolutely right about being scared of planes. Premonition or what?'

Mark was frowning fiercely now. 'What the hell are you talking about?'

'Her flight crashed over the jungle,' Paul said. 'The news is all over town.'

4

Internal and external environments in harmony; her heart humming to a rhythm set just above her. Bliss! She was back to the beginning, Sylvia thought, back to being a foetus in the womb, or further back, a unicellular creature in the primordial ooze, the same temperature as her blood.

But somebody had set the clock too fast. Aeons too fast. The ooze started to coagulate. The ground became hard. Her skin tightened. Then a prickling all over her, hardly noticeable at first, became steadily insistent, irritating. Millions of itching pinpricks. Excruciating. And the noise, no mere hum any more, but a cascade. It drilled into her skull, twanged every nerve, drove her crazy.

She had to escape the stinging and the noise, but at the first attempt to move, a sharp pain across her middle drowned every other discomfort.

I am tied down, for heaven's sake! I can't get away!

She was held down in the hardening mud, only able to lift her head for air that was too humid for relief.

Oh, please let the noise stop so I can think!

She fumbled at whatever imprisoned her and found a buckle. After several efforts she managed to undo it, disentangled herself and was off. A few steps and she bumped into something big and solid and slithered to the ground.

There was a peculiar semidarkness all around. Not that of an enclosed place. Not shade. Light but not enough of it, yet sufficient to make out her surroundings: a twilight world of buttressed pillars that rose to fantastic heights then met into a vault. A cathedral-like sauna infested with insects from which the caked mud that covered her offered little protection.

It all came back to her. Flying over the Amazon, wishing for the journey to end, yearning to explore the jungle once more, the explosion . . . she did not want to remember the rest.

My wish came true, I'm in the bloody jungle!

Fate had been good to her once more, but not without the usual twist. It allowed things to reach the nadir before it lent a hand. But she was here now, sitting against an enormous tree trunk, one of many surrounding her.

It must have been what saved her. The fall had been broken by trees and her seat had soft-landed in mud. Maybe she was suffering from concussion. It explained her irrational behaviour so far.

Rule number one in the forest: do not panic or you are lost for good.

All she had to do was to sit tight and wait for the rescue.

They do organise rescues in such cases, don't they?

But the prospect of rescue didn't seem all that inevitable, and to get hold of herself was impossible when she could hardly breathe. The moisture around her was boiling. She followed it with her eyes – up and up and up. It was going to seep out, drawn up by the sun she could not see. It was not just sucking the moisture but the air. And as she stopped following the steam and stared at the canopy, layer upon layer of green cloud, it started to move. Downwards. Pressing the air, condensing the moisture, forcing it into the ground, into the roots of the giant trees. The steam couldn't escape any other way. It was trapped in there, like her.

Don't panic. Keep on moving. Explore.

The space between the soaring tree trunks was uncluttered. There was no undergrowth to battle with. All she had to watch for were the lianas that looped and writhed in mid-space when they did not wind themselves round trees like gigantic serpents. The ground was firm and surprisingly clean. Not even a whiff of putrefaction, unlike Africa. Everything there smelled of decomposition, in and out of the forest. It was like the signature of the place, overpowering even the petrol fumes of Lagos. Here, on the rare occasion that an air current reached the understorey, there was a momentary smell of exquisite perfume from the canopy, and then the sultry stillness engulfed her again.

The scenery remained unaltered no matter how far she walked. It was as if she had never taken a single step. Another contrast with Africa. This place had not been interfered with for millions of years. There, trees were often cut down, allowing the undergrowth to go berserk in the heat and humidity, or plantations were created and then abandoned. The variation acted as a marker.

She let herself slip to the ground, too tired of walking. Where was she going anyway? There might be civilisation a short distance away, but in which direction? Better to sit and wait for rescue. But how long had she been down here already? For how long had she been unconscious? Days? Hours? Her watch had stopped and the light never altered, so she had no idea of the passage of time. There was no sun whose progress across the heavens would guide her.

Then she remembered that when night came, it would do so suddenly. She knew that much about the tropics.

Worries about the noise, the itching, the leeches, which were already competing with the insects for her blood, or any wild animals – she hadn't seen any, so far – became insignificant. She did not know where she was or the time, and sooner or later she would not be able to see at all! Now she understood what people meant when they said that the worse horror imaginable was complete disorientation.

In Africa, she had followed a bulldozed path. It had been reclaimed by the bush very quickly, of course, and every time she walked it, it appeared different, but it was a path that led from the campus and back to it. If she ever wandered from it, there was somebody around to guide her home. That was adventure in safety, with the sure knowledge that an air-conditioned house and all modern comforts – within the limitations of Africa with regular electricity cuts and running water stoppages – were a few minutes away.

The last few years in suburbia had been suffocating. She was stranded in an emotional desert; the demands of married life without any of its rewards; small children with their school runs, ballet, scouts, swimming; no relative or friend or kindred spirit for miles; no job to keep the mind alert. She had looked back at the jungle years with longing, and when Ian grew particularly wearisome, she had even dreamt of being alone in the jungle.

Her wish had been granted. She was alone, with no hope of being less alone soon, maybe never. She would sit here while her body dehydrated and the lassitude spread, her blood sucked from her by leeches and insects, and never get up again. If she had never come round after the fall, it would have been preferable to this slow death.

This too was new, sitting there feeling sorry for herself. Hadn't it always been just as she gave up hope that things began to improve? She could be rescued or she would die – and both were improvements on the present.

Slowly, her mind diffused into the gloom of the understorey that seethed and buzzed around her as if alive. The rest of her could follow, for all she cared. Thirst, hunger, pain were still there, but she experienced them with detachment, as if they were happening to somebody else. Hope was irrelevant and so was fear and the need to struggle. *Just wait for the end.*

That's being defeatist, buzzed the shadows.

'What's more defeatist?' she answered her inner voice, for even in her confused state she realised it could be nothing else. 'Dying now, or carrying on until I die of starvation, disease or a poisonous sting? Futile struggle against the inevitable is not brave.'

Pull yourself together!

It echoed so clearly in her head this time, she thought somebody else had said it and looked around hopefully.

There might have been a shadow, but it dissolved away, and what was one shadow among all the others? It was true, though. She should pull herself together. She had promised her children she would be back. Children didn't allow for mitigating circumstances. Anyway, if she had survived the crash, so could somebody else. He or she could be somewhere very near and feeling like her or even worse. They might need her help. She had some experience of jungles, even if appearances were a bit different with this one. She could find eatable plants. She was sure she would recognise most of them. In Africa, most plants she had identified were invariably described as indigenous to South America, which had made her wonder, at the time, how little seemed to have been indigenous to Africa.

First, she had to make a fire. The drop in temperature meant nightfall was near.

There were dry twigs around, and she remembered the lighter in her pocket. While looking for it, she came across the cigarettes as well. They were damp, but she could dry them by the fire. Cheat the hunger pangs by smoking and maybe drive the insects away.

Whatever light existed in the understorey suddenly disappeared, like she had expected it to do.

She sat in a pool of light, smoking. Every so often, she brought the glowing end of the cigarette near a leech and it dropped off. One burst inside her dress and covered her with blood. In spite of her revulsion, she carried on methodically clearing the pests from the parts of her body she could reach and tried not to think of the rest. She wished she had her jacket with her. Her dress left too much flesh exposed to pests, and the scarf offered little protection.

The smoke had no effect on the insects. A cloud of them buzzed above the flames. Occasionally a giant moth fell into the fire. Outside the circle of light nothing was visible, but the darkness rustled with noises of scurrying creatures. Frogs croaked, birds cried. A growl, a sniff. Everything sounded closer, clearer than during daytime, frightening.

It was strange. The only frightening places in Nigeria were outside the jungle, wherever there was a concentration of people, horrific traffic jams, crime, pollution, dead bodies by the wayside. She avoided that as much as possible.

She was not an expert in herbal medicine, in those days, but lack of synthetic drugs for her experiments drove her to seek the efficacy of local remedies, and since the University of Ife was built in the middle of the jungle, she undertook many expeditions through it, usually accompanied by Chief Elewude, the herbalist. That began her passionate love affair with jungles.

The only thing that had worried her there, was a screech ending in a sinister cackle. She used to hear it occasionally in the evening. It probably was a harmless creature, but nobody seemed to know what. That was, perhaps, why it was so terrifying. Something unknown that seemed to mock her. Don't relax completely, the jungle seemed to say. You don't know everything about me.

She certainly knew very little about this one, but she was too tired to worry about it now.

Once again, she was under the cathedral arches of a bamboo grove on a Sunday morning, the singing from the church back down on campus drifted towards her and, in case she forgot where she was, a lion roared. But there was no need to be afraid. The lion was unlikely to sneak upon her. It was kept in the University zoo. There was nothing dangerous here. All big game had been killed or captured, smaller animals eaten a long time ago, except for the odd snake or rat.

The unknown animal screeched, and she woke up to complete silence and the realisation of how reassuring the noises had been.

Fear was palpable in the darkness. Everything held its breath, sensing the prowler like her. The thumping of her heart marked its muffled footsteps. A sharp cry, almost human. Then silence again, protracted, terrifying.

When a bird called she jumped, her heart about to burst, then another answered and the frogs resumed their croaking. The danger had passed. All the creatures could breathe again – but not her.

There was something else out there, scrutinising her. She tingled all over, a hum, not unlike that of a swarm of bees, rising all around her. It was as if whatever it was had the power to charge every atom in her body, energise it, sensitise it . . . to what? It was beyond fear now. Just the profound desire for a resolution. Whatever it brought. Anything to stop her disintegrating into her component parts.

5

From the air, Mark could see the crazy path her plane had cut through the canopy like a lawnmower gone berserk.

'There is no chance of finding anyone alive in this,' Paul said, 'and they've looked long enough. We will be quite justified in taking a detour.'

Paul had waited for the promised plane all day. He dragged Mark to see a crazy Greek battling with pythons or anacondas in a mud pit, and an excursion into the bush in brand-new safari clothes as recommended by the guide. They saw their allotted amount of trees; a token waterfall; visited an Indian village to stare at the remnants of some tribe; ironically contributed to a fund for the preservation of the forest; and returned to their hotel thankful for the air-conditioning.

Still no plane.

Next day, they had the plane but no permit to fly it.

'You mean I am not allowed to view my own property?' asked Paul.

The official was unmoved. 'You can, senhor, but not today.'

Paul was furious. 'Do you think I have nothing better to do but hang around here?'

'You forget the tragedy, senhor. They have to cover the whole area. Many times. Lots of helicopters and search planes. You understand, no?'

'I thought they would have given up by now. Look! Couldn't we help?'

'You are not trained, senhor.'

'We have a plane, for Christ's sake, and how much training does one need to see a jumbo jet?'

'They found the jet, senhor.'

'Then what the . . .'

'Some bodies are missing. They were sucked out of a hole before the crash.'

'What chance is there of finding them?'

'Not much, but we must try. A couple more days, maybe. Then you can fly.'

Paul put his arm around the man's shoulder and slipped a few dollars into his shirt pocket. 'But we could still help, maybe?'

Mark could imagine what it would be like down there. He was told in Manaus that if you survived death, after a while you went mad. 'Even if there is one chance in a million,' he told Paul, 'we should try.'

As long as she was not crushed in the plane, which, of course, Mark had no way of knowing, there was hope. She could be down there. Would it be worse? Dying slowly, waiting for rescue. How long could she last? She looked so fragile. Did somebody else survive to look after her?

He'd like to believe that. But what chance of being found if everyone was like Paul?

'You are trained to believe in a chance in a million,' Paul was saying, 'but I have the controls. There is no chance, not even one in a million, of stopping me.'

Paul was right. Short of tossing him overboard, which Mark was tempted to do, he couldn't change Paul's mind. Wrestling the controls off him would be useless. He did not know how to fly the stupid thing. And it was stupid. A wreck that Paul called a survivor of the war. It looked more like made up of several bits of not quite survivors of the war. And which war were they talking about, anyway? But it seemed lovingly restored and even had parachutes. They had never been used, the owner had told them to show how reliable the thing was.

He needn't have bothered. Paul had fallen in love with it instantly and was now playing at being a veteran flying ace. What did he hope to see, even if they did fly over his darn property?

'One bit of green is just like another,' Mark said.

'There's supposed to be a river, a tributary to the Rio Negro, to be exact, and a waterfall. It should fucking well be distinguishable.'

There was a ravine, shining black in its depth, cutting through the green in graceful curves. A cloud of mist separated the wider part of the ravine from a much narrower one above. Paul flew down its length for some distance then took a sharp turn and started to drop. The green walls on either side changed to a less monotonous colour in the distance and then receded to reveal the river, wider than Mark had realised. The water was like polished metal, light skidding over it, dazzling. Where the shadow of the plane fell, it was black but elsewhere dark red, rusty at the edge of rocky banks and around sandy islands.

The river changed its mood as they flew over it, shaking itself into wakefulness, anticipating something. Mark looked ahead instinctively. They were in a cul de sac, flying straight into a solid wall of trees.

'Watch out!'

Paul didn't seem to either hear or care. There was this maniacal light in his eyes, like when he gambled fortunes on the throw of a dice or pushed his luck to the limit, sailing too close to the wind or any of the other stupid things he did for thrills.

The plane forged ahead. Mark made to grab the joystick and was roughly pushed aside. This was ridiculous. He was about to haul Paul out of his seat and try his luck at avoiding the trees now staring them in the face when Paul banked the plane, skirted the trees moments from collision and followed the curve of the water calmly, as if nothing had happened.

Now the river was swift, tumbling over rocks, whipping itself into rusty foam. A cliff of rushing water that was intercepted by rainbows reared up in front of them. Rocks guarded it, either side like gigantic gateposts, and the jungle leaned towards it as if sucked into its vortex.

'Awesome!' Paul had to scream to be heard above the noise. 'A gateway to heaven.'

Which side of the rocks was heaven? No doubt they were about to find out. This flimsy craft would never gain altitude fast enough to clear the falls.

For the second time in minutes, Mark gripped the sides of his seat. His field of vision diminished steadily. First to go were the green forest walls, leaving underneath them maddened water. Next the grey rocks ahead disappeared until nothing remained but a section of a foam wall, a segment of rainbow. Anticipating the impact, he shut his eyes though there was nothing to see as they flew into the mist.

Mark had no illusions. This was not the kind of accident one had any chance of surviving. His greatest regret was that with them gone, her chances at survival were even less, not that they had ever amounted to much.

He heard Paul's crazy scream and thought that was that, only to open his eyes the moment he realised it was a triumphal cry.

They were emerging from the mist that now swirled below them, soon to be replaced by water the colour of wine, making its lazy way over a flat ground, ignorant that its bed was about to tumble over the abyss.

'We must have cleared the cliffside by inches,' Paul said, out of breath with adrenaline rush, and Mark felt like hitting him.

'The river is more or less navigable up to the waterfall,' Paul continued. 'That's how the prospectors could come this far, and that's how we must do it if we are to see the thing properly.'

He swooped over the cloud of spray one more time as if to greet the source of such a terrific adventure, and then banked towards the monotony of the green they had come from.

'If we ever make it,' Mark said, not just to be awkward for what he had gone through but because he had noticed the fuel gauge almost at zero. He pointed it out to Paul.

Paul dismissed it. 'The man assured me he put in enough fuel. It must be a faulty gauge. For such an old bird, it's a minor defect. Did you see how it responded . . .'

Mark had no desire for going over the last bit of madness as if it were a simple thrill. 'Or the tank leaks.'

'Do you have to be such an asshole?'

'It *is* a possibility!'

Paul concentrated on weaving around enormous cloud columns advancing across the sky, skirting pillars of rain, thrilled – until the engine began to cough.

When the aircraft started to lose height rapidly, Mark grabbed the parachutes. He forced one on Paul, who wouldn't completely let go of the controls. He raised one arm then the other for Mark to strap him in.

'There isn't much response, but it's better than nothing.' Paul said. There was a slight lift. 'Whoopee! A thermal. We could make it. People have managed to guide crafts as big as jumbo jets home on hot air currents. It should be easier in this flimsy thing.' After a while he modified his optimism.'Not quite home, maybe. Just a clearing or a river would do. Anything flat.'

It was clear to anyone that those columns of cloud boded ill for such hopes, but Paul persisted. 'If the current goes round the next pillar of cloud . . .'

They were heading straight for it. Paul attempted a manoeuvre. The craft went smack into the cloud. The engine coughed one last time and shuddered to a standstill. Visibility was nil. The cloud passed them and they were going down in glorious sunshine.

Mark had already opened the door. The wind shrieked. He yanked Paul off the controls and pushed him out.

6

The feeling that she was being watched, was still there, but in daylight Sylvia could be more rational. She had been victim of her overactive imagination again. There was nothing wrong with awareness of potential dangers as long as it did not interfere with action. In her previous life when she had allowed that to happen, it had caused only some inconvenience to her. Here, it could be lethal. She had to get going, no matter what.

For lack of any other navigational aid, she followed the ants. There was a rope of them strung across the clearing. One twist of the rope, embroidered with bits of greasy cloth, was running backwards, the other, plain, going forward. She kept going until her brain, numbed by sleeplessness, registered its significance.

Cloth?

Fully alerted, she turned back, following the ants to the source of their booty. She had no idea of what to expect, but cloth meant people and she shouldn't care less who they were. Or should she? There was no time to think this out. Against her will, she kept increasing her pace in time with the hammering against her ribcage, the booming in her ears, the pulsing in her temples.

The trail stopped at a mount of black grease spotlighted in a shaft of light from above, where the canopy had been damaged recently. With so many ants crawling all over it, it seemed to boil and shimmer. Crooked fingers of vapour rippled from it, reached out, clawed at her. Heavy sweetness saturated her nose, her mouth, her hair, her clothes, her skin. A sudden spasm in her stomach doubled her up but not before she saw the chunky gold bangle sinking slowly in the ooze.

Pursued by the nauseating sweetness, still retching, she ran away. Any direction. It didn't matter. By the time exhaustion brought her to a stop, her stomach muscles ached from unproductive overexertion. She had been without food for too long. What did it matter how far she ran, anyway? It would be a long time before she could escape that smell and the haunting sight of the sinking bangle, probably never. But that was insignificant, compared to the realisation that all that black, liquifying flesh belonged to the woman that had befriended her, wanted to protect her, and whose generosity she had resented as being excessive.

She had no illusions as to her own fate. Unless she did something soon, she too would end up as a pile of black grease to be recycled by ants.

She kept walking in the semi-darkness, marking trees as she went. If she saw them again, she would know she had gone around in a circle. But there seemed to be no end to them, and she needed to keep on urging herself not to give up.

Just a little bit more. A little bit more.

Her perspiration could not evaporate in this humidity, and without this cooling effect, her temperature kept rising. At this rate she would become delirious soon, and if nothing happened to rescue her, she would die. So what was the point? Yet she persevered, obedient to some inner compulsion that overrode her pessimism until a tree trunk blocked her path.

She was blinded by light and as her eyes adjusted, she was astonished at the miraculous change to her mood, to nature, everything, that a little sunshine could bring.

Orchids, bromeliads and other epiphytes nestled on mossy cushions along the entire length of the trunk. The skylight created in the forest ceiling by the tree's demise must have been there some time. Saplings were already in competition for dominance. The strongest would reach up first to plug the opening. In the meantime, less ambitious plants put out leaves and flowered and seeded while the sunshine lasted. Among them was a pink morning glory flower: *Ipomea patatas*.

She burst into tears of joy, not only because in this monochrome world, she saw a thing of beauty, a spot of colour, but because she had found food! She had tried to grow this flower in her own garden in Ife, but the gardener confiscated it for his vegetable plot. Sweet potato, he said, was of more use to him.

She followed the meandering of the stem to find its origin and then dug with her fingers and bits of wood until she found a red tuber. She removed it, covered it with loose soil and built a fire over it.

The flavour of the sweet potato reminded her of roast chestnuts and winter at home, but it increased her thirst. Her lips were cracking. She knew all about lianas. They were plant water channels. If one cut a segment, liquid would flow out. But she had not arrived in the jungle with a survival kit. No knife or machete were available. In desperation, she scraped a handful of lichen from a tree trunk and squeezed it into her mouth.

By the way the sun was pouring vertically into the clearing, it must have been noon. The heat was strong enough to quench the noises in the canopy, but the insects attempting to devour her increased. She couldn't help scratching. It was useless saying to herself that any resulting wound could cause septicaemia. Before dehydration and fever made it impossible, she had to force herself to get up and search the undergrowth for aromatic herbs or wood for an insect repellent.

She trusted her instinct and what she had learned from Chief Elewude, the herbalist from Ife. Chief Elewude's plants, of course, didn't always work. Sometimes they did more harm than good, and his favourite solvent was urine. She certainly wasn't going to use that. Water, more than she could get from the lichens, was necessary, and the only hope resided in that something behind the bushes, not just a shadow this time but a definite shape. It disappeared too quickly for her to see clearly, but if it were an animal, she should follow it.

Animals drink by streams or water holes, don't they?

She ought to walk cautiously, not to frighten whatever it was, but it kept increasing its speed and she had to move faster to keep up with the rustling ahead of her. It seemed to be going on for ages, now at a trot, leaving no time for marking anything. Not that whether she went round in circles or kept to a straight line mattered any more.

By the time she reached another clearing she was gasping, she had a stitch, there was no water hole or stream and no animal in sight. Just a rock. She leaned against it to rest.

Since her arrival in the jungle, her clothes had been damp and were already going mildewed. Now they were sticking to her, saturated, dripping. She felt so detached she would not have reacted if she saw them dripping with blood. But the excess moisture seemed to come from the rock. Clear drops were oozing from the lichen-covered surface and trickled down, leaving rusty streaks in their wake. As the rivulets reached the ground, they made a little muddy puddle, which gave her the idea to make a container.

She gathered some mud, rolled it into a sausage and coiled it up, getting carried away with aesthetics. Eventually she came up with a shape appropriate to her high standards, piled sticks all over it and set them on fire like she had seen Nigerian women do in the bush.

When the flames died down, she sat there admiring her work of art while it cooled. It was black with the odd red streak, like a daguerreotype of a tongue of flame. If it was a little unbalanced like the prototypes she had based the manufacture on, who cared? It was not meant to sit on a flat surface but a pile of sticks. Besides, it was something tangible she had achieved, something to be proud of.

She made the potion, wetted her scarf and wiped herself all over then stretched on the ground to stare at the canopy, examining it the way she had the ceilings of palaces and mosques in Cairo, ages ago during a holiday. There were similarities. Neither was flat. Both were made of innumerable small surfaces, in this case millions of leaves, each at a different angle. The light from above ricochetted from one leaf to another at different trajectories, permanently shifting, changing with the tremor of the leaves in the breeze, hence the glaring mirror effect that prevented the eye from seeing all that life that screeched above it. Where a beam reflected from a leaf towards her eye, it dazzled her. Where it penetrated right through the mass, it created a hole in the canopy through which a theatrical spotlight fell to the forest floor. The rod of light, almost solid with insects, sparkled.

The rest of the understorey received only diffused sunshine, enough to see, and even then, not very far with all those tree trunks in the way. Of this sylvan immensity, only a few square yards were visible at any one time.

The noise in the canopy was not just a nuisance like she had thought at first. One could distinguish so many components to it. From booming and howling, especially first thing in the morning and late in the evening, to this hum. As it came nearer it turned into a rumble or more like the throb of an engine.

From almost coma to full alertness, it took seconds. Was the noise now syncopated, or was that the effect of her heart overpowering it at every beat? Brrr ... thump. Brrr ... thump. Brrr ... thump. A kettledrum joined in. Its distant booms were followed by a roll that came closer and closer, drowning the engine noise. Then a massive cloud dragged a curtain of water across the clearing over her, obliterating everything for the few seconds it took for her to be drenched, and roared away the other side.

She tried to comfort herself for the disappointment of mistaking the storm for an aircraft by looking at the positive side of things. At least she had a refreshing shower.

She bent down to scoop water from a puddle to drink, but her courage deserted her. She was not that desperate yet. She had something safer to drink. Her insect repellent was not different to a herbal tea and, having been boiled, free of most germs. She was not familiar with everything she had put into it, but the smell was deliciously lemony. As it turned out, the taste was refreshing and it revived her, gave her the urge to walk, to do something. Besides, she ought to make the progress that cooking and making potions had prevented all day.

It was getting colder and the frogs were already in full throat up in the canopy. Frogs on trees had surprised Sylvia at first, but she got used to it like she was getting used to so many things. At least their evensong was more melodious than the cacophony of birds they had partly replaced. A good accompaniment to a pleasant walk. There were a few insomniac birds still chattering, but something suddenly frightened them. Their last cry, sharp, panicky, sounded almost human, but she was not going to let her imagination get out of hand again. Two disappointments in one day were more than enough.

She could still see very well. Better than ever. Maybe she was coming to the edge of the forest or the canopy was thinner. When she looked up, it was there, if that much higher. It kept getting higher while she watched, though it felt more as if she was getting smaller. It made her feel dizzy, yet she had the energy and the confidence to keep walking.

She picked out sounds one normally never heard, crisply, her ear like a microphone hovering just off the ground: the rubbing of a beetle's elytra, the landing of a frog, the beating of a moth's wings.

Her vision, too, had narrowed to a path she could follow, a milky way in the darkness, skimming the ground on which she glided as if by magic. Out of this matrix, objects crystallised out sharply, one at a time. A blade of grass, an insect, a stick, a rotting leaf, all tinged with bluish purple as if they were being scanned by a UV beam projected from her eyes.

Purple light? It ought to mean something to her, but she

couldn't remember what and trying to concentrate was too tricky, her thoughts were too slippery, slid off each other, turned to rivers of colour, fountains of brilliant light, starbursts, purple rain.

The flames leaped high. The sap of new wood burst and sparks showered around. One landed on her bare shoulder and though she registered the pain exquisitely, she couldn't react. After walking half the night, she had expected to find herself somewhere different, yet she was sitting by the rock, legs drawn up, arms around her knees, looking at a roaring fire. She couldn't remember lighting it, nor did she have any idea for how long she had been back, only that she was not alone.

In the flickering shadows beyond the flames, there was a patch of condensed darkness. It could be anything: a crouching panther, a primate, a human. If it meant her any harm, it had plenty of time by now, and whoever, or whatever, it was had been around for some time. Since she had found herself in the forest, to be exact. She had felt a presence, saw a shadow, heard a noise but never paid enough attention, except the night before, when she nearly died of fright. Amazingly, even to her confused mind, it didn't bother her now. There was nothing she could do to defend herself, but when it moved closer, she shrank all the same.

7

Paul drifted on a hot air current over what looked like an ocean of broccoli and found it just as exhilarating as sky-diving above the Pacific. As he came closer, he noticed that each fleurette represented a tree crown floating independent of all others. All he had to do was to manoeuvre himself above a gap, pull to release the chute and pray that it worked.

By the time he realized that another tree was hiding in that gap, a second storey of canopy, so to speak, it was too late and as he crashed through it, a third appeared even denser. 'SHIT!'

He was tangled in vegetation, twirled around, slapped, grated, the harness threatened to slice through him. It was like being in a food processor. Peace followed, and he swayed back and forth like a pendulum. Beneath him the ground was invisible in the dense shade. No way to judge distance. Not that there was any time for such calculations. The chute tore, by the sound of it. He jerked further and further down when he came under gunfire. *Who the hell . . . ?*

He thrashed around in panic. After a particularly loud bang, he found himself tilted sideways and realised that the lines were snapping, one after the other, and in the confined space beneath the canopy they resembled shots, but there was no time for relief. One of the remaining lines was about to strangle him. He searched for the hunting knife he had strapped to his belt because he had thought it went well with the safari clothes, but cutting that line left him dangling like an enormous spider at the end of a single strand of web that could break at any moment.

There was no imminent chance of rescue. He could see or hear nothing of Mark who, for all he knew, would be in a similar situation or worse. His only chance was to sever the last line and pray to ... whatever ... that the forest floor was not all that far down.

The ground came at him too fast. The trees spun around. No time for bending knees and rolling or whatever one was supposed to do. His breath was knocked out of him and he stayed there stunned, half-sunk in mud.

There was no pain anywhere, but that was no guarantee of anything. He felt around for broken bones and found none. Only then did he get up groggily, thanking the rainstorm that, though it finished off the plane, soaked the earth sufficiently for him to survive the fall.

He turned round and round on the spot, trying to make sense of the environment he found himself in. It was gloomy, claustrophobic, alien, it made him feel insignificant and vulnerable. But he was not scared. Not yet, anyhow, but for the first time in his adult life, he felt mortal. Then something moved. 'Mark?'

Silence. He was alone. Alone!

He ran zigzagging between trees, stumbled on exposed roots, fell, picked himself up and ran again, ignoring the stitch on his side. In spite of years of training, he got exhausted very soon, but his fear of solitude overcame the exhaustion and he persevered until he collapsed.

Paul's eyes focused slowly on his hand. It was lying on the ground, inert, next to his face. An unfamiliar dark blemish on his skin was gradually changing shape. It grew bigger, longer, shinier ... for a while, he watched the obscene transformation with detachment. He sat up slowly, shivering. It was so cold! In the fucking tropics, and he was cold.

After lying still all night on the hard earth, he found it almost impossible to move. His brain wasn't moving any better, either. That spot on his hand, for instance. Then he grimaced with disgust. 'Shit!' He sprang to life, pulled at the creature and tore it off his hand, taking a bit of flesh with it. He brought his hand to his mouth and sucked where a few seconds ago the leech had been doing just that.

He had to find Mark and get out of this place. But what if Mark fell too far away? What if it took days to find him? Or worse, what if Mark got killed?

He didn't believe in God as such, so he prayed to whatever spirit lurked around. One couldn't look at this sepulchral place without sensing something. It was there, OK! Everywhere, it seemed. His skin crawled. He hoped it was not malevolent, though the indications were not encouraging.

'Please let me find Mark! It wasn't his fault.'

But then, if the fault was Paul's, what better punishment than to have to live with the knowledge that he had killed his only friend. No. He was not going to think of that. It was the gloom of the place that generated such stupid and depressing thoughts. He would find Mark. He had to be positive. If he couldn't do it alone, he would recruit help. There ought to be missions somewhere, native villages, scientific expeditions, prospectors, loggers or even pyromaniacs, for fuck's sake. The way one heard it about the jungle, he would be excused in thinking, one couldn't move for people. But where were they?

He wished he had never thought of that, because suddenly it felt as if all these multitudes were there staring at him from invisible hideouts, adding to that feeling of dread that kept increasing with every moment he spent in the jungle.

He scrutinised every shadow – and there were no end of shadows in this place. They took all sorts of shapes: human, bird, animal, and all vanished into the earth itself. Even the shadows of the trees shrank closer to their trunks when he took a closer look. Everywhere there was movement but no substance. Nothing he could get hold of. Physically, that is. Every instinct told him otherwise.

He shook himself together. He was behaving like a child

in the dark. He was not going to look over his shoulder again. Just decide on a direction and walk. Sooner or later something would turn up. Which direction? The one of least resistance, of course. Where his instinct told him there was less danger. He smiled. Here he was trying to take purposeful decisions, yet he allowed imaginary fears and shadows to herd him in a particular direction. There was no choice. It simply felt safer that way.

He had no idea for how long he walked, but he must have covered as much ground as during his crazy run earlier with less suffering. Panic didn't pay. But just as he was getting more self-assured, he stumbled on something that was not the usual exposed root, and the spotlight from above was unnecessary to tell him it was a body – or whose.

For what seemed ages he just sat, paralysed with terror. The jungle filled with laments, sighs, sobs, moans, protracted cries as if the shadows that pursued him all day had turned into his Erinyes, thirsty for appeasement. To touch Mark, to confirm his worst fears, would destroy him and satisfy them. Could he do it?

Paul had been stiff the day before, with falling off trees and running after Mark and lying on the ground, but it was nothing to what he felt after having to haul the Incredible Hulk around.

When Mark had stirred, Paul thought it was the happiest moment in his life, but now he had second thoughts. Mark was where he had propped him up last night against a tree buttress, around which another tree had anchored its roots in an effort to hoist itself hundreds of feet above and lift its crown to the canopy and the sun. The intertwined giants reduced Mark's powerful frame to insignificance. He was not just looking puny, for a change, but also deformed. At least the dislocated shoulder was. It gave him the appearance of a hunchback, and one could hardly see his face for insect bites.

There was a lot of pain, no doubt, but should that be an

excuse to change him from laconic to positively uncommunicative? Things were bad enough without the loneliness.

'Hey, man! Stop playing dead!'

Mark tried to move and winced.

Paul helped him up but not before he made a mental note of the twisted tree. 'Let's get the hell out of here,' he said.

This escapade was taking too long. As adventures went it wasn't too bad so far, and he would milk it for all it was worth when they got out, but when would that be? The problem was, nobody knew where to look for them, thanks to that ill-considered detour. And he hadn't even seen the place he was supposed to be purchasing. What would happen to that venture, if there was a delay in getting out and, even more importantly, what would happen to them?

'I had visions of people walking through an impenetrable jungle hacking a path with machetes,' he said to distract himself from such thoughts.

'Easier, this way.'

Paul did not anticipate a reply and, after his first shock, launched into the next observation quickly in case the impetus for communication was lost. 'That's all very well, but so far we came across nothing recognisable as food. Where are the bananas and pineapples and all the tropical fruits one expects in a jungle?'

'No light.'

Paul was relieved that he was getting somewhere. The observation had not escaped him. He just wanted the exchange to continue. 'Still, tropical fruits exist in tropical forests,' he said. 'That's where they fucking well came from in the first place. OK, there is no light here, and there might be somewhere else in this goddam place. But what about the animals? Are they afraid of the dark or something?'

No reply.

'I suppose we should be thankful we are not going to be eaten by anything.' Paul passed his tongue over his lips.

They tasted salty from his sweat making his thirst keener. 'We are more likely to die of thirst. Stupid thing is . . .' He tried to demonstrate by pulling his shirt away from his chest and heaved from the power of his own body odour, 'we are swimming in fucking moisture.'

Mark obviously thought he had done his bit at social intercourse and he would much rather be left alone to concentrate on walking. He had not complained, but Paul could imagine the throbbing pain in his shoulder and the jarring with every uneven step he took from the way his jaw was set as if he had to grind his teeth to stop himself from screaming. Nevertheless, Mark pointed up towards the canopy and the source of a shrill cacophony where the invisible perpetrators sought to establish boundaries, attract mates, signal friends, warn enemies or, just like Paul, banish the fear this place inspired.

'I mean accessible,' said Paul, irritated by a distinctive noise, even in that pandemonium, reminiscent of scraping rusty metal.

Mark indicated the insects swirling around in a rare shaft of light. 'They are accessible.'

'If that's what comes when you bother to talk, might as well save your breath,' Paul snapped. These tiny tormentors were worse than the noise, not least for the disfigurement of his face and hands.

Mark wiped the sweat from his face with his sleeve. He inhaled deeply, his nostrils flaring but obviously failed to extract sufficient relief from the humid air. He gripped the arm hanging by his side and resumed his walk, resetting his jaw, lips pressed into a thin straight line.

As the day progressed and heat intensified, the noises from above subsided. A broody silence returned to the twilight world of the forest floor. Even Paul's conversation dried up. He felt completely disembodied. Nothing registered but a shock going through his body every time his foot hit the ground, on and on until eventually he wound down to a standstill.

Mark had already slithered to the ground and closed his eyes. Paul knelt beside him. He ached all over, but at least he was not injured like Mark. There must be something he could say or do to sympathise, but how did one show emotion to a man like that? Instead he concentrated on a lone voice from above, a strange rattle that slowly built up to a crescendo and then, smash! a sudden crack of a whip.

He looked up for the aerial joker responsible and saw something glistening, probably a flitting bird. Then he realised. 'A fucking piece of metal!' he shouted scrambling to his feet. 'It's a bit of aircraft. We are walking along the flight path, and if they are looking for us they . . .'

'Whose flight path?'

Paul grimaced, but Mark was right. With increased air travel, there were many crashes over the Amazon, and in the history of aviation only a couple of people had been rescued from this jungle. If what they had been told in Manaus was right, they had rescued themselves. They managed to walk out. He forced himself up, pulling a wincing Mark with him.

All around, the shadows shifted and stirred. Invisible eyes crawled all over him, and to add to his feeling of despair he was confronted with the very same complex of trees they had left behind this morning.

He sank back to his knees, too dismayed for his customary obscenity. 'It would be the ultimate in irony if the jungle gets us,' he told Mark.

'Quite fitting,' said Mark. 'You were about to get it.'

Paul refrained from swearing at him. Obviously Mark was getting worse, and a bit of crabbiness was to be excused. 'All the same, we can't just sit around and wait for it,' he said and got up.

8

Sylvia just stared.

The fire highlighted ebony hair, cut in a pudding shape and picked out high cheekbones on a mahogany face. Two little flames danced in small, slanted eyes. As the stranger bent forward to arrange three bowls on the ground, one after the other, conjuring them out of the darkness, feathers in his earlobes threw weird shadows on his naked chest, from the centre of which a green flame burned brightly.

He raised one of the bowls to his mouth and started chanting over the narrow neck. The sound twisted in the hollow and came out as a moan, so haunting the hair on the back of Sylvia's neck stood up. It lingered in her mind long after he stopped and delayed the realisation that what he was doing by stretching his arms stiffly forward while staring into the flames between them, was making a ritualistic offer of the container. She hesitated.

He remained as still as if he had been lignified by his own magic, still holding the gourd at the full extend of his arms. The play of shadows and the answering twinkle of green from his chest that, far from animating, emphasised the immobility of the sculpted features, mesmerised her. Involuntarily, she stretched her arms towards the bowl, without a clue of what to do when she took it. He released the container in her care and returned his arms to his lap, but neither his expression nor his stare changed.

Now she concentrated on the bowl, fascinated by its decorations. There was a cross, surrounded by first a lighter and then darker border. In the corners of the cross were crude angular shapes and where the bowl narrowed, two handles protruded like ears through which passed a rough rope for a handle.

While studying the container, a vague thought entered her head, like remembering something told her a long time ago. Something very important that slowly turned to longing. She didn't know what it was exactly, only that it had nothing to do with her rescue, or hunger, or lack of safety. Finally it took shape and she could find the words to express it, but she couldn't remember under what circumstances she had heard it, felt it or said it before. It revolved and echoed in her head until it burst out of her mouth.

'I want to see everything.'

She startled herself by the unfamiliarity of her voice and its monotony.

The man didn't move.

As if to order, she slowly brought the bowl to her mouth and drank. She regretted it instantly. It was the bitterest thing she had ever tasted. More so than quinine and that, she had thought until now, was the ultimate in bitterness.

The man bent again and took the next bowl. He offered it to her in the same manner he had the first, but without the preamble of the chant. In the firelight she could see it crowned with milky froth, and the long-forgotten sour smell of palm wine wafted towards her.

She had drank that once or twice in Nigeria, not to offend whoever gave it to her, like she had to do with this man's potion now. Only this time she was lightheaded already. If this drink was anything near as potent as Nigerian wine, it would be devastating on an empty stomach.

She waved her hand as if to brush her own objections away. *Oh, it doesn't matter.* She could sleep it off, and anyway, it might help to neutralise the bitter taste from the first drink.

She subdued her retching and drank, but there was no satisfying the man. He gave her the third container. This one smelled so strongly of perfume she would rather pour it over herself, but the man's eyes were on her and she felt compelled to obey.

He resumed his imitation of a wooden statue in the lotus position and stared at the fire. Again memories of questionable origin started forming in her mind. They were so faint, mere echoes of thoughts. She struggled to capture them, focus them, invent her own words to express them, the necessary concentration making her dizzy.

Sleep, little paca. Tomorrow you will meet the puma and the hawk. They need you. But beware!

After all this effort, what did it all mean? She had never seen a real paca in her life, only an illustration. It was a brown rodent with white spots that lived in the Amazon, and she was not keen to meet with any pumas. The only word that sounded interesting was sleep. She never felt more in need of it, but the Indian was making himself comfortable as if prepared to stay there all night.

The next convulsion of her stomach muscles was too powerful for her to control. The foul mixture of whatever she had drunk was expelled violently, threatening to quench the fire.

She lay down exhausted, still retching. Her eyelids weighed tons, everything was confused, both inside her head and above it. She turned round to vomit again, gasping in pain, convulsing all over, convinced she had been poisoned.

For this wretched end, fate had intervened repeatedly to spare her throughout a life strewn with dangers and near misses.

You will see everything, still echoed in her mind. Maybe from beyond the grave was the only way to do that, and she had wished for it so fervently just a few minutes ago.

The darkness vanished as if an arc light was switched overhead. The Indian disappeared and the trees receded until there was no tree as far as the eye could see, only stunted grass. The sun beat down on her mercilessly. There was such clarity around that every blade of grass was sharply focused like in a surrealist painting.

In the vast emptiness of this landscape, she felt no bigger than a mouse. High above, a hawk glided majestically. It dipped its wings first to the left then to the right, the fanned-out tail feathers acting as a rudder. She was sure it kept her in sight and felt the stare going through her. There was no hiding place, no escape.

Her heart was beating furiously against her ribcage and she was bathed in perspiration, yet she was cold. So cold. She hugged herself while she scanned the horizon. There was taller grass in the distance. If she could reach it, she could hide from the soaring bird of prey with the terrible stare.

Progress was as slow as if she ran through treacle, but she persevered and inch by laborious inch, she approached the sanctuary. The bird followed, riding the thermal smoothly, keeping her under surveillance. A little more effort and she would make it. Safety was just a couple of steps away.

She stopped abruptly.

A sleek puma was picking its way delicately through the tall grass, heading straight for her. She could see the eyes measuring her up, icy cold, calculating, their colour metallic blue. It halted, crouched on all fours, the powerful feline body coiled up, and remained immobile, every muscle tensed, eyes unblinking, prepared to sprint. It felt forever. The tension suddenly released, the puma sprung in the air like an arrow.

Mesmerised, she watched the living missile suspended in mid-air, ears pushed flat against a sleek skull, mouth open but silent, extended limbs, arched body. The powerful beauty and deadly elegance overpowered her and she forgot to be afraid until the sharp, unsheathed claws were almost upon her.

Her heart tattooed crazily against her chest and she was aware of her short breath and the icy film of moisture all over her. She tried to move but her stomach muscles ached so badly, she remained flat until she regained her breath and her heartbeat came more or less to its normal rhythm. Then, sitting up painfully, she saw the extinct fire and steam rising all around her and realised where she was and that she must have had a nightmare. To add to her misery, she was starving, with no energy left to go about looking for food. All that was left from yesterday were the remnants of her insect repellent.

She stretched her arm for the container but then remembered last night's experience. She should not have drunk it yesterday. It gave her bad dreams which reminded her of the walk in the forest and that she had been able to see blue images in the dark.

Good coordination and blue night vision meant one thing: Ayahuasca, the dead man's vine. Its hallucinogenic alkaloids were known in her field, but nobody could prove all the effects the Indians claimed. It was possible she had used it accidentally in her insect repellent, and since it preceded the Indian, he could only have been a hallucination and all that went with him. She had been sick, of course. That too was a known side effect. But nothing else.

She had no previous experience of hallucinations, and she marvelled at how real they had appeared to her. Not so much the Indian as the wild animals. Maybe they were not even hallucinations, just dreams. Hallucinations, she was told, were irrational, but everything she had experienced was not. What would be more natural that her fear of Indians, wild animals – after all she was in the middle of the Amazon jungle – and things she had read about, would get mixed up in a dream. But she couldn't get rid of the idea that premonition was part of it. She believed in that now, after the experience of the air crash. Besides, there was scientific evidence that one of the functions of dreaming was to give advance warning of psychological or physical dangers. Only she was not sure of the warning: *they need you but beware!*

Was she supposed to be in danger from Indians and wild beasts or to help them? But how was she expected to help them in their own environment when she could not even help herself?

But she couldn't deal with such riddles right now. Her head ached so, and the bloodcurdling roar that drowned the dawn chorus and rattled her brain inside her skull, didn't help. Then there was the response to the excruciating sonic boom, to confuse her even more. But so what? She was not going to waste any energy. The forest had proved itself a merciless trickster so far. Would it be different this time?

9

Maybe, Mark thought, Paul was trying to distract him by insisting it was just another tree.

'That's all there is in this goddam place,' Paul was saying. 'What's the point of asking?'

But Mark could make out her pathetic, half-starved face in the shadows. Those beseeching eyes . . . 'Don't worry,' he tried to reassure her, 'we are in the same boat.'

'Damn right, we are,' Paul said. 'But at least I don't keep on walking into trees. Here,' and he tried to guide Mark in a different direction.

Her arm had been chewed up by wild animals by the look of the bloody shreds on what was left of it. Mark felt a physical pain at the sight, in the same part of his anatomy. 'NO!'

'I hardly touched you, for fuck's sake,' Paul said. And then calmer, 'Maybe we should rest. We are getting nowhere anyway.'

Mark let his weight down slowly on the ground in front of her and stretched his arm to touch her. She had disappeared. He looked around to find her amongst the shadows. All that was gone too. He was back at his house, the bedroom to be exact, and the only other person there was his wife. 'Nicol?'

She turned to the mirror with that contemptuous smile on her face. She was going out again. So intent on pleasure. Almost hysterical. Compensating for the boredom of having to live with him, perhaps. Living with him! Hardly that. Whose fault was it? He spent too long at work, but a doctor's wife should be prepared for long hours. Was it absolutely necessary? He could get more staff. Spend more time with her. She didn't like that. He was in her way. She needed people. Fun-loving people.

She was laughing at him. Scarlet mouth open. No mirth in the eyes. Vicious laughter, high-pitched, tearing through you.

He shut his ears to her words, but he felt them. Cruel, ugly, obscene. More so for coming from someone so immaculate. Was she beautiful? Not any more.

He felt no anger. Pity, maybe. What had he done? Better, what was he not doing? Understanding was misinterpreted as lack of care. Interest as jealousy.

'Got to you, at last, have I?' Triumphant, cruel eyes. Intent on hurting.

He must have done something very, very wrong. What? Marrying her was wrong. She didn't agree to a divorce. Terrified of it. Can't discuss it.

'I'll ruin you. You will never work again. People don't like to think their doctor is . . .'

Can't even bring himself to listen. How could she think that? 'Why, Nicol? Why?'

Mark heard his name called from a great distance. He opened his eyes. There was nobody there but Paul. He could just make him out in the gathering darkness, sitting up straight, ears cocked, sniffing the air like a restless animal.

'There is definitely something out there,' Paul said.

Mark's heart beat fast. Was it possible . . .? No. He had to get hold of himself. 'Nocturnal animals,' he said.

'As if there are any other kind of animals except nocturnal in this fucking place,' said Paul.

Mark shut his eyes, pretending to sleep to avoid having to talk, but Paul wouldn't calm down.

'There!' Paul whispered. 'Did you see that?'

Mark was confused about so many things, except for the

pain. That was real enough. And the endless walking and Paul's incessant chatter and hunger and thirst. But for the rest, reality and fantasy were mixed up.

There was no doubt that after Paul's fumbled attempt to help, his shoulder got worse. There were trapped nerves before but now a ligament must have been torn as well and inflammation set in. Bouts of fever addled his brain. That's why he saw things. Even now that he was sure he was lucid, he saw her gliding by in the ghostly light he had always visualised her in, like a little forest fairy. But what was Paul's excuse?

'Do you see a . . .' Paul gave a little laugh, 'woman?'

That he would take advantage of his delirious state and make fun of him was a little too much. 'You are unbelievable!'

It shut Paul up but it increased his own confusion. No matter how much he had desired it, the real chance of meeting another victim in this vastness was negligible. But what if Paul saw the same thing? They couldn't both have been fantasising in an identical fashion. Even if he himself hadn't seen anything, he should trust Paul's unerring instinct to smell a female anywhere. He made to get up and go after whatever it was they had seen to make sure, but Paul stopped him.

'We are both going out of our minds. You talk to trees and I see women. Next, a forest fairy is going to come and rescue us.' Paul sighed. 'What a way to go!'

He was right. If Paul was to fantasise it would be of a woman, hence the coincidence with his own vision. But Paul looked so disheartened, Mark felt sorry for him. 'Tomorrow something might turn up,' he said to cheer him up.

Above their heads the leaves were caught in a breeze and moaned in unison. Millions of sighs flew around, their melancholy chorus extinguishing any delicate hope. All that remained was the uncanny feeling that they were being watched, and not by a benevolent forest fairy.

*

Mark jackknifed into alertness and jarred his arm in the process. The pain that shot through him almost knocked him out. He was sure the scream was not generated by him, either due to the earlier nightmare or the present pain, nor was it coming from Paul, who was looking around him like a trapped animal because it was still there, building up steadily into a stupendous roar. It reverberated around the forest, magnified as it deflected from every tree trunk and hit them simultaneously from every direction.

'JESUS!' Paul's jaw dropped at the sheer volume of sound that engulfed them like a tidal wave. 'Could it be a lion?' he said when he could bring himself to speak. 'I read somewhere that lions could make an incredible noise.'

Mark was sceptical. 'From that height?' He indicated the canopy, where some movement was still visible, and made attempts to get up. Now that whatever danger had threatened them seemed to have retreated, they should get going before the heat built up.

'Have some more rest,' Paul said, refusing to stir. 'You hardly slept last night.' And as an afterthought: 'Do you miss Nicol?'

Mark started. 'What made you say that?'

'You were calling her all night. Kept me awake.'

'Sorry.'

Paul found a comfortable spot on the ground. 'You worry about who your old lady is screwing with at the moment?' he said and made a show of studying the battered toes of his shoes, for all the world unconcerned by the unsuitability of the remark.

Mark struggled to conquer his rising anger and tightened his lips to avoid saying anything he might regret later. But what a moment to choose to discuss such a thing? Did that roar unhinge him?

Paul watched him closely and added with detachment: 'If she was tempted when you were around . . .'

'By you, I suppose?' Mark couldn't help saying in spite his resolve not to give Paul the satisfaction that he as much as heard him.

'*I* did not have an affair with your wife!'

Mark was aware of a muscle in his cheek twitching, and cursed himself for being so sensitive to that real or imaginary stress on the 'I'. 'What stopped you?'

'She was your wife.'

'Aren't most of your women other men's wives?' Why, oh why, couldn't he just ignore him?

'They are not my friends,' Paul said indignantly.

Mark turned and looked at him closely, his emotional insecurity on the subject getting the better of him. 'You mean you never slept with Nicol?'

A straightforward 'yes' would have gone a long way to reassure him, but that slight hesitation before Paul said: 'Never,' lanced through him and he could not be sure whose treachery mattered to him most: his wife's or his friend's?

As if Paul was not satisfied with Mark's humiliation, he added: 'Not for lack of trying on her part.' After letting that sink in, he elaborated, 'She threw a glass of gin at me for refusing her offer.'

That was so like Nicol he needn't doubt Paul's sincerity.

'And do you know what she called me, and by implication you?' Paul continued mercilessly.

Oh, yes! Mark knew very well. He took a deep breath, not that it helped very much. His voice still sounded much more fierce that he wanted it to be. 'You are trying to bait me, aren't you?'

'Just having a conversation,' Paul said casually.

'Conversation?' If he wasn't feeling so wretched, Mark would have swatted him like an insect.

Paul looked as if studying him for a while before he said: 'It's amazing how intimidating you can look when you scowl like this,' without looking particularly intimidated. Then he waved a hand, palm upwards. 'But life would be so boring without a bit of danger.'

'As if there isn't enough of it as it is!'

But Paul carried on thinking aloud. 'It makes teasing you exhilarating, like sailing close to the wind, too near a force that if provoked would be as unstoppable as a natural disaster.' Then he bent towards Mark and added confidentially, 'Do you know that by suppressing things the way you do, the reaction when it comes could be . . .'

Mark grabbed him by the shirt front with his good hand and lifted him off the ground while Paul concluded: '. . . awesome?'

'Just make sure you are not the one to bring me to that point,' said Mark an inch from Paul's face.

'OK.'

The expression of utter submission, to say nothing of his seeming trust that he was in no real danger, made Mark almost smile and he dropped Paul unceremoniously. The man was a clown.

'Is this the time or place for this sort of thing?' Mark said eventually.

Paul lifted his shoulders. 'It had to be brought out sometime, and I could never get up the courage to say it before.'

'You counted on my being injured?'

'No. You are the lesser of two evils. I'd rather face danger from a real person than sit around and conjure up imaginary ones.'

It was true that the argument, though distasteful, had stopped Mark too from thinking that they were being spied upon, but now that impression returned with a vengeance.

10

The roar had nothing to do with it. Sylvia was getting used to the sound of howler monkeys in the mornings. They were distressingly loud but harmless. What had unsettled her was that terrified human call coming immediately afterwards: 'Jesus!'

In spite her determination to do nothing about it for fear it would be another trick of her imagination, she couldn't ignore it. Somebody out there needed help, and it did not sound like an animal.

Voices, sometimes rising in anger, sometimes muffled, guided her among the maze of tree trunks. Though breathlessly excited, she tried to moderate her expectations. But when she saw the two shadowy figures, she was astonished at her reaction.

She had thought that if anything as unlikely as meeting people should occur, she would run and claim whoever they were as saviours. Instead, she hid behind a tree buttress.

It might have had something to do with the fact that they were about to come to blows. *Men!* Besides, caution was a good thing. What if they were criminals or drug barons or . . .

Don't be so stupid. They are fellow survivors.

Two men, one woman, it would lead to trouble.

You have been reading too many books.

Still, she would lose nothing by waiting. They were not going anywhere fast.

Two snakes, side by side, glided by, almost touching her. A ripple of motion passed down their bodies. She was so captivated by how they poured over obstacles, she vaguely worried and then only about her lack of fear.

Amazing! She never saw a living thing for days, other than insects and leeches, and now they came in twos. But why did she think she ought to be scared? The animals minded their own business. She did not interfere with them, they went their way. The same with the jungle in general. She was not really afraid of it. Just thought she ought to be. Maybe she had panicked because she could not escape if she wanted to. Now there was a possibility, she could be rational.

What was she thinking about? Was there a question of her refusing to be rescued? Had she gone crazy already? For a start, she had a duty to her children. On the other hand, did the children need her? After the initial shock, they would adjust. They could live perfectly well without her. Their father would see to that and learn a thing or two on the way.

One of the men stood up with fluid, unconscious grace. The tattered clothes revealed a perfectly proportioned body that would have been extremely impressive if it were not for the fact that the other man began unfolding as if he never meant to stop.

Ajax clutched his left arm and began to walk. Adonis followed.

She had to make a decision, now.

Perhaps it would be wiser to shadow them. Even if she could assume they were perfectly safe, she lacked confidence in other ways. Utterly stupid to worry about what she looked like, under the circumstances but this was not something she could be logical about.

*

It took the best part of the day before she discovered that these men – from their accents she gathered they were citizens of the United States – were not going to lead her anywhere. They were as lost in the jungle as she had been, going through the same motions, walking around in circles, disoriented, hungry, thirsty and unable to see food or a source of water when they came across it.

Not only could they not help her, they needed her help. Without her, these innocents would starve or become so desperate they would eat the first berry they came across and poison themselves. Besides, Ajax was injured and that selfish companion of his did not seem inclined to help.

So they had the looks! She had the knowledge. They were evenly matched. She squared her shoulders, set her jaw and made to take the first step.

There was a humming noise in her head. Dizziness, most likely. Not surprising considering how long she had been without food, to say nothing of the fact that she had drugged herself in ignorance. But that was not all. She was paralysed from limbs to vocal cords. She couldn't even warn the men of her presence. Every time she tried, the hum intensified. Now it resembled the distant noise of a flock of turkeys or a number of angry people talking simultaneously. The two men were talking too, at least one of them was, but that was something separate. If she could not pick up what he was saying, right now, it was from the interference of the other noises.

A voice from the background mumble began to predominate. She could not make out words but somehow knew the meaning. It was a warning.

The men were walking away. She was going to lose them. Panic rose in her throat like last night's sickness. A couple of steps and she would not be alone any more. How could she not take them? How could she get herself in this state?

Convinced, until now, that there was nothing around but those two strangers, herself, and whatever madness existed in her mind, she was surprised to see shadows detaching themselves from tree trunks and bushes. Dozens of them. People, so cleverly disguised, she did not see them before.

They were naked but for a string around their waists. Feathers in their ears. They walked on silent feet, armed with blowpipes and machetes. One of them had a shotgun and wore shorts.

The Indians had the two white strangers completely surrounded, yet nobody bothered with her. Just when she thought she might be invisible behind the buttress, the Indian with the gun turned, fixed her with his eyes and pointed behind her.

She swung around and came face to face with the same Indian she had seen by the fire in what she had speculated was a dream or a hallucination.

He was squat, solidly built, immobile, ageless. There was no threat or encouragement on his face, no expression at all.

When she had seen him before, she had been under the impression he was naked. Now she realised that he wore something resembling shorts that had assumed the same dark brown colour as the wearer. He also wore a pendant around his neck. A rough stone, suspended from a leather thong. Embedded in its powdery matrix was a huge crystal. From its rectangular shape and the green flames it threw, it could be nothing else but an emerald, the sort of size that people out there would kill for.

Confronting him in daylight, cold sober, Sylvia was at a loss.

He went down on his haunches and signalled her to do the same.

She thought of the two people who were about to be killed, but the man's calmness communicated to her. She sat down, determined to refuse drugs this time.

Nothing happened for a while and the man's calming effect was wearing off. She fidgeted, worrying about the men and if the Indians would kill her too after they finished with them or, worse, take her to their village.

She knew that Indians went in for stealing women from

outside the tribe. They might not understand the science behind genetic variation, but they practised it all the same. There were stories of white women fulfilling that role, too. It would be the ultimate in irony if, by trying to free herself from being a suburban housewife, she ended up as a squaw, if that was what they called them here.

The Indian produced a bird cry, so convincing at first that she looked around for the bird. Suddenly they were surrounded by dozens of Indians, including the one with the gun. They looked very unhappy.

Sylvia could breathe more easily now she knew they were not stalking the two white men, until it occurred to her that they might have already dispatched them silently with their feathered arrows like the one the Indian seated in front of her began to make, producing the materials out of a pocket. There was nothing she could do but sit and wait.

The atmosphere seemed charged with the buzzing from an invisible swarm of angry bees. Like the other night, it destabilised her. She felt as if she was drowning and tried to concentrate on the chief Indian, using the calming effect of his monotonous occupation as a raft. Beneath the buzzing, she located a calmer undercurrent that gradually swelled up until it drowned everything else.

Is up to you!

There was no doubt about it. It came to her the same way thoughts filled her head last night. Nobody had said a word. The man in front of her was patiently getting on with his arrow construction and the other Indians stood mute, wrapped in their anger.

For a while she was stunned. How could it be? But there was no other explanation. She was listening to unspoken thoughts. In English?

Was it English? Were thoughts in any language? She had chosen the words to express the thought. Like those strange warnings about pumas and hawks. She had given the animals those names. She might as easily have called the one jaguar and the other eagle. What came to her mind was the idea of a big cat-like creature and a bird of prey. Now it was the idea that what happened next was up to her, and it all implied thought transfer.

She had experimented with it once in her youth at a student dinner dance. But it was only a prank, and she had the excuse of having just read Hesse.

'We can't sit here hidden behind a pillar,' her friend Jessica had said. 'Nobody would ask us to dance.'

'Let's have a couple of drinks and talk. I don't feel like dancing,' Sylvia said.

'You are saying that to save face. You are afraid in case nobody asks you, anyway.'

Sylvia was peeved. 'I can dance with whomever I chose,' she said.

'Oh, yeah! How?'

'Wait.' And she went through the performance of concentrating her thoughts on the handsomest man on the dance floor. Almost instantly, he turned around and came to ask her for a dance.

It might have been a coincidence, or the young man caught her eye and fancied his chances, like Jessica had said, but it had been scary at the time. Since then, she had read of 'beaming', that is, thought transfer as practised by some shamans in the Amazon, without giving it much credence, though it had been recorded by scientifically trained explorers. She had put it in the same category as the assertion that some Ayahuasqueros, people who used Ayahuasca, could see their animal equivalents or predict the future. It had never been scientifically verified.

Is up to you!

She stood up. The Indians around her stirred uneasily. The buzzing increased, then one spoke harshly to their leader, who then got up, took the pendant off his chest and dangled it in front of her eyes, offering it to her, tempting her. There was an intake of breath all around.

She shook her head. It was of no value to her, especially under the circumstances.

He seemed to have expected nothing less and returned it to its rightful place with a satisfied smile as if to say to his troops: I told you so. The rest of the Indians relaxed a little and opened up their ranks for her to go, the buzzing of their silent anger gone.

Was that all that was up to her? To stay or go? And what of the men? Were they given the same choice? Somehow she knew they were not, but whether they were considered a greater threat and were to die, if indeed they were not already dead, she had no way of knowing, nor did she relish having to find out.

11

Paul's dilemma was whether to open his eyes to the humiliation that he was afraid of shadows or pretend he was still asleep. To the almost constant feeling since he'd been in this place that eyes were crawling all over him, another element was added, never felt before: a strong smell of lemon blossom mixed up with something unmistakably feminine. Wishful thinking, of course, but wouldn't the presence of a woman make things more interesting? He cautiously opened his eyes, just in case and yet fully prepared to laugh at himself.

'Jeeesus!' He let his breath out slowly and closed his eyes again. When he reopened them the apparition was still there, wrapped up in haze.

This was not his idea of beauty. He liked them longer in the leg, narrower in the hip and fuller in the breast. Why should his fantasy take this turn?

He waited for the figure to dissolve but it persisted, took a few faltering steps forward, focused and lost some of its ethereal quality. She was extremely feminine, he had to admit, in an old-fashioned way reminiscent of a Grecian statue, the way her wet clothes clung to every curve. In the heat, steam rose from them and enveloped her in a wavering peplos, adding to the dream-like appearance.

He rose slowly, eyes still fastened on her for fear that if he blinked, she'd disappear. Her face reflected a succession of feelings: apprehension, relief and finally annoyance. Maybe she did not like him staring at her like that. He should say something.

'Do you speak English?' He pronounced it carefully, like one does in a foreign place.

'Do you?' she snapped back.

Paul had not lived in England for years without coming across people objecting to his calling his speech English without the prefix 'American', and it never failed to amuse him. That, combined with his relief that he was not seeing things, made him throw his head back and let out frustration, anxiety and fear, all these alien feelings he had allowed to overwhelm him in this sepulchral place.

His laughter dispersed through the forest and returned in echoes of varying resonance, creating multiple effects: gurgling, chuckling, rejoicing, mocking. She must have registered just the last by the way she shook the masses of black hair from her face, raised a stubborn chin, dark eyes flashing a warning. But as the last echoes expired in gentler tones, she relaxed, an uncertain smile on her lips.

This was his chance to take charge of the situation. He was about to begin introductions when he realised she was the nervous passenger he had seen in Miami airport. He was stunned but recovered quickly.

'Sylvia,' he said with mock urbanity, as if glad to see an old acquaintance. And then, unable to resist exhibiting his erudition as she, most probably, took him for ignorant just because he was an American, added in his best Oxbridge accent, 'How very appropriate, meeting you in a forest.'

She was genuinely surprised but not in the manner he had hoped. 'We've met . . .' It was a statement rather than a question, so she must have noticed him at the airport, after all.

Paul could hardly suppress his satisfaction for catching her out. 'Yes. I had the honour of rescuing your file in Miami Airport.'

'We were passengers on the same flight?'

'No,' said Paul.

She became defensive again. 'What are you doing here, then?'

Her tone grated and he lost his desire for confidences.

The whole truth was not necessary, anyway. 'Looking for you, as a matter of fact.'

'A rescue party?' Maybe she was right to be so contemptuous. In their state, they didn't look the part.

'It's true,' Paul persisted. 'We were looking for survivors and ended up lost too,' and added as an afterthought, 'in this Godforsaken place.'

From being still as a statue, bar the single shake of the head, she became animated, arms moving expansively as if trying to embrace the whole of the forest. 'Godforsaken? This is the best place in the world for survival. It nurtured innumerable species of life for millions of years for the simple reason that it possesses the optimal conditions for the purpose: moisture, warmth, food – provided one does not expect it wrapped up in cellophane.'

Ah, well. A nature freak spouting out some propaganda she had read. 'What about wild animals, insects, noise, unbearable heat by day, cold by night . . .' Paul counted on his fingers.

She silenced him with an imperious wave of a hand. 'You haven't been in a jungle before, have you? You swallowed the myth of the Green Hell, and you are now busy trying to live in it accordingly.'

To say that her pomposity pissed him off would be mild. But he had no chance. She was off again.

'Have you been attacked by anything?' Again, she left no space for response. She was already answering her own question, hands flying around like birds on the wing. 'They are all minding their own business and staying out of sight. You are more likely to be attacked by a human animal in a city than a wild one in the forest.' Even she must have realised she was becoming a pain in the ass because she added a bit less forcefully, hands back by her side, 'Besides, there are no big carnivores in the Amazon.'

'You are an expert, huh?'

'I can read.'

Things were bad enough without smart-alecky females. And what was she doing, staring at him like this? It was his turn to squirm under her stare, aware of his dishevelled hair, the stubble on his cheeks and the innumerable blemishes of insect bites.

Now she held his eyes. He had been told, often enough, they were his strongest feature, but her reaction was far from the usual. She frowned, startled as if frightened or, even worse, repulsed, and moved her glance quickly at something even more horrifying behind him.

Sensitised by constant feelings of dread, he turned to face some monster and came face to face, well, face to chest, with Mark, who had also awakened and was now towering over him.

12

Mark decided that it was not another bout of fever. This was reality, however improbable. Here she was, neither injured nor starved, defending the forest that obviously held no terrors for her, and it was they that needed the reassurance and, in his case, the mending. Size wasn't everything, after all.

But this wasn't a fairytale ending. They were still in the forest, all three of them. One shouldn't forget Paul. The predictable scenario was: he provoked, she admired, he mocked, she dropped her guard, he conquered. Well, she nearly dropped her guard, recovered, marshalled her defences and kicked Paul's ass. It was refreshing but wouldn't help her in the long run. She was already getting lost in those fatal eyes. Curiously, she started as if sensing the danger and looked up to him, but instead of being reassured, her vague anxiety turned to unmistakable fear.

It went through him like a scalpel, but the hurt turned instantly to fury. Not at her. How could he? At himself for looking severe, though he felt nothing of the kind. People always thought he frowned at them when he just concentrated. But his anger was as transitory as her apprehension and he looked at the face upturned towards him in fascination. He ought to say something to reassure her that he represented no threat to her. Or, in fact, anything. He had always thought she would be the kind of woman he could talk to. Now words failed. He couldn't even say hello, aloud.

He sighed. *No fear from this end, honey, no stomach for this sort of combat. I never know what to do with women. You are good, very good. A little forest fairy, like your name suggests. Fragile like a China ornament. I am too clumsy. Paul plays with them and throws them away. They don't break. I love them and they do.*

She was taking in the damage. *No sympathy, please!*

Her stance and expression changed and she walked over to him bypassing Paul without a second glance. A determined, firm step. This particular delicate ornament was underpinned in steel, betrayed by her earlier talk, her walk now, her glance. Steady, almost stern. The fleeting apprehension was but a little wobble, now overruled.

She came closer and he was drowned in the smell of lemon blossom. If he stretched his arm he could touch her. He wouldn't dare, of course, but he let his glance caress that smooth brown skin, so much of it exposed. Unlike them, protected by trousers and long-sleeved shirts, she only had her dress. It was suspended from the shoulders by two straps into which she had tucked the corners of the purple scarf as some protection for her shoulders and back. It still left her arms and bosom bare to the mercy of the insects and leeches, though they didn't seem to have taken advantage of it.

From his height he could see down between her breasts. It wasn't a cleavage. That was what his wife had. Two mountains squashed against each other, a deep, tight line between them. This was a shallow valley between two gently rising hills.

He shifted his eyes down the tiny waist, the smoothly flaring hips – and another comparison with his wife. Nicol's were as narrow as a boy's and she was terrific in trousers, but she wouldn't look half as sexy as this, in a damp dress that clung to every smooth curve. One could bruise oneself on Nicol's sharp hipbones if one got too carried away . . . *stop it!*

The whole ensemble ended in a pair of scuffed shoes, so pathetically small it brought a lump to his throat. Any moment now, she would totter off the dainty hills, bent and worn from walking, and into his arms.

He jumped out of his reverie at the sound of her voice,

apparently scolding Paul for not taking care of his shoulder. She cared!

'I tried,' Paul protested, 'and he told me to piss off for causing too much pain. You feel brave, you try!'

She looked up at Mark again, a challenging glance, and he went down obediently only to find his eyes just above the gentle rise of the triangle between her thighs. He reproached himself for his adolescent-like obsession and tried to think of the certain pain he was about to endure if she tried anything. He didn't succeed. It was the fever, of course. It made him stupid. What was the use of him getting so carried away with Paul around?

All that was forgotten as pain overwhelmed him – and she was only trying to get his shirt off. He had raised his good arm for her to pull the sleeve off, and now she was slowly and gently peeling the one from the injured arm. He dreaded to think what would happen if she tried to set the shoulder. From his experience, the operation needed a lot of strength which she couldn't possibly have. And speed. One quick sharp movement. It would concentrate the pain in the shortest time possible. That's what he would have done.

She hesitated, probably realising her lack of necessary muscle. Then, 'You hold him and I will pull,' she told Paul with sudden resolve.

'Play tug-of-war with him?' said Paul.

'Any better ideas?' she said.

'Nope.' Paul put his arms around Mark's body. 'I just hope you know what you're doing, that's all!'

'Putting a ball in a socket,' she said bluntly.

Mark could hear Paul mumbling next to his ear, 'Smartass!' and if things were not so dire, he would have smiled. Instead he felt her hands on his arm, warm and gentle, one trying to encircle the biceps and not succeeding very well, and one below the elbow. The grip was pitifully inadequate for the job. She changed her mind and wrapped her arms around it. The necessary raising of his arm, even to such low degree, was so excruciating that it meant nothing that his wrist was squashed hard against her bosom. Instead, he concentrated on taking deep breaths like he used to before a concerted effort in the stadium that would have made great demands on his energy reserves. He tried to think of anything else but what was to come and the limitations of his helper.

'Pull,' she called suddenly, and Mark felt as if a football opponent had rammed him in the stomach with a great, padded shoulder, driving the breath out of him and everything went black. He came round with not just his hand into her bosom but his face. He felt his whole body running with cold sweat and, mindful of body odour, withdrew.

The scarf had disappeared from her shoulders and was now round his neck, supporting his arm. The throbbing in his shoulder beat in time with his heart that thumped against his ribs and reverberated into his ears. He set his jaw firmly to stop being sick as wave after wave of nausea hit him. Just about every regulatory centre in his brain seemed affected and he had hunger and thirst to thank for no more embarrassing manifestations than just cold sweat, tachycardia and nausea.

Paul was replacing Mark's shirt over his shivering shoulders and, for lack of anything else, Sylvia used the damp hem of her dress to wipe his face. Mark wanted to say thank you but dared not unlock his jaw. He just gave her what he hoped was a grateful glance. He was sure she would think him deaf and dumb by now. That's why she was always addressing Paul, never himself.

'Let's help him to my base,' she said.

Base? She had a base? This woman was a treasure.

She bent over to help him up, and his desire to say something, the increased pain at her mere touch, the battle to control bodily functions, made it all come out sharp, like an army sergeant's command: 'Easy!'

She took a step back and now it was she that set her jaw, staring at him, waiting.

He felt confused for his clumsiness, certainly, but also at

why this woman had showed fear, even momentarily, when she treated both Paul and him with this amount of firmness. It was obviously not them she was scared of but something she had recognised in them. What?

13

Sylvia listened to Paul's regular breathing as he slept in the foetal position on the hard floor and Mark's restless movements against the buttress beyond the circle of firelight. She wondered at her earlier urge to defend the jungle to them as if convinced, all of a sudden, that it hadn't been that bad. Come to think of it, since she had decided not to fight it and stopped caring about escape or even survival, the jungle ceased to be her enemy. She had not, of course, admitted to them that she had found nothing eatable, so far, except for sweet potatoes, but other matters had supplanted such mundane practicalities at the time.

She had been mesmerised by Paul's eyes. They reminded her of something, certainly the colour – cobalt was what sprang to mind – but more so the expression. It was that of a cat watching its prey lazily, in full knowledge that it could not get far enough that a pounce would not bring it down.

A cat!

She turned quickly to the other man, who had finally managed to stand up behind his friend, throwing her head back to look at him.

In his turn, he was observing her from above. The mouth relaxed briefly, showing well defined lips, the outlines firmly traced as if chiselled out of granite like the rest of his features, but there were two little dimples at the corners of the mouth that betrayed a sensitivity denied by the rest of his countenance. The smile spread slowly across his face until it reached the eyes under the shadows of the brow. They took on a soft sheen, bestowing on him a benign look. He moved his head and they caught a beam of light filtering from above. They changed to a lighter brown, so light as to appear almost golden. They glinted for a second, piercingly hard, before softening under the shadow. That and the boldly sculpted nose, slightly hooked, reinforced the image of a bird of prey.

The memory of the hallucination she had had under the influence of the Indian's drink returned and with it, the chilling breath of fear all over her. She was trapped between two predators and it was too late to run. After all, what was she? The Indian had called her a paca. She certainly had viewed everything in her hallucination from the lowly point of something not bigger than a rodent.

The fear was superseded almost instantly with the satisfaction that, at last, there was proof that Ayahuasca, or a mixture of that with God knew what the Indian had given her, could induce someone to see animal equivalents and events that were yet to take place. Whether she would ever have the courage to admit that to a scientific conference and face being laughed off the podium, was another matter.

This feeling, too, was short-lived, to be replaced with annoyance. Great! They were magnificent beasts of prey and she just a mouse. It would do her insecurity an awful lot of good! But she had to brave it out. The second part of the message was, they needed her help. The hawk man in particular. Looking at him again, she felt slightly reassured. There was strength flowing from this silent giant, but that momentary flash of the eye was a warning that he was never to be taken for granted. Maybe if she were to move away from his shadow, the same strength would appear menacing. But how could she be out of range of those eyes, fixed as they were at such advantageous height?

Now they were here, she was at a loss of how to behave towards them. She couldn't even look at them. One met her eyes with that taunting look, the other stared at her as if she were a curiosity, and both made her nervous. She could not make natural conversation without looking into people's eyes. But that was not the whole story. Their presence, whether she looked at them or not, was overpowering.

Paul's comments came back to her and she cringed.

She had guided them to the rock and let them drink. Then she turned to go in search of food when it occurred to her that she did not even know their names.

'Paul and Mark.' Paul indicated appropriately.

'They fit,' she said without thinking.

Paul stared at her as if she were crazy. 'Fit what!'

'Your appearances, of course,' she said.

And so they did. One as soft as a love sigh, the other as hard, well . . . as his appearance.

'Nuts,' Paul said to Mark when he thought her out of earshot. 'Never mind. At least we have water, food with any luck, and certainly sex.'

'Leave her alone!'

She was startled at the fierceness of the remark. The pain, she supposed.

Mark added, a little more gently: 'Not your type.'

'Come on! How many types are there? She is a female, isn't she? Weird, but the only screwable thing around.'

'You are being disgusting again.'

'Just realistic. Besides, she has been alone for a while. She must be in need of . . . comfort.'

It made her mad at the time and she would never forgive him for it, but Paul was right in some respects. She had been alone for too long, and by that she did not mean the last few days like he thought. She had been chronically starved of sexual contact and that made her vulnerable to the sensuality these men exuded. Trust that brat of an

Adonis to recognise it and look at her in that insufferable way.

Mark was delirious. Talking to Nicol, whoever she was. He must be in great discomfort, but there was nothing she could do other than try to cool him down.

She went over to wipe him again, dipping the handkerchief she had found in his pocket in whatever little insect repellent remained. The warmth of his brow penetrated the cloth. The unshaven cheeks were like sandpaper and as she bent over him, she couldn't help smelling his sweaty body. Normally she would have found it repelling, but now the musky scent excited her. The insects bomb-dived on his chest and she wetted the cloth once more.

Under the golden suntan, granite muscles pushed and bulged against the elastic skin, reminiscent not of the restrained musculature of a Greek statue like Paul's, but the exuberant glorification of the male anatomy in a Michelangelo painting.

He moaned as she came close to his shoulder. It was swollen, the overlaying skin discoloured. Perhaps in the morning she could find the right plant to ease the pain and reduce the inflammation. At least, there was no open wound to get infected.

She went back to the fire and wished for some advice, but there was no message from the other side of silence. Or did that phenomenon occur only under the influence of Ayahuasca?

As a pharmacologist, she had great respect for drugs. She never touched anything unnecessarily, only painkillers when pain was unbearable and antibiotics in cases of severe infection. The so-called recreational drugs she had experimented with on laboratory animals, never on herself. She knew that anything that had an effect through the brain was addictive and harmful, no matter what the folklore was among those that indulged in it. There was no safe drug.

Besides, in the course of her career she had met too many casualties. Now someone was experimenting with her.

She could not have refused the shaman, of course. It might have caused offence and she needed him on her side, but next time she should get more information from him, somehow. This beaming business was limiting and far too passive.

'Don't you need sleep?' It came out of the darkness suddenly, and she jumped. 'Sorry! I didn't mean to startle you.'

So the silent giant felt better and made the effort, at last, to talk to her. If he had waited for her to make the first move, they would never talk to each other. But what a voice! A rich, resonant bass, welling out of the barrel of his chest, soothing.

'I had enough sleep the last few days,' she said.

'Don't worry. Everything will be fine.'

She felt immersed up to the neck in honey. Well, honey that had trickled over gravel, gathering sand on its way, just noticeable in the lower register. She was ready to believe anything spoken like that, though she knew that there was plenty to worry about. Things might turn out fine in the end if she did as she was told, and that's where the danger crept in. She was not very good at that. Not that she understood exactly what she was told. She had a feeling that what the shaman meant by it was up to her, had nothing to do with her being free to go or stay, but whether these men lived or died, and that was too much responsibility.

She couldn't tell Mark any of it. 'They must have given up looking for me,' she said instead, and then for encouragement, 'but, of course, they will be searching for you two.'

'We were way off course.'

For once, she thought of something without blurting it out loud: *I wonder why?*

'You were going to a Medicinal Plant Conference, I understand,' Mark said.

She could not help showing her irritation. 'You two seem very well informed.'

'Paul makes sure he always is about everything. That's the secret of his success.'

'And I bet he is very successful.' So arrogant, he could be nothing else.

'Oh, yes!'

Mark bent forward and she could pick out his outlines. The fire illuminated just the forehead, the side of the nose and the lower lip. It looked very dramatic.

'It must have been very hard for you, all alone,' he continued.

'Only to start with,' she said, then she decided she could trust him with the inessentials, at least. 'Food is still a bit of a problem. "Not on sweet potato alone, liveth man".' His chuckle was awkward, as if he hadn't enough practice. Somehow, it embarrassed her and she thoughtlessly added, 'Anyway, there were compensations.'

She regretted saying it instantly, but it made a lot of sense. For the first time in her life she was free: no money worries, no stress, no emotional demands. She could think uninterruptedly for as long as she wished without someone filling the silence with drivel in the name of small talk. She was master of her own actions. She had no responsibilities. If it weren't for the fact that she missed the children, and the worry about how they were coping without her, she would be happy. Perhaps happy was the wrong word. She was less unhappy here than any other place she had known. She could not tell him all that, either.

'There is so much beauty, unspoilt by the baseness and greed of man,' she said, 'Not for long. They haven't reached this far yet.'

Then it occurred to her that these two strangers might be the harbingers. Obviously, they hadn't come here to rescue her. The Indians must know something, hence their attitude towards the men.

She tried to veer in a different direction. 'There is great satisfaction in using my knowledge of plants for something more practical than writing scientific papers, and the absence of people can only be a bonus. Oh!' She realised too late. 'I, er . . . didn't mean it like this. I meant crowds. You know?'

'I know,' he said and there was sadness in his voice. 'They make you feel so claustrophobic, you want to run away.'

A soulmate too? The thought encouraged her to open up. 'When I was young, people represented cosiness and security. I wanted to join them, only to find out I was even more lonely, so that I escaped to feel lonely again. It took a lifetime to learn to live with it. But the last few days, after the first panic, I was surprised to find how un-lonely I was.'

'I thought you were married,' Mark said. 'How could you have been that lonely before?'

She looked at her ring, a dead giveaway. 'Is marriage a guarantee against loneliness?'

'No,' he said sadly, 'and I should know.'

So Nicol was the wife. She tried to change the subject or they'll end up exchanging marital horror stories. 'Can I ask some questions, too?'

He inched nearer, amused. She interpreted that as yes. 'You and Paul . . .'

A metallic glint from under the eyebrow; the face hardened; the body stiffened.

Sensitive on the subject, she thought. She was quite safe in their company, after all. Did she feel a little, just a little, disappointed? No! It belied the vibrations she was picking up from both of them. She was not that naïve. But somebody must have voiced what she had thought momentarily, hence the defensive posture. She continued smoothly, however, as if she had noticed nothing.

'What are you doing here? Other than looking for me, of course? Business or pleasure?'

'Paul was on business.' There was more sand than honey in his voice.

'And you?'

A shadow passed over his features and his eyes lengthened, focusing some place beyond her head, in the darkness.

Without meaning to, she had poked at exposed nerves. The stupid thing was, she was not curious. She just thought she ought to show some interest. People were forever telling her she was too selfish to bother about anyone's business, but whenever she tried, she made a mess.

She should keep to tried and tested methods: maintain her distance. After all, she had been warned that these people were a threat. In which case, wouldn't it be better to leave them to it? Why saddle herself again with responsibilities, emotional upheavals and the rest of it, now she had found how their absence could be such a liberating experience? It would be dangerous, but liberty had its price, though she had not assumed any responsibility voluntarily. It was imposed on her by the Indian. How would he react to any shirking? But surely, he only meant for her to help the injured man and show them how to get food and water, not become their slave. Once they could take care of themselves she was free to leave them, possible only if she had not enmeshed herself in any way before then.

14

Paul was reclining by the rock, studying its markings moodily. Something was bothering him, Mark thought. Severe hunger pangs, most probably, if his own stomach was anything to go by. He would prefer to leave it at that, but silence intensified his worries.

At dawn, Sylvia had got up and left. Nothing remarkable in that, except that she looked upset about something and a couple of hours had elapsed since her departure and she was nowhere to be seen. What if their presence was making her nervous, in spite all the bluster or, maybe, hence all the bluster. All the indications were there. The way she turned to squash some flippant remark from Paul, only to catch his eyes and get flustered; avoiding his own eyes; her consternation at Paul's knowing smile whenever he caught her surreptitiously looking at him. Even worse, she might have overheard Paul's remarks yesterday. That alone would make her feel sufficiently threatened for her to go and never come back.

Last night he had meant to reassure her. He intended to explain about Paul, tell her not to take him seriously or she would let herself in for a lot of bruising. Paul was not bad, not even unkind, just careless with people's feelings. Instead, he reinforced her suspicions that there was something between him and Paul other than friendship.

He had thought of following her, but there seemed to be a chasm between his brain and his limbs. He couldn't move from the wedge of root that supported him. This fever was causing too much trouble. He was holding everyone up.

They had to get out fast or things could get worse. Malnutrition, illness, entanglements, desperation, reversion of civilised standards . . .

'What's up?' he asked Paul reluctantly.

'Last night,' Paul said, 'I wasn't asleep. I heard.' He then turned viciously on Mark. 'You are such an asshole! You showed so much sensitivity when she mentioned our names in tandem, you gave her the wrong impression.'

As if Mark needed him to point that out.

'I don't mind what she thinks of you,' Paul continued. 'It serves you right for trying to sweet-talk her, but my own reputation is at stake.'

'I thought you don't care about such things.'

This infuriated Paul even more. 'Why should I care if she thinks I am a faggot? Better people than her assume that, and I don't give a shit.'

'Why then?'

Paul threw his arms up in the air. 'That's just it! It's enough to drive one crazy.'

He suddenly saw the joke and started laughing. Then one rude remark followed another and Mark lost patience and stopped responding. His uneasiness about Sylvia returned mixed up with something else.

Paul sulked for a while then said: 'You are as good company as she is.'

'Maybe we find something to worry about in this situation,' Mark said.

'I worry too, you know. Where is the next lay going to come from, for instance.'

Trust Paul to think of nothing else. No wonder she couldn't bear their company. 'I thought you believe that women can't keep their hands off you.'

'Not all, obviously. Sylvia can't stand me.'

'Do you blame her? She rescued us, cleaned us, fed us, and all you want is to use her like a whore, which is the only kind of woman you know anything about.'

'They are all whores!' Paul sat bolt upright. 'They are out for what they can get. Why does Nicol put up with you and your precious work that keeps you away all hours? Your money. She can have a prestigious house, belong to the best clubs and screw around with whoever she fancies.' He pointed an emphatic finger at Mark. 'You are a fool. You won't catch me doing that.' Now he stubbed the finger at himself. 'I know they are not after me for my big blue eyes. They would spread out their legs just as easily if I were sixty and had a pot belly, like they do with my father. It's money and the power that it provides that they are after.'

It was the first time that Mark had seen Paul like that, and the effect was to exorcise his own fury. 'You are annoyed because you can't do without women. It's a bit unsettling to find you are so dependent, isn't it? Right now, all you need is to be laid. You will soon become your usual sunny self.' He instantly regretted the last bit.

Paul calmed down as suddenly as he had flared up. His face reflected surprise, followed by shame. 'I have every intention of being laid,' he said, looking away.

Mark hesitated for a while before saying: 'Perhaps you cannot sweep her off her feet as easily as all that. Your money is of no use to anyone here, and she might want something more than good looks and lightheartedness.' That, of course, was wishful thinking on his part.

'She will prefer your more sedate ways and mature charm, no doubt?'

'I am not available.' Mark hoped he did not sound as regretful as he felt.

'Remaining faithful to good old Nicol?'

'Don't start that again!'

The day was getting on and she was still not back. Paul fidgeted, but it was no use Mark letting him go in search of her. He, too, could get lost.

'We have to trust she knows her way around,' he tried to reassure Paul, though he himself was anything but.

'We could both go and look for her,' suggested Paul pacing up and down.

'And if she came back, there would be nobody here,' said Mark.

Paul smelled the air. He gave a good impression of a stalked animal, and as if to reinforce Mark's impression he said: 'We can't just stay here like sitting ducks.'

So Paul felt it too. For some time now, from the moment she had left, in fact, Mark fancied that they were under scrutiny again, but he asked innocently, 'Are we being hunted?'

'I've no idea,' Paul said irritably.

A new thought struck Mark. 'Why don't we feel this,' he waved his good arm around vaguely, unable to find the right word to describe the feeling, 'when she is around?'

Paul's voice went up a few octaves. 'I don't know.' Then he thought for a while. 'Why? Do you think it had been her, all along, following us around?'

'Don't be stupid!'

'What then? Do you think we have turned her into some form of mother figure, that's why we feel safer when she is around?' He stopped in his trucks. 'Nope, or I could be accused of incestuous thoughts.' He resumed pacing. 'I just can't stand this any more.' Then he turned to Mark, his jaw stubbornly set. 'I am going off to find her. You stay in case she comes back.'

Mark still didn't agree. There was nothing he could do, but instead of wishing Paul good luck, what came out was, 'If I thought for a moment that you sent her off by making her feel unsafe with us, I will kill you!'

Paul turned back and stared at Mark, seriously for a change. 'Man, I only teased,' he said eventually.

'She doesn't know that.'

Paul remained thoughtful. 'She knows more than you think.'

'What do you mean?'

'I've no idea.' He looked confused. 'It just came to me.'

'You are crazy.'

'There is so much I feel but don't understand any more, I agree with you. But . . .' Paul raised his arms, '. . . the way she looks at people as if she is tapping into them...' He dropped his arms shamefaced and turned to leave the clearing. 'She gives me the creeps.'

Mark had the creeps too, but only in her absence, as if she had the power to ward off evil. Since he did not believe in evil, he was as confused as Paul. Why should grown-up men feel safer in the presence of such a fragile-looking woman? And what was the nature of that hazard? One thing he was sure of: if they were surrounded by danger, as was confirmed by every fibre in his body, they shouldn't split up like this.

'Wait,' he shouted and staggered after Paul.

15

In the coolness of the morning with the mist rising all around, occasionally penetrated by a lance of sunlight, Sylvia might as well have been walking in a temperate woodland. But it wasn't long before she was reminded of where she was.

There was a violent disturbance amongst the tree crowns, a burst of activity and indignant screeching. Something must have scared a troop of monkeys, by the sound of it. Small branches and leaves rained down. Heavier fruit thudded on the invisible ground. What seemed a squadron of butterflies spiralled out of harm's way. She jumped up to grasp one but it turned out to be a blossom, its bruised petals emanating a heavy perfume.

The mist began its upward drift towards the hidden sun, revealing the usual colours of the understorey. Brown earth. Bare tree trunks that occasionally displayed the odd streak of dusty bronze, reflected the delicate tracery of a fern, or provided the neutral contrast to the vivid green of a climber flattening itself against them, determined to scale their smoothness. Then she was startled by a splash of blood against wood. It turned out to be a passion flower and it made her day. The first time she had seen red since her arrival here.

She retraced her steps in a much better mood. There was no need for dramatics. She could handle the situation. Neither of the two men was a brute. Paul was a spoiled brat, that was all, and somebody should put him in his place, though she could see how people hadn't so far. It must have been damned hard to be unpleasant to such a beautiful creature. But she could do it. It wasn't as if she was likely to fall in love with him. The only emotion his appearance stirred was the same as the sight of the passion flower. The constriction in the throat one feels before a work of art or a beautiful sunset and, even then, only occasionally when he took certain poses that, she ought to admit, seemed more part of him rather than contrived. Such feelings had nothing to do with desire and free of that, she could cope. Anyway, men who talked too much of sex were the least dangerous. It betrayed an underlining insecurity. All the same, the sooner they got out of here the better.

By now the children would have been told she was dead. No hope of her keeping her promise to be back soon. But she meant to be back, sometime. If she tried to follow the Indian's instructions, such as they were, it might be never.

Since their last meeting, the chief Indian's presence was all around her like a warning or a threat. She couldn't tell which, only that she was meant to stay within its influence, and it made her feel claustrophobic. But if all three of them put their minds to it . . .

She heard Paul and Mark talking and was about to advertise her approach. She didn't want to hear everything they said. Ignorance had its advantages. But voices carried too well in the forest and it was too late. 'They are all whores!' She had to restrain herself from bursting in on them and giving them a piece of her mind. Instead, she turned on her heels and walked blindly away, her pace increasing with her rising anger.

If she was in two minds about abandoning them this soon, they made up her mind now. It would be impossible to cooperate with them. Sure, Mark had defended her, but even he had to say he was not available as if she were there just to destroy his precious marriage that, from what Paul said, didn't seem all that precious. That was his problem, though. Hers was to find a way out by herself, fast. She would strike along new territory. Keep on going and to hell with all of them. Yanks and Indians.

Blinded in fury, she nearly stepped on a container. Then she saw that the chief Indian was standing there, and if it were not for the gourd to make her stop and look, she would never have noticed him.

They just stared at each other until she thought she ought to do something, and she tried to concentrate her thoughts on a message, using sign language as well, to make doubly sure. *Help me to get out!*

He just stared at her. Whatever made her think that she could project her thoughts to him? On the other hand, she was getting a message, but it took a while to understand what he was trying to convey.

Not ready. Not ready, echoed in her head.

Oh, yes she was!

He spread out his arms, pretending to fly, at the same time he frowned and looked from under his brows. He bent one arm, beating the air with the other ineffectually then pointed at the gourd and straightened the bent arm, both arms now beating strongly. A professional mimic couldn't have done it better.

'He has to mend before I can go?'

He shook his head and put a fist to his heart. That, obviously, was not ready. Then he went down and folded himself like a cat, lazy, yawning. Suddenly he sat up, rubbed his stomach, snarled, his fingers crooked like claws and then slapped his hands sharply.

When the puma was hungry, it would pounce just like any other cat. *Tell me about it!*

The Indian smiled at her, showing blackened teeth, and walked off. Just a few steps, and he blended into the background.

There was no point running after him, but if the chief was here, so would the rest of the tribe be, and she had a fair idea of what they made of all this. They had no reason to trust intruders to their world. So were the three of them safe or in danger? What did the shaman mean by: 'not ready'? For a start, nobody was readier than Paul. He would cause a lot of trouble if they could not get out soon. The chief himself had indicated as much, and Mark was injured. Who knew if she had done the right thing with his shoulder? She wasn't an expert. She did what she thought was logical, using whatever knowledge of anatomy she remembered, and hoped she did not trap any nerves. Suppose she'd crippled him for ever.

But apart from Mark's health, was there need to worry? What did the Indian's appearance mean, if not to reassure her? Why offer medicine unless he wished them well?

She picked up the gourd and made to turn back, then remembered why she was here in the first place. Those men thought of her only as a whore, and she had no intention of going back to them and waiting until they were ready. The Indian had said nothing about her not being ready.

She didn't need anybody. She could make it alone. If there were Indians around, there was a stream or a river nearby. How else could they survive? If she discovered that, she would find a way out. She shouldn't be chained to the rock and certainly not to the men. They were not her responsibility. They could find their way out when they were ready.

For years and years she had been unable to do what she wanted, thinking that other people depended on her. She was not going to start that again. Nobody really needed her except, perhaps, the children.

The more she argued the merits of her going her own way, the more doubt enter her mind.

I have to go back. I have to go back.

'I don't have to do anything I don't want to!' she screamed in frustration.

I have to go back. Over and over and over until it became not just a thought but a belief, a necessity. It was absolutely essential she should go back but she couldn't do it now, even if she wanted to. Since she had meant to leave the men for good, she thought it unnecessary to mark her way.

Once she realised that, the panic of the first day in the forest returned. The immensity of the place pressed on her.

She couldn't breathe. The will to walk deserted her. There was nowhere to go. She was lost.

The Indian reappeared like a *deus ex machina*. She ran towards him, but he turned around and started to walk. He was too fast for her. She had to break into a trot to keep up, but he disappeared behind a tree. She was now running as fast as the terrain and her legs allowed until she caught a glimpse of his back, glistening with sweat. Determined not to let it out of her sight, she looked at nothing but the mesmerising play of shadows on the muscles moving rhythmically with his brisk walk. It didn't matter that she was gasping for breath, her throat was dry, there was a stitch on her side, sweat fell into her eyes or that she felt dizzy. She kept moving.

But surely all this was unnecessary. She could rest. If the Indian wanted her to go somewhere, he would be back. And where was the guarantee that he was leading her where she wanted to go? But she could not stop or get rid of the anxiety that she might lose sight of the Indian, that she might not get back. *In time*, it suddenly occurred to her, and she stumbled. If they had to hurry so much, there ought to be a reason.

The Indian stopped and signed urgently, confirming her fear. She picked herself up and resumed the run. *Oh, God! Let us be in time.* She was sure it had to do with Mark and Paul, and that it would be her fault if anything went wrong.

16

That this search was anything but a useless exercise, Paul had no doubt, but anything was better than just sitting around and imagining things that go bump in the dark. Not that his imagination was less active now. He felt like being pursued by an invisible Argus, but he ignored it and concentrated on tracking her down.

Considering that the earth was as hard as concrete, there was no chance of footprints. What else would a scout do? There was a torn leaf on a climber. So what? But then a few paces further along, there was a bent fern frond and further still, a scratch on a tree trunk. Too consistent to be other than a trail. Whoever made it meant to be followed. Intriguing. She must have known they would come searching, correction, he would come searching for her. Mark was too ill. So that's how the cookie crumbled!

He was beginning to enjoy this game of hide and seek when all markings evaporated. She must be somewhere near. Certainly, whatever was stalking him, and he had an idea now who it must have been all along, was very close, and if it meant what he thought it did, he would forgive her his earlier anxiety. Not that he would let on about that.

There was a muffled sound behind him and he turned, expecting to see her. It was only Mark. He certainly would spoil things. But his initial annoyance was replaced by a doubt. What if it wasn't her that had left the markings? What if they had been lured into a trap?

He couldn't shake the idea off. The sense of uncertainty grew with every step he took, convincing him that he should go no further. He stopped and looked over his shoulder for the reassuring sight of Mark, who was motionless, listening as if he too felt the icy breath of death in the air. Yes, death. Paul had no doubt. All around them, the shadows became menacing. Another step forward would be their last.

He was no coward. On the contrary, people accused him of a death wish because of the chances he was prepared to take in everything. Business or pleasure. They couldn't be more wrong. He pushed things to the limit because he instinctively knew where the limit was, and he never went beyond that. And here he had reached that limit.

Stillness all around, absolute silence. It was unbearable. Something had frightened all life away. Something invisible, insubstantial. The atavistic fear of the unknown, of evil spirits and unnatural powers, awoke from the deep recesses of his brain and his hair stood on end but only briefly. More recent faculties took over. This was real. What was unsettling was that he could not see it. Whoever he, she or they were, only had to show themselves and he and Mark could deal with them. Maybe they knew that. Hence the undercover surveillance. Then it occurred to him that Sylvia was alone. No matter how contrary she was, physically she would present no danger to anybody. There would be no need for this amount of precaution before they attacked her. *Oh, God, no!*

Mark was right. He ought to be grateful. She had led them to the clearing as if she were guiding them home. And she had water in a container, for heaven's sake! Enough water to wash, even, and she had set Mark's shoulder promptly with ruthless efficiency. Yet, for some reason, she brought out the worst in him. That did not mean he had a desire to cause any pain or that he found her uninteresting. Far from it. When Mark tried his macho thing with her, she just stood there and stared until he apologised. Obviously, she wouldn't take any shit from him, and if that did not make her unusual, nothing would. Mark took giving orders and having them accepted for granted without question. It all promised to be quite entertaining at first. Now, he was not so sure. Interesting, yes, confusing, certainly, but entertaining, definitely not. Whatever. The last thing he wanted was for something to have happened to her. And if Mark was right, it would be his fault.

He wished he could take back all those things he had said about sex, which he did just to annoy Mark, who was becoming so protective towards her. Since then, every time she looked at him he felt like he used to as a child when he swore in front of Nanny. He couldn't, as he did then, say: 'Sorry, I didn't mean it,' and nobody was going to make him feel better by telling him he was an angel with a little devil inside him and all he had to do was pray. He prayed that Sylvia never heard his conversation with Mark – but who to? Nanny had not succeeded in either driving the little devil out or making her Irish God real to him. The nearest to religion he came was the belief that each place had its own spirit, and the spirit of this place, right now, seemed to be breathing down his neck.

A rhythmic thud in the distance interrupted such thoughts. It was approaching, accompanied by heavy breathing. A trotting animal in pursuit or being pursued, perhaps. There was a rustle all around like a shifting of numerous unseen bodies and the invisible circle of menace shuttered.

Animals! It was such a relief. That's who the unseen enemy had been all along, too well camouflaged. They never saw them until something disturbed them. Not that he could see them now, no matter how hard he tried. All he could detect were shadows rearranging themselves and making him dizzy. Yet further into the darkness another shadow drifted by, and beyond, another advanced, bobbing up and down. It stopped, desperate panting filling the space, and then it disappeared. Not the noise, though. Whatever it was still wheezed.

Mark, in one of his legendary bursts of energy, dashed towards the noise and Paul made way for him to pass for fear of being steamrolled.

This was no time for heroics. If you cannot identify the

danger, you don't approach it. But Mark was going full tilt for it and Paul had no option but follow.

Mark came to an abrupt stop. Paul careered into him and they both ended up in a pile, cursing and swearing. Mark seemed in agony from the collision, but Paul couldn't blame himself. It was not his fault Mark accelerated from zero to the speed of a bullet and back again without warning. To make it worse, Paul thought somebody was laughing at them, but that was impossible because the only other person there was Sylvia, and she was on her knees, clasping something to herself, trying to catch her breath.

She raised her head and stared at them as if at ghosts. Eventually she said between gasps, 'Thank God . . . I am . . . in time.'

'What the hell?' Paul said in exasperation, picking himself up. She had nearly caused a major injury, and all for fear of the approaching night. 'I thought you must have been attacked by some beast, at least!'

She turned vicious. 'Yes,' she said, 'a bloody puma,' and swatted both Mark's and Paul's helping hands, sobbing.

Mark pulled her up, anyway. 'It's all right now. Don't cry.'

She stepped back astonished. 'But I never cry!'

'Oh boy!' Paul rolled his eyes.

Mark gave him a stern look then turned to her and said gently, 'You should not wander off on your own. It could be dangerous. You yourself said you've been attacked.'

She shook her head. 'You don't understand.' And then said in her usual emphatic way, 'I have to go where I can be alone. I can't be with people twenty-four hours a day. It would drive me crazy.'

It would drive Paul crazy if he were not. 'You resent our presence?' he said.

'Usually,' she said, 'I mark the trees to guide me back, but today I . . . er . . . forgot.'

That, significantly, didn't answer his question, and Mark's frown meant he had registered the implication too. It certainly annoyed Paul, and he couldn't help expressing his contempt with the whole thing. 'So you couldn't run back to us when danger threatened. We have our uses after all, pity about the intrusion.'

She tossed her hair defiantly. 'It's you who were threatened, not me.'

'You mentioned a puma if I'm not mistaken?' Paul said. 'I presume you actually saw it?' The sarcastic tone only marginally helped his humiliation. They had felt threatened and didn't even see anything.

She was staring at him in her peculiar way. 'Yes, I have seen it,' she said with a lopsided smile, 'but it can't catch me unless I want it to.'

She was crazy. He didn't know why he bothered to say any more, but he did. 'You, of course, can outsmart a puma!'

She was still staring and smiling. 'I think so!' she said very slowly.

Mad. The woman was mad.

'It is true we were stalked by something too . . .' Mark began.

'I know,' she said.

Mark frowned. 'Do you know what it was?' he said carefully. 'We haven't seen anything definite.'

She opened her mouth to speak then looked around for something or somebody. She fastened her eyes at a spot among the elusive shadows behind them. Paul turned. There was nothing but maybe some bees if the buzzing was anything to go by, and even that receded and blended into the background noise. Yet she concentrated as if listening, transported and in the shadows, almost as insubstantial as when he had first seen her, she seemed to embody the spirit of this place, or if not, to be in close communion with it. 'I only know the danger is there and that . . . together . . . it would be safer,' she said picking her words carefully.

'We can't face it without you, is what you mean,' said Paul. His absurd thought of spirits was proof that her craziness was catching, and it intensified his resentment. Everything she said or did either humiliated or confused him. And now she was looking at him as if she could read his mind and was returning his distaste in equal measure. His mind! What was left of it. What he needed was a clear head and positive action, impossible when one spent whatever little energy was left from starvation, chasing shadows and crazed females. Let him get some food in his belly and he would soon teach the little bitch a lesson.

'I have no doubt you are very brave and you will put up a fight. That's the problem,' she said. 'You just can't win.'

'And you can,' said Paul.

'No,' she said looking extremely tired suddenly. 'But then I am not going to fight, and neither are you if I can help it. Nothing will hurt us if we show we are harmless.'

Paul gave a mirthless chuckle. 'That's a good theory. Are the beasts out there aware of it, I wonder.'

17

The boom of a howler monkey cleared the throat of the canopy that now picked up its dawn chorus of whistles and cooings and cacklings. Mark shivered in the clammy cocoon of his clothes. His tongue seemed to be stuck to the roof of his mouth. The first attempt to dislodge it brought an intense sensation of bitterness. Then something started tugging at his shoulder and at last he managed to emerge completely from under thick layers of sleep to another painful morning. Paul was still asleep by the remnants of the fire, and Sylvia, nowhere to be seen.

It had been his first real rest since the accident, but the effect of the herbal remedy she had given him last night was wearing off. All that remained was the taste. It had made him wish he had never accepted it. He only complied, not out of any belief in its efficacy, but so as not to insult her. After all, she had endangered her life to get it. Now he was glad he had. At least he got some rest and the pain, though still present, was less intense.

He couldn't remember being ill before, save for the occasional football injury. A lot of pain for a short while and that was that. It had to happen now that it was so important. No wonder she resented them being around. All Paul cared for was for the earliest opportunity to lay her, and Mark was absolutely useless.

He didn't know much about the place but he could at least hunt, for fuck's sake. Isn't that what men were supposed to do in the wild? They hadn't seen any animals simply because they were not going to hang around at the approach of three people talking and crashing about. Now, even if he could creep up on them, what could he do with a useless arm?

Then he remembered yesterday's conversation. But surely, she had only meant big game, and he was not so stupid as to attack a puma. For a start he had no weapons, to say nothing of the fact that it was useless as food. And that brought him back to the needs of his stomach. Its nagging complaint was as constant as the pain in his shoulder and had been present for just as long.

Paul woke up too and poked at the remnants of the fire, trying to revive it. He was talking about Sylvia. She was driving him nuts. Well, she was driving Mark nuts too, for different reasons.

What sort of a woman was she? He had told Paul that the only women he knew anything about were whores but his own knowledge was no more extensive, especially since he was an only child with no sisters to grow up with.

He knew all about women's bodies, of course and their capacity to withstand suffering and then wipe it off their memory which gave them the ability to face it again and again. Physically fragile some of them might look, weak they were not.

He learned to look at them as different because it was the difference he, as a doctor, dealt with. Their anatomy and its function. Never thought of their feelings, their soul, their secret thoughts. He doubted his wife had any. Whatever little she thought of she aired freely, and the rest was drowned in alcoholic fumes.

He watched Sylvia return from her wanderings loaded with plant material. Yesterday's fright was obviously forgotten, together with his advice. She circumnavigated Paul without a glance as if he were a piece of wood or a stone. No glance towards himself, either, but he'd rather be ignored than pitied.

She began silently the process of making her insect repellent, and the place was redolent of aroma with a predominant accent on lemons which he thought of as her signature smell. Yet there were no lemons in her collection of ingredients. Just grasses, bark and leaves which she put in the pot, and a couple of flowers which she didn't.

Paul picked up a flower whose elongated petals hung down like thin twisted ribbons. 'How beautiful,' he said.

She looked at him for the first time since her return. 'Deadly,' she said and after a little pause, 'like most beautiful things in the jungle.'

Paul let it drop. 'So why use it?' he said suspiciously.

'I am not,' she said. 'I can admire beauty without ulterior motives.'

But Paul had plenty of motives, as he stared down her cleavage, from the way he ignored any inferences that might have been drawn from her comments and tried hard to be pleasant and complimentary. Either that or he was trying to make amends about his rudeness yesterday.

Mark could understand how Paul's pride might have been hurt, but she was only trying to help. It would have been nicer, of course, if she asked for assistance. It was not enough to have told them she did not need them, she demonstrated it with every act. Why couldn't she at least tell them what it was that threatened them so they could avoid it, instead of having to rely on her? To be in control or as a protection? Was it possible she mistrusted them that much?

The heat from the fire and the steaming pot was becoming very uncomfortable. Sylvia looked flushed. Perspiration trickled down her neck where Mark's glance, just like Paul's, followed it. When she bent in that way of hers, straight from the hips, knees locked, he caught his breath. The front of her dress gaped open and he could see the breasts tumbling down, the dark pink tips pressing lightly against the material. The demarcation of darker skin unprotected by cloth traced two circles at the fullest part, leaving the lower halves luminescent cream. The contrast was intoxicating. He checked a sigh and almost felt them, elastically firm, fitting snugly into his cupped hands. He was no better than Paul, of course, but there was something about her that made his wife look like a dummy in a dress shop window.

Paul, unable to draw her in further conversation, made his request for food in the politest way possible and Mark realised that maybe hunger pangs, rather than lust or regret, were responsible for the compliments.

'Do you know the real reason I am here?' Sylvia said. 'I was running away from having to feed somebody all the time and having to stay put and listen to unwelcome drivel. I have no intention of getting into that trap again. You want food? Go get it!'

Why so harsh? Had she heard Paul's rude comments? If she did, she must have heard about his wife, too. He hoped not.

After a while she relented. 'OK Let us all go look for food.'

Mark stood up stiffly.

'How is the shoulder?' Her manner was kinder towards him. Felt sorry for him being a cripple, he supposed.

'Maybe she does not think you a faggot after all and fancies her chances,' Paul whispered in Mark's ear.

Mark ignored him. 'Better, thanks,' he said to Sylvia.

She walked ahead and Paul put his hands in his pockets and went along for the ride. 'If she wants my help, she has to ask,' he said to Mark. 'Then I will tell her to hop it like she told me.'

With the heat rising steadily, they all grew tired very soon and Paul's temper deteriorated. When she tapped a fallen tree before sitting down, it burst out. 'What did you expect to find it in it?' he said. 'Our long-awaited breakfast?'

Earlier on when he tried to flatter her, she tore him apart, now he shouted at her and she smiled. 'I just didn't want to offer myself as somebody else's breakfast,' she said.

Paul sighed. 'Like who?'

'The tree could have been full of ants,' she said.

'Just like a woman!' Paul said. 'A forest full of unseen wild beasts, it's OK but ants?'

'You'll learn,' she said getting up.

Her mood continued to improve as the men's bewilderment increased. Nothing was what it appeared to be. Deception was the order of the forest. Roots became snakes, snakes roots. A glowing yellow cigar with black bands wrapped around it turned out to be a giant caterpillar. An enormous flower exploded when Paul inspected it as the butterflies that composed it took to the wing. She laughed for the first time since they met her. A silent kind of laughter like her sobbing, only her chest moving, forcing out short breaths. Just like a woman, Mark thought, echoing Paul's earlier remark. He was not applying it to Sylvia alone, but to the jungle as a whole. Just like a woman: enchanting, confusing, deceptive. Paul obviously was in no mood for such esoteric thoughts. He was more concerned at being, as he interpreted it, laughed at. She shrugged to show she didn't give a damn for his pout and walked ahead.

Paul hacked viciously at a bush in his frustration and only then saw the red berries. He had no time for anything else.

'I wouldn't if I were you,' she warned without turning, as if she had eyes at the back of her head. 'It's *Rauwolfia*.'

That was a name Mark had heard of before. Anyone with the most rudimentary knowledge of pharmacology had.

'What would it do to me?' Paul asked.

She was already absorbed in something else, so Mark volunteered the answer. 'Dampen your ebullient spirits,' he said.

Sylvia turned to stare at Mark, interested. 'How did you know that?'

'Don't tell me you spend the nights flirting,' Paul continued, 'and he never said he too was a doctor?'

Mark rolled his eyes, despairing at him, and she tossed her head and walked off again. 'Perhaps I should keep some of those berries. They might come in handy, after all. Useful for all sorts of mania,' she said. Still, she thought it fit to explain. 'I am not a medical doctor. I taught Pharmacology before I had the children. I became a plant expert by default.'

'That explains a lot,' said Paul. 'A schoolmarm!'

She turned, eyes blazing. 'Except that I am used to dealing with people a bit older than you seem to be.'

Paul made a comic grimace. 'Ouch!'

His insolent smile infuriated her even more and she stalked off, only to stumble over a root.

Paul rushed to put his arms around her, ostensibly to stop her from falling and pressed her against his chest, smiling wickedly down at her. She didn't move.

Mark grimaced. Oh, brother! How predictable. It all had been nothing but the obligatory sparring prior to surrender. Just like a woman, OK!

18

She remained still in his arms and Paul felt the warmth of her body through the flimsy dress. He could not call her beautiful. She had dark eyes, a delicate nose and a well-formed mouth, the upper lip on the one side slightly fuller than the other. Charming, in fact. If he were to kiss her, and probably he would if Mark weren't there, he would be tempted to bite it. It just lent itself to it. But her complexion was swarthy, the jaw on the square side and too determined. She gave the appearance of beauty, nevertheless, he was at a loss to explain.

He passed his tongue over his parched lips and bent closer, breathing in the smell from the gap between the breasts, a mixture of lemons and something unmistakably feminine from further down. His want became a torment, his blood raced, engorging him, leaving him gasping for breath. She must have felt it, too. In Paul's experience, women liked it and you progressed from there, or after the first excitement they pretended offence and slapped you, and you progressed from there. He was ready for the latter but it was, perhaps, too much to hope she would do the expected thing. She never had done, so far.

She suddenly blushed furiously and withdrew in confusion. He almost felt sorry for her. She was as inexperienced as a schoolgirl and as insecure. All that efficiency and authoritative manner was a front. Her strategy had been to put him off by being bossy. She was shy of Mark, or afraid. It was amazing how her manner changed from downright rudeness and arrogance towards himself to almost diffidence when she addressed Mark.

Was it Mark's imposing appearance that commanded respect, or had she guessed of the catastrophic temper lurking behind his customary mildness, waiting to burst out? Admittedly, it only did under severe provocation, but it made all those who knew him well or had the misfortune to have witnessed it, mindful of taking him too much for granted.

No. She was no coward, whatever else she was. Just impressed by the acres of bare chest. All those pectorals. One could understand how women could get sidetracked like that. Even experienced travellers like Nicol got lost there, temporarily.

Now she was parting the undergrowth seeking something, pretending nothing had happened. She squatted down to dig.

Paul changed his mind about withdrawal of labour. He ought to pay for his keep, at least. 'OK, I will dig.'

'I thought you were afraid of getting your manicure all messed up,' she said.

Paul clenched his teeth. He was an easygoing person and avoided unpleasantness as long as possible, but she was pushing too hard. Now she was studying him closely, waiting for a reaction, her eyes holding his steady. He shrugged. Let it pass. The little bitch was enjoying herself. He was not going to give her the additional satisfaction of knowing she was bugging him.

He found the roots, swollen into pink irregular ovals, and was about to take them all up.

'No need to kill the plant,' she said, taking over. She lifted a couple of tubers, piled the earth back and patted it down.

The effort had brought beads of perspiration to her face. She tried to wipe them off and the dirt on her hands mixed with the moisture. The resulting smudges transformed her into an urchin and his resentment began to melt, but he resisted it. His accumulated anger burst out. That much about her expertise. 'We've spent all morning, and other than a couple of poisonous plants and a potato, we found nothing.'

'And an orchid,' she said, 'look.'

She was making fun of him, and if that was an orchid he was a Red Indian. The flowers were so small, he could hardly see them. 'They are larger and more flamboyant than that,' he said. He knew about orchids, if nothing else. Women were always impressed at his choice of them as presents.

'Those are the showy vulgarities of the species,' she said contemptuously. 'This,' and her tone turned to a caress, 'is a little lady.'

'And of what use is it?' Paul said. 'Can it feed us?'

She looked at him perplexed. 'Not our stomachs, but surely doesn't it feed your soul to see something so miraculous?' She lifted a droopy blossom with a fingernail. The fingers of the other hand flattered around it like butterflies after its nectar, her face flashed, eyes sparkling. She went into raptures while describing the pink, urn shaped base extending into a creamy lip; the way the pink petals curved back to expose the opening, how that was guarded by a diminutive red tongue, suspended there by an invisible hair in front of golden stamens protruding from the depths. She blew gently as a demonstration, the little tongue shivered and Paul had a hard-on. Now he knew what made her appear beautiful: an underlying sensuality she was at pains to conceal, for whatever reason, and into which he wouldn't mind tapping.

A surreptitious glance at Mark convinced him he was not alone in being aroused by the sight of her unrestrained passion, be it at a flower. Mark's face was set and expressionless, but that was how he registered strong emotions, and the eyes spoke volumes. Not only did Paul have to fight her resistance but face competition as well. It certainly was a challenge.

Both of them staring at her speechless embarrassed her, and she withdrew, one could almost see it, into her shell.

Paul thought he ought to say something. 'You have a thing for flowers, huh?'

'About beauty,' she corrected and felt bound to add 'all kinds of,' letting her glance roam all over him. It disconcerted him. *Him!*

'You go back,' she said. 'I must look for a plant with anti-inflammatory properties for Mark, and I can do it better alone.'

'It's not necessary,' said Mark, 'I already feel much better.'

'Not for long,' she said.

'But if we keep returning back to the same place, how are we to get anywhere?' Mark insisted.

She looked away from him before she said, 'We can't get anywhere until you get better,' as if she knew it would embarrass him.

Paul realised she just wanted to get rid of them so that she would be alone, and he walked back even angrier than when he started this exhausting expedition that had produced hardly enough food for one, let alone three people.

What the hell did she think she was playing at? She spoke to him rudely, yet all the time made references to his looks. It wasn't the first time she stared at him with that peculiar expression she had when she studied the stupid flower.

He had no doubts about his appearance. He knew women liked him. He liked them. He chose nice, clean-cut, uncomplicated girls who took his advances as lightly as they were given. Bimbos, Mark called them. So what? He wasn't looking for mental stimulation from that quarter.

If only this one could relax and take a tumble in the bush, life would be more tolerable. Instead she was as approachable as a prickly pear. He smiled spitefully. She looked like one too. Short and dumpy. He thought the idea so original, he had to tell Mark.

Mark frowned. 'That's unkind.'

'I know that!'

The memory of the embrace came back and his longing returned. He wanted her. Only because he needed a woman and she was the only one around. So fucking intense! No sense of humour. A charming gesture, a joke or a compliment that made other women fall into his arms, only caused her to bristle and eye him suspiciously.

Still, she was not indifferent to him, obviously, and he could wear her resistance down, but he was not used to having to persuade women. They were always willing. What made her so immune? Or was she? She was just playing hard to get. She should be lucky if he paid her any attention at all. Perhaps, clever broad that she was, seeing the lack of competition, she was taking revenge. The little bitch, far from being naïve as he had thought, teased him!

He still wondered what it would be like with her. Probably a pain in the butt. She might want to analyse the metaphysics of sexuality or something. Or would she? His instincts about women were never wrong, and he had a strong feeling she could turn out to be rather surprising. Maybe he should change his approach. Come from a more unexpected angle. Surprise her.

19

Sylvia watched Paul trying to cook the potatoes. The penny had dropped, at last, that she was not going to ask for help. It should be something they realised on their own. True, Mark couldn't do much, but Paul should. Yet he waited until he starved and she was not there to cook, to get the message.

He looked up suddenly and she shifted her eyes quickly, unwilling to face that smile again. It had taken a lot of effort not to hit him this morning. She couldn't guarantee the same success now, with her resentment increased tenfold. No matter what the acoustics in the understorey, it was too much of a coincidence that she should hear every abuse he uttered. She was meant to hear it. He couldn't wait for her to put enough distance between them before he spouted out his aphorisms. This last time, too preoccupied with more important things, all she caught was one word. No need for more to know in what context it was used. And the answer from Mark: 'Unkind'. She winced at the memory. Damn right it was unkind.

'Can one only find potatoes around here?' Paul was saying now, and when she forced herself to look at him again, he was smiling at her pleasantly, the eyes softening to smoky blue in the shadow of the unruly fringe.

In spite herself, she felt flattered. 'So far, but there are lots of things that one ought to find around here. I am sure we will come across them soon,' and all the time she was trying to imagine what he would look like without the prickly beard sprouting on his face. She had a vivid picture of a smooth, hard masculine cheek as if her hand was actually caressing it, and missed a heartbeat just like when he had held her in his arms this morning. Come to think of it, it had been more than missing a heartbeat. She had gone weak in the knees and her stomach had sunk to somewhere in the region of her lower pelvis.

Ridiculous! It was not he that had caused the reaction. It was a reflex. She would have reacted the same with any man. Well, not just any man. Only one that was not repulsive or objectionable to her. Damn! She could count the men she did not find objectionable on the fingers of one hand, and they all had been people she became very intimate with. Once they were acceptable, no other barrier existed. How would she feel if it were Mark? He was watching her as usual, and a smile travelled by degrees from the corner of his mouth to the velvet of the eyes as if he guessed her thoughts.

Damn! Damn! Damn! No wonder she wished she had never met either of them. At least when alone she did not have to consider complicated things like relationships and sex. Just survival. She still had to think of that, only in triplicate. They brought no advantages with them. Only problems.

'I'll try that brew again,' Mark said.

Was there a resentful grimace on Paul's face that she had turned to Mark? Was Mark needing the tea or trying to draw her attention away from Paul, or, more to the point, was she being paranoid?

'So you trust me now?' she asked Mark, remembering his token resistance the first time she had offered him a herbal remedy and his condescension: 'If you insist on using me as a guinea pig.'

'I'm no fool,' Mark said, whatever that meant.

Paul brought the potatoes over, cut in quarters, arranged tastefully on a broad leaf. He was not entirely useless, after all. 'I didn't know they taught catering in English Public Schools,' she said.

Paul nearly dropped the potatoes. 'How the hell do you know that?'

She didn't. Sarcasm was the quickest form of defence she could come up with against his charm offensive. The form it took surprised her as much as him. But she began explaining, all the same, more for her own sake than his. 'The odd phrase here and there, the American accent slipping now and then. The sort of thing one doesn't pick up from the occasional visit to England.'

Paul plonked the potatoes down. 'Anything else you know about me?'

His discomfiture was gratifying, coming so soon after her appalling weakness at a mere glance from him, so she tried to look mysterious. 'Quite a lot, I would imagine.'

'Like?' Head lowered, Paul peered at her from under the fringe. No softness now, more his usual cat look. He was not going to let her off that lightly.

She stalled. 'That would be telling.'

'You mean I've called your bluff?' That cursed smile again.

'Remember, you asked for this,' she warned, unable to resist his challenge yet fully aware of how foolish the whole thing was. 'Let's see.' She stared at him as if his eyes were a crystal ball. 'Privileged background, pots of money, always had what you wanted.' All that was obvious to anybody, and Paul's sarcastic smile said as much. 'Except, perhaps, love.' This came out against her will but she carried on, talking fast, to cover up her embarrassment. 'Been a little rascal all your life. Got away with it. Parents didn't have much time. Others too intimidated with looks and money.' She noticed that Paul was not smiling anymore. Good! 'You were sent away to study in England to learn some discipline, as a status symbol or just to be out of the way.' Now he was frowning. 'You grew up to be adored by ladies and envied by men. You are a bit cynical, no, very cynical. It suits you if people think you superficial or frivolous. It gives you an advantage. Could be ruthless, if need be . . .'

'I wouldn't have thought,' Paul said, 'that you were the type to read gossip magazines.'

So! He was famous enough to be in magazines. No wonder... 'I have never read anything about you,' she said. 'Just observation. Have I been a little too close?'

Mark ventured into the exchange. 'Bang on.'

'What can you observe about him?' Paul said, passing the buck with some relief.

She looked at Mark for a way out.

'There is nothing to see,' Mark said.

Oh yes there was. A child could tell. A stable home, comfortable background, not over-privileged but lacking in nothing. Did all the right things, probably played for the school. She needn't say anything except that his smile was so smug. So secure in the thought that she could not fathom him. 'He married his high school sweetheart,' she blurted out.

'And?' Paul prodded her on.

She took a deep breath, her heartbeat gone crazy. 'She did not fit in with the career but he was too decent to discard her.' Another pause. No help from anyone. 'Perhaps he still lives with her. Perhaps she left for somebody less demanding. If she did, he remarried...' From Mark's expression she was in for it, so what difference did it make any more? 'But after unwrapping the package, found the content missing.' And there it was, if nothing else, at least, wishful thinking. But she had said enough. Private things for which, she was sure, both men resented her.

Mark seemed to be making great efforts not to respond, and Paul's face was a picture to behold in more ways than the obvious. She could see thoughts fleeting across it while he furiously assessed the situation. Obviously, he did not enjoy having the tables turned on him. He wanted to know everybody's business and made sure nobody knew his, or probably fed them the wrong leads. When he spoke his voice was neutral, careful not to protest too much, she supposed, and hence confirm everything.

'You said women adore me and yet I have everything but love,' he said. 'It makes no sense.'

Damn him! He homed in on the only detail she wanted to ignore. 'I just said that for effect.' That should put an end to the whole thing.

'No you didn't!' A lot of resentment was compressed in this short sentence and two pools of blue lava smouldered from behind Paul's fringe.

'Look,' she said, 'you make me say things and then you get annoyed.'

Paul tried to prove her wrong by attempting a smile that did not reach the eyes, where the lava had solidified into cold steel. 'I'm curious, that's all.'

She resigned herself to the inevitable. 'You are rich and very good-looking. Very lucky, people might say, but...' the contempt flickering at the corner of his mouth relaunched her on her reckless way. 'How can you be sure if your money and looks get you everything or whether it is because of you? I mean, people fawn on wealth and power. Women are flattered to be seen out with an elegant escort, a rich one at that, but do they care for you?' She pointed a finger at Paul's chest. 'Do they know you? What is in there?' This time she actually stubbed at his chest. 'You wouldn't show them, would you?' She felt excited. No, angry, for some reason. She couldn't get it all out fast enough. 'Why? Because nobody took you in their arms as a child and loved you for being Paul. They have always indulged you because you were a pretty, rich boy. What does that mean?' Paul was squirming, but she had him fixed in her sights. 'It was not your mother that brought you up but a paid servant, reverential to your privileged position. Right?'

A black hole opened between them into which all sound, together with her anger and resentment, disappeared. Across it, Paul's pale face. After an appalling interval, his croaky voice bridged the gap. 'Right. I was raised by a nanny and a butler,' he said and her ridiculous pomposity was punctured. She deflated a little bit more with each word that followed, pronounced distinct yet softly: 'But they loved me.'

Depression, the natural consequence to any great surge of excitement, enveloped Sylvia like a black cloak. 'I got carried away. I had no right.'

Paul cleared his throat. 'I asked you, and you warned me.' His voice steadied. 'You implied that what nobody else sees . . . I mean . . . you assume there is something.'

'I normally wouldn't,' she said. 'You would not have come close enough or stayed around long enough for me to see anything. Anyway,' she continued in the absence of any comment, 'you're taking this too seriously. It was just a guessing game. I don't know anything. I just felt my way around and it sort of developed. I can't explain it.'

'You are frightening, that's what you are,' Paul said just above a whisper and then as he turned to go, louder. 'Frightening!'

'Don't knock it,' she said after him. 'Without things we can't explain, you would still be lost and hungry.'

Paul stopped in mid-stride. He turned slowly, his eyes narrow slits. 'It would have been too much of a coincidence, wouldn't it? You didn't just stumble on us. You knew!' It sounded like an accusation.

She back-pedalled. 'Premonition,' she said, realising that the Indian would be displeased if the men were told about his involvement. Didn't he say 'not ready'?

Paul was back to his previous form. 'Bullshit! Premonition warns of an unspecified something, not what or where, and in a place like this, boy, do you have to know the precise where. So how?' and sarcastically, 'The spirits told you?'

She hesitated. 'In a . . . way.'

'Oh, shit!' Paul raised his arms to indicate he was giving up. 'I said it as a joke. You bloody well meant it!' And then he said spitefully: 'If this were Hollywood, I would come across a gorgeous damsel in distress. Instead, I found a bloody witch.'

All her contrition evaporated. 'She found you. Remember that!'

She heard what he mumbled under his breath as he left: 'Fuck you!' But she did not blame him. She had been carried away by a passion resembling the first stages of intoxication. It usually happened when she discussed anything she felt strongly about. Only this time, she was not expostulating about a pet subject but the life of strangers of whom she knew nothing except what she could glean from their manner, appearance and snatches of conversation, yet she had spoken with conviction, as if she had an insight into their mind. It would appear frightening like Paul had said.

Still, she resented being called a witch. She could not explain to them what had happened in a way that would appear better. Of course, she ought not to have been hurt just because somebody found her unattractive, but she had been sensitised to the accusation since childhood. Her mother had coined the simile Paul had used earlier and Mark thought it unkind, not untrue.

'It's this gloomy place,' said Mark. 'It makes people superstitious. Don't worry.' He nodded in the direction Paul had taken. 'He will be all right soon. Paul cannot stay unhappy or bad-tempered for long.'

'I am glad you are not superstitious,' she said.

Mark remained quiet for a while. 'No, but . . .' he said at last, '. . . it is unsettling to find someone seeing right through you, even by accident.' He gave her his golden eagle stare. 'Or was it an accident? Did Paul tell you about my marriages?'

'No. I thought you were the type to marry your high school sweetheart.' She did not mean to be so frank and laughed lamely to cover up. 'You know?'

He raised an inquiring eyebrow.

She searched for words, trying to escape the morass and sinking in deeper. 'The sort of man women would not allow to stay a bachelor for long. Especially high school girls.'

He let it sink in, before: 'But she left me all the same.'

'That was to be expected,' she blurted out. He waited for an explanation and she was forced to comply. 'I mean, when people marry young before they know their minds fully . . . as a rule, such marriages end up in divorce.'

'And the second marriage?'

She lifted her shoulders. 'As I've said. The sort of man women find, er . . . challenging.' She could hardly say irresistible, which was what she felt.

'For a while,' he said. 'They both changed their minds pretty quickly. As a husband, I must be a great disappointment.'

'To the tone-deaf, even a Stradivarius would be disappointing.'

He just stared, astonished, and she went to mess with the fire and the pot and generally keep busy before she got into worse trouble. Why on earth did she say that? Her situation was complicated enough and more than dangerous, as it was, without the 'come on'. What would she do if he responded?

20

Mark wondered what Sylvia had meant. Probably that he had married the wrong women, nothing more. She was right though about high school, if not quite the sweetheart bit. Involvement in sport threw him in the company of his team mates, and the only girls he got to know were cheer leaders and groupies attracted to the glamour of successful sport. He was basically shy of girls, and he only went with whoever threw herself at him. When one got pregnant, he did the right thing. It was no great sacrifice. At least he didn't have to put himself out to find a sexual partner. She became bored with his new career and left, just like Sylvia had guessed.

Paul was back from Europe by then, and Mark got sucked into his dizzy social life. Paul was surrounded with glamorous women, and inevitably some of the fallout came Mark's way. He was taken in by Nicol's beauty and yes, the packet, as Sylvia put it, was empty. But to be fair, if one bought something on the strength of the packaging alone, one hadn't the right to complain about the content.

Sure, men envied him his wife's beauty, but they didn't have to live with her. Physically there was nothing much there, either. That might have been a compensation. Nicol considered sex as an expression of homage to her looks. It was that, rather than sexual appetite, that determined her promiscuity.

With Sylvia, it wouldn't be a matter of disappointment after opening the package, more bewilderment at the collection of pieces of puzzle. One would not necessarily make any sense from the picture that emerged, only that it might be worth the trouble.

So far, he was just confused. At times he thought of her as a helpless child playing at being tough and needing his protection. From what, he had no idea, since she could take good care of herself. Better than him, anyway.

A different feeling was creeping on him now that he had witnessed the kind of enthusiasm that could explode out of her spontaneously and passionately before she withdrew behind her prickles. They had nothing to do with irritating needles as Paul had implied, but exposed nerve endings, sensitive to just about everything.

He felt the need for some contact. Verbal would do unless she decided to nurse him again. He wouldn't mind that at all, right now.

Could he take some of her comments as encouragement, or would that be wishful thinking?

'Do you believe in extra-sensory perception?' he asked her. Not the subject he should have chosen, perhaps, but he could not dismiss what had occurred. It might have been, like he had told her, that the gloom of the forest made everyone superstitious but observation alone did not explain all she had said.

She stopped what she was doing, hesitated briefly and then came closer. 'Like you, I am a scientist and, no matter how I look at it, the only satisfactory answer is bound to be scientific.' She gave him a dazzling smile. 'Radio waves?' as if she just had a revelation.

'What?'

'With the right receiver, you pick them up.' She sat next to him. 'Why can't the brain transmit through the air like a wireless?'

He was watching the intense expression on her face and forgot about rigorous debate. He said vaguely, 'Not quite wireless. The brain is an electrical circuit that transmits messages from one part of the body to another via the nerves, the wires, if you like.'

She shook her head vigorously in agreement. 'And we

know that because we can measure the current across a nerve and we can study transmission by chemical agents across a gap between nerves. I did many a time,' she said, getting excited. Obviously, she had expected that response and she was ready for it. 'We have not devised a means yet to pick up and demonstrate the impulse outside the body. It doesn't mean it's not there.'

So she had thought it out and came to a logical and physical explanation. She would.

'But only exceptional people, those with the right receiver so to speak, can pick them up, I suppose,' he said.

'Maybe we all could, but only people living at the edge of survival cultivated the skill, kept it alive while others, in comfort, could afford to neglect it. If we were to stay here long enough, even Paul would be surprised at what he learned about himself and what he could do that he previously thought impossible. Then I won't look to him like a witch.'

So she was still smarting from Paul's accusation. She also implied that she had lived dangerously or had picked up the skill quicker than them. But he didn't care what they were talking about, really. Only that they were talking. So he said casually: 'Have you always believed in it?'

She, on the other hand, was very serious. 'I always thought that language was such a clumsy way to pass messages to other people. Abstract sounds relying on the skill of the speaker and the interpretational powers of the listener. No wonder there is so much misunderstanding in the world.' She shrugged. 'As a child I thought transmitting pictures would be more effective. Even better than thought transfer, not that I knew anything about that,' and curiously added, 'then.'

Mark frowned in his effort to concentrate on what she was saying rather than the passionate face in front of him. 'A strange child!'

She laughed as if he had paid her a compliment. 'They explained it by the fact that I had experienced death, came back from it, so to speak. I had seen the other side.'

This conversation was becoming more weird by the minute. 'Did you?'

'Not really. I appeared to have died, sufficiently so for the doctor to give a death certificate.'

'Necrolepsis,' he said automatically as if she required his diagnosis, which he should have known she wouldn't.

She didn't seem to mind. 'I think necrophania is a better term,' she said casually. 'It's the same thing. My father was unable to bear the thought of having me buried, so he snatched me up and ran away. By next morning I was breathing again.'

'Thank God for that!'

She dismissed it with a flick of the hand as if it made no difference, one way or the other. 'When I was old enough, my father told me not to pay attention to such superstitions. It was all to do with heredity. You see...' her face was inches from his now, '... an ancestor of mine, some Italian princess, had the same thing happen to her, a few times. She was taken for a witch and they drove a stake through her heart in the end, to make sure she remained dead.'

Mark's head was reeling. 'Italian princess? I thought you were English.'

She laughed again, a carefree laughter. 'Do I look English?'

That permanently suntanned face and mobile hands should have told him a long time ago.

'I was born in Cyprus,' she continued, 'from mixed ancestry, what my father called noble-looking Greek peasants and peasant-looking Italian aristocrats.' Her hand perched lightly on his knee and she added confidentially, 'One of my direct ancestors was a Barberini, the black sheep of a Florentine noble family. Well, Venetian originally, but they settled in Florence. He became a pirate.' She seemed quite proud of that. 'After a life of bloodshed, pillaging and raping, he settled on the island. My father said it was him we have to thank for being restless and losing our temper so monumentally.'

He was thinking of trapping her hand with his but before

he could gather the courage, it flew off in another direction like her speech.

'According to my Greek grandmother, it's his side of the family, too, I have to thank for my looks,' she said. 'Her side were blue-eyed blondes. They couldn't read or write but, like my grandmother, could recite Homer and guard their genes jealously through generations until my mother broke the cycle. Grandma couldn't forgive her that. Breaking traditions had terrible consequences and . . .' bitterness crept in her voice, '. . . one only had to look at me to see.'

'What did she mean by that?' said Mark, getting more perplexed by the second.

'I was short and dark and both my mother and grandmother never forgave my ugliness. "I am blessed with a cactus fruit," my mother used to lament to the neighbours, referring to my . . . er . . . compactness.'

Mark started and she fixed him with those feverish eyes.

'That's right! My mother beat Paul to it.'

Was there anything they said she didn't know about?

'I can't believe anyone would think you ugly,' Mark said.

There was a strange expression on her face now. Suspicion, maybe. 'Why? Do you think I am as beautiful as, say, your wife?'

He wished she had never mentioned his wife. She couldn't be further from all this. At the moment he regretted ever meeting Nicol, and it was without the slightest remorse that he said, 'To quote you on orchids: she is the showy vulgarity of the species, you are a little lady.'

She took offence. 'That's very kind of you, but I don't need it. I don't rely on appearances for anything.'

'Quite right. With all the knowledge, personality, colourful ancestry, you don't have to, but it doesn't mean you are unattractive.' What a stupid thing to say! Not unattractive. She was a little gem, but to say that would take more courage than he had.

Her look was contemptuous. 'Tell me truthfully that if I were not the only female around, you would be sitting there talking about extra-sensory perceptions and my ancestry.'

'Maybe not, but only because I couldn't corner you, or even if I did, I would never have dared,' he said truthfully. 'You are rather . . . formidable.'

Her eyes opened wide. '*I* am formidable?'

'Oh, you mean my size. People are wary of that but I don't rely on my appearance, either. I don't believe in violence. Well, not unless I am provoked. I mean, a lot and even then . . . I only meant to defend myself and . . .' Shit! How did he get on to that?

Suddenly she was calm. 'It's OK,' she said touching his sleeve again.

He didn't like to talk about himself and especially about that incident, but she already knew so much, it didn't seem to matter.

'I just saw this boy being bullied,' he said. 'I didn't know it was Paul, then. He seemed so much out of his depth in that rough neighbourhood, and there were a lot of them. I threw one off Paul and he produced a knife. I only hit him once.'

The familiar picture swam before his eyes. The unnatural turn of the head, the terrible immobility.

'I can never forget the boy's face,' he continued, 'nor that due to me, he never grew to be a man.' He was silent for a while. She never uttered a word and he never dared to look at her expression.

'I decided to give up sport and become a doctor,' he said. 'I felt that if I learned to save lives, it would, somehow, help.' He took a deep breath. 'It doesn't. I have killed a man, and what I wanted to do was to work for the poor and underprivileged. You know? All this idealistic stuff.'

He glanced at her, but there was no disgust in her face. She just looked kindly at him and he carried on. 'I ended up getting rich by treating even richer people who, if it were not me, they could afford another doctor. I mean to do something about it, but life . . . I'm married. It's not just me. Well, it might be an excuse. I don't know.'

'Is that how you met Paul?'

'Yes. I suppose he feels obliged to me. We don't have

anything in common.' He felt such a traitor. 'Don't get me wrong,' he tried to put things right. 'Paul is much more than he pretends to be, but I don't have to tell you that.'

'We all make use of whatever we are given in life. He has the looks and exploits them, I suppose, to get his way.'

Did she realise just how right she was?

'But,' she continued, 'nobody in his right mind should take big cats for granted, however cuddly they may look. When necessity arises and only then, they move into action and one had better not get caught in the way.'

Mark looked at her confused again. 'Big cats?'

She blushed. 'It's just that he reminds me of a puma or a jaguar, that's all.' She must have noticed his astonishment and tried to justify it. 'I've read, somewhere, that the Amazon Indians give an animal equivalent to everybody.' Then after another break, 'I suppose, when one lives in the same environment, one develops similar habits.'

'It makes sense,' he said and she seemed relieved. Why relieved? Could there be another explanation that she didn't want anybody to know about? He was being absurd. Maybe he would start behaving like a primitive forest dweller soon. 'Do you have an animal equivalent for me?' he asked lightly.

There was no hesitation. 'A hawk. An eagle. Something like that.'

He smiled. 'Not as dangerous as a puma, then?'

'I don't know about that! You can hide from a puma.' She was serious.

'And yourself?'

'A paca.' Again it came instantly. No thought required.

'What's that?'

'A rabbit-like creature.'

He frowned in concentration. 'You feel threatened?'

She laughed. 'This place is swarming with them. Have you caught any?'

'I see!' Did he? Was she trying to tell him something?

'We were talking of how tough Paul is, in spite of appearances,' she said, obviously unwilling for any more revelations.

'He's not just tough.' Mark returned reluctantly to their original subject. 'He can be thoughtful and kind and loyal and many other things, but he would never have had time for someone like me if it were not for the fact that he thinks he owes me his life. I could be very boring.'

'Boring?'

'I don't like talking and he lives for it.'

'You are doing quite well right now.'

He felt his face getting hot. 'Yeah! I don't know why.'

'Don't apologise.'

'I am not. It's just that since I've been here, I feel as if my whole personality is changing.'

'Oh yes,' she said as if she just had a revelation. 'You are getting ready.'

'Ready for what?'

She suddenly became confused. 'I . . . have no idea. I just remembered something, somebody said.'

'Who? Paul?'

'No.' A curtain fell behind the eyes, a withdrawal.

'There is nobody else here.'

She stood up. He didn't want her to go so he said the first thing that came to his mind. 'How come you went to England?'

It worked. 'I went to university there.' She settled down again. 'I was expected to study literature, philosophy or art, those being my favourite subjects. Especially art. But I decided to escape my fate,' she gave a little laugh, 'and did sciences instead.' She looked at him as if requiring his understanding on that. 'In this modern world, one should know something about science, I thought.'

'I suppose so.'

'I get as much satisfaction at the end of a good piece of research as I would after finishing a painting, for one can paint or read philosophy whether one has a degree or not. If anything, one is freer of fashions and theories to develop just what interests them.' She was up again. 'And then I messed it all up by getting married. But enough about me. Paul is unsafe out there on his own.'

'You seem to manage.'

'That's different,' she said.

'Of course,' Mark said, stung. 'He, like me, lacks your experience.'

'No. My immunity.'

She walked off, leaving him even more perplexed and frustrated. And why didn't *he* worry about Paul's inexperience or lack of immunity to whatever? It hadn't yet come to that, surely.

21

As he prowled around the forest like he had done yesterday and the day before, Paul wondered at the verticality of the place. Everything pulled the eye up. The tree trunks that like an infinity of cage bars hemmed him in, pointed up. The lances of sunlight, the noises in the canopy, all drew the glance up. There was nowhere else to look unchecked.

He had been brought up by the ocean and missed the sense of expanse. The water, the sky. The ability to let his eyes travel to the horizon, the dazzle of the sun, the salty breath of the sea on his skin. He wanted to sail, fly, socialise, make love. Instead, he was condemned to sit around admiring orchids with those two for company. They were driving him crazy. Mark was a reliable friend, but as a conversationalist he left a lot to be desired. As for her!

The cramps in his stomach reminded him he was hungry. He had left without eating, but the prospect of yet more sweet potato drove him nuts. Their diet was in need of improvement. Some meat, for a start.

Now that he knew that the invisible spies were animals trying to suss out if they either posed a threat, or more likely, if they were a suitable prey, he walked cautiously to catch them out, but all he came up with was something as innocuous as a rabbit that soon disappeared into the ground itself.

He leaned against a tree to rest and jumped back instantly. 'What the fuck?' He was on fire. His body was crawling with ants, every sting burning and he furiously tried to brush them off. She had predicted even that. 'You will learn,' she had said. That's all he needed to make his day!

There should be a way out of this hell. Why was Sylvia so reluctant to press on? Her excuse was lack of water. The only source, so far, was the rock and until they had found an alternative, she said, they could not afford to leave it. Couldn't she see that it also meant that without a stream or a river, there wasn't sufficient break in the canopy hence no light and no undergrowth necessary to feed animals in any numbers that would make them accessible? Without plants or game, there was no hope of human settlements, and their chances of being discovered by Indians, or any other group of people, were nil. How long could they last on the diminishing amount of sweet potatoes, the only thing she could find with all her so-called skills, without moving on?

There was always the canopy, of course, with birds and other animals, to say nothing of fruits and nuts. If he could climb high enough, he might also be able to see any break in the canopy that would indicate a river. But how could he climb? The tree trunks were smooth and regular as if turned on a lathe and soared up hundreds of feet into the air. Occasionally they sported clusters of small flowers and nothing else to give any support for climbing. Unless, of course, he imitated Tarzan! He grasped a liana. 'Shit!'

His palms were lacerated before he noticed the vicious spines. Still cursing, he kept on searching until he found a smooth one, but it was slippery with slimy fungus. That much about Tarzan.

He turned around quickly. Was that laughter? Was that female spying on him? But it didn't sound like her and certainly not like Mark, who didn't waste any energy on such frivolities, anyway. The forest itself was laughing at him. Here he was, wandering all day and all he had managed was to get stung by ants, cut his hands, get thoroughly depressed and nothing to show for it. Not even a sweet fucking potato, and he had reached that invisible barrier again, beyond which his instincts told him he couldn't venture. It was as if some power kept them prisoners, and if so, she was in collusion with it. The day before yesterday when he had reached such a point, she appeared out of nowhere to guide him back. He had strayed into a big animal's marked territory, she said or some bullshit like that. What did she have to gain out of keeping them here?

It was dark by the time he returned, and the other two had already lit a fire. He looked at Sylvia and felt something akin to loathing. But no matter how humiliating, he had to accept the sweet potato she had saved for him, sure, no doubt, he could come up with nothing.

His bed was a pile of tobacco leaves, not just because she had said they were good as snake protection but because most other leaves had razor-sharp edges. He tossed and turned in the darkness for ages, unable to relax. What he was desperate for was the comfort of a woman's touch. He longed for the release of tension and peace to his aching body her softness would bring. There was no such comfort to be found in that little prickly bush. To top it all, he heard a groan from her direction.

'No sooner is one vaguely on the way to recovery, the next comes down,' she said. 'It's like being home with kids again.'

'I am not sick,' Paul snarled.

'Then what's wrong?' She found him in the dark and felt his face. 'You are burning,' she said, suddenly concerned. 'Do you want some water?'

His arms shot up involuntarily. 'You know what I want,' he said, grasping her by the shoulders. 'What we both need.' His voice was such a fierce whisper, he frightened himself.

She pulled away. 'No!'

'What do you have against it?'

She sounded more sad than angry. 'An overestimated pastime.'

'You don't like it?' The only female for miles, and she had to be frigid.

'Sometimes,' she said.

'But not now?'

'Not under the circumstances.'

He relaxed. 'Oh, you mean Mark. He is asleep.' He wished he could be sure of that.

She moved away and back to the fire, and he followed her.

'Look,' he said. 'We might have to stay in here for a while. How long do you thing you can keep it up?' He looked at her closely. 'Is there, er . . . something wrong?' Not PC exactly, but better than asking outright if she were a dyke.

'The monumental ego of the man!' she hissed. 'If a woman doesn't want him, there must be something wrong with her.'

'Then why do you look at me the way you do? Why throw hints about my appearance?'

She turned sharply. 'You completely misunderstood.'

'Have I?'

'Yes! I may think you are beautiful . . .'

He didn't think much to that. 'What you mean, perhaps, is attractive or something like that.'

'No. Attractive is personal. It involves emotion. Beauty is abstract, an idea, something universal.'

'So you've read Plato,' he said with disgust.

She sighed but persevered. 'One may see something and say it's beautiful, but one may or may not desire it.'

'You talk as if I was an inanimate object!'

'Sorry, I did not mean that. What I was trying to say . . .'

'You made yourself perfectly clear,' he interrupted.

She suddenly looked tired. 'I doubt it.'

Paul was in two minds as to whether he should stay or withdraw in a huff. He stayed. He disliked the lonely darkness even more than her conversation. Instead, he changed his line of approach.

'You must love him very much,' he said.

She was startled. 'Who?'

What sensitive spot had he touched there? But he pretended to have noticed nothing. 'Your husband.'

She gave a shrug and let him interpret it any way he chose.

'You enjoy making love to him, of course.'

She just stared.

He persevered. 'You said that sex was overrated but you enjoyed it sometimes. So have you enjoyed it with him?' He was asking for trouble, but what the heck.

'Not particularly.'

The casualness of her remark confused him, but he pressed on. 'Somebody else, then?'

She thought for a while, a dead giveaway there was nothing earth-shattering to remember. 'Maybe. But even then . . .'

'What did you expect?'

'It's nothing more than just another appetite,' she said angrily, 'like hunger and thirst. We don't make so much of those, and they are more vital to our existence.' She waved a hand dismissively. 'I know all about the need to procreate and all that, but people do not think of children every time they fornicate.' She tapped her head. 'Most of it is brainwashing. Nobody wants to accept it for what it is: a brute instinct. They have to involve love,' another flick of the hand, 'whatever that is. They want to believe it is something special that sets them above animals. Those that fail to think so are made to feel inadequate, so the majority convince themselves it is a wonderful experience.' Her contempt increased with every pronouncement. 'They build myths around it; get obsessed by it; they have to prove they are as good as they think others are.' She turned on him viciously. 'How many people have you met that are willing to admit they are no good at it, or don't like it?'

'You!'

'I don't give a damn if people think I am frigid or inadequate. I accept it for what it is. A means for begetting children.' And more quietly, 'It could be pleasant at best, but nothing to write home about. I can take it or leave it, mostly leave it. I hate pretence or compromise.'

'Don't you compromise when you make love with your husband if, as you say, you don't even like it?'

He nailed her, and they both knew it.

'I didn't like hurting his feelings,' she said lamely. 'Men's egos are ever so vulnerable. Brainwashing work better on them.'

'You mean you would oblige a man if you thought you might hurt his feelings?' he said.

It was amusing to watch her trying to extricate herself. 'Not any man,' she said.

Boy, was she screwed up! 'You want to be swept off your feet. Earth moving and all that. Maybe you haven't met the right man yet.'

'I am not that romantic. As I just said, earth moving and all that is a fiction.'

'Wow! The men in your life have a lot to answer for!'

'You can put me right, no doubt?'

He looked her straight in the eyes. 'Why don't we find out? You have nothing to lose.'

'Oh yes I do!'

'What?'

'My pride.'

His exasperation overcame any remaining manners.'How the fuck does that come into it?'

'I don't want to be used by a man because I happen to be the only . . . let's see if I remember it correctly . . . the only screwable thing around.'

That demolished him. 'Ah! You heard.'

'Was I not meant to?' she said sarcastically. 'Anyway, I could work it out for myself.'

'I am sorry!' He tried to sound convincing. 'People often say things they don't mean.'

'Sure.'

'If it was not for my er . . . indiscretion, would you have?'

'No.'

Ah, well. She could not be any clearer than that. But he was not a quitter.

'You said sex is like hunger and thirst,' he said. 'You are desperately hungry, you eat sweet potato day after day. You are horny, you put up with what's available.' Oh, shit! He didn't mean it like that. 'I mean you may have to put up with one of us.'

'It's not as straightforward as all that,' she said. 'Look I don't want you to think that I am playing hard to get.'

'Oh, yeah! What do you call this?'

'I am not that perverted,' she said, ignoring the insult. 'Regardless of what I said, I find you, yes, attractive if sometimes annoying. I am only human, and one susceptible to external appearances at that. However, there are three of us.'

'I thought it would come to that, sooner or later.'

'We must survive.' She was now staring blankly at the fire, her voice flat. 'For that, we must keep relations between all three stable, or as nearly as possible. Sex complicates matters. It introduces unpleasantness, jealousies, antagonisms.' She turned and looked at him earnestly. 'Suppose we remain in here for a long time. If I allied with you, it leaves Mark out.' She put a hand to her breast. 'God forbid that I should think myself irresistible, but how would it feel if one man is frustrated when the other fornicates with the only woman around?' She pointed at him. 'How would you like it? Wouldn't it cause friction?'

'If we stayed here long enough, how do you think it would be with two frustrated men?'

She looked back to the fire. They both fell silent for a long time.

Paul broke the silence first, tentatively. 'I suppose you have moral objections to er . . . making love to both of us?' He braced himself for outrage, at least.

'I have no moral scruples whatsoever,' she said. 'What determines my actions, I hope, is logic.' To prove it, she remained calm. 'Logically speaking, there is no reason at all why I should not have sex with both of you.' Then she said with more animation, 'By the way, do not insult my intelligence by using the word love. It has nothing to do with it. We are talking sex here.'

He exhaled. 'Then there should be no problem.'

'But there is.'

'I don't understand. You just said . . .'

'You forget conditioning.'

'Huh?'

'Men are conditioned to expect monopoly from a woman or else treat her as a whore. I have no intention whatsoever to either assign exclusive rights of my body to anyone or assume the role of a whore.'

'A moment ago you said you have no morality, and now you use a moralistic term like whore.'

'I just don't like being used.'

He had never talked to anyone who complicated matters more than her. 'When two people have sex, they use each other. Or even better, they give and take. It should be simple. Something that gives pleasure and fulfils a necessity.'

'We have already agreed that it was neither a pleasure nor a necessity to me.'

'So it seems,' he sighed. He always thought intellectual broads were a pain in the butt.

She relaxed and smiled, as if gracious to a defeated foe. 'You don't even like me,' she said. 'I bet I am nothing to what you are used to.'

'What would that be?'

'Slick, sanitised, standardised American beauties with big boobs and legs up to their armpits.'

Bullseye! But he laughed. 'I hope I have a more universal taste than that. I find no woman unattractive. They all have their merits.'

'Even me?' She flashed her eyelashes at him in a caricature of flirting.

'Yes,' he said and, strangely enough, meant it.

She had a shot at being coy. 'And I thought my appearance would protect me. Was I wrong?'

'I find you fascinating.' To his surprise, he meant this too.

She looked coldly at him, all pretence gone.

'Because, for once, you want something you cannot have,' she said.

Was she tempting him to prove her wrong, or something? She talked so big, but what was she? 'The mouse that roars,' he said and thrilled at the way she was startled, her eyes dilating in fear and at the same time disgusted with himself that he should have sunk this low as to find scaring a woman exciting.

22

Her only salvation was the Indian, Sylvia thought as she walked towards the frontier marked for them, hoping to meet him. She knew where it was from watching Paul. The fact that he sensed it was a revelation. But it was the kind of challenge he wouldn't be able to resist for long. She had a hell of a time trying to turn him back the other day. Yet all the Indian had to do was to break the siege or, even better, act as a guide and they would be out. They were ready now, surely. Mark was better. And what did he want from Paul? To pounce? Well he did, in a way.

She marked the tree trunks purposefully with the knife she had borrowed from Paul, without his permission, since he was asleep at the time, her mind still preoccupied with him. He never disguised the fact that he disliked her, found her ugly and objectionable, but in the absence of anything better he thought all he had to do was snap his fingers and she would be grateful. She was scared, and it had been unwise to show it, but not of Paul. After all, Mark might have been asleep but only feet away. Though was he any better? He was kinder, yet his stare was worse than Paul's advances. Maybe he saw right through the carapace to the disgusting mess underneath. He was laughing at her, just like Paul.

She had been that close to falling prey to Paul. It was the analogy of cat and mouse that brought her to her senses. She was frightened of her weakness. She had began to question why she refused him. An acceptance would stop him being difficult and probably give her some pleasure, the argument went. Now, of course, she realised that to get involved with someone like Paul would mean emotional suicide. She had been involved with a beautiful man before. It was not an experience she wanted to repeat. Not that Paul had any involvement in mind and, in spite of all she had said to him, sex without involvement was beyond her.

Paul was right, of course. None of the men in her life, not even her husband, gave her any emotional security, let alone sexual fulfilment, and, yes; she was romantic. She still dreamt of a man she could rely on, somebody big and strong who could also understand *her*, for a change, somebody to whom it wouldn't be so humiliating to submit, somebody like . . .

Was she so naïve to hope for a hero? Mark certainly looked the part, built on such a heroic scale, but so what? One never knew what he was thinking and though his silence could be interpreted as depth, he could as easily have nothing to say.

She cringed when she thought Mark might have overheard her conversation with Paul last night. How could she have allowed herself to so artlessly think aloud in the presence of strangers? And what was the point in thinking about either of them? Sooner or later they would get out and go their own ways, and that would be that. Anything that might occur here would be out of necessity, not real attraction.

There was no need to look to know the Indian was there. She could smell him and feel the kind of peace he always induced in her. She sat down, spreading her legs in front of her, unable to squat like him. He had brought a pile of strips, some kind of vegetable matter and began to plait them into a rope. She picked one up. It looked like bark but very thin and flexible. He watched her for a while, registered her curiosity and got up.

He made a couple of slashes on the tree trunk and peeled off strips as easily as banana skin. That was impressive, but even more so was the sharp knife he had used. Something else he must have got by contact with white people. So where were they, or the mission, a trade post, whatever?

She tried to concentrate on that and see if he responded, but he returned and continued his complicated work oblivious to everything.

She pointed at the knife and gestured. Where did he get it from?

A waste of time. She picked up a few strips and tried a simple plait. Just three strands, the only kind she knew. The result was quite strong, and by adding another strip, every time one ran out she could extend it to any length she wanted. With lots of them, maybe, she could make a hammock. She was not very skilful at macramé but not completely ignorant. It shouldn't be too difficult.

She continued plaiting. The sheer monotony of the task was soothing. In her numbed mind two ideas were forming completely disconnected. About loving the forest, about climbing trees. And as she plaited the strips of bark, the ideas wove into each other, grew inextricably linked. *If one climbed trees, one would love the forest.* But she loved the forest and she had never climbed trees, nor was she likely to, in this place. *If they climbed the trees, they would love the forest.* That was better. *If he climbed trees, he would like the forest.* That was even better, though she did not know why. It just was. All their problems would be solved. She sighed with satisfaction and continued her work, side by side with the Indian.

He suddenly got up and signed that she should stay where she was. He disappeared for a while and came back with a bowl. Her heart sank, but when he took his place next to her, to her relief, he downed most of the drink. He was thirsty, that's all. It was not going to be another drug-taking session. She watched him closely, all the same. Nothing happened. So when later he took another swig and offered her some, she felt safe. She drank a little. It was not too bad. Quite refreshing, in fact.

They worked and drank in silence until she became so drowsy, her eyelids needed propping up. Last night had been long and sleepless, and the monotonous work didn't help. She ought to be going back. She started to rise, but once on her feet she didn't stop. She was getting higher and higher as if someone was pulling at her arms, enough to strain her shoulders. She was hauled so high, she could look at the forest floor as if from a tree top.

A puma that from this height looked no bigger than a kitten, prowled around and around the tree trunk, measuring it up. Then it took a leap at it. It slithered down, its claws grating the bark. It tried again, this time ending on its back. More prowling and another assault and so on.

It occurred to her that perhaps what the animal was doing was trying to get to her. Instead of being frightened, she felt its frustration and willed it to succeed. But the puma gave up and walked away. Only a short distance though, for Indians with arrows blocked its path on every side, forcing it back to the tree, its only escape to climb out of reach. It renewed its efforts frantically until it succeeded. It passed by her, perched just above her and dangled a paw to grab her. It snarled at her or at something further down. She turned to look. There was nothing beneath her but void and a figure she had seen many times before, disappearing into it: a rag doll. Yet the air wheezed by her own ears, her body made of lead, following the doll, becoming the doll.

She jerked into consciousness, alone, her heart pounding, covered in sweat. Except for the buzzing insects, everything was still. The heat was unbearable, the steam rising. After a while, she realised that even for midday, it was too quiet.

She picked up her ropes and extra strips of bark and headed back to the men, walking cautiously, paying attention to her markings. All the time, she was fearful that she was followed, and not by somebody as friendly as the shaman. Her hands instinctively held tightly to Paul's knife, though she kept repeating to herself that surely the shaman wouldn't let anyone hurt her.

Her path was blocked by several Indians. More of them materialised from the shadows all around. There followed a lot of commotion and gesticulation. One walked towards her threateningly. She backed against a tree. He kept pointing at her knife. The Indian obviously wanted it, but she couldn't afford to give it to him. It was one of the two tools they possessed: her lighter and Paul's knife.

She pointed to his arrows, another man's machete and the gun the man with the shorts held. She tried to convey that they had tools, she only had the knife. She put it against her chest to show how she valued it.

The man in front of her was literally hopping mad. He bent forward, said something inches from her face and jumped back, thrusting his pelvis forward and moving it from side to side. His penis, suspended from the string around his waist, swung back and forth.

The rest laughed and the man with the gun came forward and said between bouts of mirth, 'He say, you no son. No cojones.'

She stared at him. 'Cojones?'

The gunman pointed at her attacker's scrotum. 'Cojones.'

She didn't understand the significance of that but all the same turned to the man who, amazingly, had spoken in English, and said, 'Tell him there are disadvantages to having cojones.' She realised 'disadvantages' wouldn't be something he understood and corrected it to 'bad thing'.

He translated, and everybody fell about laughing. The man in front of her advanced even closer, carrying on with his obscene dance and trying to grab her knife. She was tempted to demonstrate just what she meant and, as always, gave in to the temptation instantly without a thought for the consequences.

Her knee made contact with the swinging cojones which, due to the Indian's compact stature, were conveniently at the right height, and he crumbled.

There followed a terrible silence. She was ready for any amount of violence, cursing herself for allowing her piratical ancestry to determine her reactions.

The translator was the first to do anything. He shook his

head up and down as if he had, at last, understood something. 'You his son. Yes,' he said. Then he said something to the Indians, who, were still staring at her shocked, and then all, including the interpreter, roared.

Sylvia looked stupidly from one to the other for a while until she too was infected and laughed until there were tears in her eyes.

In all the excitement the prostrate Indian launched at the knife, grabbed it and ran, pursued by his peers' laughter. Before he disappeared into the shadows, he turned. There was a flash of steel. Sylvia watched its trajectory, a jerky image like in early motion pictures, as it passed from light to shadow, from sunbeam to sunbeam. Everyone stood still, holding their breath, or it all took as little time as between one breath and the next. There certainly wasn't enough time for her to move. She gasped a silent scream as the sharp point embedded itself into her flesh.

The Indians looked at each other and then en masse scampered off like gazelles that had picked up the scent of a lion, and vanished within seconds, leaving her there bleeding.

23

The moment Sylvia was out of the way to look for herbs or food, or whatever else she did, Mark kicked Paul awake.

Paul jumped up swearing, looked at Mark and retreated. 'OK. So you heard, and now you know I am an asshole.' He spread out his arms. 'I know! Do you think I am proud of it? Put it down to inexperience. Have I ever had to proposition a woman before?' He withdrew even further as Mark advanced. 'Look, man! I said I am sorry and it was an even battle. Did you hear what she did to my ego?'

'You are right. You are an asshole. You can't tell a lady from a whore. But try that again and I'll kill you. Do you hear?'

'Hey! What's with the chivalry? I insulted your wife and you did nothing but a little frowning, and now you want to kill me?'

'Nicol *is* a whore. This one isn't. Get it?'

Paul peered at him through untidy hair, out of which he was picking bits of leaf. 'If you feel like that, why didn't you stop me last night?'

'I wouldn't have done anything to embarrass her more. But had you laid a finger on her . . .'

'Come on! You don't really think I would stoop to that! For Christ's sake!'

'I don't put anything past you after last night.'

'Oh, thanks!' But the pout turned to Paul's more usual mischievous expression. 'Trust you to play it all wrong. You should have done it when she was around. A knight in white armour and all that shit. She is romantic, our little

Sylvia, never mind the tough talk.' Then conspiratorially, 'I hope you will not sit around waiting for her to proposition you. She would have slept with me by then, and only do it for the sake of fairness.'

Paul was on the ground with blood pouring from his nose, and Mark didn't even realise he had put any force behind his right fist. He was left-handed, anyway.

Paul picked himself up. Icy blue shafts pierced through the tangle of hair falling over his face. 'I can't defend myself. Not with you injured. I am not the utter shit you think me.' He wiped the blood with the back of his hand, and only then did Mark notice the lacerations on his palm. 'But don't even dream of doing anything like this once you get better.'

It was Mark's turn to feel a jerk. 'I'm sorry. It just happened before I even thought about it, but you have been asking for it for ages. Just let it be. Let's concentrate on what is important. Look for a stream, a river, a path. Any sensible direction to walk to.'

'I think I have found it,' said Paul.

'Then what are we waiting for?'

'It seems, her permission. We might disturb some fucking animal's territory or something. We are prisoners to her madness or some motive I haven't worked out yet.'

'It's you who is crazy. She wants to go as much as we do. She suffers as much, and what's more, she has a young family out there.' She wasn't mad but knew something they didn't. She implied that something she was immune to threatened them. What she was doing was for their protection, and that was humiliating to say the least. She didn't trust them to act like grown-ups.

When Sylvia came back and threw her burden down, Mark saw the bloodstains on her dress. She trusted them with nothing, not even the simplest task. Probably for fear of being under obligation. What about them? 'Has it ever occurred to you,' he said, 'to ask anybody for help?'

She was taken aback, he would have said scared, if she hadn't looked frightened before he shouted at her. He changed his tone. 'No need to hurt yourself with us around to help.'

She looked down at her skirt and two red blotches appeared on her otherwise white face. 'It's just a scratch.'

'We are quite capable of gathering sticks,' Paul said. 'We even managed to build the fire without you.'

'Hammocks,' she said. 'Or will be, one of these days.'

Mark noticed for the first time that what she had brought looked like bark and, more remarkably, rope. That confirmed it, of course. He was a jerk. He was shouting at her when all she was doing was looking after their interests. He gestured at the bloodstains. 'Can I have a look? I don't have to tell you that even a scratch is dangerous in this environment.'

She sat down, brushing his request away. 'It's my fault.'

She wouldn't accept his help as a doctor, let alone a man. Boy, did he always misjudge women!

'Besides,' Paul said, 'we might see you bleed and mistake you for an ordinary human.'

Mark took his frustration out on Paul. 'Oh, shut up!'

He knelt by her and she obediently, for once, lifted her skirt above the knee. He sucked in his breath. The lips of the wound pouted into a kiss. There was hardly any bleeding by now, but it was deep enough to have penetrated the thigh muscle and should be very painful. His wife created havoc at a pinprick. This one was trying to hide a stab wound, and he was supposed to understand women! 'How did it happen?' he said.

'The blade slipped. I am sorry!'

'And you would have said nothing about it if I hadn't noticed?' Mark asked.

'Superwomen don't cry,' said Paul.

'My behaviour has nothing to do with pride, being superwoman or shit.' Whatever had subdued her before was gone. 'I simply do instinctively what has served me well all my life. The jungle is not all that different to anywhere else I've been. I have always obeyed my instincts and managed to just survive.'

'Would your survival be endangered by acknowledging that you hurt?' said Paul. 'I hurt.' He showed his swollen hands. 'Mark hurts. We don't mind admitting it.'

She sighed and said in a tired voice, 'I bet as a child, somebody kissed you better and took care of you when you were hurt. I got smacked for being careless or, worse, accused of trying to attract attention.' And she added indignantly, 'I was too bright a kid to think that attracting anyone's attention was a desirable thing.'

Instinctively Mark put his hand on her shoulders. It seemed to calm her down. 'I am so sorry,' he said. He should have kept quiet. She stiffened again.

'And I did not say it for sympathy, either,' she said. 'Just to put the record straight.' But she didn't move away, and as his hand slipped down her bare arm, she relaxed enough to smile.

He wanted to pull her towards him but that would be going too far, too fast. Instead he moved to her neck, his fingers kneading where the muscles felt hard and knotted.

'I seem to inspire people to give the worst possible interpretation to anything I do,' she said.

She looked sad. Mark moved his hands down her back to reassure her. She closed her eyes and he had the feeling she was about to rest her head on his shoulder, at least he hoped she would, but she gently disengaged his hand and leaned back against a tree trunk.

Mark cleaned the wound with boiled water like he had done with Paul's hands, the most rudimentary of disinfectant procedures. There was nothing else. If she couldn't stop the certain infection with her herbal medicines, he would have to resort to more drastic measures, which he would much rather not do.

She didn't even flinch, just carried on talking. 'Do you know how I found out about right and wrong as a child?' It was a rhetorical question, so Mark carried on with what he was doing, glancing occasionally in her direction to see if he was hurting her. She gave a little shrug and continued,

'By being accused of something, first. Then I looked it up in a dictionary.'

Mark bound her thigh with her own scarf. He didn't need it anymore. His shoulder was much better, as long as he did not move his arm too much.

She brought up her knees and rested her chin on them, arms around her legs, her favourite posture, and stared at Paul, who was quiet for a change, his hands under his armpits. 'What's wrong?' she said gently, as if to show there were no hard feelings after last night.

Paul extended his arms, palms up. 'They sting like hell.'

She did not look at his hands straight away. It was her stare at the shoulders and arms that brought to Mark's attention how the contours of Paul's muscles were picked out by the theatrical light and brought out into high relief. 'What have you been doing?' she said, eventually.

'Pretending to be Tarzan,' Paul said sheepishly. He tacked his hands under his arms again. 'The only hope for anything worthwhile to eat is up there,' and he pointed his chin to the canopy. 'I thought of using a liana to climb.'

She gave a little start as if her wound suddenly hurt. 'Oh,' she said.

Paul showed her his hands again. 'But they are spiny,' and tacking them away, 'or slippery.'

'And sometimes poisonous.' she said.

Paul rolled his eyes. 'Now she tells me!'

She chuckled. 'Some are quite safe, and natives in Africa climb trees with the aid of slings made from them. I suppose they do something similar here. I'll show you.'

Paul looked at her thoughtfully. 'I don't know what we would have done without you.'

She blushed. 'I'm not trying to impress, you know.'

'I know.' Paul hesitated. 'I'm only teasing, most of the time.' Another break. 'Look, I am sorry about last night. It's unpardonable. I don't know what came over me.'

She threw a surreptitious look at Mark. He kept his face still.

'It's OK. He knows,' said Paul.

Mark signed behind her back for Paul to stop at that.

Sylvia got up. 'We have to see to those hands before sepsis sets in.'

'Mark did,' said Paul.

It didn't seem to impress her much. 'As a doctor, he was taught to rely exclusively on synthetic drugs.'

'Might as well,' Mark said to stop her going out there again. 'Or people like Paul will be the poorer.'

The bait worked. 'Oh?'

'He owns a drug company, among others,' Mark explained.

'Have an interest in one,' Paul corrected.

'A very large one,' added Mark.

She kept looking from one to the other.

'Maybe,' Paul said, 'you can work for me when we get out. We could market these wonderful plants you know so much about. Drugs from nature and all that. It would go down a treat with the Greens. Give me a break from their pestering about raping forests and what have you.'

'Do you?' she said.

Paul realised his mistake too late and said warily, 'I just have an interest in a mineral company here.'

'And was busy taking it completely over when all this happened.' Mark moved his arm around to indicate their predicament.

'This explains things much better,' she said without great surprise.

Paul looked like a little boy about to be sent to the headmaster's office. 'Now that I spilled the beans, you will have another reason to stomp on me.'

'I don't stomp on people!' she said, but without her usual snap.

'Maybe not people. Just me,' Paul said.

'Sorry, it's just that you keep on teasing, as you call it. Anyway, why do you think I should stomp on you now?' She had her head to one side, staring at him with the kind of indulgence one shows to contrite, naughty children.

Paul was watching her warily. 'I thought with your love for nature, you would be outraged.'

'I can appreciate that raw materials are needed,' she said reasonably. 'There is a profit to be made, and somebody will make it.'

Paul looked sceptical. 'You . . . condone it?'

'I think wholesale destruction of the forest for short-term interest is unwise, but all living things exploit their environment. It's a matter of balance. They get it right, they survive, they get it wrong, they perish. It's as simple as that. Symbiosis or parasitism but,' she gave a shrug, 'between us, the parasites are no endangered species. There must be a balancing factor somewhere.'

'I thought, in the case of Greens, emotion not reasoning is the operative word,' said Paul. 'You are one, aren't you?'

'If by Green you mean interested parties using scare tactics, the panic of the ignorant masses and the reflex reactions of the even more ignorant politicians, no thanks!' she said.

It was too much for Paul. He threw his head back and his laughter bounced from tree trunk to tree trunk. 'God,' he said after wiping his eyes with the back of his hand, 'is there nothing safe? You just demolished the most recent and hence most sacred of cows.'

'I bet those who come to complain to you about the forest do so in their fume-belching cars,' she said. 'Have they thought what they would do without electricity or the latest consumer goods in their favourite supermarket, I wonder?'

'That's what I tell them,' Paul said, 'but I did not expect it from you, not after I saw the love you squander, er . . . sorry, lavish on living things here. Don't you want to protect them?'

'Yes, but from both ends of the spectrum,' she said. 'I'd much rather people didn't deforest the Earth for their raw materials or to create a farm for a couple of years, but, in my view, the so-called conservationists are responsible for a lot of damage too.'

Mark was about to say that was going a bit too far, but she was getting into her stride and obviously enjoying herself. 'Nature is bountiful, merciless and just.' From a closed fist she brought out one finger after the other. 'Whatever cannot compete gets eliminated.' Now both palms opened, face down. 'Evolution is relentless. Interference with it, catastrophic. It's arrogant of us to think we could apply compassion to it, or worse still, try to correct it.' She mimicked some imaginary nature lover: '"This animal species is threatened with extinction, let's save it. Dear me! Too many of this species now ate all the trees and made the forest into a desert. Everything else is getting extinct."' Mark couldn't keep up with the hands anymore. They were all over the place. 'Let's make it green again with conifers. Surprise, surprise, too much acidity is killing whatever managed to survive...' Paul's laughter interrupted the flow. She set her jaw. 'I deserve to be ridiculed,' she said, 'for trying to discuss things with a man who cannot take anything seriously and another who would never allow any expression of personal conviction.'

Paul sobered up. 'Since when is laughter a capital offence?' Then he changed his mind about protest and continued with the argument. 'I was about to say that the thing most missing from modern debate, is common sense. Leave Nature alone and it will take care of itself, is what you implied. I could go along with that. What I don't like,' and he stared at Mark, 'is to be preached at...'

Sylvia continued from where she thought he had left off: '... by film stars and pop singers who couldn't survive a day in the wild. It's the in thing to support a cause. Today, the dolphin, tomorrow, the whale, the day after, the Amazonian jungle.'

'Right,' said Paul. 'Let's also hear it from the fisherman and the jungle dweller and why not the industrialist and the workers in his factory?' He was looking at Sylvia with a new-found respect.

Mark kept out of it, still smarting from the assumption that he had no opinions because he didn't air them as freely as her, and sensing it, she turned to him. 'Sorry,' she said. 'I got carried away with things. Nobody bothered to challenge me, and it made me feel foolish.'

'Maybe we agree,' Mark said.

'Or are being condescending. My argument had its weaknesses,' she said.

'If you know that why...' began Paul but she seemed impatient to answer before he finished, like people who rarely have the chance to talk and when they do, they have to express as much as possible quickly before the opportunity disappears.

'I feel things only vaguely,' she said. 'Keep them ureconstructed in my head until there is a need to find the words for it. And even then, I need some resistance to work against for a watertight argument. Otherwise it comes out all sloppy.'

'We are not argumentative enough?' said Paul.

'About frivolous things, yes, but nothing serious,' she said. 'After all, I am a superstitious female, a witch.' Then she turned up the intensity. 'I can assure you, I believe there is nothing here that can't be explained with physics and chemistry and a little bit of anthropology.'

'And I will be the happiest of men if we could seriously discuss why you insist we remain here like prisoners,' said Paul.

'You could answer that better yourself,' she said. 'I've seen you. You walk up to a point and come back. Why? A modern man brought up in a sophisticated society in every possible comfort would have been unequipped to recognise what you did. But I guess you were bored in your safety and had to play with death for kicks. That's the only thing that would explain how you managed to tap skills inherited from remote ancestors. So it is not I that stops you going, but your own atavistic instincts. You want to live, and you will stay until the danger passes.' Then more quietly, 'It will soon.' And after a pause, 'But you have to learn to climb trees first.'

Paul was thoughtful for a while, trying to make sense of

it all. 'You mean to get food, so we have the strength for a long haul?' he said at last.

'Yes,' she said doubtfully, 'and so that you fall in love with the jungle.'

'Now who is being frivolous?' said Paul. 'If I was going to climb a tree, it would be to find food, not to fall in love.'

'There is no way out unless you do,' she said.

Paul seemed to have no idea how to take it any more than Mark did. She looked too serious for it to be a joke. 'You say the weirdest things,' then he smiled, 'but that's your charm.'

She smiled back. 'I never thought witches could be charming.'

'Wasn't Circe suppose to be a charmer?' Paul said, keeping the lighthearted tone going.

'Are you afraid I might change you into a pig?' she said.

'Could you please find something a bit better?' Paul wrinkled his nose. 'I hate pigs.'

'Would a puma do?' she said.

'A great improvement, I think.'

She chuckled. 'I'll see what I can do.'

'Good. Then I will climb a tree,' said Paul 'and we will find that goddam river.'

Mark didn't join in their new-found bonhomie. He was too busy trying to work out her change of policy. It had worked wonders, but what brought it about? Surely it couldn't be Paul's lamentable behaviour last night. More and more, things didn't add up. The wound was too deep for a mere slip of a knife. She spent too long out there on her own, always bringing back something new, she never made or found when anyone was watching, and avoided looking one in the eye if asked about it. Now she had Paul eating out of her hand. And as for the connection between climbing trees and their ability to get out, it was anyone's guess.

24

Paul had gained experience and confidence in climbing trees the last few days but those were trials. This time he chose a tree big enough to get him into the canopy. His arms couldn't go round the trunk and he spread them as wide as he could, flattening his chest against it. The sling encircled both the tree and him.

He searched with his fingers for the slightest roughness on the bark and when he found it, he clung desperately while inch by inch he moved his feet up the trunk. The shoe leather was slippery. Bare toes would have been preferable, but he did not dare go barefoot for fear of stepping on a camouflaged snake. Even so, he occasionally stamped a foot on the tree trunk, hoping the vibration would scare the snakes away. That was Sylvia's advice when walking on the forest floor. That or tapping with a stick, neither of which she bothered practising herself.

With every tap of his foot, he risked his shoe disintegrating. Both shoes and clothes were already mildewed and threatened to fall off his body. The friction with the tree bark and the sling didn't help.

As his feet moved a few steps up the tree, the sling slackened. Supporting himself against the sling and gripping with his feet, he could afford to let go with his hands and tried to move the sling a bit higher. And again, a few steps to slacken the sling, push it higher and so forth. A few feet from the ground his fingers were numb, his shoulders ached and his feet had cramp.

He looked up and despaired. The first branch was still as

far away as when he began. Looking down was a little more encouraging. Sylvia and Mark were getting smaller. He saw how anxious they both looked and smiled down reassuringly, not that he himself felt particularly confident. He took a deep breath and persevered, creeping higher and higher until it seemed wiser not to look down.

By the time the first branch was within reach, he was too exhausted. The air was so hot and humid he could hardly breathe, and perspiration was running down his body in rivulets. Everything around him swayed, including the tree trunk. Dizziness, he supposed. He shook his head to get rid of it and took deep breaths to extract some oxygen. But the solid tree trunk kept on the move and only in one direction. The green umbrella of the crown had resolved itself into millions of large leaves, all caught in the breeze, moving en masse against a bright sky. He could feel the strain in the wood. Nothing this solid could bend this far without cracking. He shut his eyes, waiting for the explosion as the tree snapped. The tree creaked and groaned and shivered. When he thought he couldn't take much more of this, it stopped and Paul took a deep breath, but his heartbeat had no time to come to some sensible rate of beating when the tree went into motion again, this time in the opposite direction.

He had no choice but to put up with the swaying and get hold of that branch. He wiped the sweat from his eyes against his upper sleeve and cautiously extended an arm. The entire length of the branch was covered with epiphytes, leaving no bark visible. To get a grip, he rubbed his hand back and forth to dislodge the aerial plants, but could not pull himself up. He sat on the sling to rest and then uncoiled the rope made of bark, one end of which he had tied to his waist. He threw the free end over the branch and tied it to himself. Now he felt reasonably secure to let go with both hands and grasped the branch again. He transferred all his weight to his arms and dangled in mid-air.

He groaned with the agony that shot through his shoulders, but there was no turning back. The manoeuvre had to be completed. Desperation made him call on reserves of strength he didn't know he had. His breath came in agonising gasps, his shoulder and arm muscles bulged, about to burst through his skin, his veins stood out like ropes. He pushed that little bit more, raised himself enough to bend over the branch and take some weight on his chest. With a last heave, he put a leg over it.

Astride the branch, both arms resting on the bark in front of him, his eyes closed, bathed in perspiration, he thanked the forest spirit. He made it, though all his muscles quivered uncontrollably and he shivered in the tropical heat.

Eventually he raised his head. No way was he going to look down. He was dizzy as it was. In what felt like slow motion, he moved his hand to grasp a leafy branch and steadied himself enough to look around.

This was a different world to the forest floor, more like he had expected a jungle to be. Masses of epiphytic plants draped everywhere, their roots dangling; gaudy flowers wafted powerful perfumes; colourful birds darted around; iridescent insects buzzed; and above all, there was light. Dazzling, life-giving, glorious sunshine! Starved of most sensory stimulants for so long and now all his senses bombarded simultaneously gave him a high, more powerful than from any drug he had experimented with.

He forgot all about his exhaustion and terror. This was Paradise. What would Sylvia make of it if she ever dared to climb up here?

The thought of Sylvia punctured his euphoria. Everything she did or said the last few days conveyed forgiveness for his nocturnal lapse in taste, but it didn't make him feel better. No matter how lonely or frustrated he had been, he should never have made such a naïve approach. He deserved the mauling of his ego and losing the respect of Mark, the only real friend he ever had.

'For once you want something you cannot have,' she had said. If it were just that, it wouldn't have been so terrible, but from having everything he ever wanted to nothing he could possibly want was a bit harsh. It wasn't a matter of the smartest clothes, the most exclusive restaurants, fast cars, his own jet, properties around the world and the prettiest women, people saying 'Yes sir!' to his every utterance. He would settle now for a hamburger, a coke, a shave, a bed and the good opinion of just the one woman and Mark.

He shook himself out of it. He had this place now. For the time being, this was *his* world, *his* kingdom. It would take Mark a long time with his weakened shoulder to be able to climb, and Sylvia would never have sufficient strength.

It took him a while to realise that the green mass suspended to his right was not of plant origin but a sloth hanging upside down, its fur green with fungus, blending perfectly into the foliage. Paul's clothes were fungusy, so if he stayed still, would he blend as well in the background? It seemed he did, because the animals and birds that scattered away with the noise of his approach were now returning.

After a while, he felt eyes on his back like he had done so often on the forest floor. He turned. A monkey scurried away. More animals he could not identify caught the monkey's apprehension and scampered off too. He laughed. The difference light makes!

He moved along the branch cautiously to gather some of the fruit the monkey was feeding on, before he frightened it off, and put them inside his shirt. Fruit alone had to suffice for the time being. They had not been successful manufacturing bows and arrows. Sylvia knew the theory of how to make them, having seen them in Africa, but in practice they never flew true. She said they required animal gut to bind feathers at the ends. Catch-22. To get the gut they needed animals, which they couldn't get without arrows. Tied with bark, they were as crude and as accurate as brandishing a stick. Which made him think about that toucan in front of him.

Paul had initially mistaken the gaudy colours of the cumbersome beak for a bright bloom, but the frog-like croak betrayed its presence and now he could make out the black body and yellow throat quite distinctly. It was not entirely impossible to strike it. Any bit of branch would do. But he hesitated. What right did he have . . .? On the other hand, a few more days on sweet potatoes and he would never have sufficient strength to climb trees again. He carefully broke off a brittle branch, took aim and knocked the bird off its perch, making sure he didn't look down to see what became of it for fear of getting dizzy. Still, the toucan's fate bothered him and he caught himself philosophising about it. Out there, in his previous life, to succeed, one had to stand out above the rest, to make noise. Here, one had to blend in, be quiet like the sloth, or one ended up like the toucan: dead.

There was nothing else to do up there, yet he was reluctant to descend into the gloom. He sat for a while, observing life all around him. It didn't take him long to realise how lucky he had been to climb this particular tree. All sorts of animals came to feed on it, always by the same way, and departed along an equally fixed route, so much so that the branches bearing the traffic were devoid of epiphytic plants or other obstructions, forming aerial highways. If this tree, this roadside diner, were to be taken out, the disruption would be tragic, considering the amount of plant and animal life it supported, as well as the part it played in the road network. But it would be temporary. Just beneath it, there was its successor, ready to spring into place. What he had been planning, though, was the removal of thousands of such trees and their seedlings and all undergrowth. The enormity of his proposed crime suddenly hit home, and so did the conversation he had with Sylvia the other day. He was to climb a tree and fall in love.

At least she gave him credit that if he saw the canopy, he would appreciate the significance of any damage to the ecosystem, but that also begged several questions. Was this some elaborate game to teach him the value of trees? And how could this lesson help them to escape? To propitiate the forest was the implication, and at the same time she negated anything that could not be explained in physical terms. Spirits were mentioned once, by him, as it happened, and she had qualified her answer: 'In a way.' What way? He sighed. He couldn't make head or tail of the woman.

He thought the descent would be easier. Gravity would be on his side, but with already overtaxed muscles, a controlled manoeuvre was out of the question.

Once he began, it was too late to correct his mistake. As he picked up speed, his hands and legs chafed against the bark with no time to get a grip on anything. The sling would fray, for sure, but any attempt to put the brakes on resulted in destroying whatever was left of his shoes, to no benefit.

He desperately looked for anything that would come to his rescue and break his inevitable fall, and noticed what was happening to the sloth, but there was no time to think about that now.

The green around him moved faster and faster, finally zipping by, and the Doppler shift of bird noises like emergency sirens intensified the sense of impending danger.

25

Sylvia wished she could see what was happening, but the tree was too high and lower branches from neighbouring trees obscured whatever vision she might have had, to say nothing of the glare. She still stared upwards, to no avail. The back of her neck ached, and that brought on a terrible headache.

'I would have gone up there myself,' Mark said through clenched teeth, 'if it weren't for this darn shoulder.'

'It can't be helped,' she said. It would have been as anxious for her if he did.

'Paul is unreliable,' Mark continued. 'He takes everything as a game invented for his pleasure. He is likely to do something stupid up there, and it would be my fault for not stopping him.'

No, it wouldn't. It would be her fault. She had encouraged Paul to climb the tree when she refused to expose herself to the same danger. And for what? Dream interpretations and omens?

Maybe all this business with the chief was just in her mind. But where else would it be? Everything humans perceived, be it touch, smell, taste or sound, was in their mind. It was the mind that processed and interpreted all messages, whatever the source.

She was not sure, however, of that interpretation. She thought the Indian warned her against venturing out before he had decided they were ready, and that, somehow, involved Paul climbing trees. And was the dream just that, or had the shaman tricked her in taking a drug again? In the vision, the puma had appeared safe. It was she that had fallen. She couldn't interpret that. But what if it had been nothing more than empathy? She had identified with the frustration at the initial failure, felt relief at the puma's eventual success and finally experienced the horror of its fall.

She wished she could tell Mark how worried she was and why. He would put his arms around her and she would press her cheek against his chest. Those marvellous hands would slide all over her back again. She would feel reassured and comforted, like she did the other day, his open palm moving down her back, radiating a wave of luxurious warmth. She had unwound, her tense headache eased and she wished it would never end, yet she ended it herself because it was gradually turning to sensuality.

Why had she thought him intimidating before? He was really kind and gentle. Perhaps she had never been intimidated – just shy. Why shy?

Then it hit her. She was unused to the presence of a mature man. Her husband never grew up. He had remained just as she had first met him. After so many years, the unfamiliar presence of a man threw her into confusion.

Of course, she couldn't do anything now, for fear of being accused of encouraging something more, at a moment like this.

That was the problem with men. They could not understand a woman's desire for touch without the need for sex. How many times when she had felt like today, lonely and vulnerable, she had sought to approach her husband, who instantly translated it as a call for him to perform his duty.

That was how he always considered love-making. An unpleasant duty that he avoided as much as he could. If she tried to explain that she was not after sex, he misunderstood and lost whatever little confidence he had in his prowess – and if she said nothing, she felt humiliated. In the end, she gave up altogether. For a tactile person like her, to learn to live without human touch was very hard. Living in such an emotional desert for so long, no wonder she was vulnerable to the slightest show of affection.

She felt so sorry for herself, she wanted to cry.

'I am sorry,' said Mark. 'I shouldn't be talking like this. He'll be OK'

I need a cuddle. Instead she nodded. She was being unreasonable. He was near, he was most sympathetic, and his voice as comforting as his touch would ever be.

There was a flurry up in the canopy and something was coming down, too fast for comfort. She shut her eyes, unable to witness what she was sure would follow: the limp body of Paul, waving its arms around like a rag doll.

The thud at her feet was too insignificant to be that of a man's body. She opened her eyes slowly. There was a shattered orange beak, the black streak at its base bracketing a small pool of blue, from the centre of which a dark eye stared blankly at her. She let out her breath in relief, but it was a while before her pulse stopped ringing in her ears and her body became ready to obey any commands.

There was another commotion behind her, this time a stir of air like a heavy sigh and a soft thud. She jumped. A turkey vulture folded up its enormous wings and stared at her imperiously. It was already staking its claim to the victim at her feet.

Sylvia bent down and picked up the corpse. The vulture took a couple of hops to register its disapproval and took off, the beat of its wings sending a draught of chilled air over Sylvia's perspiring body.

'Other than a couple of broken bones,' she said to Mark, 'the bird seems OK.' And as an excuse to end the agony of waiting, she went off to prepare a toucan barbecue. There was nothing useful she could do by standing under the tree.

Sylvia slowly built up the fire and lit it. She filled the pot from the oozing rock. It took ages, but she was in no hurry. After balancing it in the middle of the fire she waited for the water to boil, staring at the flames. For seeing pictures in, it was as good as staring at clouds. How long ago since she had seen a cloud? Would she ever see one again?

Her children's faces appeared in the flames, eyes anxious. 'Come back soon, Mummy' – 'Cross my heart'.

Was she going to do it by sacrificing other people?

There was no profit in that line of thought, so she took the bird and dipped it in the hot water. After that, the feathers came off easily. With Paul's knife she made an incision in the loose skin above the breast and removed the crop, cut off the anus and reached into the cavity to remove the internal organs.

The gall bladder glistened like an emerald in the liver folds, and care had to be taken detaching it. A puncture would release bile and make the liver bitter. It was too valuable a source of iron and vitamins to be wasted like that. She split the gizzard in two to remove the grid and fibre and so saved an extra bit of flesh. There were three hungry people to be satisfied out of this one bird. The intestines, too, could be of use. She washed them and kept them soaking in cold water in a small gourd. If wound around objects while wet, they would shrink and fuse on drying and make secure bindings.

What little was left, like the crop and trimmings, she threw as far away from her as was consistent with her wish to see what happened. She didn't have long to wait. The vulture's keen sense of smell guided it down within minutes. It kept a weary eye on her while making for the offal. Two more vultures circled a couple of times and landed heavily nearby. There was an ill-tempered dispute involving a lot of hopping and pecking, but honour was saved by all getting a scrap, and when they left not a trace remained. The jungles's refuse disposal unit had done its job.

She sharpened a stick and skewered the bird onto it. She was debating whether to start cooking now, or wait until Paul came down. The fears that the necessary, if unpleasant, occupation had soothed, returned, and when she heard Mark's horrified cry she was ready to believe the worst.

26

Sylvia looked terrified when the bird fell from the tree, and Mark had to keep his own panic under control not to make things worse. He was glad she had decided to go, though he wouldn't dream of doing so himself. There wasn't much he could do standing there, other than pick up the pieces if the worst came to the worst, but one never knew.

A black shadow blotted out the glare above him and he heard the flapping of giant wings. The atavistic fear of the Angel of Death passed briefly through his mind but he was not that far maddened yet, that such thoughts would last for any length of time. He had to get a grip on himself.

There was a flash of white breast feathers. Enormous black and white striped wings flapped. The bird was inverted, presenting Mark with its sable back as it shot upwards, talons first. There was a sickening crunch, a little pathetic squeal, laborious flapping, a draught of air disturbing the leaves, then all was quiet.

Mark beat his fist against the tree trunk in impotent fury. An agent of death, after all. The sharp pain brought back some sense. There was another disturbance above him then a protracted scream of terror and Paul came into view, sliding down the trunk. At this speed, he would hit the ground any moment now. The rope tied to his waist was already trailing within reach.

No thought was involved in what Mark did, just reflexes. He grabbed the rope and ran away from the trunk, pulling. Paul was jerked backwards and the sling tightened against the trunk, acting as a brake, but only for a while. One by one the fibres in the sling were snapping and Paul started coming down again, but nothing like as fast as he would have had there been no brake.

Mark ran back and plucked Paul off the tree before he hit the ground and held him in his arms, his cheeks wet with tears. Before he had time to be embarrassed by this show of emotion, he realised Paul was unable to stand on his own feet. His legs shook uncontrollably, which legitimised Mark's embrace. He half-carried, half-dragged Paul back to base and Sylvia took over.

Far from smirking or wisecracking, as one would have expected from him, Paul submitted quietly to Sylvia's massage, except for the odd swear word when the pain got too much. But the agony of his muscles didn't stop him eating. It was, after all, their first real meal since they had found themselves in the jungle. Barbecued game, roast sweet potato and fruit for afters. Only then did Paul sleep, and when he got up the next day he was so stiff he couldn't move a muscle.

Mark forced him to do some mild exercise and ignored the abuse.

'Fucking Nazi! Does it give you pleasure to torture me?' Paul turned on Sylvia. 'Just laugh, why not? Only I just risked my life for you two.'

That's right, thought Mark. He did risk his life, and why should he? 'Next time, I'll go,' he said.

There was no pleasing Paul. 'One of us risking his neck is enough,' he said. 'Besides, you are heavier than me. It would take much more strength to haul that bulk of yours up the tree, and your arm is not strong enough yet.'

'It will never be strong enough if I never use it,' said Mark.

'In good time, if you must,' Paul said, 'but it's no use trying just any old tree. If you want to meet people, you go to clubs or restaurants. The same up there. Trees with ripe fruit would be where most animals will gather...' He noticed Sylvia's smile. 'What are you smirking at?'

'Quite the naturalist already, I see,' she said.

Paul smiled for the first time since his adventure. 'In case you're wondering, yes, I did fall in love. It's paradise up there.'

'Then why are you in such a foul mood?' Mark said.

Paul's face darkened. 'Because cruelty and death are part of paradise too, like everywhere else.'

'You regret having to kill the bird,' Sylvia said. 'I can understand that.'

Paul frowned for a second. 'The bird?' and then, remembering, 'Oh, yeah. I suppose I was a bit, but that's not what I was talking about. I lost a friend, up there.' He looked at their puzzled faces. 'A sloth. He was a bit on the quiet side, but I'm used to friends like that,' and he smirked at Mark, who just grunted.

'What happened to him?' asked Sylvia.

'The eagle got him.'

Mark was in no mood to laugh at himself for thinking an eagle could carry away a human. His mental state bothered him. Was he going soft in the head?

By next day Paul was physically much better but still moody and irritable. At least he had an excuse. But Sylvia did not utter a word all day, fidgeted around, made some effort to go and look for food and gave up. Nobody felt hungry anyway. Mark, too, lacked the energy to get off the ground, let alone do anything.

They had all spent too long in this gloomy world. Today was more dismal than ever. The atmosphere pressed on his chest, heavy with humidity, unbreathable. He wiped the sweat from his eyes and wished it would rain and get it over with, but nothing seemed to happen. There was a slight breeze, enough for a moment's respite, and the oppression returned with a vengeance. A little longer and he would scream – if he could find the energy.

Time passed. The forest sighed as if it, too, was suffering. There was a sussuration of leaves but no freshness, no relief. A distant drum beat a bass tremolo. Mark felt the vibration through the ground. The wind picked up. Sylvia suddenly stood still and listened. She might have heard the distant rumble, too, but why did she walk towards it? He forced himself out of his apathy. 'Where are you going?'

She turned and mumbled something like 'I have to.'

Dysphoria transmuted into anger, but the only outward sign was a raised eyebrow to show his disapproval. When she ignored it, he made a half-hearted effort to get up and follow her. He changed his mind. It was none of his business if she wanted to be alone all the time, even in a storm. And come to think of it, why all this indignation at her independence? He accused women of relying too much on men, and when they did not, he resented it. Inconsistent or what?

Yet he sensed that he was letting her expose herself to danger in the storm, alone, neither because he was angry at her independence, nor out of respect for it, but because something beyond his comprehension was stopping him. A whisper in his mind that she belonged to the forest and it would not harm one of its own.

When he had time to digest that, he was appalled. It was so fatalistic and superstitious. He was becoming a pagan, after all, some throwback to a remote ancestry, like Paul and his instincts. He had allowed the forest to affect him. Primitive thoughts sprang up unbidden: extrasensory perceptions, angels of death, destiny. What next? Yet he couldn't help another idea slowly surfacing from some dark well in his soul, and it hurt much more than his perceived vulnerability to superstition: whatever was to happen excluded him. Just him.

'Why did the stupid woman choose this moment to go walkies?' Paul shouted to be heard above the gathering storm.

'We are not protected where we are,' Mark screamed back.

'At least we are together. Why does she always have to do something different?'

'You needn't do anything.'

Paul agreed. 'Why should I worry if you don't?'

He huddled next to Mark between two buttresses, prepared like him to sit out the storm. But he began to fidget and curse. Suddenly he stood up. 'I have to do it,' he said and stumbled into the open.

He was sluiced by rain, buffeted in the wind, one moment under an arc light, the next in darkness. He would be blinded in both cases, Mark thought. He would have no idea where to go, either. The whole exercise was useless. But he made no effort to stop him.

27

Sylvia would rather not have had the drink the Indian offered, especially with a storm coming on. She might need her wits about her, but he gave her no choice, and though he had separated her from her companions, he went afterwards, leaving her standing there, legs apart, bracing herself for the worst yet looking forward to it.

Stormy weather had always fascinated her. She remembered in her childhood the excitement at nights when the wind howled and the sea moaned outside her window. How, on wintry days, she sat by the sea to watch the raging waters lash the coast, ignoring her father's comment: 'It's like you prefer an angry person to a smiling one.'

As a grown woman in Africa, she found excuses to walk out whenever there was a tropical storm, but doors opened and people called her in or cars stopped and offered lifts, and no one would let her go in the bush alone.

She could not have explained without appearing crazy, that she needed no protection from a storm, that she enjoyed it, it was as if the turmoil in her soul found release. The warring elements outside expressed all the frustrations, confusions and ferment within, leaving her calm and restful afterwards.

But she was not prepared for what was happening now. The lightning came in a thin straight line. It turned the forest white for a second. A deafening boom shook the forest. Secondary rumbles receded further and further away. Stronger winds were unleashed all round. The trees, already animated, went frantic, waving their branches and groaning in anguished protest.

There was a tremendous explosion too close for comfort, followed closely by a roar, coming towards her. She waited helplessly. A tree must have lost the battle with the elements. Such a giant crashing down would destroy everything in its path, including her. In all the mayhem, it was impossible to determine the direction. She could as easily run towards it as away from it.

The forest wall in front of her cleaved in two. It was too late to run. The tree crown intruded into what had been a large clearing. It elbowed aside lesser trees on the periphery and shattered the aspirations of straggling seedlings for a future takeover. It spread and freed its branches, filling the gap, and then flopped down. The giant's expiring breath blew Sylvia out of the way to make room for the tips to rest inches from her.

As she tried to pick herself up, another ominous growl rolled through the tunnel the fallen tree had left behind. A wave of water advanced and hit her like a brick wall. What followed was a frenzy of lightning, thunder, wind and water, an elemental orgy that defied comprehension.

Her initial terror was replaced slowly by a sense of power as if she herself orchestrated the turbulence, this battle of the elements: the wind howled at her command, the water was let loose at her bidding, the trees bent their heads in reverence to her wishes.

She threw her head back and let out a triumphant laugh that drowned in the noise of the storm. There was nobody to curb her freedom to enjoy the tempest, to communicate with the elements, to release the inner conflicts, to rid herself of frustration and unrest. Yet at the same time she had a longing for sharing. It would be even better to worship the elements with another human being, one that preferably felt the same way. But who was there that felt the same way?

She stood up with great difficulty and lifted her face towards the sky, reeling in the force of the wind. The rain stung her. All her willpower concentrated on an image. She couldn't pin it down. It kept changing, flickering like bad reception on a television screen. She stretched her arms to the laden sky and screamed a name as if by doing so, she could focus the image. Her voice, inaudible in the roar of the tempest, reverberated through her body and echoed in her mind, but it didn't sound like the name she had called. She tried and tried. Then she felt someone's presence and turned.

The figure was indistinct, shrouded in a watery curtain. She was convinced it was there in answer to her call, and it reinforced her delusion of power until it began to move. There was something strange about it. Another image kept superimposing upon it. The two images sometimes blended, sometimes replaced one another. Both were uncannily similar: the same supple grace, the same sinuous way of stalking, the same placid indolence, disguising the ruthlessness, the same cobalt eyes, pinning her down, the same savage sleekness and menacing beauty.

The puma coiled up a few paces from Sylvia. A voice in her head warned 'This is too dangerous. You cannot handle it. Run away!'

She could not move. She waited for the fury of the sprint she knew would follow. The feline eyes did not blink or shift their stare, not even in this rain. Every muscle was taut. The tension reached breaking point, then the paws shot up and now it was too late to run away.

But it was Paul bending over her, his eyes dilated, narrow cobalt rims surrounding black holes. There were his fingers digging into her flesh, his lips that parted a fraction away from hers. She felt his short, laboured breath on her face, sheltered from the rain by his head.

The strain was unbearable. Before she crumbled up under its pressure, his lips pressed hard on hers, demanding, and she groaned at the sudden force. His tongue pressed against her teeth seeking entrance, and when it thrust into her mouth the pit of her stomach sank, her knees gave way and they both tumbled to the ground.

As they rolled in the mud, she clung to him desperately. He tore at her clothes, seeking her out urgently, impatiently, making a growling noise at the back of his throat. She fought frantically, not to escape but to be one with him, her vehemence equal to his, her needs as demanding and overpowering, craving appeasement with the same compulsion. It was a savage struggle, in tune with the tempest all around them if anything the storm paled to insignificance as they surrendered to the primitive greed of their bodies.

When he came he let out a cry, half in relief, half in triumph, before he collapsed, his weight crushing her. He took a few gulps of air, his heart thundering against her chest, and then rolled over on his back.

He opened his mouth to let rainwater fall in it. His Adam's apple moved convulsively up and down. Even when the rain stopped, he remained stretched out star-like in the mud. It was a long time before he raised himself onto his elbows to look at her as she lay there, half-sunk in mud.

His head to one side, he said 'Lady, if that is what you do when you don't like it, what could you have done if you did? Blow my head off?'

She sat up and drew her knees up to her chest, clasping them with both arms. 'I am no hypocrite. I will not pretend I didn't like it.'

He went on his knees and grasped her head in both hands. 'I don't know about earth-moving, but I thought the sky fell on me,' he whispered.

'It did,' she said, pointing at all the devastation around.

They both laughed, foreheads touching, then Paul became serious. 'I never felt like this before and, though I say so myself, I am not exactly inexperienced.' He lay back again, his arms under his head. 'You were right, of course.'

'About what?'

'About not settling for mediocrity. Aiming for perfection. You didn't fool me. All that cynicism about love and sex was disappointment. You expected more, knew there was more, and were not satisfied with what you had.' He waved a hand above his head. 'You were right. I might have mocked you, but deep down I have sensed your frustration.' He tucked his hand behind his head again. 'Perhaps I was searching for the same thing myself. It was not just promiscuity, but a quest. There ought to have been something more and I had to find it.'

'And have you?' She couldn't help being sarcastic, but if he noticed, he chose to ignore it.

'Oh yes!' he said with utter conviction.

She felt apprehensive. 'Don't make too much of this,' she warned herself more than him. 'The circumstances were such. It can't be repeated.'

He sat bolt upright. 'Don't!' he said with vehemence, his eyes darting blue fire. 'Don't try to destroy it by explaining it away.'

He was right, but she could never stop herself from dissecting things. 'I could never perform premeditatedly,' she said. 'It must be spontaneous. Try and sit it out and see how often one is swept by spontaneity. There are aphrodisiacs, of course. With me it is the urgency of my partner. I got carried away on somebody else's wave of enthusiasm.' And she had mentioned nothing of drugs and Indians and storms.

'It was not a mere response, baby. It was an equal partnership.'

It suddenly occurred to her that the Indian had a hand in all this. She could not, as yet, explain why he should wish such a thing, but she felt manipulated.

She turned her anger on Paul. 'Don't get carried away.'

'But I am carried away. I love you.' He raised his arms and shouted at the top of his voice: 'I LOVE YOU!'

'Yes Paul.'

He deflated. 'Christ! The first time I tell a woman I love her and she says 'Yes, Paul' as if I had just announced it was a nice morning.'

'Paul, please! In your own words, I am not your type. Just the only . . .'

'Stop!' He put a hand on her mouth. 'That was before.

Things have changed. Yes, we were influenced by circumstances, but it was you and me. It seemed to be the right combination.' He removed his hand from her mouth and smiled. 'Even if it never reaches the same peak again, we have attained it together, once. You and me.' He stressed it by pointing first at her chest then at his. 'People live and die without ever experiencing anything like this, so don't go and throw it all away.'

'What did you feel when you had a sweet potato after a few days starvation? Wasn't it the best food you've ever had? And what do you think of it now?'

'Honey, I know what lust is. I had it before and I satisfied it before. I know how it feels.' He stared from behind his wet hair, the eyes losing all their previous intensity for a more relaxed playfulness. 'I didn't have to say anything. You don't believe me anyway.' Then he pretended to tidy his hair so she did not look at him as closely as she was aware she did. 'He isn't going to make the first move, and you are not the kind to ask for it. You are stuck with me. So why should I lie?'

Was it that obvious? And, come to think of it, whatever happened to Mark? Why had he let Paul come out searching for her alone or, more to the point, why didn't he come, alone? But she was not going to discuss that. 'How can anyone change his tastes so fast? Or have I bewitched you?' she said.

He chuckled. 'From the very beginning. I just struggled like hell against it, hence all the abuse. I am just as scared of love and commitment as you are. The surprise is, you didn't see it a mile away. Look at the imagery. Cactus fruit, I couldn't handle you. Witch, I couldn't resist you. Not my type?' He turn his palms up. 'What is my type? The women I screwed and dropped like hot potatoes? If they were my type, then why didn't I choose one?'

What was this? A personality transplant? And how was she to handle it?

28

Paul couldn't bear the silence and thought of going hunting just to escape, but not before he had trimmed the arrow feathers. They were glued to the notched end of the slim wooden shaft by the dried gut. No joint was visible. Balancing the arrows was a matter of trial and error, but he was almost there.

'My!' he said. 'We are moody this morning.'

He had to admit that the frequent rains were becoming a bit of a nuisance. Last night the fire had been washed out again, and they huddled close to each other for some warmth. It proved far from cosy, with Mark giving a good impersonation of a statue, expressionless, surrounded by an impenetrable wall of silence. His depression infected Sylvia. This morning she still looked absolutely miserable in her damp clothes. All their efforts to restart the fire had failed, and she sat staring disconsolately at the wet ashes.

Mark revived somewhat and grimly, his habitual expression of late, moved the fingers of his injured arm, flexed the arm itself, rotated the shoulder. The grimace told Paul the shoulder, at least, was still painful but everything seemed in working order.

'The arm better?' Paul said.

Mark condescended to speak. 'Well enough not to be the excuse for remaining here any longer. I can't stand this place.'

Paul put the arrows aside and picked up the bow. It had been much easier to manufacture. A length of doubly twisted gut, with loops at either end, passed over the two points of a stave. As the gut dried and shrank, increasing the tension, it bent. He could even get a note out of the string. He plucked it just for the satisfaction and pride it gave him. Using the note as a key, he whistled a tune. He, at least, was happy. What did Mark mean he couldn't stand it here? 'This is *the* life,' Paul said, interrupting his song. 'A real adventure. Holiday with attitude.'

He ignored Mark's disgusted look, fully aware that he was getting on his nerves. Frivolity, he called it. But hey! They couldn't all sit around contemplating their navels. Mark must have realised, somehow, what had happened, hence the disapproval. But what right did he have to disapprove? He was neither husband nor lover, yet he succeeded in making both Paul and Sylvia feel uncomfortable in his presence, guilty even.

One of the things that puzzled Paul was Mark's behaviour when Sylvia left at the first signs of the storm. He seemed quite content, this time of all times, to let her endanger her life, and he was supposed to be the Good Samaritan. Nobody ever thought of Paul as anything other than a selfish brat. Not that Paul had any interest in running after her, either, which led to the second and more serious puzzle. He still couldn't explain to himself what made him leave. Sex, for once, was the last thing on his mind. In all that pandemonium, he thought he heard her call. It didn't seem strange at the time, and as she kept calling, he was only too grateful for the guidance. In that storm, God knew where he would have ended if he had walked unaided.

He shivered, remembering the light in the clearing. So eerie. Only her ghostly silhouette was visible. She was standing by the fallen tree, arms stretched above her head, mouth open as if shouting to the wind. With her clothes plastered to her body, she looked like a naked Maenad going through a ritual, and all Paul wanted was to run away.

She had sensed his presence and turned around slowly. Her eyes glowed like burning coals against the darkened face, a maniacal look in them, not, as he first thought, anger at being interrupted at whatever she was doing, but triumph.

Looking at her now, shivering in her wet rags, brought him back to reality. What he had thought was an inexplicable force pulling him towards her, was nothing but the sight of a woman as close to being naked as possible without taking her clothes off, and his hormones. The rest was nothing but tricks of light and an overactive imagination. And just like his instincts had told him, she was full of surprises.

The incident had a great effect on his outlook though she remained her usual moody, volatile, self-willed and contradictory self. In a way, she fitted so perfectly in this environment, she embodied the place. One could not imagine her anywhere else, and he loved her. He didn't give shit if Mark thought him no better than a moonstruck calf.

He got up and gave her his brightest smile. 'I might as well go and do something, before it starts raining again,' he said.

From the amount of screeching, a monkey war was taking place up there, not directly above Paul's head but near enough for him to hear the thudding of something hitting the ground. Probably fruit shaken down in the melee. Something useful, he hoped.

There was no need to hurry. Whatever it was wouldn't walk away. He stopped to tie his shoelaces, passing them under the shoe to hold the sole together, and froze. There was no mistaking the heavy breathing. Then crunching, rustling, like something rolling around on a bed of leaves and the unmistakable smacking, popping sound of an open kiss.

It sounded just next to him but the way noises carried in the forest, it could be anywhere: around the next tree or several hundred metres away in any direction.

He was devastated. He knew it would happen sooner or later and had thought he wouldn't care. But the idea that they just waited for him to leave and then threw themselves at each other was disgusting. That they had lulled him by acting cool towards each other was underhand. And what did they think they were doing? Man, it sounded like bloody animals. He had experience with her fierceness when aroused, and Mark hadn't done it for God knows how long, and when he eventually came around to anything, he invariably went over the top. He was grunting like a pig!

Well, get on with it, man! Stop just thrashing around and get on with it. It's killing me!

That they were not getting on with it, he gathered from the lack of any sort of rhythm to the noise, though distance could distort things. Now his imagination filled in the gaps. His heartbeat provided the rhythm. He ought to run away but he couldn't, as if he needed this punishment. He was drawn to it, had to make sure, and the only excuse he could find for this perversity was that the great hulk could hurt her.

He tried to be quiet but every dry leaf he stepped on exploded, he tripped on every half-exposed root, his footfall thudded on the ground as if he were the giant in Jack and the Beanstalk. Then he rounded the next tree and he was overwhelmed by the sense of the ridiculous, shame at his foolishness and inadequacy as a hunter, but above all, relief. It hadn't happened yet. It might never happen.

Three or four wild pigs that had been feeding on fallen fruit scattered around and blended into the forest instantly they smelled him. It happened too quickly for them to have seen anything.

He had gone to find some food. For the first time since being here, he came across real game. Four-footed. On the ground. Pigs, for Christ's sake. Pigs! And what did he do? No time to even think of bows and arrows, let alone use them. He wished he could see through smell and hearing like the animals. Then he might have stood a chance.

To date, other than the odd bird up a tree, he had killed nothing, and he was in no mood for climbing a tree now.

They had to make do with roots and leaves and a potato if they were lucky.

He rooted among the pigs' leftovers and competed with ants and flies that swarmed everywhere for fruits that were only sticky, bruised and overripe. The rest had been popped open, sucked dry or trampled underfoot. As he walked back he smiled at the irony of fate. A man with so much money he couldn't be bothered to find the exact amount was thankful for a handful of flyblown fruit whose identity he didn't even know. But this kind of musing was replaced with something even closer to his heart when he caught a snatch of conversation: 'I can't force you.'

Was Sylvia throwing herself at Mark? Women were often attracted to him. The strong, silent type, admired in theory if impossible to live with, and he was the only person that could make Paul feel insecure, though they had never been in direct competition before, hunting different territories as a rule. But Mark had no idea what to do with women, not even his own wife. Paul could wait for him to do what he was an expert in doing: putting women off with some inane remark. And it didn't take long. 'Can't promise anything.' Well, now! Her answer was indistinct but the tone was low and ominous, consistent with hurt pride. What if she succeeded in overcoming Mark's stupidity? For that's all it was. One had only to see the way his eyes followed her everywhere to know how he felt. At last, he had found someone like himself. They both thought on similar lines. Rather, they thought too much. They analysed everything to distraction. Tortured themselves with self-criticism and doubts. It didn't solve any problems, simply increased the confusion. Nothing, of course, was black and white, but thinking too much about it only threw light on a multitude of possibilities, limiting action.

On second thoughts, he shouldn't wait for her to find out how inadequate at relationships Mark was and run back to him. Not his style. Besides, he had enough of tiptoeing around not to upset Mark. It was not as if he was afraid of him!

29

Mark watched Sylvia spread the soaked ashes around to let the water evaporate in the rising heat of the day, and couldn't help feeling cheated. One didn't have to be a genius to know what Paul's recent metamorphosis meant. It was not the sudden disappearance of moodiness that chafed, his lighthearted laughter, always easily provoked, now resounding constantly around the forest, nor that he was relaxed, charming and obliging. The possessive look in his eyes every time he looked at Sylvia was the killer. But Mark had expected her to be able to see through amorous, frivolous, fickle Paul. Perhaps she knew there was no chance of avoiding him indefinitely and gave in. Paul was determined to have his way, and whatever he wanted he always took.

How had he managed to tolerate Paul all these years? Just habit, probably, like everything else he did. He got stuck in routines and never took the initiative to change anything. Better late than never. But he should at least inform her of his plans, except that she avoided eye contact as if she knew what he wanted to say and didn't wish to hear it. Or maybe she was nervous being left alone with him. She would be right. He had to exercise great self-discipline to avoid doing something stupid. For how long could he retain his control in this environment? The veneer of civilisation could easily crack in the absence of social controls. It hurt his pride to consider himself capable of anything like that, but then a few weeks ago, it would have been inconceivable that such a thought would enter his head, but it did. There was no time to lose.

'I was thinking of setting off on my own,' he said.

He might as well have hit her, she jumped up so suddenly. 'That's madness! You cannot wonder off on your own.' She hesitated for a moment then said: 'We must stick together. We'll all go.'

The bitterness spilled out before he could check it. 'I didn't think you and Paul wanted to leave this idyllic life.'

She blushed. 'So that's it.'

'You had to choose, I suppose and, understandably, you chose Paul,' he said. 'Your prerogative.'

'If I had to choose, which I didn't,' she said, 'I couldn't possibly have chosen Paul.'

Mark lifted his eyebrows in a silent question.

She brought out of a clenched fist, one finger after the other. 'He is too young, too beautiful and too rich.'

'I should have thought those were precisely the reasons that make him so eligible.'

She gestured in exasperation. 'If I fell for that, I would need my head examined.'

'But you slept with him.'

'I had no choice.'

He felt the blood drain from his face. 'You don't mean . . .?'

'No.' While he was still recovering from the shock, she continued in the same confused and confusing strain. 'I simply obeyed . . .' she corrected impatiently, '. . . responded to somebody's affection.'

'And you would have, no doubt,' he said sarcastically, 'responded to mine, if I gave it?'

'You never showed any inclination. I can't force you.'

He took a step forward then checked himself. 'You puzzle me,' he said. 'You are all-knowing, you can guess people's lives by just looking at them, their thoughts, but when it comes to this, you suddenly become naïve. What is the matter? Do you require everyone on their knees offering eternal love, so that you can feel emotionally secure? What of their security?'

He had been wrong to think she was nervous of him, like he was wrong with so many other things. She flew at him, both barrels blazing. 'You act jealous with me with whom you have no relationship at all, but not with your own wife.'

So she knew about that too. 'But then I am not in love with my wife.'

It was out now. He couldn't have been any clearer than that about his feelings. His heart beat crazily. He had given it to her. What would she do with it?

But the only thing she could find to say, and that almost brutally, was, 'Then why are you married to her?'

He was furious with himself at that needless revelation, and as self-punishment he proceeded to make things worse. 'She is good for public relations and while she is around, I am free of ambitious nurses and romantic patients,' he said.

'Great! And she?'

'She wants the freedom to love whom she wishes, and lots of money. She has both. It's a fair arrangement.'

'Christ!'

He tried to retrieve the situation. 'I just wish things were different. That we met under different circumstances.'

'That's how things are, and we'd better make the most of them if we are to survive.'

Her reasonableness had the opposite effect on him. 'You mean you don't give a shit about either of us, but you are putting up with the situation for the sake of survival?' And he did not need a degree in psychology to know he had hurt her.

'Don't try to judge things with the standards of a society that does not exist in this place,' she said.

But like a man who, having committed one crime, found that the subsequent ones were easy and inevitable, he asked her outright: 'You told Paul once that you would either sleep with neither or both of us.' He saw her wince, but his excuse in persisting – there had to be excuses, even in

183

madness – was that he had to clarify matters. 'Would you do it if we were two different men?'

She abandoned any effort to remain calm and reasonable. 'Since we started this conversation, you have thought it fit to insult me,' she said. 'You insinuated all sorts of things. There is no need for any of that, and I don't have to take it.'

'I am sorry. I didn't mean to hurt you.' And that was a lie. Of course he meant to hurt her and himself and the whole world. He hesitated then stretched his hand towards her, and as his fingers brushed her cheek, the whole world stood still. 'It's not what you think,' he tried to explain. 'Unlike Paul, I can do without a woman, it's just that you are so different . . .' He could have done with some encouragement, but she cringed. Didn't like being different. Maybe she took it for weird. *Change tracks.* 'I never thought I would be so . . .' *What? Vulnerable, stupid, susceptible?* He panicked. He had already told her he loved her without any other response but some vague understanding that, on the grounds of survival, she might put up with him. He was tempted, of course. He was obsessed with the woman but then he would let the beast out, and he was not sure he could control it. She would find out just how unworthy he was of her sacrifice, for that's all it was. 'What do you expect from me?' he said, exasperated.

The whole effect he was desperate to create shattered. She stiffened. Two laser beams scanned his face. 'Nothing, except that you should not leave this place on your own.'

'I can't promise anything . . .'

Her voice, just above a whisper, chilled him like an icy shower. 'I'm damned if I am going to let you kill everyone because you took it into your head to split us up to prove some point.' She forcefully pointed a finger to the ground, a gesture designed to anchor him to the spot. 'We are staying together, and you are bloody well going to put up with it.'

She turned to go but Mark grabbed her arm. 'I will kill everyone? How? Do you know something I don't?'

She shook him off. 'Before you accuse me of anything else, think about it. People stand a better chance if they work together.'

Mark was unconvinced, not with the argument itself, which was indisputable, but her motives. 'If we must work together, shouldn't we all know what's going on?'

Still that menacing undertone. 'Earlier, I said I had no choice. It's not true. I have a choice between the safety of all three of us or just my own. Maybe I chose wrong. I need to rethink it.'

Mark had no time to digest that or to respond.

'Don't worry, honey,' Paul addressed Sylvia as he burst in on them. 'They say knights in white armour protect women from everything except themselves. Mark would go one further and protect you only from himself.' If he had stopped there, Mark would have let it go but, as usual, he took that step too far, testing things. 'What am I saying? If he lived in the Middle Ages he wouldn't be a knight in any kind of armour. A hermit, more likely. Or he would have joined some ascetic religious order.' His smile broadened. 'Not that he has any aversion to the pleasures of the flesh, as many a nurse will verify. Just to martyr himself. Hence marrying Nicol and now refusing . . .'

Mark hit out but made sure he used his injured arm. He meant to express his frustration, not to cause damage, and he was surprised that Paul fell. That, and the jarring pain in his shoulder, brought him to his senses.

Paul picked himself up slowly. He took a threatening stance, legs apart, fists clenched. Paul wouldn't back down now as a matter of honour. Mark's mind was on what Sylvia had said and wanted this stupidity to end. 'I am sorry,' he said. 'OK?'

'No,' said Paul. 'If you are frustrated, play with yourself, not punch me for relief.'

'Don't push it, Paul,' Mark said and turned to Sylvia, who was now staring at him in disbelief. He didn't blame her. It was as if everything he said or did today was designed to diminish any respect she might have had for him.

'I told you I would not let it pass the next time round,' said Paul and put his hand on Mark's shoulder, unfortunately the injured one, now throbbing like mad after the exertion and spun him around. Mark, maddened with pain, both physical and emotional, reacted instinctively but still expected Paul to at least duck, but he was too slow.

Paul put his hand on a tree trunk to stop himself from losing his balance yet again, and shook his head to clear it. He regained his composure and narrowed his eyes to size the situation coolly as if he were back boxing in the gym. But Mark was familiar with his tactics. Many of his opponents, even those that had the advantage of size, could lose their temper and hit out blindly, like he had done so stupidly, when Paul taunted them, which he always did. Paul, on the other hand, grew calm and calculating. He measured his opponent, found his weak point and went in for the kill, not unlike in business.

Mark was determined to shut out whatever Paul was saying now and kept his body relaxed, his arms hanging loosely, ready, but only to contain Paul. He had been angry with him, and a tap here or there might have vented his resentments. It was over now. But just when Mark thought that Paul too realised that, he lunged at him. Mark avoided him easily enough, but before he could calculate his next move, Paul kicked sideways, aiming at Mark's abdomen, and whirled away quickly, out of harm's way. Mark doubled up, recovered quickly but decided not to go after Paul, who knew better than to let a bigger man close to him.

He had underestimated Paul. The diet and constant exercise from climbing trees gave extra leanness and strength to his muscles, not that he had ever carried extra weight. He had always taken care of his body, and he was not going to misjudge Mark's reach again, after being hit twice.

Mark watched as Paul danced around, took a shot, moved out and back again, just avoiding him until he got fed up with the whole thing. He let out a shout that froze Paul for an instant and threw himself at Paul, parried his blow with his weak left arm, ignoring the pain, and brought the full force of the right into the middle of Paul's body, aiming at the pit of the stomach and beyond, the solar plexus. He was not a surgeon for nothing.

Paul's jaw dropped when he realised that he had no control over his body. His paralysed legs gave way under him and he started to keel. Mark put his arms around him, holding him in a vice, both to stop Paul from falling and to restrain him when he recovered enough for any retaliation. 'There is no point to this,' he said. 'I know the workings of your body and can stop you whenever I want to.'

'Fucking bastard!' Paul gasped, but his aggression evaporated, his pride hurt.

It must have been an unfamiliar feeling for Paul to taste defeat, once he came out and declared war. He never did unless he was sure of success. That was Paul's excuse for avoiding a match whenever Mark asked to partner him in a friendly. 'There isn't such a thing as a friendly,' Paul used to say. 'One of us has to win, and I saw nobody fight with you and come out a winner.'

'This is too much of a cliché, and by golly it's not going to happen here,' Sylvia was saying through clenched teeth. 'Don't you even think of following me, either of you, or you will end up dead!'

Mark let go of Paul, who sank to the ground. 'You said we had to stick together,' he reminded her, afraid she might take it into her head to run away for good.

'That was for the benefit of you two,' she said. 'I am not in any danger.' And left.

Mark sighed. What could a man do with this woman, he helped Paul to his feet. 'No hard feelings, huh? I am not coming between you two. She chose you, and that's that.'

Paul sat down, obviously still feeling weak. 'I wish I was as sure of that as you,' he said. 'I just happened upon her when she was in the right mood, and now she sits around waiting for another inspiration.'

Every time anyone said anything about that business, confusion increased. 'You didn't happen upon her, you went searching for her,' Mark said and sat next to Paul, 'though, I must admit, it was a strange time for romantic encounters.'

'Tell me about it.'

'So, what made you go?'

'I just felt I had to, against my better judgement. Why didn't you go?'

'I felt I shouldn't, against my better judgement.'

They both kept quiet for a while. Then Paul got up a bit too suddenly and staggered.

'OK man?' Mark got up too.

'Oh, fine! I just love being a punchbag. Makes me feel useful.'

Mark shifted uncomfortably. 'We better go find Sylvia and apologise for all this childishness, I suppose,' he said. 'Do you realise that this would be just the thing to send her in an even more unpredictable direction?'

Paul set off, quoting as he went: 'Who is Silvia? What is she, that all the swain . . .'

Mark followed, shaking his head.

They returned just before nightfall empty-handed, and Mark built a fire large enough so that the smell of burned wood, the light, the generated warmth, would guide her back.

Every rustle beyond the fire, every growl, every slithering, things that they had got so used to, that never even registered any more, became ominous again. She had been out there alone before, but never in the dark. And why couldn't Paul keep things to himself? The belief that sharing a worry halved it was nonsense. It magnified it.

After exhausting all the possible dangers she could be facing, Paul expressed what probably had been preying on his mind since she had left. 'Do you think she meant what she said?' When Mark did not answer, he frowned and said, 'She could kill us any time she wants to. She knows all the poisons around here.'

'She said we would be killed, not that she would kill us. She is usually precise. There is something else out there,' and Mark added bitterly, 'she obviously doesn't trust me. I thought you might have come to a better understanding.'

Paul gave a lopsided smile. 'Understanding! She calls the shots, man. I do as I'm told.'

30

The more Sylvia thought about the fight, the angrier she got and the faster she walked. When she found the Indian she had to make it clear, if he didn't know already, that things had reached a climax and something had to be done.

She had expected more from Mark, though she had an inkling of his potential for violence. She still felt the bruise on her arm where he had held her, and if that was his weak hand, what would his strong one be like? Paul had found out, poor thing. It had happened so quickly, she hardly saw Mark move. Paul was on the floor and Mark was still standing there, head slightly bent, with only a hard metallic glint escaping from the shadows of his eyebrows. And before that, how dared he speak to her the way he did? He was in no position to know how she felt about him, she had never shown anything, so he had no right to treat her as if she had broken a promise or betrayed him.

She slowed a bit to catch her breath and realised that she had followed no markings, nor had she marked anything on the way. If the Indian found something better to do, she would be in real trouble. As if she didn't have enough worries.

Mark implied he loved her. Rubbish! He was hard up and stooped to using love to make believe he was better than Paul. She was not ashamed for what had happened with Paul, anyway, though she still worried whether Paul came as a result of her bidding or it was just a coincidence. No matter what, there was nothing she could complain about. Well . . . other than that he was not Mark.

It was Mark she had wanted. She respected him, then, she was almost in awe of him, she trusted him, at least more than she did Paul. Feeling like that, she should have automatically called to him, not Paul. But, no matter what, the final image in her head was Paul's image. She had called a name. It turned out to be Paul's name. Why? She had responded to Paul's affection, she had told Mark, but wasn't it truer to say his looks and, why not, admiration for his unexpected behaviour? Once Paul felt the hunger pangs and nobody to rely on but himself, he took up the challenge, to everyone's benefit. It was so effortless, so enjoyable to him, nothing more than recreation. He had given the impression of a spoilt young man, used to getting everything without lifting a manicured finger. Now the fingers were rough and callous. His clothes hung in tatters over a body still as graceful and supple as a puma's, the skin, exposed to the strong light in the canopy, like mahogany, and the pale eyes, in contrast, even more cat-like.

His face flitted in front of her with that tantalising under the fringe glance, his growing beard adding years and emphasising the sensuous mouth, the dark hair, unruly over the wide forehead, a cheekbone glowing golden in a shaft of light. But she found the strength to shake the image off and continued her walk, following a vague smell of woodfire. She had not been walking aimlessly like she had thought, hoping the Indian would intercept her. She was unconsciously following that smell, but any guidance was welcomed right now.

As for Paul, he was really so uncomplicated, almost innocent. He wanted something, he asked for it. If denied he sulked, when given it he felt grateful. He even said he loved her, poor darling! Mark, however, was the unknown. One could never be prepared for it, or include it into any calculation. Maybe her subconscious played games with her. She had sensed that Mark could not be commanded, could not be influenced by her, would not have responded. Mark's injury might have been a hindrance to her purposes.

In other words, what happened with Paul was not as spontaneous as she pretended to him.

And what about the Indian's potions? Could she have explained to Mark that it was possible somebody had manipulated things so the most restless of the two men was kept content? It didn't make her feel too good admitting it to herself, let alone to anyone else.

She sniffed the air. It must be her imagination. She was so hungry she was dreaming of roast pork. It was some poor animal, most likely, hit by the lightning last night, like the little monkey they had seen the other day, still grasping in its charred fingers a burned-out branch. They were thankful to the deluge for once, for putting out the fire before it spread and incinerated them as well, in their green tomb.

She continued her musings from where she had left off. What were her real feelings for Mark? No better than a schoolgirl's crush on an older man, and he was not even older than her. She endowed him with solidity and reliability, with subterranean depths, and took him completely for granted. Nothing he could do would surprise her. If he was to perform a miracle in front of her, she wouldn't bat an eyelid. After all, it was only natural that a man built on such a heroic scale should do heroic things. It was natural that one should rely on him and find comfort in his shadow. She gave a little laugh. It was also natural that he might throw the odd thunderbolt from his Olympian heights now and then.

If one was to believe everything Paul had said about Nicol, one could also understand Mark's insecurity. All the same, he went too far and, whether nervous or not of him, once she had embarked on confrontation, there was no drawing back, and now it was too late for anything. There had been one moment of hope, and he took insurance out.

She came to a standstill. The smell of wood fire and roast pork was now intense. Maybe, without realising it, she had walked around in a circle, back to their base. She didn't stay around long enough to find what Paul had brought back from his expedition, but now she was hungry enough to sacrifice her pride in return for a mouthful of whatever it was.

Paul, Mark. What could a woman do between these two? Ignore them both? Love them both, but how when each demanded exclusivity? That reminded her of her two children, and she felt as if a hand squeezed her heart. She had tried so hard not to think about them. Nothing could be gained by it. But the wound was there, aching permanently whether she let thoughts surface or not. She loved them both equally, but they had no use for that, either. 'Who do you like most, Mummy?' 'I love you both most,' and the little faces would fall. Human nature.

She was still following her nose, disregarding the lack of familiar signs. What she did notice, however, were unfamiliar sounds: banging, rustling, chattering. Whether they were caused by a troop of monkeys, birds, humans, she could not tell but that smell was unbearable, irresistible. She had been hungry for so long, she had forgotten what it was like to be satiated. Even when Paul got the odd bird, it hadn't been enough, not for all three, and she had always felt that she deserved the smallest portion since she was the smallest in size. Nobody admitted openly they were hungry, but nobody was going to argue if one refused part of their own portion. This time she would not be so noble.

When she stumbled into the clearing, all noise stopped. Everyone stared at her. The men, except the shaman and the English-speaking Indian, had just a braid around their waist, their penises suspended from it by the foreskin like the one who had boasted to her of his cojones. A few had red markings on their faces, nearly all bright feathers in their ear lobes. Naked women stood in groups, some with babies on their hips. A few looked in their early teens. Others were shrivelled old women, their breasts empty pouches. Sylvia guessed it was not due to age, just too harsh a life, too many pregnancies.

Then everyone started to talk simultaneously and a giggling girl offered Sylvia something to drink. The shaman said something abruptly. Everyone was silenced. The man who spoke English came up to Sylvia.

'You drink with him. You his son,' he said, pointing at the shaman.

He had made this mistake before, she ought to correct him. 'You mean daughter.'

'Daughter!' He grimaced contemptuously and continued in his staccato voice: 'She woman. Woman have no the gift. Only man. You have gift, you man. Spirit say son come from the sky with gift.'

Men! 'No cojones,' she said.

He started giggling. 'Yes, cojones,' and tapped his head.

'Where did you learn English?'

'At mission by the river.'

There was frenzied activity everywhere. Around a central pole, staves were driven into the ground. Hammocks were hung, one end tied to the central pole, the other to one of the peripheral ones. Leafy branches formed the roof. Some people went to bed almost the moment the hammocks were put up, two at the time, each taking a place opposite the other. It made sense, Sylvia supposed, or the central pole would collapse. Women, some still suckling their young, were masticating leaves and spitting them in containers. Sylvia had read that was how alcoholic beverages were made, letting the salivary enzymes do the fermentation. A few men were sitting around the fire, waiting for a small wild pig to roast, hair and all. A couple of them did not wait. They just hacked a piece off and ate, fat and blood oozing between their fingers. A little boy with a parrot on his shoulder stood apart and stared blankly at her. The rest of the children played or chased pet animals.

Sylvia did not hear a sound, only the word 'Mission'.

'Near here?' she said softly as if not to disturb anything, not to tempt fate.

'Very far.'

There was an apprehensive murmur from the direction of the boy with the parrot, but Sylvia couldn't be sure. His mouth hadn't moved and the bird seemed asleep. Her interpreter followed her look and volunteered the information, but the sentence was too complicated for his simple English and she had to fill the gaps. The boy was his son and the chief's successor or honorary son, like her, or after her. 'He too young now,' he said. He also told her that all this activity will be taking place somewhere else the following evening. They were to leave at dawn. Now they were taking it in turns to eat or drink or sleep.

She tried to ask him the direction of the mission. It didn't matter how far it was. He became agitated. 'No good for you. No good.' One arm waved in the direction of the boy, the other of the chief. 'They say you stay with us.'

One man after another began to fall to the ground, rolling around in the dirt, drunk or worse. They were making animal noises, pretending to be pigs or frogs, or squawked like parrots. Those not drunk or drugged yet were staring at her: the strange man that looked like a woman. The shaman was preparing the three gourds.

The interpreter made to go then turned back as if he remembered something. 'When you drink, you say "I want to see everything". You see. Then you come with us.'

Somebody had cut off a chunk of meat and was offering it to her. The skin on the outside was charred, the meat inside still bloody. She didn't care. Nor did she bother if the juices run down her chin and onto her chest. Her fellow diners were in a worse state. Their bare bodies were sleek with fat, and those were the sober ones. What the bodies of the others were smeared with was better ignored.

She started worrying about the chief's potion. She could still remember the bitterness and the vomiting. The first time she had something like enough to eat, and she was going to lose it. Besides, if the shaman took a little bit too much drink and passed out, and he looked well on his way, the other Indians might forget she was meant to be his son. Their eyes were eloquent enough and didn't leave much to the imagination.

How stupid she had been to leave Paul and Mark in a huff. They wanted the same thing as the Indians, but they were gentlemen. Such civilised values, comparatively recent and superficial, could easily erode, but they were still able to understand no, even if their arboreal ancestry was already beckoning. This lot wouldn't.

31

She returned at dawn, exhausted. Her eyes didn't focus properly and she looked confused.

Where would Sylvia find a drink, or anything else, Paul wondered. It was more likely she was ill. Sooner or later one of them would be. It was surprising it didn't happen earlier, considering the conditions. And what could Mark do with no drugs or even basic hygiene?

While Mark made her sit by the embers of last night's fire, Paul threw a log on it and the flames shot up. She came closer to them, gathering her rags around her body, and began to fall apart: her muscles twitched, her teeth chattered, her breathing became convulsive. Her effort to control things without success was pitiful. Then, to Paul's horror, she extended her hand towards the fire. To impose discipline to a shattered nervous system with a shock, perhaps.

Mark pulled her away from the fire and she shrank from him, eyes round with terror. Paul came over to reassure her, with the same result.

'You are ill,' said Mark. 'You need help.'

She shook her head and made herself into a ball, a little animal licking its own wounds. They were likely to cause more harm by interfering, and anyway the trembling slowly subsided and her breathing became more regular. At last, she looked up.

'Free to go,' she said in a husky voice.

'I don't want to go anywhere, anymore,' Mark said.

'We,' she said, 'we are free to go.'

'Go where?' Paul said.

'They left,' she said. 'Upped sticks and went before dawn.' She took a deep breath. 'We can go anywhere we like. No choice but follow the water. We couldn't get lost. He said so.'

Paul looked at Mark, puzzled. Then at her. 'Who?'

'She is delirious,' Mark said and signed to Paul to keep quiet. 'We will talk about it later,' he said to Sylvia. 'You are tired now.'

'No,' she said. 'Just drugged to the eyeballs. Part of the ritual before they left for a new camp. They have to avoid the water, you see.'

Paul was bewildered. 'Are you talking about Indians? You saw Indians?'

'Why didn't you say anything?' Mark said, and Paul thought he sounded a bit too severe and nudged him, but Mark kept on. 'This sort of thing has been going on for a while, hasn't it? It would explain a lot of puzzling things.'

'He didn't want me to say anything.' She straightened herself as if to show no regret for her deception. 'I can see his point. What would you have done if you knew they were all around us, altering markings, forcing us to go in circles, making sure we never left? Being aggressive men,' and she stared from one man to the other pointedly, 'as you have proven earlier, you would try to fight them, and we would all end up with poison arrows in our backs. As it is, they delayed us until we learned how to take care of ourselves before the long journey. You see, from now on they can't help us.'

'Did they help before?' said Paul.

'The shaman did. He helped me find you. Gave me drugs for Mark's arm. Warned me of the tribesmen. They were not all thrilled with our presence.' She singled Paul out with a glance. 'I have a feeling they know why you are here. They have contact with the outside world. I noticed a couple of them wore shorts. Filthy and torn, but shorts. Knives, too. Where did they find them, unless they've come into contact with civilisation? For a start, they know of a mission by the river.' Before Paul had a chance to get excited, she waved her hand, dismissing it. 'It's very far.'

'The shaman can speak English, I suppose,' said Mark.

'No. Maybe broken Portuguese, but I don't understand it,' she said.

'Don't tell me you speak his language,' said Paul. It wouldn't have surprised him if she said yes.

'I didn't speak with him, but . . . he could make himself understood.'

'Telepathy?' said Mark.

She shrugged. 'He drugged me and I saw things. Other times he made me feel certain things. I put the words. It's difficult to understand. He . . . sort of . . . beamed messages. This time there was somebody there who spoke English. He told me of the mission.'

Paul was alerted. 'Can *you* beam messages?'

'I think so, but before you call me a witch again, you are capable of picking them up,' she said.

'Oh!' Paul said and thought about the day of the storm. How naïve he had been, but now things were falling into place, one after the other.

She looked at him closely. 'Any regrets?'

'No!' Paul said.

'So how do we get out now?' said Mark. 'Follow the water, you said. Isn't it what we've been trying to find all the time, with no success?'

'It will find us,' she said.

'You have to be a bit clearer than that,' Mark said.

Sylvia looked perplexed. 'How can I? I don't know. All I saw was an awful lot of water. A sea, a large lake? I don't know. There was mist in the distance and a rainbow.' She looked at Paul. 'I could see the puma's silhouette against the sunset.'

'He would,' said Mark, nodding in Paul's direction. 'He is a survivor in any kind of jungle. Concrete or emerald.'

Paul couldn't see the connection.

'Just the puma?' Mark again.

She looked away. 'A big bird was flying above him and the paca . . .'

'There you are,' Mark interrupted triumphantly, 'we will all make it.'

'No,' she said. 'You see, the bird . . .'

'Ah,' said Mark. 'The eagle didn't quite make it?'

Sylvia stared at him for a while, sad. 'I only saw the eagle drop the paca on the rocks, at least it was looking at it from above as if it had before it flew away.'

'No!' Mark said sharply. 'You don't really believe we will go and leave you behind, or that I would . . . drop you?'

She looked away. 'Not everything can be taken literally.'

Metaphorically speaking, Mark had already dropped her by refusing her offer, Paul supposed, but he couldn't wait for Mark's protest, or anything else. 'Could somebody, please, explain to me what the hell is going on here? What is the significance of the menagerie?'

'She had a hallucination,' Mark said, but avoided his eyes.

Paul became more suspicious. 'I never knew people interpreted hallucinations.'

Mark signalled that it was unwise to persist. When he saw that Paul was not going to be put off that easily, he said, 'I'll explain later when she is better.'

Sylvia pulled herself together and tried to reassure them. 'Other than feeling stiff everywhere and having a headache, I am fine.'

'Sorry,' said Mark. 'There isn't much I can do, except this.' He felt the knotted muscles at the back of her neck and kneaded them. She winced initially, but then bowed her head and submitted. 'The Indians,' he said, 'they haven't hurt you in any way . . .'

She closed her eyes in pleasure, almost purring. 'No,' she said dreamily. 'They were too spaced out for anything like that.' She smiled, her eyes still closed. 'Besides, it would have been unwise to take liberties with the chief's son.'

Paul and Mark looked at each other, puzzled. 'Son?' from both.

Now that Mark had stopped what he was doing, she

opened her eyes. 'I was adopted by their shaman,' she said, still smiling beatifically. 'He is convinced I am a man.'

'Even a drug-crazed shaman could see what sex you are,' said Paul pointing at her rags which left nothing to the imagination.

'He doesn't go by appearances,' she said. 'He planned a safe career for me, as a caretaker shaman until his successor grows up, and a shaman can't be female. To let me come back to you, I had to promise to go only as far as the rainbows.'

'And then?' said Mark.

She shrugged. 'I will either die or go back to him.'

'You don't believe that!' from both Mark and Paul.

Another shrug. But Mark went back to massaging her back and she melted again, contented. 'I'll let you know when I think about it,' she said playfully.

Paul suppressed his resentment at their intimacy now and his exclusion from shared knowledge before. He gathered their possessions ready for the trek and whatever adventures, real or imaginary, it brought with it.

32

Mark thought that their few possessions – the pot, a couple of gourds, the hammocks, ropes, bows and arrows – shared between two men, would weigh nothing. After a few hours of trekking, out of breath and drenched in perspiration, he changed his mind but persevered. Paul could hardly keep up, since he thought it fit to stop every few steps to scratch bear-fashion against a tree. Sylvia lagged even further behind, and Mark couldn't bring himself to show enthusiasm with any of the marvels she pointed out. Granted, the sight of a pair of brightly coloured parakeets was unexpected and their aerial acrobatics, well . . . exhausting to even look at.

'Isn't it incredible?' she said.

'Not as incredible as your ability for so much talk in this heat,' Paul said, which was something, coming from him. And when she tossed her hair and let herself fall further back, he added, 'Don't sulk, and keep up.' But he stopped to wipe the sweat from his face and scratch again, to give her time to catch up. 'Don't you find this humidity uncomfortable?' he said.

'It's perfect,' she replied. 'Comforting, like a womb.'

Paul threw up his arms and resumed walking.

'What's the hurry?' she said, trying to quicken her pace to catch up, and getting out of breath like them. 'Striding along at your pace won't get us anywhere.'

'While sauntering along at yours will, I suppose,' said Paul.

'That's right!' she said. 'You get hot, irritable and tired, and need rest more often. At my pace, I can observe my surroundings, preserve my energy and keep on going when you are all puffed out.'

Time passed with no sign that they were getting anywhere, and Sylvia's enthusiasm evaporated. 'Don't you ever get hungry or anything? Speaking for myself, I could eat a horse.'

It was an excuse, of course, so that she might not admit she was too tired to take another step. There was nothing to eat, as she very well knew. They had hoped to find something on the way, but so far without success. She didn't fool Paul either, by the sly smile he gave her, though he was a bit too quick to lay down his burden. Mark had no choice but to follow his example.

'And you had better not look at me like that,' she told both of them. 'You are glad that somebody else had suggested a break and you can preserve your macho images.'

Mark listened to the little quarrel that followed between Paul and her, which was nothing if not proof of their intimacy, with a twinge of jealousy and bent down to pick up his things, but neither of them moved. What was this? A strike? At this rate, they would get nowhere. Of course, she was not keen on getting out, was she? She had a decision to make, not that she would discuss it with anybody, and she was prevaricating. He had to be firm.

He turned to say something and noticed their eyes fastened on a stick lying on the ground between them. What now? He took a step closer and noticed how rigid they became and stopped. Did the stick move? Now part of it was raised. It had a head. The forked tongue flickered, tasting the air, smelling their fear. Thankfully, Mark was behind it. If only he could reach that fallen branch.

In slow motion, careful not to disturb the air, to make a noise, anything that would hasten a strike, he stretched. The snake sensed something. A few more inches of its body were raised off the ground. Its head moved like a periscope, tongue flickering. He had to do something. He straightened up as noiselessly as he could, raising the stick above his head. His muscles tensed. Perspiration poured off him as if he were a melting statue. By now, his hair had grown so long and tangled, it formed cat tails. They dripped from the tips into his eyes. His heart beat crazily. He couldn't possibly see what to hit. He blinked to clear his vision. When he could focus again, the snake had drawn its head back, forming a sinister S, ready to strike towards Sylvia.

There was a hiss, a swish, a slight thump, Mark in a batsman's stance, arms at the furthest extend of a swing, and the snake was flying like a brown ribbon through the air. As it landed, Mark ran at it and hit it again and again, his terror turned to rage.

Sylvia shot up and grabbed his arm. He could see how pale she was even through the water works. She, too, was dripping with sweat. 'It's dead now,' she said.

'Then it doesn't matter how much I hit it.'

'Yes it does.' She snatched the stick away from him. 'Food,' she said.

Mark busied himself with the fire. He had tried to keep some wood shavings dry in his pocket for the purpose, but they were damp. Paul tried to help by blowing. There was smoke everywhere, stinging their eyes and making them water.

Sylvia was babbling away excitedly about Africa while she prepared the snake. He had never heard her speak so much – to cover the fact that her hands were still shaking, probably, or to lighten the obvious depression in Paul and him after the expenditure of so much adrenaline. 'My gardener caught a snake outside my kitchen, once,' she was saying. 'I looked out the window and there he was, trailing a string with a five-foot snake at the end of it, its mouth held open with a stick. 'A strange pet, Michael,' I said. He looked at me as though I were crazy. 'Food,' he said.'

The fire caught eventually. Sylvia finished skewering the meat on a stick and passed it for Mark to turn above the fire. Mark silently watched the meat bubbling in the flames and Paul looked preoccupied, but she continued with her prattle, regardless. 'To realise just how valuable snake meat is to Africans, you have to travel around. If they run over a person on the road, they keep going. Not worth . . .' She stopped short, as if she remembered something too unpleasant, and shook her head to dislodge it. Or maybe she had realised she was talking too much. She finished half-heartedly: 'But if all traffic comes to a standstill and people race out of the cars to be the first on the scene, you can bet your last penny somebody has run over a snake.'

Paul accepted the bits of snake Sylvia distributed around on a broad leaf and started laughing as if she had just delivered the punchline to a good joke. With rest and food Mark, too, was feeling much better. But now that they had cheered up, Sylvia's mood was fast running the opposite way. He didn't know what to say to cheer her up, so he gave the signal to get going.

Enormous raindrops started to fall at large intervals. One here, one there. Where they hit the ground they raised a big bubble, which on bursting released a strong earthy smell. But what was the point in stopping for shelter? They were not exactly dry as it was. The tree trunks, the lichen, their clothes and shoes, or whatever remained of them, were damp and green. The only dry place was the ground. Every drop of water in the thin soil was utilised by the roots of the forest giants and left it bone-dry between rains. It had turned as hard as concrete and cracked into jagged-edged geometrical patterns.

The raindrops got closer and closer until the heavens opened. It flooded the hard ground. Instead of sinking into the thirsty soil, the water ran in dirty brown swirls down a slight incline, only to meet more water and slowly retreat back towards them. They had to stop.

The rain didn't last long, but when it moved on it left them in several inches of water, their few possessions floating around them. Worse still, the water seemed static, having nowhere to run. Mark had to admit defeat.

'With a bit more rain,' he said, 'the water will rise. We might have to retreat to higher ground.'

Paul was horrified. 'Go backwards?'

'What do you propose?' said Mark. 'Keep on course and drown?'

'It looks like a valley basin and that's where rivers are to be found, right?' Paul insisted. 'It might take a while, but the water will fall. It's only natural.'

'This,' Sylvia said, speaking for the first time since they ate the snake and looking even more depressed, 'must be what the Indians were fleeing from. They know which part of the forest floods during the rainy season.'

'Don't worry,' Mark said. 'It would take a while for it to become impassable. We will take it as it comes.'

'I was thinking of the night ahead,' she said and hugged herself, shivering.

This wasn't like her. She had never griped about anything before. A matter of pride, Mark supposed, for there were lots of things she could have complained about. 'Everything will look better in the morning,' he said, while Paul sighed and splashed down into the water. 'For now, let's hang the hammocks and try and get some sleep.'

Paul half-heartedly got up and helped him tie the hammocks, and Mark lifted Sylvia into one. He was surprised at how light she was. They all had lost weight, but she had so much less to lose. On the move they needed all the strength they could muster.

He was drifting off to sleep when Sylvia began screaming, and he tipped out of the hammock in his hurry. He wasn't sure what she was saying, the way she was chewing up her words. Something about dolls, which made no sense at all, but then she felt hot and clammy in the chilly night.

'A slight fever, nothing too serious,' he tried to reassure Paul, but he knew, only too well, that slight fevers could turn into serious ones.

*

By morning conditions had improved but only slightly. The water subsided, leaving the soil slushy. Their shoes fell apart when they tried to walk and they trudged barefoot, the mud oozing between their toes. The temperature rose steeply and the understorey turned to a sauna. Worse of all, the insects seemed to have multiplied overnight, and what normally was a nuisance became a torment.

With the effort needed to lift their feet out of the mud and hardly any sleep the previous night, they tired quickly. Sylvia looked awful. Mark offered to carry her, but she refused point blank. 'If you can walk, so can I,' she said but held grimly onto his arm, all the same, for fear of the ignominy of ending face down in the mud.

Nobody talked after that, not even Paul. The earth started to cake over and the walking became easier, if they did not mind sharp roots and spiky leaves on bare feet. Heads down, they trudged along. For a change, they were making good progress. Sooner or later . . . and then he heard the growl and was shocked into alertness, adrenaline pumping through his veins, faced with the primordial dilemma of flight or fight.

33

She had been here once before. In a dream. Was this a dream? It had to be. Or delirium. Didn't Mark say she had a slight fever? Maybe it was getting worse. The puma was perplexed and unhappy, though. If she touched it, would it turn into Paul? But she couldn't move. *Talk*, a voice in her head said, soothingly, quietly, over and over. *Talk, talk.*

But Paul was standing next to her, and so was Mark. Both were rooted to the ground, as indecisive as the animal. There was no doubt about it now. It was real. *Talk, talk.*

The puma blinked lazily. It bared its teeth half-heartedly as a preliminary warning. It was trying to make up its mind whether they were enemies or prey. If they showed aggression it would attack, if they fled it would give chase. They stood no chance either way. But . . . if not too hungry, it might leave them in peace. How to communicate this to the rest without breaking the stalemate? Mark mustn't do any of his heroics. No matter how fast his reflexes, he had no adequate weapons. *Talk, talk.*

Her knees gave way. She went down slowly. She rested her hands on the ground, eye to eye with the beast. Mark made to move. She grabbed his leg. 'No,' she said as calmly as the voice in her head that kept saying over and over, *Talk, talk.*

'You are beautiful!' she told the puma, imitating the voice. 'I love you, you know that, don't you?'

The puma looked at her puzzled, and for a moment Sylvia thought it purred. She was not sure if big cats were supposed to purr. Whoever heard of a purring lion? But this cat did. *Talk, talk.* Sylvia resumed talking, meaningless things, and when she ran out of words, the cat snarled. *Talk, talk.* What about?

A picture flashed before her eyes: intense light, a sparkling white house, a single tree in the yard, a soft breeze laden with hymenocallis growing in an old oil tin. Grandma in black, hands folded under her pinny, the corners of her kerchief thrown over the top of her head, reciting. Sylvia repeated after her, letting the words roll off her tongue like water over pebbles, word flowing into word, smooth, rhythmic and comforting like a lullaby. The animal yawned. Sylvia continued, on and on, until the puma got so bored it turned around and walked away slowly.

'I had a hallucination,' Paul said. 'None of this really happened, right?'

'What?' She sat on the ground, exhausted. The shadowless objects in her vicinity were so sharply focused they seemed alive: a sharp-toothed leaf, a clot of earth, a brown stick.

'How . . .?' Mark left the sentence unfinished. She knew what he meant.

'The Indian,' she said. 'He can't be all that far away.'

'So,' said Paul, 'if it was him talking, where did he learn Greek?'

'You speak Greek?' Her heart fluttered. Wouldn't it be just wonderful . . .

'No, but I did a bit of Classical Greek,' said Paul. 'It never sounded quite like that . . .'

'That's because you never learned it from a Greek,' she said.

'It still doesn't explain why the Indian inspired you to talk in Greek,' Paul said.

'He didn't put words in my mouth. Just the idea of talking calmly to the animal. I couldn't think of what to say, so Grandma's training came in handy.'

The mention of Grandma brought back the childhood memories again. The light and smells of her homeland. Grandma's voice reciting. 'How can you remember so much, Grandma?' little Sylvia asked. 'No books,' Grandma said. 'Books make memory obsolete.'

She had read a lot of books since then and remembered very little, but she had never read the *Odyssey*. She never needed to. When she was very lonely or very frightened or very depressed, Grandma whispered it in her ear and she repeated it after her like she used to then. But it would be of no use in replacing her longing for her homeland, or England, her heart skipped, or her children. The Indian had tried to impress upon her, during their last meeting, the danger of her leaving the forest. She could still see the snarling puma, the soaring eagle, both framed against a rainbow, and in the shadows the dead paca on the rocks. Maybe this was the last time the Indian could help.

They saw the puma again a few days later, from a safe distance this time. It was stealthily stalking a deer through the reeds of a small swamp. To Sylvia it was a repeat performance, but the men stood with mouths open, fascinated. The creature crouched, and when it launched itself into the air, it circumscribed an arch fifteen feet high and at least that much again in length. It literally hurled itself at its victim.

'Christ!' Paul said as the puma buried its teeth into its victim's throat. 'Am I glad you hypnotised the beast the other day. I wouldn't fancy the deer's fate one little bit!'

'Maybe it prefers swamp deer,' Sylvia said. 'And the puma's behaviour was not all good news. It is obviously unfamiliar with man, or it would have avoided us or attacked. We are nowhere near human habitation.'

But the more disheartened she became, the more optimistic Paul was. 'Have you noticed that we come across more and more animals now? I saw all sorts of creatures, but before I even thought of using bows and arrows they disappeared. Maybe we are nearer a permanent source of water, and with you boring them stiff with poetry and Mark's skill of matching animal reflexes, we might be able to feed ourselves better than ever before.'

'Hey! That was pure panic, not skill,' said Mark.

'Whatever. We will reach a river in no time,' Paul insisted.

'But not in time,' Sylvia said.

'Time for what?' said Paul.

'The flood,' she said.

Paul laughed. 'You are dramatising things as usual,' he said. 'A few rains and a tiny swamp do not a flood make.'

He changed his mind with the next rain, which just didn't stop, and by then Sylvia was in no mood to say I told you so.

For how long it had been raining she lost count. Day after day after day, it poured, with no promise for any relief. They talked in shouts to be heard above the deluge until they went hoarse and gave up. They trudged through the mud until they couldn't lift their feet any more, and then huddled together for warmth, to no avail. Food was the last thing on their minds.

Sylvia was close to a nervous breakdown. In the end she refused to wade through the brackish water, and Mark carried her under his arm like a parcel while she kicked and screamed until she got too exhausted even for that.

Still it rained and the swamp spread, forcing them to climb back to higher ground. The only comfort was that the insects had disappeared for the duration of the rain.

In a brief break between rainstorms, the forest turned to a horror movie set. Steam rose from everywhere. In the misty swirls the giant trees looked as if floating in mid-space. Sylvia could see Mark's legless torso and Paul's head and shoulders. To them, she probably was invisible.

She felt awful, covered in mud from head to toe, and there were no words to describe the viciousness and tenacity of the insects that reappeared and bred furiously in so much stagnant water.

Mark kept talking of horrible diseases unless they went

deeper into the forest, away from the spreading swamp. Thankfully, even he realised they couldn't avoid it altogether. They had to keep the drowned world in sight. Follow the water, the Indian had said.

34

All the time, Paul kept thinking of a river that would channel the water into its bed. He visualised it as a road through the jungle with verges on either side to make walking easier. But when they came across it they nearly missed it, it was so completely covered in vegetation.

River was too grandiose a word for it, more a wide stream running over an almost completely flat floor. The water hardly moved, hence the mat-forming plants. Only the force of more water with every rain pushed it sluggishly on. Aquatic plants floated on its surface, trees and vines scrambled for water near its edges, arching over it into a green umbrella, the longed-for glimpse of the sky still forbidden them. Far from it being a road through the jungle, it made progress even more difficult.

'Why don't we walk through the water,' Paul said. 'It doesn't look very deep.'

Mark disagreed. 'How do you know what lurks under there?'

Paul pushed the vegetation aside with his hand as if to find out. The water was the colour of wine, crystal clear and transparent. No silt, no sediment.

'With this colour, it must be a tributary of the Rio Negro,' said Mark.

'That really pinpoints us on the map,' said Paul, 'give or take a thousand miles.'

But they could at least wash. And when Sylvia worried about the piranhas, it was quite satisfactory to be able to give some advice for a change. 'Keep on splashing,' he said.

'I was told by a fisherman in Manaus that it scares them off.' She was staring at him sceptically, but even so, he couldn't help teasing her. 'I am not so sure one should trust him all that much. Some of his toes were missing.'

'Thanks for the reassurance,' said Sylvia.

Paul laughed and explained that the man didn't lose his toes in the water but in the boat where he threw his catch and then, like a fool, walked all over thrashing piranhas.

They all went their own way, grateful for some privacy after so many days imprisoned in mud together, but it didn't take long for Paul to find out that he still didn't like being alone and he sought out Sylvia. He found her, or whatever little of her emerged from the cocoon of mud, huddled behind a rock, covered in nothing but her long hair.

Paul crept up to her and suddenly put his arms around her. She gave a little startled scream. He lifted her, a pathetic handful of bones, weighing nothing, onto a tree trunk that was bending over the water. To his amazement, she was crying.

'What's wrong?' he said.

'I've nothing to wear.'

It sounded so incongruous under the circumstances that he couldn't help laughing, and even she gave a little smile. The first for ages. Her role of late had been that of Cassandra. Nothing but predictions of gloom and disaster.

'My clothes came off with the mud. I couldn't salvage a single scrap,' she said wiping the tears with the back of a hand, and then arranged her long hair to cover her breasts. She kept the other in her lap.

He was about to ask if it mattered. He had seen her naked before and Mark was a doctor, but he realised that, to a woman, it did matter. His shirt was made of tougher material than her dress and still held together, just. He put it round her shoulders, brushing off any protests about needing it at nights, and threaded her arms through the sleeves. They fell beyond her hands, so he rolled them up for her. The rest of the shirt swamped her. He was about to button her up, then changed his mind.

He put his arms around her body, inside the shirt and stood between her legs. She glanced around, on the lookout for Mark, as always. 'He is further down the river,' he said. 'He can't see us.'

'What if he returns?'

'If he is a gentleman, he'll look the other way.'

Perhaps Mark had left them alone on purpose. That man didn't deserve this world. No competitive instinct at all. One wouldn't catch Paul being so selfless.

She was pushing him away, laughing self-consciously. 'Paul! Don't you ever think of anything else?'

'No! And you are basically too shy of your body unless carried away by something, which again relies on luck. It can be a stumbling block to your education.'

'You find me lacking in experience?'

'You know a lot about the power of your brain and you dissect your feelings to distraction, but you are ignorant of the power of your body.'

'You mean I am naïve about sex.'

'You rely too much on spontaneous reactions, which of course can be very exciting, but ignore the pleasure of experimenting and improving on things.'

'I thought you had enjoyed it.'

'And so I did. But who knows what can be discovered with a bit of effort? One would miss a lot in life, sitting around waiting for inspiration and spontaneity.'

'What if I don't want to, right now?' she said.

'Then I will be a very sorry lover, if I couldn't make you want to.'

And so she did very soon, and it would have been a great pleasure, considering how long it had been since they made love, if it didn't feel so perverse. She felt so small in his arms it was like making love to a child, in more ways than one. Other than embracing his waist with her legs, for which she had no choice, the way she was sitting on the trunk, she took no part in the proceedings. It was entirely his show. Nothing like what had happened that day in the storm. Mark's long shadow was coming between them for sure. In a way, Paul wished that Mark had overcome his stupidity and made love to her and got it over with. Then she might realise that Mark was too complicated for any normal relationship.

Did Mark abstain out of masochism or because Paul had told him he had not made love to his wife out of respect for their friendship, and Mark was reciprocating? If so, Paul felt guilty because he had lied. He had made love to Mark's wife. Once. Since they got married, that is.

It wasn't his fault. Nothing more than a reflex reaction to the proximity of a beautiful woman. She had accosted him, he tried jokingly to parry her advances – not an easy task with a determined woman – she touched him, he responded. That was all. He didn't even enjoy it. Nicol was too much in love with herself to care about giving pleasure to anyone else. He had avoided her since, to her fury. How could anyone resist her? If it was vented by throwing the odd drink at him, like he had admitted to Mark, it wouldn't have been so bad. Instead, she spread lies. She couldn't accuse him of being an outright faggot, there was too much evidence to the contrary. Instead, she claimed he was bisexual and that Mark was among his lovers. This, coming from the wife, gave the story some credence. He could not explain all that to her husband, so he lied.

To Sylvia he said, 'Hasn't Mark ever made any advances?'

Sylvia looked at him suspiciously. 'No.'

'Does it bother you?'

She pushed him away and jumped off the tree trunk. 'Don't you start that, too!'

'What?'

'Accusing me of things,' she said, pulling the shirt around her.

'Is that what he does?' He gave him too much credit, the bastard! 'I wouldn't pay any attention. He is jealous. It's wrong, I suppose, if you sleep with me, but it would be fine with him. Some people are like that.'

'Aren't you like that?'

'I was never vulnerable to bouts of jealousy,' he lied. He had been, just the once. The day of the pigs.

'You can afford it, I suppose. I can't imagine you are in the habit of losing to other men. The shoe is on the other foot, more like.'

'I have experienced a lot of things for the first time in this place. Before, I didn't have any reason to be jealous. Now, I can't afford to. If I forced you to choose between Mark and me, I would be playing to lose. I don't often do that.'

'What makes you say that?' she said, surprised. 'You know there is nothing between Mark and me.'

'There is everything between you two, bar sex, and that only for the moment. But unlike you two, I don't go in for analysing things too much. It is so. Fine. As long as I am not left out.'

'But I never said or did anything that would justify all this.'

Suddenly he felt bitter. 'What he thinks, what he feels, what he says, are of great importance. The same from me can be dismissed. I couldn't possibly mean it. You don't even believe it when I say I love you.'

'One loves a person above all others. There are no others,' she said patiently.

'Back to that again. I have never regretted saying anything in all my life as much as that. I didn't know you then.'

Her heavy eyebrows gathered. Against her deathly pale face, they were as black as ebony. From under their shadow, her eyes sparkled as if on fire. Her hair stood on end. He could almost hear the crackle of electricity. The hand that held her shirt together trembled. 'And you don't know me now,' she spat out before she swept past him and stumbled downriver as fast as the rocky ground would allow.

After a few seconds of stupefaction at the volcanic eruption, Paul followed. He tried to steady her when she missed her footing. She beat him away, which unsteadied her even more and she landed on her butt. 'You thought it wasn't as much fun as the first time, and you blame Mark,' she screamed at him and allowed no time for him to put in a protest. 'It's nothing to do with him. If you must blame somebody, blame my bloody husband.' She took another swipe at him when he tried to help her up. 'I told you. I need to be drunk or drugged and God knows what else to overcome the inhibitions and complexes he created in fifteen years.' She clawed at the shirt, seeking her body. 'I'm shy of my body, am I? He made me loathe it! Sex? It was a dirty word, never to be mentioned. It was something one did fumbling in the dark without a word, in case one acknowledged it was taking place. I hated it! I HATED IT!'

She started sobbing and pushed him away when he tried to comfort her and then Mark was there and Paul thought he was about to kill him for making her cry.

But first, Mark turned to her. 'OK?' he said.

'I am not OK and it was not Paul's fault and I do not want your interference.' She took a deep breath. 'Do you know when things go bad for me?' she said just a few decibels lower. 'Whenever I act against my instincts. "Marry me",' Ian said, and I told him the truth. I was not the marrying kind. But I let him persuade me and I ended up in hell. The same here.' She spread out her arms to encompass everything. 'I know that the jungle is friendly to me, as long as I don't try to fight it or treat it like a prison to escape from. What do I do? I follow you two through bogs and floods and God knows what, until I can't take it any more. Why?'

'Because you want to get out,' said Mark.

'No. You two want to get out. And here,' she said, kicking at the water and splashing it all over Mark, 'is the stream that would lead to a river and to the people you miss so much. Go find them. I am not coming. There is nothing out there for me. Nothing!'

35

Mark put his hands on her shoulders to make her sit down, and his touch had its usual miraculous effect. He seemed to do it a lot lately. When she was angry, when she was depressed, when she was tense, and it worked every time.

'You are upset and tired,' said Mark calmly. 'As you said, here is the stream and it will not be too long now, so we could take a rest. You will feel better about everything, then.'

'You don't understand,' she said quietly. 'I tried, but beyond this,' and she swept her hands to show the trees, 'I see nothing. There is nothing out there. Nothing!' She looked down and stamped her foot on a rock with each word. 'The-rocks-are-the-end-of-the-road.'

Mark shut his eyes as if she had slapped him. 'You don't really believe I would harm you?' And when she couldn't find anything to say, he added: 'You are a scientist. A realist. Telepathy is one thing, but this,' he shrugged, 'is too ... fatalistic.'

She sighed. Once Ian looked just like this, and she relented and married him. Maybe, she would relent now and it could be fatal this time, but that too might be part of the scheme. She gave a half-hearted laugh. 'I tell you what. Why don't we get drunk?'

'If only!' said Paul. 'I would give an arm for a drink.'

'Nothing so drastic is necessary. Just get up that tree,' and she pointed downstream at a palm by the shore, 'tap the flower stalk, tie a gourd under it and wait. The juices pour in the gourd and ferment,' she said. 'It only takes a few hours.'

Paul stared at her. 'If it's that easy, why haven't we done it before?'

'I never saw that kind of palm before in this place, and I never felt like getting drunk before. Does it answer your question?'

'I'll do it,' said Mark.

'I am very sorry about earlier. I didn't realise . . .' Paul said the moment Mark left. 'Is that why you are unenthusiastic about getting out? Because of your husband?'

There was no point telling him that enthusiasm had nothing to do with it and she was thoroughly ashamed of herself. Things were hard enough without her contribution. If she were them, she wouldn't be this patient.

'Just divorce him. It's easier,' he said and kicked at a pebble as if in demonstration.

'That was what I tried to do. Get back to my career, earn enough money to bring up the children, be free of him. It would be no good just hoping for maintenance. I couldn't get anything out of him when I was married, let alone if I left him, whatever the law says. But I ended up in here.'

'You don't have to worry about that any more. I have more money than I know what to do with.'

'That's very nice. But how does it help me?'

He looked down at her soberly. 'It would all be yours too, when we marry.'

She felt a lump in her throat. 'You don't need to offer me anything, darling.'

'It's yours, anyway. It won't be much use to me without you.'

She reached up and took his hand affectionately. 'Wait until we get out.'

'You think I will change my mind the moment I get back to civilisation. Return to my old ways.' He waved his hand. 'That's all behind me now. I grew up a lot, lately.'

She didn't mean to hurt him. 'I know. But I still can't marry you.'

'Because you don't love me?' Eyes narrowed, waiting.

'Maybe I care too much. I don't want you to end up with someone like me.' She gave a little laugh. 'I'll drive you crazy in a matter of weeks. You need a woman of your own background, your own age, outgoing, sporty, somebody who could entertain your business associates,' she took a deep breath, 'somebody as beautiful as you.'

'You are condemning me to marry a clone!' he said, suddenly very angry. 'I don't want a woman like Mark's wife, immaculately beautiful, like all the other immaculate beauties in our social circle, all products of the same plastic surgeon, dress designer and hairdresser, flitting from expensive club to expensive club, flirting with tennis instructors, hairdressers and beach boys, bored in their luxury and empty in the head.' It all poured out, and then he took a deep breath. 'I want a real woman.'

'An older woman, who can't even make small talk, with two kids.'

'And one that is difficult, temperamental, unpredictable and downright stubborn.' He sat next to her, smiling. 'Let's put the record straight.'

'Then why on earth . . .'

'Because of your passion, baby,' he said. 'Passion about flowers, animals, storms, passion about everything. I'll never be bored with you. I'll never know what you would do next. What you would get passionate about. You are different to anyone I've ever met.' He bent nearer to her. 'And, most important of all, I love you.'

There was no mistaking the sincerity in those sapphire eyes, and it was very tempting, but still she could not visualise herself in any scenario that featured a life of luxury with an ex-playboy, no matter how much she would have given for anything as unlikely as that a few months or even weeks ago.

'I'll tell you what,' she said. 'You propose like this once we are out, and I will not be responsible for my actions. I'll snap you up before you have time to say bimbo, let alone go out with one.'

He laughed. 'Is that a promise?'
'Provided you promise me something too.'
'Anything!'
'Wait until you know what it is, first. If . . . now don't say anything, just hear me out. If you make it out and I don't, look out for my children. Make sure they are OK.'
'We will all three make it, or none will,' he said emphatically.
'Yes, I know. But just in case. Will you promise?'
'Of course, but . . .'
She put a hand over his mouth. 'That's all.'

The trouble with drink was that it made her very tactile and under the present circumstances it wasn't much use. The person she most wanted to finger had reached the silly stage of drunkenness and it would have been so easy to lay her hands on him, had it not been for Paul, who had turned downright lecherous and she had to fight him off. If Mark noticed through the palm wine fumes in his brain and bolted, he'd leave her empty-handed. She didn't give a damn about having sex with Mark. She coveted his touch.

What had annoyed her earlier with Paul was that she had let him make love to her because she had no good reason to say no. That had reminded her of her husband, hence all the anger. For sex to be of any use to her, she had to be in a state where no thought process was possible. Otherwise, she felt humiliated. The loss of sovereignty over her body, the invasion of her privacy, made the act abhorrent. Was that an indication that she had never been in love with anyone she had sex with so far? Would it be different with Mark? She couldn't be sure. The mechanics would be the same. The role of the woman in sex was submissive, demeaning. Full stop.

Stupidly enough, she still wanted to touch Mark's hand. Could one be in love with somebody's hands? And his voice, of course, and then maybe the rest of him. But primarily his hands. And they were only just there. If she sidled up to him and put her hand 'accidentally' near his . . .

'Oh, Paul, for Christ's sake!' she said impatiently as Paul tumbled over her.

Mark lurched to his feet. 'I'm not used to drink,' he said. 'I need cold water on my face,' and off he ran, like she thought he would and she could have killed Paul, except the silly thing looked so innocent and sorry, he had scared Mark off.

If the river was so near, as Mark thought, this would probably be the last chance she would ever have of saying goodbye to Paul. Or maybe she was too frustrated at losing her prime victim or too drunk, and all objections to intimacy were overruled or . . . who the hell cared any more?

'How about throwing all my inhibitions to the wind and getting to see you properly?' she said.

'For a moment I thought you were going to suggest something a little more intimate.' Paul was slurring his speech a little, but he didn't look as far gone as he had pretended earlier.

'Really see,' she said. 'The way babies do.'

'Well, there is not much hidden. Here it is.' He spread out his arms to show that he only had a pair of torn trousers on.

'Take them off.'

He complied, but took that for an invitation he could understand better and opened his arms.

'Uh-uh! You are not allowed to move a muscle,' she said.

'Oh, shit!' But he submissively spread star-fashion on the rocks.

She stretched her hands to his face and let her fingertips trace its contours, went over those marvellous cheekbones. She bent down. Her lips touched his eyelids, his nose, his mouth. Her tongue traced the line of his lips then followed the muscles of his neck to the pit at its base. This being a favourite spot she lingered there, kissing it, tracing it with her tongue, feeling his Adam's apple moving as he swallowed. She moved to the shoulders and chest, her hands gliding down his arms, the fingers seeking out hard muscles under the smooth elastic skin. She rubbed her cheek against the taut belly, followed the groove of the hip bone and kissed the transparent skin of the groin, feeling the blue vein throbbing under her lips. She let her hands move to his thighs.

There were three areas of the male anatomy that she found particularly enticing: a freshly shaven flat cheek – she hadn't seen one for ages and probably would never see one again – the hollow of the neck and above all, the groove between the *adductor longus* and *gracilis* muscles, on the upper inner thigh. The genitals themselves were not arousing to look at. But her hands lingering on his thighs were driving Paul restless.

'You are killing me,' he groaned. 'Do something or I'll forget my promise.'

She ran her finger up the shaft of his penis to feel the contrast between the satiny skin and the hardness underneath, and Paul gasped and all discipline was lost after that. It didn't seem to matter all that much now because she seemed to be in charge, or drunk, or both.

'Is that what you call seeing?' he said after a while.

She smiled. 'I thought I had explained. Didn't I say like a baby? They see with all their senses.' She gave him a fleeting kiss before getting up, their bodies separating with a squelchy noise. 'I just wanted to commit everything to memory.'

'I will always be there.'

No he wouldn't, and sooner than he realised. She felt it in every cell of her body. One day soon he would let go of her, just like she knew Mark would or already did, after a fashion. 'Can't promise anything,' he had said. Paul, of course, promised everything, but the result would be just the same.

36

Mark had a head for heights and his arms were getting stronger by the day. A vine bound round both feet was sufficient for a reasonable grip, and he could dispense with Paul's sling and ropes. Not that he needed to look for food up trees. With so much water around, life was plentiful at ground level, but it got him out of their way without making a drama of it. It also gave him the chance to think, not an easy task under Paul's constant verbal barrage.

He crept up the trunk, but soon the repetitive motion became routine and he allowed his mind to stray to other matters. That fixation of Sylvia's that he would drop her literally or metaphorically. No wonder she was getting closer to Paul. His inability to say what he felt didn't help.

It was exasperating not to be able to relate to anyone. The only person he had ever been close to was Paul. Never having been in love, he married both times for convenience. In a way, life had been rather simple. Suddenly, at his age, he found his happiness in the hands of somebody else. It was frightening and confusing. He couldn't handle his feelings or reactions. Hard words came out when all he wanted was to say something nice. He certainly had not meant to say he couldn't promise her anything, that day. Of course he could. He loved her. If they ever escaped the jungle and she left her husband and Paul, he would divorce his wife and marry her. But by what right could he expect her to agree?

He was already amongst the branches and hadn't even noticed. He hoisted himself onto a sturdy branch to watch life all around him, like he had done several times lately. It was not much different to anywhere else, like Paul had said. There was the struggle to find food, to protect one's territory, to find a mate, to safeguard one's young. Occasionally death would strike out of the blue. There was brutality and unparalleled savagery, but also cooperation and associations of the most extraordinary nature. All was aimed single-mindedly at one goal: survival of the species, not necessarily the individual. One could learn a lot up here. For instance, how to adapt to the prevailing circumstances, not react according to some conditioning from another world. Sylvia had told him as much, but it took him this long to realise.

At the thought of her, a wave of love overwhelmed him. A delicious ache. Nothing had changed, of course, in the short time he had spent up the tree. He was not any nearer knowing how to confide in her. She still liked Paul. But something had shifted. He was at peace with the world.

It was good to be in love. To have somebody to care for. Somebody whose existence made it all worth while. Better than his indifference to everything before he met her. Even that ache felt reassuring. You had to be alive to feel pain. And she was not completely apathetic towards him, if the way she melted into his arms whenever he touched her was anything to go by.

The close proximity of her body invariably excited him too much. Knowing that he was either unresponsive or uncontrollable, he panicked and withdrew to hide his confusion. He thought he saw hurt in her eyes. Yet it was hard to believe she cared for him. After all, she was Paul's lover, though she had said she had no choice about it.

He was sure Paul had not forced her, but sooner or later he would have stooped to that if there was no other way to get her. It was unreasonable to expect Paul to settle for celibacy, no matter how good her arguments. It would also be unreasonable, however sincere Paul seemed now, that he would pass by any temptations once they got out. Nobody could change that much. And he, Mark, would be there to cherish her, the way Paul couldn't possibly do.

Paul would throw money at her of course, and jewels and God knew what else, but she didn't seem the type to settle for just that. The only thing now was to get safely out, and here the same cloud appeared on his mental horizon as it did whenever he tried to be positive about things.

Why did she keep saying she saw nothing beyond the jungle? How was her vision to be interpreted? Certainly he would never do anything to harm her or leave the forest without her. That much he could be sure about.

He scampered from branch to branch, intending to get above the canopy. This stream had to join a river sooner or later. It was only from up there he could see a sign to add impetus to their grovel through this green tunnel. He emerged into the sunlight and hope was restored. She was unwell, hence all the depression. Of course they would get out. All three of them. Then the word 'unwell' registered. In this climate, without any medicines, how long before any mild indisposition developed into something serious?

It was not until well into the next day that they spotted the window of light at the end of their green tunnel and ran towards it, hungry for open space.

'The sky, the sky!' Paul parodied as they emerged into the open.

They lifted their faces to the cerulean dome. White lozenges of cloud with fiery lace fringes floated across it sedately. The wind ruffled the surface of the water, carrying the river's humid breath to greet them. A short distance from the river's edge, rocky islands sparkled with rubies that turned out to be red crabs creeping sideways, and hovering above them like miniature helicopters were crudely painted red and black dragonflies. On the shore itself, trees desperate for water anchored themselves on any stony fragment they could find or gripped smoothly rounded boulders with knurled exposed roots like bony fingers. And then the undergrowth went into riot, and with it all associated life. None of the restraint of the understorey inside the forest here. Intense colour burst from everywhere, reflected from the water, dazzled: flowers flaunted themselves in electric purple and flaming red; birds in brilliant turquoise or orange plumage; iridescent blue butterflies, almost as big as birds; yellow and black bumblebees, the size of Brazil nuts.

Sylvia walked along the bank, happier than Mark had ever seen her, exclaiming with delight, 'So that's where all those plants I was looking for have been all the time.' She spread out her arms, twirling around and saying, as if reciting from a poem, 'Where the current deposited the seeds, where there is sunshine and water to nourish them.'

Mark and Paul went after crabs, wading through the water to avoid the blistering rocks. Paul parked on a rocky island and cracked the shells open, impatient for the meat, while Mark returned to the shore for driftwood to make the fire. By the time he was back, the others were already busy eating.

'They were broiled on the rocks,' Sylvia said. 'No need for fire. It would make us even hotter.'

Sunshine, both direct and reflected from water, heat radiating from the rocks, steam from everywhere, had turned the place into a sauna, hotter than anything they had experienced in the womb of the forest. Mark thought of Sylvia's recurrent bouts of mild fever. It wouldn't do her any good. 'We had better take shelter under the trees,' he said, 'or we will get sunstroke.'

Sylvia got up first and hopped from one stone to the next quickly, to stop the soles of her feet burning, and slipped. Mark caught her before she landed backside first in a rocky pool.

'Thanks,' she said, flashing a smile up at him, and waded ahead, squinting against the glare, to find a flatter launching pad. 'Over there,' she shouted, and Paul splashed after her.

Mark hung back to push the hair out of his eyes. It was so long and tangled up, it became a nuisance. He wiped his brow with the back of his arm and then shaded his eyes to see what she was on about.

From her angle it might have looked like a flat stone submerged in dazzling water; from Mark's, it definitely didn't. He lurched forward. 'DON'T!'

She turned to look at him, surprised, one leg already outstretched. To balance herself, she planted it firmly down. There was a sudden movement under her, a splash of water, and she was airborne. The way she was falling, upside down, she was about to smash her skull on the rocks and Mark was too far back to catch her, no matter how fast he moved.

Paul, just behind her, tried to break the fall but staggered backwards and into deep water, with her on top.

Mark was on the scene within seconds. The rusty water was too disturbed for him to see clearly, and it took a while to spot the cayman. The animal, in its surprise at the sudden attack on its noonday basking, had moved some distance from the shore. Now it swept its powerful tail in an arc through the foam and made a sharp turn. The tail swung from side to side, propelling it forward. Its snout cleaved the surface of the water as it zoomed towards the two floundering figures. Mark tried to haul them out but Sylvia, either through inability to swim or injury, sank beneath the rusty foam.

37

Paul saw the cayman coming at him, but he had to find her. He could hardly accept Mark's help and leave her as a bait while he saved his skin. But the water was too disturbed to see from above. He held his breath and dived. It was not easier from below, especially since he was whisked around in a vortex. He spread his arms to drag the water for her blindly, to no avail, came up took a breath and dived again. Now he could just make her out, a shadowy figure somersaulting in the water, tangled up in her own hair that floated around her like seaweed. Beyond her, giant jaws flashed white against the rusty foam, closing in.

He grabbed her hair and yanked. She was propelled into him, driving out whatever breath he had left, and knocked him against the rocks. The water here was shallower and he staggered on shore, dragging her after him.

There was a lot of thrashing still in the water, as if the animal had gone mad for losing its prey. Sylvia was coughing up water. He patted her back, dismissing her thanks while looking for Mark, surprised at his inactivity. He was nowhere to be seen.

The cayman was now emerging from the water. The head came up first, vertically, the underside pearl-white. Sylvia screamed and retreated backwards like Paul, as the animal kept rising, showering water around, a grotesque Aphrodite. First came the shoulders, then extended forelegs, white belly, hind legs twitching. It finally rested on the surface of the water on the tip of its tail, before, amazingly, it started gliding forward towards the shallows and the rocks where he and Sylvia sat.

It took Paul a while to realise that the brown necklace around the cayman was formed by Mark's arms in a vice-like grip. The animal beat its tail and both beast and Mark fell backwards. Now Mark was under the thrashing cayman. He didn't let go, though, wrestling with the beast until he managed to turn around and pin it under him. 'Do something, you fucking idiot,' he shouted at Paul. 'Get the knife.'

Paul still bewildered, searched for the knife. 'It wouldn't even scratch it. Look at that skin,' he said, but the knife was not in his waistband. He must have dropped it in the water.

With Mark's urgent screams after him he dived, hoping it wouldn't be so hopeless a search with the principal agitators out of the water. Nothing doing. He came up and had a glimpse of Mark shaking to bits on top of the animal, while Sylvia, in her efforts to immobilise the tail, was swiped off and floundered on the rocks. He dived again. The water was calmer and clearer. He saw the knife but ran out of breath. He came up, took another gulp and tried again, succeeded in retrieving it and dragged himself towards the tangle of twitching beast and humans.

'Here!' Mark screamed while trying to keep the animal still. 'Behind the skull. Hammer it in with a stone, if you have to. Just sever the spinal cord.'

The whole thing was crazy. No way could Paul hold the knife still with one hand while trying to get hold of a rock with the other. The blade kept slipping from the scaly skin as the animal struggled. Mark was getting impatient and screamed abuse, scared, probably, of letting his grip slip through exhaustion. With an animal this maddened and frightened, they would all be in the shit. He took hold of the knife's handle in both hands and managed to nip the skin between two armoured plates. Sylvia abandoned her rocking seat on the reptile's tail, picked up a stone and hammered it in. The animal lurched once or twice. Mark let go of the cayman and twisted the blade. There was a shudder and the cayman went limp.

Mark got up, bruised, scratched, breathing in gasps from the exertion, but no serious harm was done and an awful lot of good. Perseus had saved Andromeda from the fearful monster yet again, and boy, was she grateful! Taking care of Mark's bleeding chest, so tenderly.

One couldn't sit around moping, though, so Paul built a fire, heat or no heat, and threw the cayman on top of it, skin, guts and all. He was never a good cook and certainly knew nothing about cayman preparation.

'Lobster,' said Sylvia later. 'Definitely tastes of lobster.' She bent towards Paul and patted his greasy hand with her equally greasy one. 'But next time don't forget the garlic butter and breadcrumbs.'

Paul flicked away bits of food that had got into his beard. Eating caymans without cutlery was not a delicate operation. 'You two,' he said, 'you look like pigs.'

All three laughed and Paul regretted the sulking earlier. After all, she had said thank you to him. If it sounded a bit offhand, she was choking at the time, and he did not need any mending like Mark.

Upriver, the clouds looked like giant meringues floating in a pool of raspberry sauce, the next moment the light was switched off, turning them to drab caymans swimming in mud.

Without the protection of the canopy, the temperature fluctuation was more pronounced, and the scorching day was followed by a chilly night. They huddled together for warmth. Sylvia squashed small between the two men, Mark wrapped like a cloak around her back and she in turn curled up against Paul's side.

The prospect of being out of the jungle, now so close, instead of filling Paul with joy, unsettled him. He stared at the sky for hours. With no glare from habitation for God knew how many miles, the Milky Way stood stark against the black sky. He thought the shadows in it resembled animals. There certainly was a bird and a puma, but where was the paca? He wished upon a shooting star to the accompaniment of buzzing insects. *Let us all stay together, like this, in and out of the jungle. Sylvia, Mark and me.*

He was still awake to see the pink pool reemerging down river. Out of it a creamy sun rose slowly. For a while the sky was splashed with shocking pink before it was slowly bleached to almost white. The greenery that had emerged from darkness on either side of the river converged to form sparkling solid walls, transforming it into a canyon, with no end in sight. Paul's spirits sank, the lowest in his memory.

Sylvia stirred, and he wished the opposite of what he had wished during the night: that Mark was someplace else and she would help to bring him up from the pits.

Paul took Sylvia's arm to stop her slipping. She didn't seem to have the strength to negotiate the granite boulders on the riverside any more. Maybe she had sunstroke. This endless walking in the blaring sun was getting them all down. He too would have given anything to stay in one place, but it was ages before Mark gave the signal. He let go of Sylvia's arm and she dropped in the shade of a tree, where the stones were cooler.

'We need a boat, a raft, anything that floats,' Paul said, falling next to her, 'or we are fighting a losing battle.'

Mark looked at him quizzically. 'We will fell trees with the knife, I suppose?'

'I could do without smart-alecky remarks right now,' Paul said through clenched teeth.

'Has it occurred to you that we came across nothing and nobody because the river isn't navigable?' Mark said.

Yes, it had occurred to Paul, and it was disheartening. He wished for a car and an open road. He possessed lots of cars but only one he called his own. 'I wonder who has my car,' he said wistfully. 'Do you think they have decided I'm dead and sold it off?'

'Was it a sports Jaguar, by any chance?' Sylvia said.

The comment annoyed him though she was probably

trying to lighten up the atmosphere, not that she herself looked very light, but then everything annoyed him right now. 'It's no point asking, "How do you know",' he said.

'It's just that you look like a Jaguar man,' she said and tried to smile.

'And what are you?' Paul snapped. 'A Mini woman?'

He regretted it instantly, knowing how references to her size bothered her, but she decided not to take offence. 'Very funny!'

'Well?' Paul said more gently. 'What car do you drive?'

She found something of interest on the opposite bank of the river. 'I don't drive,' she said quietly.

'Everybody knows how to drive,' Paul said. 'It's not that hard.'

She became defensive. 'I know how to drive. I just don't like to.'

'You prefer a chauffeur?' said Paul.

She rolled her eyes. 'It happened in Africa,' she said. 'We were driving through the bush on a road still under construction. There was red dust everywhere. The whole thing was crazy.' She transferred her interest to her hands, examining the poor state of her nails. 'I saw this child hit by a car but our driver wouldn't stop, no matter what I did. He insisted that the whole thing was in my mind before reminding me that the first rule for all expatriates or drivers with expatriate passengers was not to stop for any accident, or they would be blamed for it.' She found a piece of a broken nail sticking out and started gnawing. 'I cannot get the picture out of my mind.' She realised what she was doing and sat on her hands, her head bent. 'Every time I sit behind the wheel, I see the little body rising through the red haze, flaying about limply, like a rag doll before disappearing back into the dust. I know how irrational it seems,' she turned to them for understanding 'but I become so ill and trembly and sweaty, I'm bound to hit someone. I can't take the chance.'

'Have you thought of a psychiatrist?' said Paul.

She seemed to hesitate, then. 'Maybe it's a kind of

premonition. I don't want to block it out. My husband, like you I'm sure, thinks I'm crazy, but I don't care.' Then she said more resolutely, 'I'm not going to endanger anyone's life just to prove something.'

'It's not the end of the world,' said Mark, apparently concentrating on something else.

'Try telling that to my husband,' Sylvia said. 'Though I am not sure he doesn't really cherish the idea, deep down. It's the only thing he can claim to do better than me, and boy, does he make sure I know how skilful he is and how stupid I am. But I still won't drive.'

'I don't think I like your husband very much,' said Paul.

'Shh! Do you hear that?' Mark said. 'If we are to have another storm, we shouldn't sit so near the water's edge. Besides, we are more exposed here than we were in the forest. We need some shelter.'

A percussion orchestra in the distance was now in full swing and kept coming closer. Flashes of lightning were succeeded by darkness. The wind rose. It creased the water, blew spray from the waves, bent smaller trees, whipped palm fonds around. By the time the explosions and fireworks were overhead, they had constructed a shelter with fallen branches and palm leaves.

The rain came like a grey mist from the forest. It bounced off the water for a while, then all was quiet. The columns of clouds glided to the horizon, where they crowded themselves impersonating a distant mountain range, leaving behind them everything sparkling. Blue and yellow macaws came out to play. Parakeets squawked. A solitary egret landed gracefully on a half-submerged tree trunk, polished to the texture of marble. It reflected in the water as if in a black mirror.

Then out of the stillness they started to distinguish the original sound Mark had drawn their attention to before the storm. Nothing like booming drums. More of a continuous rush. The storm had blown too far to have anything to do with it.

Paul got up. 'It sounds like rapids. I'll go ahead and

scout,' he said. 'I'll be faster without having to carry any clutter.'

'I hope you are not talking about me,' said Sylvia.

'I mean pots and ropes and things,' he said irritably, and as he left he heard Sylvia say, 'Whatever happened to Paul's sense of humour?'

38

The sun was high, the light intense, the shadows deep and the silence was broken only by the drone of insects. There was a siesta time for all creatures, including the cayman, who basked in the noonday sun. Sylvia had been told caymans were safe as long as they were not disturbed, but she was not sure that the cayman was aware of the theory, and after her recent experience she kept a respectful distance.

She liked this time of day, despite the heat, because it made her feel as if in all the starkness and stillness she could hear and see everything to the minutest detail. She squinted in the bright light reflected from the water.

Mark was fishing upstream. He was using a stick for a rod, a long string from a palm leaf for a line, and the hook he had carved from one of the bones of the eaten cayman. She marvelled at the degree of immobility he could achieve when in silent meditation. His long hair and beard, bleached by the sun into a rich gold, shone like a beacon. He looked like a lighthouse built from the rocks he was sitting on. She wondered what he was thinking about.

Mindful of piranhas, she splashed in the shallow edge of the water towards him. He looked up. A slow smile spread over his face, lighting it up. She smiled back and sat by him.

'Got anything?' Her voice shattered the silence like a stone the surface of a still pond.

'My line is too obvious. It takes very stupid or very greedy fish to bite. They are rare.' He said it lazily, pointing at his one and only catch before turning back to the water.

His shoulder was burned to a coppery colour, unlike her arms and legs, which were more a chocolate brown. She wanted to put her head on it but didn't dare, in case he withdrew again. She could do without the humiliation. 'Have you done much fishing before?' she said.

'I used to take my son fishing.'

She had no idea he had a son, but there were so many things he never talked about. 'Do you miss him a lot?'

'Sometimes. He lives with his mother, my first wife. I only saw him during vacation. Fishing was one of our more quiet pursuits.'

'Is that why you looked so preoccupied? Thinking of those days?'

'I was thinking of the rocks and what you said about being dropped on them.'

She laughed carelessly. 'I am a cat with nine lives. I survive everything. Poverty, wars, car accidents, air crashes. I will survive a few rocks.' But a shiver passed through her, and she stood up so that he wouldn't notice. 'A suicidal fish took the bait and you haven't even realised,' she said.

He jumped into action. The fish, about a foot long and half that in width with a blunt head and disproportionately large jaws, thrashed around where he had thrown it. She looked away, unable to watch the death struggle, even that of a piranha. He noticed. 'I hate it too,' he said, 'but sometimes it is inevitable.'

'What I hate witnessing is the struggle against the inevitable.'

He abandoned the fish and stood behind her, putting reassuring arms around her waist. She forgot all about being on guard against rejection and leaned back on him, relaxing to the touch, melting against the heat of his chest. Neither spoke.

There was a different feel being close to him now. Outwardly, nothing had changed. He still spoke little, and there were times when he withdrew behind a wall of silence. But whilst before she sensed a struggle behind the closed doors, now the silence had the serenity of meditation. Then, she had wanted to be admitted in, to be part of whatever caused the strife. Now, she could stand unobtrusively by and let the waves of calmness that radiated around him wash over her. She felt secure and relaxed, an experience unfamiliar to her until now. It needed a lot of confidence, it was said, to be silent in the presence of another person. She felt that with Mark.

She used to be silent in the presence of her husband, but the reasons were different. It had nothing to do with mental communication, ease or familiarity. It was a protective shield against the stress signals he sent in every direction like spiked rays. Perhaps that was his way of communicating frustration at her silence, but his speeches, expressing views invariably bigoted, stunned her into silence. Yet he was a mild person with everybody else. His worse side surfaced only in her presence. If that was his way of eliciting her response, he failed by overdoing it. Even remembering his words now, brought a kind of spiritual weariness over her. 'Shoot them!' he would say forcefully whenever there was a mention of old, disabled, black, khaki or Muslim. 'Real people,' he used to say about white Anglo-Saxon Protestants. Yet, she had reminded him once or twice before she had given up, he had married neither an Anglo-Saxon nor a Protestant. 'It doesn't count now we are married,' he would say, as if marriage alone had elevated her to that exalted state.

Mark turned her around and lifted her chin with forefinger and thumb. 'Everything OK?' he inquired gently and when she smiled, he bent down slowly and buried his face in her hair. 'You are so beautiful,' he said as he let his hand move down her body.

Right then, she was inclined to agree with him, but there was no time to savour the moment because Paul was on his way back, wading through the water, looking unusually subdued. She hoped it was not because he saw her in Mark's arms, but he absentmindedly kicked a floating log out of his way. In its turn, the log collided with something looking like an animal's head, just showing above water, too small to be that of a cayman. Sylvia did not think much of it. Most animals they came across lately seemed to be able to swim, even sloths. They had to, with the place about to flood out for months on end.

The head surfaced and started to roll over the trunk, followed by the rest of the animal, on and on and on, at least thirty feet of snake body, the diameter of a small tree. If that was terrible, Paul's passivity was worse. Not even when he lost his footing and fell right in the anaconda's path did he respond.

Mark made what looked like the fastest sprint in his life, over rocks and through the water to grab Paul by the hair and drag him away before he got entangled with the snake, without the slightest assistance from Paul. Mark had to haul him out, just as the snake slithered inches from them. Still retreating on his backside, he dragged Paul away in case the snake changed its mind, but it slipped by just as unconcerned as Paul, who drew himself into a ball and fell asleep.

'Is he in shock?' Sylvia asked, out of breath, having just covered the distance.

Mark looked at Paul shivering on the hot stones, worried. 'It's more serious than that.'

They couldn't afford for any of them to fall ill. They had to keep moving ahead of the encroaching water, which after weeks of rain was making the river spread out behind them, submerging the lower parts of trees and covering completely all other vegetation. Even this noonday break was unwise, and if it were not for her getting tired so quickly, they would not have stopped.

'How do you feel?' Mark asked when Paul opened his eyes, but Paul just clenched his teeth to keep them from chattering.

'It might be a chill,' said Sylvia, hoping. 'All these cold damp nights.'

But Paul's temperature kept rising, no matter how much Sylvia bathed him with cold water. Delirium set in. Mark prodded around Paul's abdomen, discovered the enlarged spleen, and their worst fears were realised. 'Malaria,' he said.

Sylvia did not want to believe it. 'Can't be. Not here!'

Mark spread his arms around. 'There is enough stagnant water for mosquitoes to breed.'

'Breeding isn't the operative word,' she said. 'Transmit is. But from what?'

The significance of Paul's illness suddenly hit her. Human habitation couldn't be too far away. As the mosquito flies, so to speak. 'Oh, my God! We've made it!' She started to laugh, then looked at Paul and threw herself at the limp body. 'Sorry, sorry, sorry! I didn't mean to rejoice at your illness. It's just that for a moment . . .' But Paul was too far gone to hear any of it.

Sylvia took turns with Mark to fan and wash Paul, trying to keep his temperature down, unsuccessfully. She was furious with herself. 'It's so stupid! We are probably surrounded with cinchona trees and I can't even recognise them. I've never seen one. Only heard about them.' She knew it was a small tree with opposite leaves and flowers like those of lilacs but pale pink.

'It's better than nothing,' Mark said. 'We could look.'

'The description fits several things. Coffee, for a start.'

'Trial and error. It's better than sitting around and watching him die.'

Sylvia prayed that the Indian who had abandoned her for weeks, would appear again or, at least, inspire her to find the cinchona tree. But she kept being drawn to the noise Paul had said might be rapids.

She clambered over tangled roots and rocks along the shallow edge of the river. The water became progressively turbulent and swift. Surface plants were swept aside. The noise grew louder and louder until it became thunderous. Boulders hewn out of the rocky sides that now grew higher and higher, were strewed across the current. The dark waters churned between them into rusty foam. She could feel spray in the air. By the time she rounded a rocky outcrop, she found that the whole of the river had been whipped into a froth, and in the distance it disappeared into the mist.

Her path was now blocked by a striated rock formation. She veered to the side, sliding from flat surface down to flat surface, like great granite steps, until she reached the edge of the cliff. She flattened herself against a rock, only just peeping over the brim.

The chasm into which the foamy waters cascaded was guarded on either side by granite pillars, part of the formation she was resting on. Trees and bushes leaned precariously towards the precipice, sucked in by the vacuum created by the rushing waters. Plants, permanently washed by the spray, clung desperately to outcrops, nodding their heads constantly, and down below, even more turbulent water rose into the air to meet the one coming down, and as the two met there was nothing but vapour and spray, rising hundreds of feet, the water droplets splitting the light into rainbows.

A long way down, the water gradually calmed until it formed a black ribbon that tunnelled through the green, disappearing into infinity. Styx itself, that used the air to pull at her and beckon towards its ebony bosom.

The feeling of death crouching down there intensified. Death for a lot of people: the Indians, their Shaman, herself. It was waiting, had been there a long time. *The Puma brought it with him. The Puma brought it with him.*

She whipped around and saw the shaman high up above her, squatting on the rocks, glistening with spray. She had wished for him so that he would help save Paul's life. How could she ask him now if he was blaming Paul for so many people's murder?

The Indian skipped down the rocks and came towards her. *The Puma is our last hope.* That was contradictory, to say the least. *The Puma must not die.* Well, what was he going to do about it? He took a small leather bag from a thong around his neck, next to his emerald, and gave it to her.

The Puma and the Hawk, they will help because of you. The Puma must not die.

She opened the leather pouch. It was full of ground bark. Meanwhile the Indian took the green pendant from around his neck and put it around hers. *Safer with you.* Wasn't she supposed to be in danger, too? He shrugged his shoulders in the universal gesture of puzzlement. He was doing what he had to do. He didn't know why.

She turned back, disturbed and confused, unable to grasp the significance of the conflicting messages. Maybe the shaman didn't either.

Once she left the big rocks behind and started to walk in the shallow edge of calmer water, she saw Mark in the distance running towards her, obviously very upset. He wouldn't have left Paul unattended, unless . . . *Oh, my God! It's too late.*

She just stood still, trying to come to terms with the enormity of it, hoping against hope she was wrong. He saw her and stopped too. He took a deep breath, making a visible effort to get his emotions under control.

'Please say it isn't true,' she begged. 'He can't be. Not Paul!' Paul personified life, vitality, happiness. People like him were meant to spread joy all around them. It was a sin, an obscenity for him to die so young.

39

Mark stopped, puzzled with Sylvia's reaction at the sight of him until he realised how it must have looked to her. He came forward and put his arms on her shoulders. 'No, no. Nothing happened to Paul. I mean, nothing worse. It's just that you took so long, I thought something might have happened to you.'

His touch seemed to have acted as a catalyst. She broke down completely and cried there on his chest, sobbing convulsively, gasping for breath. His hands ran up and down her back, trying to soothe her, but it didn't work this time. And when it was all out and there was nothing but the odd shudder running through her body, he pushed her back and wiped her cheeks with his fingers.

'He must mean so much to you,' he said.

'I could live without him. I would miss his laughter, but I could be happy to know he is there, somewhere, giving love and joy to everyone around him. I could let him go. I would never let go of somebody I . . .' She stopped.

She was confusing him again. She was trying to tell him she was not in love with Paul. That, of course, did not necessarily mean he was the beneficiary, but all the same he started pulling her towards him. As he pressed her against him he felt something hard between them. He drew back. There was a rough green stone and a leather pouch around her neck.

'You saw the Indian,' he stated.

She looked down at the two objects as if she just remembered. 'Yes. It's medicine for Paul.'

'Surely not the stone?'

'No. That's just a goodbye present.'

'So he too thinks we are almost there. He said anything about . . .'

'No!'

She always blushed when she lied, so the Indian still thought Mark would kill her.

'He told me his people are in danger,' she said. 'He, too, and that was Paul's fault. But he still thinks Paul and you can help, and he wouldn't have given me this,' she pointed at the stone, 'unless he thought I would stay alive, at least long enough to be of some use. This is a seal of office, something his people value.'

He supposed that the Indian, if he had contact with the outside world, could know that Paul had designs on the jungle, and that, of course, would not help his people. But even if Paul changed his mind, Pandora's box had been opened. Somebody else would develop the area. How could Paul, and even less he, help now? And what did she mean by 'live long enough'?

Mark cleaned Paul and forced some liquid down him, relying on Paul's ability to swallow instinctively, but all the time he worried about Sylvia. He stole a glance at her sitting nearby, and his heart sank. She had lost so much weight she looked like a starved urchin.

He set about cooking the fish he had caught earlier. Wrapped in leaves and placed on the embers, it took only minutes to be done. When he opened the parcel the flesh was succulent, the aroma delicate, just perfect, but it didn't seem to tempt her.

'What's wrong?' he said. 'Don't you like it?'

'I am eating it, aren't I?'

'You are messing it up and pushing it about, but eating it, no.'

'I am not very hungry.'

'You said that the last time.'

'Well, I've been so lazy and without exercise, I haven't developed an appetite.'

'And that's another thing. It's unlike you to be so lethargic.' He put his food down. 'You are not getting ill on me too, are you?'

He touched her face, pulled her eyelids down, felt behind the ears, under the armpits. It tickled her, and she pushed him away giggling. 'There is nothing wrong.'

He was frowning. 'Nothing quite wrong and nothing quite right.'

'I feel fine.'

She kept her hands on his bare chest. His shirt had been donated to Paul. She slid her palms down to his waist. It drove him crazy.

'Hey,' she said. 'Has anybody told you what a beautiful man you are?'

He couldn't believe his ears. What was she up to? Or was she delirious? 'You got the wrong guy, honey! Paul is beautiful.'

'Indisputably.' She smiled, her head to one side. She was flirting with him! 'But tell me, why do you give him an inferiority complex?'

'I am a few inches taller, that's all.'

'You mean as good as, only more of it?'

'Hey!' he said, embarrassed. 'You are only trying to stop me from a thorough examination.'

'God forbid! By the way, the next set of glands are in a more interesting place.'

The only time she unquestionably gave him an invitation, and he was prevented from responding by professional ethics.

There was nothing seriously wrong. Her temperature was just a little too high, her glands slightly enlarged. There was some kind of infection, but either at the very beginning or very mild. He had no way to run any tests, to say nothing of the fact that he was no expert in tropical diseases. It could be due to any one of the myriad of bugs that flourished in a climate like this.

She was serious again. Enormous dark eyes like a bush baby. Wise and sad. He had seen such eyes before, in sick babies, pregnant mothers, terminally ill patients. No! He was not going to start that, too. He walked back to Paul and turned him on his side. He varied his position regularly to prevent sores.

'Paul is really getting better all the time,' he said, in case that was an additional source of worry to her. 'The fever is gone. It's just down to exhaustion and anaemia, now. He will be up in no time.'

'I know,' she said in a dreamy voice.

'Then what is it? No more bad premonitions, I hope.'

'I was just thinking of the word "love".'

She was slipping into dangerous waters again. 'Oh yes?'

'All my life, I never found the appropriate occasion to use it,' she said.

He avoided turning to look at her. 'You surely used it to your kids, at least,' he said evenly.

'There is a specific word for that kind of feeling in Greek,' she said. 'A different word in every case. Between friends, children to parents, parents to children and so forth.'

'But there must have been somebody, sometime. Your husband, for instance.'

'My husband is terrified of any expression of sentiment, especially love. He says "Crap" and runs away, even if it's only on television. I couldn't have used it even if I had felt it, and what I had for him was fondness, until he turned it to resentment by being so very . . . well, that's neither here nor there.' There was no resentment or sadness, now. The tone was merely reflective.

He turned to look at her. 'Nobody else?'

She just raised her shoulders to portray indifference. It was all lost somewhere in the past. 'There were men I cared for, men I was attracted to, even one I actually lusted after, for a while. I used the right word. Never love.'

Well, she had to have a past. He did. No need to get

rattled by it. Still, he hated whoever it was she had lusted after. 'Honest,' he said flatly.

'Naïve,' she corrected. 'To be so honest in sentimental matters is unwise and complicates life, but I stubbornly stuck to my principles, no matter what the cost, and for what it is worth now, I am not very proud of it!'

'What word did you think appropriate to use with Paul?' Maybe he shouldn't have mentioned that, but he couldn't help it.

'No word at all,' she said dispassionately. 'I don't know how or why it happened with him, but I didn't have to say anything. Afterwards he said he loved me, and I think at the time he might even have meant it, in the English sense of the word. Sort of all-embracing, covering any one of all sorts of sentiments. I avoided the subject for lack of the exact word. Anyway, he wouldn't have believed me.'

'Why?'

'He is fully aware of how I felt about...' she moved uncomfortably and then took a deep breath. '... you, before I even acknowledged it myself.'

Did he, now? But take it nice and easy. Don't show anything. 'And what is the appropriate word for that?' It all went according to plan, except for the distinct pronunciation of 'appropriate'.

The languorous tone disappeared to be replaced by exasperation. 'What the hell do you think I've been trying to say for the last half hour? Do you imagine it's that easy after all these years?' She stood up and for the first time in ages, she used her hands for emphasis. 'I want you to know it's important to me. It might be, for all I know, the only chance I have of ever saying it. It's not emotional blackmail. It's not an exchange. It's un-con-di-tio-nal.' Then she said quietly, her eyes even more widely opened, as if she had surprised herself, 'I love you.'

He covered the distance between them in a stride. He knew he frowned and looked threatening when emotional, but he was not prepared for her panic.'What I meant is, it doesn't matter whether you can promise anything or...' she stuttered.

His hand was over her mouth. Even to himself, he sounded fierce. 'That was *my* attempt to use a word *I* have difficulty in using.' He took a deep breath to calm himself and then let her go, in case he choked her. 'I meant I could only promise you myself, and I didn't know whether it was of any earthly use to anyone. I love you. I did from the moment I first saw you at the airport.'

Her jaw dropped. 'The airport?'

'Yes. Before you were the only woman around. Afterwards I could have gone with any number of beautiful women, but I couldn't bring myself to do it. I was obsessed with you and I thought then, that there was not a hope in hell that I would ever see you again. When I was told you might have died in the air crash, it was like the world had ended. And then, there you were in the forest and I never dared to tell you how I felt, because not knowing was better than outright rejection. And now... now, even I believe in destiny.'

She suddenly looked startled. 'Destiny?' She stared into mid-space for a while. 'Mark, what university did you go to?'

He was completely at a loss. 'Does it matter?'

'Oh yes!' she said, her face intense.

'I was never too adventurous. I stayed in California.'

'Berkeley?' and when he nodded, 'I thought as much.' She looked crushed, like she had lost something precious, but soon drew the tattered shirt around her and squared her jaw. 'Better late than never,' she said, then looked up at him and burst out laughing.

He must have looked foolish just staring like that, ignorant of what to think or how to respond .

'I am glad you can see the funny side of it,' said a croaky voice behind them.

Mark didn't know whether to be glad Paul was conscious or angry at him for eavesdropping. Sylvia had solved the dilemma already.

'Has it been minutes, hours or days?' she said, advancing threateningly towards Paul. Anger had overcome her lethargy, and Mark wondered if she had not been ill at all, just bored to death with him. Maybe she needed someone like Paul to keep her on her toes.

'I don't know,' said Paul carelessly. 'Things came and went like in a dream, but I thought that some bits were too ridiculous for that.'

Sylvia fumed. 'What is so ridiculous, precisely?'

Paul eased his emaciated frame around. His skin was yellow, his lips powdery and cracked, his beard and long hair lank, but there was nothing pitiful about him because of the two pools of blue light shining out of his face. 'Precisely,' he said, 'the idea that you don't love me.' He shifted again. Protruding bones could be very uncomfortable. 'Let's see. You care enough to nurse me back to health, you like me, you find me "beautiful" – your words not mine – you are attracted to me, and whether you are prepared to admit it or not in his presence, you have enjoyed the sex, at least most of the time.' He took a few breaths to recover his strength, after such a long speech in his condition, and added, 'Any one of these things wouldn't, of course, constitute love, but taken altogether...' he shrugged. 'What the fuck is love, if not all that?'

Sylvia stood there speechless. What could she say? What Paul was telling her was true. Painfully, devastatingly true. For a moment, Mark hated him.

'Sorry, old man.' Paul turned towards him and grinned. 'You had your chance to get rid of me and didn't take it.'

It hit the spot so accurately, Mark felt as if his momentary thought had been as good as the act and was mortified.

Sylvia found her speech. 'I refused your proposal!' As if that answered all the questions raised by Paul's statement.

But it was something Mark was not aware of: either that Paul had asked her to marry him, or that she had refused! She had told him once she wouldn't marry him, but that was to a hypothetical question, put by himself not Paul. No woman would actually refuse Paul, surely?

'That was just cowardice.' Paul dismissed it with a flick of the hand. 'You are afraid of the few years between us, and any competition out there.'

'Yes,' she said. 'I would if I ever contemplated the possibility. But I didn't. I am extremely fond of you, and so is Mark. I wouldn't want any harm to come to you, and so would Mark. And I think you are beautiful . . .'

'Don't progress to the next step honey, you will scare the hell out of him,' Paul said leering, and Mark could have throttled him.

'Shut up, Paul!' She suddenly appeared to grow in stature. 'I never felt ashamed to admire beauty in anyone, male or female, and I am not a lesbian. Neither is he a homosexual, or you, come to think of it. That's the problem, if you ask me.' What the hell did she mean by that? But there was no time for Mark to think this one out before she got on with the next bit. 'Before you go around making fun, I know,' she stressed the last word, and with her wild hair, feverish eyes, one hand clasping the oversized shirt around her body, the other extended, bony finger pointing at Paul, she looked Pythian, 'I know you made use of the attraction you inspire in both sexes to get anything you want. I don't know if you actually slept with men, or care, but you have used their desire for you to your own ends.'

'That makes me no better than a tease,' Paul said through clenched teeth, eyes just two slits letting out steely shafts of light.

'That makes you ruthless,' she pronounced.

Paul lay down exhausted. 'You are not getting rid of me that easily. Besides, don't forget the spirits of the forest and the tempest. They decreed I should be part of things. You said so. You said there was no other choice!'

She ignored all that. 'Why?' she frowned, perplexed. 'Why is it that important to you? You have so much waiting for you out there.'

'Because I love you, both of you, and being obnoxious to me doesn't help. And there is nothing of any value out there.'

It devastated Sylvia. She knelt by Paul. 'Don't say that!

You have family, friends, lovers, money, power. Is all that nothing?'

'Money! Power!' He sniggered. 'It was no guarantee against finding myself here, like this.' He stretched out his arms for them to see. 'I might as well be as poor as any refugee in Africa. Family? My parents probably gave a champagne party to celebrate my disappearance and hurried to declare me dead to get at the loot.'

'It's theirs too, isn't it?' she said, confused.

'No way! Grandmother was not inspired to trust either of them with the family fortune. I inherited everything, and they never forgave me. They have money, but it's never enough for the kind of lives they live.' His voice became that of a sick old man. 'Nanny cared. She put her formidable self between me and my mother's "degenerate young men", as she called them. So much so, she forgot about my father's mistresses. When she found out, she screamed blue murder. At least she had the comfort that it was the lesser of two evils.'

Mark felt cold. He had never suspected. Sylvia said, 'Oh my God!'

Paul dismissed that too. 'They call it child abuse now, it was simple initiation then. I might be ten years your junior, but I have at least ten years start on both of you. In sexual and emotional matters, you are both immature, hence all that drivel about love. It doesn't have to be perfect, one hundred per cent. A good approximation is enough. And by those standards, you both love me.' He closed his eyes, prepared to rest. 'You are my only family. So what are you going to do about it?'

Sylvia frowned for some time then said, just above a whisper, 'I love you both, you love us both, he loves us both. All chiefs with no little Indian in sight. What a pity.'

Mark felt dizzy with the word "love" tossed about all over the place, and he didn't even want to start thinking of what she meant by chiefs and Indians.

40

Paul pretended sleep not to witness their agony. Sylvia was right to call him ruthless. He just proved it. He knew what his words would do, but all was fair in love etc. Wasn't it? Only she forgot to say coward, too. He retreated and left them in the shit.

All this time at death's door, he sensed so much. She thought she had refused marriage. But she was already married to him. There was no doubt in his mind. Something told him. The same something that made him follow her that day in the storm, that directed his steps towards her. And she knew he would go. She expected him.

They might laugh at him for mentioning the spirits of the forest, but not everything could be analysed and rationalised. He lived a primitive enough life now to feel these forces, unprotected and uninsulated as he was from the modern world. One could not live so close to nature and not appreciate its mystical compulsions. One obeyed or perished. And if the elemental gods of the jungle had willed their union, wouldn't ignoring it be a hubris? She should understand that.

His life had changed from that day in the storm. The old Paul had died. The values he had lived by did not hold true any more. He learned to rely only on himself and his two companions. Not money, position, prestige or property. Maybe the jungle had been good to him.

He started drifting off. *All chiefs with no little Indian in sight.* He would work it out, some other time.

*

He woke to terrified cries and Mark's disembodied voice, repeating over and over, soothingly, 'It's OK now, it was just a dream. I'm here.'

It had happened too many times recently, and once his heartbeat got back to normal, Paul was going back to sleep when he realised it had nothing to do with him. He was not delirious. But he could see nothing. All was black, not even a glow of embers from the fire. It must have been very late at night. 'What's going on?' he called into the darkness.

'Nothing. Go back to sleep. Sylvia had a nightmare.' Mark's voice.

Paul was scared. 'She is not ill?'

'No. Just a bad dream. There are a lot lately.'

'Why?'

'Falling out of an aircraft is very traumatic, especially for an acrophobic. She suppressed it until now, but these things have a way of surfacing sooner or later.'

'They have to be triggered off by something.'

'She has seen the cliffs down the river. She knows we have to climb them. It worries her. And then that story of the child being hit by a car, she told us about the other day gets mixed up in it somehow.'

'Did I have nightmares recently, too?'

'Lots.'

'Poor Mark!'

When Paul opened his eyes again, it was a fresh day. Misty, clammy. He could smell the vegetation in the river nearby, the wood fire Mark was tending and heard the constant rush of water in the distance.

'Acquired immunity,' Mark was saying.

'The potion contained quinine.' Sylvia's voice.

'Keep the bark for the next time,' Mark, jokingly. 'If he responds again, we will have positive proof.'

'I hope there is no next time,' said Paul, sitting up. He felt weak, but most of all annoyed at the delay his illness had caused. He was determined to make it up, but his legs wobbled when he tried to stand.

Mark steadied him. 'Your first day on your feet, we have to take it easy.'

'Fuck that.'

Paul forced himself to walk, but all the time worried about what decision Mark and Sylvia might have come to. What would become of them? He could not contemplate the possibility of Sylvia going back to her family in England or, worse still, setting off into the sunset with Mark, a more probable outcome.

Nobody had referred to yesterday's discussion. He wasn't even sure it took place. It might have been a delirium, like so many he had and, being the most recent, he remembered it.

The falls were awesome, but the black ribbon in the distance that made Sylvia shiver, held no terrors for Paul. It was a link to salvation. He thought of boats chugging back and forth, ferrying tourists to view the falls from a safe distance, settlements all along the banks, even a camp for his own people, busy studying the area.

'There couldn't be two such waterfalls in the same part of the jungle,' he said, 'We made it back to where I had wanted to be all along. My own property.' Then addressing Sylvia in particular, 'It doesn't feel quite right, I know. Not any more. But I'll think about it later.'

They moved away from the falls to a relatively quiet spot where they could hear themselves talk. Paul was delirious with excitement. He took Sylvia in his arms. 'We made it!'

'I hate to burst your bubble, but have you seen the drop?' she said despondently. 'It would take a mountaineer to negotiate it. I crawled on all fours to go up an incline of forty-five degrees.'

Mark was subdued too. 'We will think about that tomorrow. Let's have a rest.'

'We can't be this close and sit around having rests,' Paul argued.

'Neither you nor Sylvia are strong enough for the task. Not yet,' said Mark severely. 'I am going to inspect the site for the easiest route. You stay put.'

Poor Mark. He had two semi-invalids to worry about.

'I don't suppose you would like . . .' Paul began, when Mark was gone.

'No,' Sylvia interrupted. 'You are ill and you want to climb down that cliff tomorrow.'

She was right, of course. 'Oh, well. Tell me about yourself then.'

'You know everything. We lived together long enough.'

'Under the shadow of death. What are you like in normal circumstances. What would the man in your life give you, for instance, to make you happy?'

'A bunch of deep red carnations with a strong smell of cloves. Original Spanish, I believe they are. I don't like overcultivated varieties without perfume. They are soulless.'

'Suppose he wanted to buy you a perfume.'

'Rive Gauche. There is a hint of masculinity about it. More prestigious and expensive ones are usually too feminine. Too cloying.'

'And if he wanted to be extravagant and buy you jewels?'

She laughed. 'Nobody I know ever felt like that.'

He touched the stone hanging from her neck. 'You wear the Indian's present and used to have a ring. Where is it, by the way?'

'I lost it.' She looked at her fingers. No ring would have stayed on them, they were so stick-like. 'But it was only a wedding ring, I don't usually wear jewellery, and this,' she touched the rough emerald, 'hardly qualifies. But once,' she smiled as if caught doing something naughty, 'I saw something I really liked. A work of art. I forget the name of the designer. A gold bangle, matt, the texture of satin, and wouldn't you believe it? It was in the shape of a leaping puma with two little diamonds for eyes. I must have always liked pumas.' She smiled at him and he rolled his eyes. 'I couldn't have worn it,' she added with regret. 'It was too chunky. It wouldn't be me. But it would have given me great pleasure to look at every so often. I asked the salesman to take Polaroid pictures and left them about the house as a heavy hint for my wedding anniversary, but I still got the microwave oven he thought I really needed.'

Paul groaned. 'He is not one of those husbands!'

'I am afraid so.'

'You would wear diamonds, though? All women I know like diamonds.'

'Not clusters or great big enormous multi-faceted solitaires. Just a medium-size one, in an emerald cut. Or pearls. Definitely pearls. Drop earrings or a pendant. Not strings.'

'I don't need to ask about a dress. It would be satin, dropping in heavy folds, sensuous.'

'You are taking the piss,' she said, pushing him playfully.

'Not at all. Doing research. Where would you like to dine, as a treat?'

'It has to be French. I like all nationalities of food, but only the French take it seriously enough. There is a little place near the Pompidou Centre. Very insignificant from the outside. Just five tables inside. You have to know the right people to get to hear about it. But the customers at each table feel they are the only people there and at least royalty, the service is so impeccable. And the food! Divine.'

'Let's go home. What kind of car?'

'Chauffeur-driven but not flashy.'

'And the home is . . .'

'Spacious, big windows letting in plenty of light. Simply furnished. Some Chinese furniture.'

He was startled. 'Why Chinese?'

'Gleaming mahogany, meticulously carved, and the chairs are small enough for my legs to reach the ground.'

'You never hesitated once.'

'I know what I like, but I'm no sybarite. I've been without anything for so long. I am a woman, after all. I fantasise about such things. I don't actually possess satins and diamonds, or even pearls. I never had the money. People always managed to relieve me of it, especially my husband.' Then she seemed to regret saying that and tried to find excuses. 'He feels insecure, he is careful with money, probably because he never found out how much constitutes security.'

He wouldn't put it past her to go back to him. Duty and all that. But he couldn't help testing the ground. 'Some time soon, we will be able to do all these things.'

'If there is a tomorrow, we might talk of it again,' she said soberly.

He wanted to return to the earlier lightheartedness, so he continued what she had thought was a game. 'So not a sybarite.'

'I don't like being too conspicuous, with or without luxury.'

He nearly choked trying to control his laughter. 'Oh yeah!'

'Even the Indians recognised that. You are a sleek puma, he is a proud eagle, and I a bloody mouse,' she said resentfully.

'A pretty little rabbit actually, too quick to catch, but when you do, ever so delicious!'

'How the hell do you know?'

'Mark and I caught one, but he explained all about animal equivalents and things and we thought it a bit er . . . indelicate to tell you.'

'But you ate it all the same. That says a lot,' she said, tossing her hair.

'About being insignificant and inconspicuous. Tell me, do you sit unnoticed at parties, for instance?'

'Something like that. In deepest Cheshire where I live, they have this ritual where the women gather in one corner talking about babies and diets, and the men in another, impressing each other about their cars and jobs. I sit apart and observe them. It's fun.'

'But it doesn't stay that way, right?'

'Well, somebody feels sorry and comes to condescend all over me. You know the sort of thing. It sounds like a compliment, but it puts you in your place. He compliments your colouring, your accent . . .'

'But then he makes a pass at you.'

'Then things get interesting because we get into an argument and other people get involved and . . .'

'And *then* he makes a pass at you.'

She sat up straight, fully alert, eyes sparkling. 'Don't think that I have never questioned it. Do I do it to impress? Do I want to appear clever? No! I can't resist it because . . . because it's the most enjoyable thing in life.' She waved her arm about. 'More than jewels and clothes and things.'

'An epicurean rather than a sybarite then.'

She chuckled. 'Not quite. Yes, I wouldn't mind a bit of luxury and a good argument now and then, but I don't think that's all there should be to life. Too selfish. One might be content for a while, but then . . .' she trailed off.

Paul never thought that material possessions, which he could certainly provide, could be enough. 'So, security and happiness isn't the answer.'

'Happiness . . .' she said and left it to hang there for a while, thinking. Then, '. . . is the peak that follows the trough of unhappiness. On a plateau, it would disappear.'

'You want a dose of unhappiness at regular intervals?' he said.

'I am not looking for happiness. It's something one feels now and then, like unhappiness. Life is full of both.'

'What is it you want out of life, then?'

'To justify my existence. Biologically speaking, of course, we are here just to reproduce, but any animal can do that. By those terms the most successful creature is the virus. A duplicating machine. A human should be able to contribute something more. Make a difference.'

'Not all that inconspicuous, then. You make a difference, you stand out.'

'Ah!' she said. 'Now you have me. Would I be doing it for the betterment of society or my personal glory? That is, if I had the necessary talent to do anything.' And before he could respond, 'Any luck?' she asked the returning Mark.

'Difficult but do-able,' said Mark.

41

Sylvia messed about with the pot making a herbal tea, but her mind was elsewhere. 'I had a beautiful idea,' she said. 'Why don't you two go ahead . . .'

'No!' They didn't let her finish, as if they both had expected it.

'But you could bring help,' she tried again.

'No!' From both again.

'I couldn't possibly downsail those bloody rocks,' she said, almost in tears. 'I couldn't.'

'We will use ropes,' said Mark.

'I still have to climb. And anyway, I can live in the jungle on my own. I did before you came.'

Mark was getting impatient. 'You were stronger, then, and healthier.'

'The Indian would help,' she insisted.

'Not if he believes you will die, anyway. He keeps filling your head with morbid ideas,' said Mark.

She tried to reason with him. 'The only way to make sense of all the different things he says is to look at them as possibilities, not certainties. He is telling us there is danger.'

'There is no way you are staying here alone.' Mark was adamant. 'How do we know how long it would take? And Indians have been known to abduct white people. How would we ever find you?'

She turned to Paul, who was reclining by the fire, for help. 'No,' he said.

She stamped her foot. 'I am not a coward.'

'Nobody said you were,' said Mark. 'It isn't brave of us. We are not afraid of heights, that's all.'

She kept on, as if he hadn't spoken. 'I don't give a shit about death. It's not that.'

Mark changed his tactics and came up to her. He pushed the damp hair away from her face. 'It's illogical, I know, but that's what phobias are, and I know you will do it.'

'I might kill all of us, if I panic. Have you thought of that?' she said.

'Let's put it this way,' said Paul, sitting up, 'we'd rather die than leave you behind. All right?'

'Oh, go to sleep,' she said, annoyed.

'I can't. I am too excited,' Paul said.

'Have this. It will make you sleep.' She gave him the drink she had been making.

Paul accepted it but refrained from drinking. 'Aren't you having any?'

'I'll have to, or I'll spend the night screaming. Mark needs some sleep too, for a change, and between us, we haven't let him have a peaceful night for ages.'

'I don't mind,' said Mark and took the drink from her.

It was too late for Paul. He had drunk his the moment she had said she would.

'You will discuss matters behind my back, to say nothing about finding better ways to get a good night's sleep,' he said jokingly, but he did not sound too convincing.

Sylvia was too depressed to even bother to refute it. Before Mark had time to boost the fire, she curled herself into a ball and pretended to sleep.

A few days ago she had cried out of relief for Paul being alive, she cried for her children whom she would never see again, she cried for the Indian and his people. Afterwards, with Paul making such slow recovery, she had plenty of time to think of the Indian's warning. How would it be, dying? Would there be suffering? Death, as such, was acceptable if it came suddenly, swiftly. Just oblivion. But to sit around waiting for it, to look death in the face, the idea of pain . . . It would take such courage. Did she have it? She needed something overpowering to obliterate these fears, even if it meant sacrificing her pride, and that had given her the courage to talk to Mark yesterday. She didn't want to die without ever having sex with the only man she ever loved. It hadn't worked.

Now she felt like crying for herself. For the lost opportunity, the lost years she could have had with Mark, tears of bitterness that she couldn't alleviate with thoughts of revenge. Even that was denied her. Suddenly, she was not prepared to sit around and wait to die. She was not going to lose him again. He was everything to her. Not because of the heroic scale of his build, or the magnificence of his presence, but because he was already part of her. He had always been part of her. As long as he was there, she was safe. That's what the dream meant. If she let him drop her, she would die. But she wouldn't let it happen. She would hold on to him. She turned so she could snuggle up to him.

'OK?' he said.

So he was awake too. That was her last opportunity. 'I just found out what I couldn't and wouldn't let go of. You remember? We talked about it the other day,' she said.

'Yes?'

Well, she couldn't keep something, unless she had it first. So what the heck! Might as well, they were almost invisible to each other in the dark. Still, it took a lot of courage. 'You,' she said. 'I wouldn't let *you* go.'

The silence that followed stretched and stretched. He had said he loved her, but he had also shown that he was afraid of total commitment. What if he got scared at her intensity? She was sure she sounded intense but, unable to see his expression, she could make his silence into whatever she wanted to.

She felt Mark bent over her, waiting. He was giving her time to withdraw, if she so wished. He wasn't to know there was no turning back. For either of them. Then his lips just brushed hers, almost reverentially. He sighed something, she thought he said 'Please', and she put her arms around his neck, her own Big Friendly Giant.

She was not prepared for the speed with which things progressed from then on. He simply erupted. He was everywhere simultaneously, fire spread from his touch, and in no time she was engulfed in acres of rippling flesh, struggling for breath, for control, for something. And then it was over. He rolled off her quickly, lay there panting, mumbling something vaguely sounding like 'Sorry' and went into a state of catatonia.

It flattered her, to start with, that a person with his restraint should want her sufficiently to get so carried away. If it was not for the fact that she nearly suffocated, he would have carried her along with him. Of course, he had been without a woman for a long time but still ... Paul, bless him, had been in the same boat, but then Paul was basic, uninhibited and sensual, like a baby, with the same total abandonment to pleasure. He even had that habit of making a noise at the back of his throat like gurgling, that she found so exciting. It seemed almost a perversion to refuse him, like withholding food from an infant. But he wasn't selfish. He didn't just take his pleasure and leave her. On the contrary, he was all for sharing.

Maybe she had been wrong about Mark. Fireworks there might have been, a volcanic eruption, to be exact, but it was still humiliating, the anticlimax even worse. She had desired him because he seemed out of reach. With a man that inspired some respect, she thought she would be more submissive. But she didn't like that role one little bit.

The shaman was right to call her his son. There was something about her not sufficiently feminine. Since she was a young girl, boys had sensed that but didn't quite know what. They just said she was different. They talked of things in front of her they never said in front of other girls, and everyone that fell in love with her later was a lame duck. Emotionally insecure, suicidal, sexually disoriented. What did that make her?

She had never desired women sexually, either, so she did not have the excuse of being a lesbian. She never related well to women, though. Most feminine preoccupations exasperated her. Women, understandably, resented her. They felt beatific about being pregnant. She called it brainwashing. It was nothing but a gross invasion of one's body. Birth was a necessary evil, the price of having your own children, not the magical experience they talked about.

She loved her children fiercely once she had had them, but didn't share the experience with anyone else. She never went gaga over other people's babies. All children, including her own, were selfish, savage monsters one had to gently guide towards some semblance of civilisation and hope that, through education and experience, they would learn the secret of peaceful coexistence and what, one day, would separate them from animals: creativity.

And she couldn't understand why, now that technology freed women from the sink, they had to invent new tyrannies, like torturing and starving themselves to attain some absurd ideal of slimness that had nothing to do with health, the usual excuse. After all, the longest-living humans were 'plump' women – 'plump' of course, in reference to today's fashion, weight erroneously set too low to what nature intended.

She found it easier to talk to men. They made better friends, as far as she was concerned, shared more of her interests. Intellectually, they were more objective. First and foremost, she was a person. Hormones had only to do with sex and procreation, and she would never allow them to dictate every aspect of behaviour or thought.

Maybe there was nothing wrong with her. Just the way she was guided into adulthood. Not as gently as she had tried to do with her own kids.

Her mother was no monster. Just uneducated, very beautiful and trapped in an unhappy marriage. She had nothing in common with her husband. She looked to her children for salvation, especially her first-born, a son.

'So he is the only one to get pocket money,' her mother would say. 'He is the eldest and he will repay it handsomely when he grows up. A successful businessman like his uncle. He'll rescue us all. Wait and see.'

He never did, but she wasn't to know that.

'I hoped for a beautiful daughter,' her mother also said, the corners of her mouth turning down as they always did when she assumed her martyr look. 'And if not a blonde, at least she shouldn't have crossed eyes and a birthmark on the lip.' She sighed. 'It's not much to ask.'

Sylvia didn't think she looked all that bad now, and to most mothers she wouldn't have been such a terrible shock. Both defects were easily remedied. As it happened, when Sylvia grew up the lip mark disappeared almost completely, and her eye defect only showed if she looked over her shoulder. Of course, she never did now. As a child, she got a slap every time she turned her head.

'Look straight! Do you have to remind me all the time you are a reject?'

About her worst defect, Sylvia only learned a few years back when her mother, contrite of her behaviour towards her daughter, tried to explain the reasons.

'The other children cried,' her mother said. 'Your eldest brother nearly drove me round the bend with his tantrums. You were so independent from the start.' Mother always used the word 'independent' as if mentioning a terrible sin, her face assuming the expression of somebody eating lemons. 'You ate when I had time to feed you. At a few months old, you learned to help yourself to a bottle or any food within reach. I don't remember singing a lullaby to you. You made little noises to yourself. It gave me more time to see to the needs of the other children, but that meant we never bonded. And then you died . . . Well, what was one to think? Afterwards you spent so much time at grandma's. We got used to you not being there. All of us.'

'Why did you send me to grandma's?' Sylvia asked.

'When your father made money he spent it all at once on luxuries. Mostly, he made nothing. What do you expect from an artist?' That, too, it seemed, was a sin. 'It was hard to pay the rent and keep a growing family clothed and fed.

Grandma offered to take you off my hands to ease the burden.'

Sylvia's inability to cooperate with people started then.

'Don't you dare speak to the village children,' grandma would say. 'I don't want you learning to talk like a peasant. What would your parents think?'

But Sylvia was never lonely. Grandma filled her head with Greek mythology. It became her whole world. The clouds, the stones, the trees, the well in the yard, were full of gods and monsters so real she could even talk to them, but soon learned to keep it a secret. Grandma understood, but her two unmarried daughters didn't. Sylvia called them Scylla and Charybdis. If she escaped punishment from one, the other got her. They believed in discipline for its own sake. Most of the time Sylvia didn't know what she was being punished for. Now they boasted that whatever she had achieved in her life was due to their strict upbringing.

The only contact she had with other children was when they asked for help. It was surprising how much more one learned by having to explain it to others. She remembered how she had run all the way home with her first school report. Even her aunts would be impressed. 'I got ARISTA in everything,' she boasted.

The blows came from right and left. She had to put her hands over her head to protect it, and grandma tried to hide her under her pinny.

'She hasn't done anything wrong,' grandma said.

'Pride,' the aunts said. 'If she puffs herself up like that at the first little success, will she be able to get a good mark next year?'

That kind of training didn't help in Sylvia's future career. Never mind how good a scientist one may be, one can't get very far if nobody knows about it. And she knew she was good. They had not managed to teach her humility.

At the age of eight she became ill. They shipped her off to her mother.

'Everyone will blame us, if anything happened,' said Scylla.

'After all we've done for her,' said Charybdis.

Her mother was annoyed. 'I have enough trouble with a new baby.'

For the rest of the kids it was tough, without extra competition. And that was something Sylvia knew nothing about. She did not know how to fight over who was to have new shoes or clothes or who was to get first at the food, when there was any, and that meant going without, making do, inventing. What she was doing now in the jungle.

At the new school, she thought all she needed to do was smile and the other kids would like her. They thought her an imbecile.

'Is your sister a bit backward?' they would ask her eldest brother.

'She's just come from a village. She doesn't know anything.'

'Oh, poor little thing!'

Sylvia sat at the back of the class and hoped nobody would notice her, and nobody did until the first exam. Then the teacher called her.

'Are you a foreigner?' she said.

'No.'

'Strange name. Where did you go to school?'

'Zeno's birthplace,' Sylvia said.

The teacher smiled. 'And do you know who he was?'

'A Stoic philosopher. He believed we have to submit to divine reason.'

'You learned that in Kitium village school?'

'No, but they taught me to read.'

The teacher seemed impressed and made Sylvia sit in the front of the class, where they could have a chat when the other kids were busy taking notes.

From then on everyone called the teacher Sylvia's Aunt. Sometimes she would leave the class and ask Sylvia to take over. 'Any problems, ask Sylvia.'

The other children liked her, not as a friend but as a go-between the staff and pupils.

Because life at school was so good compared to that at

home, she used to walk back very slowly, to delay the unpleasantness, and that was when this protective instinct she inspired in strangers caused so much trouble. If it was a bit too hot, which was often in Cyprus, or if it rained, a rare delight, housewives would run out and take her in and protect her from sunstroke or pneumonia or whatever their fertile imagination conjured up, and called her mother to come and collect her.

'Attention-seeking,' mother said, giving her a slap when they got home.

Things hadn't changed that much. Last year she visited Cyprus and thought of doing a spot of window shopping. Nothing doing. A shopkeeper came out. 'Sit down and have a drink while I get a taxi. It's so tiring walking in this heat.'

It was her husband this time who got impatient. 'Can't you do anything alone?'

Life was so comical. Sylvia was never more alone than when with him.

Punishments stopped abruptly at thirteen. Her mother said they could not afford school fees for all the children. Sylvia found jobs for every bit of spare time and earned money to sent herself to a classical school, and since she was old enough to work, she made it quite clear that nobody had a right to raise a hand at her. She enforced the ban with such viciousness nobody tried it again after the first time. They called her bitch and witch and a cactus fruit, but from a safe distance.

If she felt a certain bitterness now, it was not that she had to work from such a young age, but why. The last year at school, she thought she was old enough to pay her own fees rather than hand the money to her mother.

'What fees?' the secretary said. 'You had a scholarship since year one.'

Her mother's excuse was, 'We needed the money for your brother. He would feel inferior to his friends, otherwise. I don't want him growing up as unsociable as you.'

'But there never was time for friends. I had to work,' said Sylvia.

'What about Sundays?'

'People don't wear uniforms on Sundays, and I have no other clothes.'

'You would have, if you had let me apprentice you to a dressmaker. She was willing to take you without a fee, but no, you wanted education. What good is it for a woman, do you think? In your case, though, one never knows. With your attitude, you will never get a husband.'

'I don't want a husband.'

'No, you are afraid it might help the rest of the family. Where were you when your uncle sent his friend around? Rich as Croesus, willing to take you without dowry, and you aren't exactly a beauty.'

'I am not for sale to rich old men.'

'That's what you need. A mature man that can manage a weirdo like you. Teach you respect. Now is too late. Everyone says, "If she is so headstrong at sixteen, what will she be like at twenty?" Do you think anyone would want you in their family?'

'I am going to leave this place.'

'As long as you don't expect me to send you money, good riddance. But don't think I'll have you back when you end up with a bastard. Because that's what will happen if you go alone, with no money.'

She was robbed of any credit for intelligence, too. Her school friends thought anyone could be good at school if they had no life, like her, spending every second doing homework. Because, of course, she never admitted to going out to work. As for doing homework, it was a joke. Her mother forbade it. 'It's only an excuse for shirking housework. And you do enjoy putting your brothers to shame.'

Her brothers were not bad at school, just not exceptional, like it said on Sylvia's reports.

Then fate's attempt to bring her in contact with Mark was frustrated. Maybe she never fell in love so that the mistake could be corrected in the future. If things were still not working out, it must be her fault.

She was not the submissive type, fine, but had she been, she wouldn't have survived this far. So she had to meet the challenge in her true colours, not as a woman someone was supposed to conquer.

42

Mark pushed his fingers through his hair impatiently. What was happening to him? Was he going crazy? He had never loved anyone as much as he loved her, and it was normal that he should want her. What was not normal, what he felt so guilty about, what he could not accept, was what had occurred when he was making love to her. He shuddered at the recollection of the conflicting feelings. The physically tormenting pleasure, the soul-destroying triumph.

Normally, she seemed so self-assured, self-sufficient, her mind as sharp as a dissecting knife and as destructive. She towered over them. She dominated them. She could be intimidating even. One imbued her with supernatural powers, forgot her size. But there, under his body, she felt so small, frail, vulnerable.

The pit of his stomach sank. That softness! That unexpected yieldingness! He put his arm over his eyes and groaned as a surge of desire racked his body and again he felt the helplessness of the tiny body struggling underneath him. It had unleashed such lust, nothing at that moment had mattered but the gratification of it at any cost. The contrast of his physical superiority and her vulnerability drove him mad. This primitive assertion of power fuelled a perverse hedonism that rendered him capable of crushing her, to appease the overwhelming demands of a primeval beast inside him that reared its ugly head. How could he face her again? How could he tell her how he felt, what she meant to him, after that performance? That could never, should never be forgiven.

'It couldn't be as bad as all that!' she said.

Mark felt queasy. He was just a clumsy oaf. 'I didn't mean to hurt you.' Maybe he meant to hurt her. After all, one didn't hurt people one didn't care about, though he was not sure of anything any more.

She looked away, embarrassed. 'I got a bit out of breath and the stones dug in my back, but I wasn't hurt.'

Mark smiled bitterly. He would rather she complained. He would have preferred it if she were angry or even abusive. He needed to be punished. Sitting there, small and fragile, she only helped to intensify his guilt. Probably she was too disgusted for anger. He certainly was disgusted with himself. 'You were right to be afraid of me after all,' he said.

'Damn right,' she said, suddenly losing her temper. 'I have always steered clear of total commitment. I built up an image of the person I would give it to, so impossible that there was no chance of ever meeting him, and then you came along and spoilt everything. It was enough to scare anyone off.'

He sat up. What was she saying? Christ! Not after what had happened. But, of course, she had no idea what had been going through his mind when they made love. It was not so much what he did but what he thought, how he felt. 'What you have recognised might be a small part of me,' he said. 'There might be others you know nothing about that might shock you.'

She laughed. 'I hope there are other aspects of you. You would be impossible, otherwise. Thoroughly boring. Besides, I got to know another you just now.'

He winced. 'You mean the savage beast?'

'You've been without a woman for some time.'

'No!' he interrupted. 'What happened was not because you were a representative of your sex but because of you.'

She looked at him closely. 'Are you depressed because you thought you hurt me?'

'What other reason would I have?'

'I thought I disappointed you.'

'Oh my God!' He drew her into his arms. 'I'm so stupid!' But he held her gently, to reassure her that he was not always clumsy.

'I am not made of china,' she said, 'nor do I relish the role of victim.'

Mark laughed and held her closer. Forget sex. He should make her feel secure. Then she wouldn't have all these nightmares. They were unsettling him too. He could carry her down those cliffs in his arms if he had to, she didn't weigh much. He would do everything to avoid any accidents. Maybe he shouldn't carry her. After all, so many things she had predicted happened. He would trust her to Paul. She had never said anything about Paul dropping her.

He rubbed her back and bare arms, and he could tell she liked it. She was almost purring. Perhaps they could make love again. Gently. He could control it this time. But that would be asking too much. He just kissed her hair. She turned and offered her lips. He couldn't resist that. It was a warm, deep, kiss and stirred up things too much. He had to let go, but she wouldn't.

'You are a passionate man, Mark, who spends all his energies trying to tame himself,' she whispered. 'Why do the Indians think you are a proud bird? You are meant to fly, not be put in a self-made cage.'

She didn't know what she could unleash with talk like that. 'What would we be if we didn't at least try to put a check to anything? Savages?'

'Wrong question. It's what we wouldn't be. We wouldn't be neurotic. We wouldn't be frustrated. It's the suppression that causes problems. Twists things.'

'I'm twisted?'

'You shore emotions up until the dam bursts. And I cause problems too, with all sorts of inappropriate sensibilities. Not any more. Tonight of all nights, you are allowed to treat me neither as something fragile nor as prey. Tonight we both fly.'

*

She was lying quiet in his arms. From her breathing he could tell she was awake. Exhausted, like him, but not enough to sleep.

He felt wonderful. Nothing like the last time. No triumph or conquest. No guilt. Only the glory of sharing something precious. 'Tonight of all nights'. Was it a form of farewell? He had talked of destiny the other day, and he believed it. Would it all be for a couple of embraces, a night of passion, and that's that? As it was, he regretted all those arid years without her. He didn't want one more day of that. Never again. 'We were meant to be together,' he whispered in her ear. 'Nothing will come between us now. I won't let it.'

'We were,' she said 'and something has already come between us. The waste, Mark! The waste of all these years!'

So much like what he had felt, but what had come between them? Paul? 'I don't understand.'

She spoke quietly. 'The last year in school I was offered a scholarship. It was for Berkeley. Same time as you must have been there. At the last moment, my headmaster changed his mind. I was a woman. Medicine takes a long time. I could meet somebody, get married and never return. A boy got it because he would come back,' she gave a little laugh. 'He never did, of course. He is still there, with a quiverful of Californian kids. I was angry at the time. Now I am bitter.'

'I could kill the bastard,' said Mark.

'He is dead, and he had sent an apology, years later, at a school reunion, just before he died. At the time, I forgave him. I had made it on my own. I was proud of that. I gained so much more through hardship and all that crap. Now, I am not that charitable.'

Mark drew her closer. 'But no matter what, here we are. Do you think it will all have been for so little? We will make it, my love. We will!'

'Will you file for a divorce when we get out?' Paul asked Sylvia while they were getting ready for the climb.

'Is this the moment?' asked Mark.

'Later we will be busy and then, with any luck, out of the jungle,' said Paul.

She remained speechless for a long time, busy cooking something. She insisted they should eat first. Anything for a delay. 'We are not out yet,' she said eventually.

'As good as,' Paul insisted and then added, 'which one of us are you going to marry when you do?' She looked at him sharply, but he still ploughed on. 'Somebody has to say it, and one could never rely on Mark. He would prevaricate for ever.'

'I went through aversion therapy,' she said. 'I am not meant for marriage, anyway.'

Mark was double-checking the ropes and though he knew Paul's timing was up the creek and had said so, he still couldn't help making a comment. 'I wouldn't say that. In a way you have been married to us, these last few months.'

Sylvia looked at Mark, surprised. She let it sink in for a while then said, 'And you find me easy to live with?' The tone was definitely sardonic.

'Why should you be easy? Are we easy? said Mark.

'Speak for yourself. I am very easy,' said Paul.

Sylvia smiled indulgently at Paul, but it was to Mark she answered. 'Do you feel as if you are married to me?' She held his eyes.

Mark looked back as steadily. 'More so than if we signed a contract in front of witnesses,' he said with conviction.

'Bigamy?' said Sylvia, dishing out a stew of fish and sweet potatoes.

Mark put down the ropes and started eating, not that he had any appetite. He wanted to get the climbing over with first, but maybe she was right. They needed some sustenance. It would be a lot of hard work.

'To start with,' he said, swallowing, 'it worried me, as you very well know.' He ignored Paul's guffaw. 'I thought a lot since then.' He put his plate down to concentrate on the subject. 'In any ordinary marriage people share their spouses. They share them with,' he ticked off, 'relatives, friends, careers, hobbies, children and society at large. The relationship is diluted. Here the three of us share everything together. We are together all day, every day. We've got to know each other as much as it is possible to know other people without social commitments or other preoccupations. Our relationship is total.' He moved a hand horizontally, palm facing down, to show how total. 'Impossible out there. We have almost become one. Each thinks of the others. How many modern marriages have that? How much closer could people get? They say if one shares a hardship with somebody, it makes them life-long friends. We three have shared dangers, hardships, faced death, day after day. We have forged an indissoluble bond, stronger than any marriage.'

'Trust you to turn the subject into an abstraction,' said Paul. 'You are not talking of marriage as I understand it, otherwise it would be a three-way sexual affair, and don't tell me you can handle that?'

'Look,' said Mark, aware he was frowning again, but he had Paul's attention. 'We will think of that when the time comes.'

'And nobody mentioned yet,' Sylvia said, 'anything about other commitments and families on different continents.' That was, of course, meant only for Mark. Paul had no commitments anywhere, and she knew it.

43

The descent began gently enough. Paul jumped down the first ledge and Mark handed Sylvia down to him. She complained she was trussed like a chicken, and Mark burst out laughing. Like everything he rarely did, when he bothered, he executed it rather well and to the full, the same with his laughter enough to gladden anyone's heart. But Paul wasn't in the mood to let his heart be gladdened. Now he realised why, all the time he had known Mark, he had been afraid of competing with him. The only time that mattered, Mark would sweep him aside, as he had done when he highjacked the argument earlier on.

Paul had never heard him speak at such length and with so much conviction before. It was a miracle or, like Mark had said, they had spent too long in each other's company. What was he, Paul, doing, for instance, analysing Mark's laughter at a time like this, when they were about to attempt the most perilous act yet and he had been appointed responsible for somebody else's life, as well as his own?

Things became more difficult by the minute. Bare rocks were piled everywhere. Knurled roots clawed at them in a desperate attempt to retain a foothold, ignoring lack of soil or excess moisture. The spray made everything slippery. Paul saw snakes everywhere. Some turned out to be roots, some not. He had thought he knew all about the viciousness of insects, by now. All that had been just a tease, compared to the swarms of flies infesting this place. They left droplets of blood on his skin that burned and itched. There was nothing he could do to relieve the pain. He needed both hands to cling to any roughness on the rocks he could find. And he could not communicate with the others any more, for the noise of tumbling water.

There was one good thing in all this misery: Sylvia had too many distractions to worry about heights. Even she would agree, now, that this place could suddenly turn into a green hell.

Once they had left the piled rocks behind to tackle the cliff side itself, things became even more hairy. He dropped onto a narrow ledge and tried to guide Sylvia's feet from one precarious foothold to an almost nonexistent one, so that she could land next to him. Mark above them was letting down more rope. He threw down the ropes attached to Paul and Sylvia, when she was safely on the ledge, and only then did he follow.

Waiting for Mark to reach them, Paul shouted encouragement in Sylvia's ear. He put his ear next to her mouth to hear what she was saying.

'My arms are coming off,' she said, but so dispassionately it might have been happening to somebody else. It was happening to him, anyway. Mark was motioning him to make his way to the next ledge down. He found the strength to try and, once more or less safe, helped Sylvia.

This was repeated, for how long Paul couldn't say, except that every attempt seemed to be the last he could manage, and yet he kept going until he just couldn't move any more. As for Sylvia, she was being literally winched by rope from ledge to ledge in the end, rather than climbing. She had no grip or strength left to hang onto anything. Paul perched on yet another ledge and held her until Mark arrived.

Mark's was the hardest job, constantly bearing all their weight. He should have been too tired, but didn't show it. Only relief.

'We've almost made it,' Mark screamed at them. 'A bit of rest and one last push.'

They were half-devoured by insects, soaked in the spray, hungry and exhausted, but they stared at the trees below them, almost within reach now, noting the fascinating variation of green, the flamboyant brilliance of the flowers, picked at by the light, drops of water on them turning to diamonds, rubies, sapphires. Hope was rekindled, new strength was found where they had thought none remained.

Mark checked the rope round Sylvia's waist and along its length to see if any bit was getting frayed from rubbing against rocks. Then he secured Paul's rope around both a tree stump and himself and Paul began the process again, the rope fed to him slowly and steadily. And so on. They were creeping down, inch by painful inch, until the light began to fade. Only sombre green remained, turning ever gloomier by the minute.

Paul saw the churning waters below him darken. The black river further down disappeared in a sepulchral tunnel. Their means of escape, their hope of reaching the outside world, didn't appear either promising or inspiring any more. What mattered now was to find a dry spot and light a fire, but even that prospect seemed a long way away.

Mark had thrown the ropes down and was slowly descending towards them. Paul couldn't wait for him before the next manoeuvre. He could lower Sylvia on the next ledge by himself. It was only a few feet below. After that, there was just one long drop to the riverside. Saving a few minutes would make the difference between negotiating the last hurdle in the light of the setting sun or darkness. That would be too dangerous, if not fatal.

Sylvia couldn't care less what he did. There were two hectic spots colouring her otherwise grey face. Her eyes were lifeless. She looked about to pass out, and that added urgency to Paul's decision to get it all over with as soon as possible.

He lowered her carefully, his hands around her wrists. She was too stupefied by tiredness to protest, even when suspended above the precipice. But he had to make her look for the ledge, to make sure she landed safely. He kept telling her to. 'Look where you put your feet. Don't give up on me now.' She was not responding, and he screamed at her. 'LOOK!'

She was startled and turned to look, but not at the ledge like he was urging her to, but the long drop to the rocky river bank. Then she stared back at him, her eyes enormous.

'The ledge,' he shouted. 'Look at the ledge for your feet. It's wide enough. It's safe. Trust me!'

Her pupils began to rise towards the top of her head and the eyelids to descend. He was staring at two semicircles of pearly eyeballs. At the same time, he sensed that whatever little tone still existed in her wrist had gone. A few dozen pounds turned to tons. He tried desperately to hold on to the limp figure suspended over the abyss, grunting in agony with the pain in his joints. This time his arms were really coming off. No way could he summon the strength to lift her up, no way could he let go and hope she would land on the ledge.

In panic, he turned to Mark for help, but he was still hanging above him in mid-manoeuvre. He screamed at him to hurry, but his voice was drowned in the roar of the water. He had to put up with the excruciating pain in his shoulder joints until Mark came down. But Paul's hands were wet, or numb, or just too tired. Her wrists were slipping from his grasp, millimetre by millimetre. His throat hurt from screaming, trying to wake her, make her respond.

'HOLD ON!'

She kept slipping. He now held her palms. Just a curl in her fingers would help. Delay things a little. Mark would be there any moment now. But the lifeless fingers were slipping through his.

Then he was grasping at nothing but air. The unbearable burden had gone. All the noise stopped. The nightmare unfolded in slow motion, as if to allow him to experience the horror that much longer, to see every detail that much clearer, to remember it, for ever.

She landed on the ledge like he had hoped she would. There was a second of irrational relief. The legs buckled. She fell backwards, softly, smoothly. Her limbs waved sinuously, the rope tied to her waist twisting after her in graceful curves. She looked like an astronaut on a space walk whose umbilical chord had been severed. She was falling in space as if for ever, spotlighted by the sun's dying rays.

Ages afterwards, he was still on his ledge on all fours, staring at her on the ground below him, unable to take it in. Then he heard the inhuman scream and turned slowly, and there above him, looking down, his face a mask of horror, flapping his arms desperately like a giant bird about to take off, stood Mark.

They had carried her to a dry spot protected from the spray, and Paul was ineffectually trying to light a fire. Maybe if she got warm she would come around. Mark was trying to breathe life into her, pressing on her ribs, one, two, three, four, five, and back to her mouth. On and on. Paul watched, stupefied. He kept thinking about her ribs. Mark would break them if he went on like that. Aeons later, he aroused himself enough to pull at Mark.

'Stop it! You'll hurt her.' His own voice sounded unfamiliar, cracked.

Mark still pushed at her ribs and blew in her mouth, steadily, rhythmically. He hardly looked human. Just an automaton in action, pushing and blowing, pushing and blowing and with time the pushing became harder.

Paul shouted this time, with total disregard to the pain in his throat, 'You are breaking her ribs.'

Mark snapped out of it. He put his left hand over her chest and brought his right fist hard onto it. Nothing. Again and again. Nothing. Then he went mad, calling and shaking her. Paul blinked in disbelief when Mark slapped her face.

'Come on! You can't do that! You can't give up now. Not now!' Mark kept saying.

When would it have been the right time? Paul thought. Was there a right time? In old age, maybe?

Mark eventually sat back in despair, the limp body in his arms. It suddenly hit Paul. 'I killed her!' he said, amazed. 'She let go of me, but it's no excuse. *I* killed her. Me! Not you, like she saw in her dream.' But, of course, all she had seen was Mark looking down at the dead body on the rocks and had assumed that he had dropped her.

Mark's voice was a hoarse whisper, no inflection to it. 'We are both responsible, me mostly. I was so cowardly to take the responsibility, I left it to someone weakened by illness. Only ... maybe whatever happened, happened before she had hit the ground. She must have been fully relaxed. Nothing is broken. The bruises could have happened any time during the day.'

Whatever happened, happened before she hit the rock. Yes. She had looked down and panicked. Can somebody actually die of fear?

'Is it possible, she is not dead?' Paul was grasping at straws.

'I can't detect pulse or heartbeat or breathing. But my fingers are raw and dead to everything, my ears deafened from the noise all day. I don't know. I have no more accurate instruments than these.' Mark opened up his bleeding hands for Paul to see.

Paul looked at his own hands. They were torn and bloody, one nail hanging loose. It throbbed, but the physical pain couldn't compete with the mental suffering.

'But it's possible, isn't it? It's possible,' he said. 'She fainted with fright, or she is in a coma. She had a concussion.' Any of these possibilities would suffice. It could happen.

His motives were selfish, of course. He just couldn't face the responsibility, the guilt. Joint guilt, Mark had said. Yes. She could have survived perfectly well on her own. She could face hunger, loneliness, wild beasts. She could have studied nature and probably even been adopted by the Indians. She could have lived to a ripe old age but for the misfortune of meeting them. She couldn't survive them! They forced her to cover enormous distances until she weakened and succumbed to infections she probably wouldn't otherwise have caught, they didn't listen when she begged them to go ahead for help. All that he could share with Mark. But *he* had suspended her over the abyss. *He* had dropped her. *He* had put the finishing touch.

Mark said nothing. He just stared into the darkness, a hand absently stroking the hair off the bloodless face. Somehow, it didn't seem to bode well for all the hopes Paul was trying to nurture in this, the longest night in his life.

He tried to run back into the forest, but at every turn a solid shadow blocked him. There was no escape. Not even the forest wanted him.

44

Mark knew all about pain, professionally speaking. If you want to relieve it in one part of the body, you cause more somewhere else. The brain gets confused and shuts off.

The pain was coming at him from so many directions, he felt numb everywhere. He registered things that his brain refused to deal with. They remained uninterpreted sensations. The throbbing in his hands, fatigued muscles, lacerations and insect bites all over him, a lifeless body in his arms.

Paul, on the ground next to him, had his elbows on flexed knees and clutched at his head. There were Indians standing all around, silent. How long they had been there he could not remember.

One of the Indians detached himself from the rest, walked towards Sylvia, stretched his hand to touch her, and Mark came back from limbo with a bump. He grasped fiercely at the wrist. Then he realised the man was going for the stone around her neck. It was his, anyway, so Mark tried to pull it over her head to give it back but the Indian stopped him and slipped it, instead, under her shirt and buttoned the collar. Obviously the stone had to be hidden. Mark had no idea why. Let it be so.

The Indian gesticulated towards the river. When Mark ignored him, he went over to Paul and prodded him until he looked up, and again pointed at the river. Paul did not move either. The Indian started to walk towards it, beckoning them to come with him.

Paul eventually got up and shuffled after the Indian.

When he returned, minutes later, there was more purpose in his step.

'A canoe,' he croaked.

Mark got up smartly. They'd better hurry. Go. Before the body started to decompose in this heat. At the same time, he disgusted himself for having thought of her as a body. But he had seen it all before. The flesh going soapy, the hair coming off, the smell. He wouldn't submit her to that indignity. He had thought of a burial, but couldn't bring himself to do it. Not here. Not where he could not come to visit her.

The Indian was now trying to delay them. He was busy organising some kind of a drinking ceremony, and was making signs that they should wait. Mark picked up the body and tried to evade him. It wasn't easy. The Indian was clacking like a hen, flapping his arms, walking back and forth in front of him. The other Indians, still standing at a distance, were getting agitated.

'Better do it quickly and get rid of him,' said Paul.

Another Indian came forward. 'You must say, I want to see everything,' he advised.

Mark saw all he wanted to see. More than he wanted to see. But he repeated it anyway, to keep him happy. Paul was advised to do the same. They both sat in front of the first Indian and accepted the drink. It tasted bitter, but it was a feeling. The first for a while. As they made to get up again the Indian gave them something else to drink, as if to wash the bitterness away.

Paul was retching and Mark wanted to be gone. This time he would not listen to anything else. He had no time to sit down and sleep, like they kept telling him to do by miming. He had to go.

His stomach lurched and he vomited. Paul was writhing around, clasping at his stomach. Mark managed to stagger to his feet. He felt unsteady. Maybe he needed to sleep this off, but he fought it. He lifted Sylvia and put her over his shoulder, holding her behind the knees like he used to do with his sleeping son when he was small. She felt no bigger.

He grasped Paul by the arm with his free hand and propelled him to the shore.

As in a dream, he threw Paul and Sylvia in the canoe, freed it from the bank and jumped in himself. Somebody pressed a wooden pole at him. He grasped it and pushed hard.

The water was fast and the canoe was swept downstream, guided round obstacles by currents and the minimal effort from him. As the water slowly returned to calm, Mark equally slowly left his body and could look down indifferently. He was really flying up there in the moist air. Normally his eyesight was good, but he had never seen anything as well focused as this before: crystal clear, sharp.

The river below him was black glass. Everything reflected into it; the rocks and bushes at the edge, the knurled roots, the lianas, an exposed branch reaching out from the water like a drowning man's hand that had turned to ivory, a metallic blue kingfisher searching for prey, the canoe sitting dangerously low in the water, hardly capable of carrying their weight. It made its way lazily on the still water, just creasing the surface, the wrinkles slowly spreading on the water behind it in ever-increasing arcs. There seemed to be no current at all to aid it.

Everything was perfectly still. Paul crouched at the bow, Sylvia on the floor of the craft, where he had deposited her, half-submerged in water.

Then Mark felt the wind on his face. He seemed to have moved on, and now he was looking down at the undulating canopy. It whizzed under him and he felt dizzy. A hole appeared in the green mass. Something stood in the middle. Mark started to fall towards it. The air rushed at him, whistling in his ears. The clearing got bigger and bigger. The speck grew into a boy. There was a parrot on his shoulder.

Mark got even dizzier. He felt his stomach muscles contract and he was back in the boat, bending over the side to be sick. The canoe nearly capsized. His head was aching, but he took the pole again and pushed. The hull scraped the sand.

Paul woke up, and when they got stuck he came out on the shallow bank with him to free the boat. Back on board, Paul paddled with his hands, occasionally pushing a floating tree trunk out of the way, signing to left or right to avoid sandbanks until they came to a deeper part of the river. Even then, they had to watch out for small floating islands of greenery as well as tree trunks and sometimes a ponderous manatee, paddling around in the river. Eels and snakes were everywhere, swimming with such grace Sylvia would have been delighted.

By midday the light reflecting from the water was blinding, the heat so intense they had to seek the riverbank and some refuge under the trees. Caymans were basking in the sun, only feet away. They ignored them. No words were exchanged, both acting instinctively, in unison, as if reading each other's thoughts.

After eating some crab meat to keep up their strength for the rest of the journey, they just watched shoals of oval fish with black lines on their sides swim back and forth until the sun came down lower.

Back in the boat they made the same slow progress as before. The sweat poured off them in streams. By the time the sun started setting, they were still nowhere.

The surface of the water turned to gold. Pink dolphins jumped ahead of their canoe, showering gold flakes all around them. The slanting rays of light played tricks on the forest wall on either side. A single leaf among a sea of green turned silver, a flower sparkled like a ruby, a liana came alive, a root writhed by the water's edge. The sky eventually turned black with only a smear of the palest pink at the horizon, where the sun had set.

They interrupted the journey again, found a dry spot away from the water and brought Sylvia out. Neither made the fire or thought of food. They were exhausted.

Mark wanted to shut his eyes and wouldn't have minded if he never opened them again. But it was a luxury he couldn't afford. She wouldn't have liked him to abandon Paul like that. He looked suicidal, though Mark couldn't think of anything remotely comforting to say. Then he remembered that Sylvia had always maintained that when things couldn't get worse, something always turned up.

'Tomorrow,' he said, and his voice sounded like that of a stranger, 'we will come across something or someone and be rescued.'

Paul looked up at him, some light returning to his eyes. 'And we will take her to a hospital, and all this would be no more than a bad dream.' He looked to Mark for some reassurance, and when he did not get it said, 'I mean, people are known to come out of coma.'

'Maybe,' Mark said just to keep up his hopes, though he was not sure if that was not worse than the truth.

45

In the dark, Paul thought of the vivid dream he had, at the beginning of the canoe journey.

He had been back in deep forest. His viewpoint was somehow lower than normal, and he could see every exposed root and fallen leaf, every labouring ant or beetle. His shoulders brushed against undergrowth. He was searching for something, he didn't know what.

He felt deliriously happy when he came across the huddled figure in the shadows, knees drawn up, arms around legs, unmistakably Sylvia. The dark hair framed a face so gaunt it escaped being a skull by the yellow, taut skin that covered it. Through deep sockets, the eyes shone enormous, at the same level as his, yet he had the impression that he was standing up. There was a lot of pain in those eyes. Physical pain that had been there so long, it gave her the sad expression of a Byzantine icon.

'Nothing can hurt you for long,' she said, 'because of the power of your laughter. Your gift for happiness. But Mark . . . he is better here with me.'

Paul felt a cold shiver down his spine. Was it a warning? Was Mark to go next? It was bad enough now. But why wasn't Mark showing more grief? He had not uttered a word all day, but he looked detached and not so absolutely devastated as earlier this morning. Maybe he too was hopeful.

Paul wanted to believe that more than anything else in

the world, but as night progressed, he lost faith. There was no hope, and he did not want to face the outside world. If only he too were dead, but it didn't happen by just wishing. He was so unhappy, the mental pain became physical, but anguish alone never killed anybody. He didn't feel as if he were about to die. That would be too neat and easy. Nothing in life was that easy. To kill himself was out of the question. Mark had enough trauma as it was. There was no way out. He was trapped. He wanted to cry, but he had no tears. The pain was beyond outward expression, but there was a scream in his head, that deafened him.

It was late afternoon the next day, the light at its most tricky, when they rounded a corner and saw a vision that at any other time would have filled Paul with joy: sprawling huts, a more substantial wooden structure in the middle, a few tents on one side slightly aloof from the more inferior shelter, some Indian children squealing by the river side. It was no figment of his imagination. They had been spotted. A cassocked figure was waving at them.

Over there was everything Paul had been hoping for all these months. It meant also that life as he had lived it with his two companions was coming to an end. It had already done so, of course, with Sylvia's death.

It was not just the end of the present, but the past catching up with him. A past he could not altogether disown. It had repercussions. He might never be able to silence them. Scores of people would be affected, whatever he decided to do.

Life in the jungle had changed him. Could he fit back in the old environment? Could he continue from where he had left before the accident? The three of them had faced hardships, fear, death, but compared to life in the civilised world, it seemed so simple. Primitive needs were easy to satisfy. A little food, some water, a kind of shelter. That was all. Decisions were easy and inevitable.

'We have to go, I suppose,' he told Mark.

The priest came to the edge to help them disembark – a noble-looking man but with leathery skin from exposure to the sun and knurled hands that seized the boat like grab hooks to pull it out of the water. His mournful eyes were round with amazement at the sight of the white savages and the body.

Only then did Paul realise what a shocking picture they must have presented. Dirty, unkept, indecently clad, thin, like victims of a concentration camp. It took him a while to explain to the incredulous priest who they were. He employed a few Spanish phrases in case the priest did not speak English. Of course he should have tried Portuguese, but what the heck. He knew no Portuguese.

The priest threw his hands in the air, his eyes heavenward. 'Miracle! miracle!' Then he recovered and said in good English, 'God truly looks after you. We have visitors. From America. They are out there,' he waved an arm in the direction of the forest interior. And in a more subdued voice, a shadow fleeting briefly over his intelligent features, 'They are looking for samples.' Then he beamed again. 'But they have a radio.'

He bustled around, shooing curious Indian children and some of their parents that gathered to gape at the white men who looked more like them, except for the hairiness and the height. He seemed at a loss as to what they might need first. Food, drink, clothes? He started doing one thing then stopped and began something else, getting all flustered and muttering to himself. 'Milegre!' Then, looking at Sylvia and thinking she was unconscious, 'You need medicine, yes? Never enough medicine here,' he moaned, 'or a doctor,' and pointed at the pot-bellied children.

'Don't the American visitors have medicines for themselves?' Paul asked.

The priest looked at him and shrugged his shoulders, pulling the corners of his mouth down, his palms facing the heavens. Obviously the priest was not too fond of his American guests, yet he was so good to the new arrivals and he must have realised, they, too, were Americans.

With the fading light the visitors returned from their expedition in two jeeps. Three men in dusty khaki uniforms and stout boots with a few Indian helpers laden down with ropes, drills and pickaxes in one jeep and a couple of armed thugs in the other.

'Bodyguards?' said Paul. 'As a protection from what, precisely?'

A glance at the logo printed on the front of the uniforms of the three men, and if Paul had any doubts, they were dispelled. It was the name of the mineral company he was in the process of appropriating before the crash. If everything went smoothly after the accident, he was now these men's boss, a fact he was not in a hurry to admit to the priest. No wonder the poor man disliked his visitors. They were about to destroy the land belonging to his flock. But there was no hope of keeping his secret for long.

'What are you guys doing in this goddam place?' said the man that had introduced himself as MacIntyre.

'Air crash,' said Paul.

'Never heard of any since our golden playboy took one gamble too many,' but he hadn't even finished before he realised and changed expression. 'Mr Alexander, sir!' And then there was a lot of 'Gee!' and 'Get hold of that,' and backslapping from the others. But they were scientists, after all, and got down to practicalities pretty soon.

They made available everything they possessed, food, drink, clothes, but nothing seemed right. Everyone's clothes were too large for Paul and too short for Mark, the food, too processed and either tasteless or overpowering. Paul turned with longing to the tins of beer and Coke, condensation running all over them, as they came out of the cool box run by the generator. An irresistible sight. Something he had longed for since the accident. But the beer was too bitter and the Coke too sweet. His taste buds had become too subtle on jungle fare.

'There is a backup team in Manaus,' Coogan was saying, at least that was what Paul thought he had called himself, 'and Danny here will radio, straight away.'

'I don't think they can risk a plane before dawn,' Danny said, pointing at red flashes in the distance. 'There will be a storm tonight, but they could be getting things ready for your reception. Fax your folks and things. Get whatever medical supplies or personnel they need.'

Paul had no interest in folks and things. 'Where will it land?' The only flat expanse was the river and even that had too many sand banks and floating tree trunks.

'There is an area cleared further in the bush.' Coogan pointed at a dirt road leading to it.

They were all sorry about Sylvia. 'After all this time. One day, just one more day.'

Paul changed the subject. He couldn't bear anyone else discussing her. 'Who is in charge of the company now?'

'Your father,' Danny said. 'Came out of retirement. It was the least he could do. He thought you died trying to secure the deal. He did it for you.'

For him and the future profits, thought Paul.

The men became technical. Paul gathered from the jargon that the investigation of the rock formations was very encouraging, but everything pointed out to the real wealth lying somewhere beyond the falls.

He was devastated. The more that was known, the less easy it was to stop. He certainly could not allow the destruction of the forest, now that he had lived in it for so long and learned to love it. Especially beyond the falls. That was home, selfish as it sounded, because it really belonged to the Indians that had helped them, when they could have got rid of them so easily by simply not raising a finger. Then he saw the thugs huddled up together, some distance away. 'What's with the morons?' he said.

'We are told the Indians aren't too keen on us, but frankly, sometimes I think we have more to fear from our protectors,' said MacIntyre.

'Why don't you sack them?' It seemed so simple to Paul.

'Ah,' said Coogan, 'then we are guaranteed something will happen.'

'I don't believe it!' Paul said. 'Are we talking protection here?'

'Something like that,' said Coogan.

There was so much Paul had to sort out, he didn't know where to begin.

He refused the invitation for them to share the tents. The priest had laid Sylvia on a mat in his makeshift church, and they ought to stay with her.

The Indian who had shown them the canoe came into the church late at night. He ignored Paul and Mark sitting by Sylvia's side, and made straight for a spot beside her head. The priest did not show great surprise, but he looked outside nervously and then shut the door.

'Is he hiding from anyone?' Paul asked.

'The vultures,' said the priest.

Paul was puzzled. 'The geologists? Absurd!'

'They are the hunters,' the priest said slowly, as if tired of these explanations. 'They destroy. The vultures follow them for the pickings.' He ticked them one by one on his fingers. 'Land for illegal crops, captive markets with the workforce that has to follow any development, running child prostitution the local tribes will provide, willingly or not.' He sat at Sylvia's feet.

'That is appalling,' said Paul. 'Do they know that? The company, I mean.'

The priest looked at him. Was he not the company? Paul shifted uncomfortably. The priest took pity.

'Maybe you people don't realise the full extent of the damage you cause,' he said. 'You think you would just destroy some trees. And that is bad enough, of course, but you never see the human cost.'

'I'll do anything I can,' said Paul miserably.

'Ah!' The priest gave a half-smile. 'I forgot. You know something of the forest now. You understand.' He shuffled nearer as if to talk confidentially. 'Only one thing can help. Public opinion. Nobody wants bad publicity. The bigger the company, the more effective . . .' He slapped his forehead. 'But, of course, you know all that.' He nodded towards the Indian. 'He thinks if he could create enough trouble, even get killed, as many such people have been, somebody might listen. But it's no good getting killed here. Nobody would see. Nobody would care. He has to get out.'

'He can come with us in the morning,' said Paul, 'but I gather he speaks no English.'

'I am sorry to say, not even Portuguese. Just the odd word. But there are a lot of Indians who do. People who left the forest but still are not ashamed to fight for the rights of those who did not. One of them can interpret. But to take him out tomorrow . . .' the priest shook his head, 'he must remain alive tonight.'

'They wouldn't try to kill him here!' said Paul.

The priest raised his hands in exasperation. 'They tried it before. There is no law here, and where it does, Indians are no priority, not compared to foreign exchange or, God forgive them, what they call progress.'

'I will make sure he is safe,' Paul said.

The priest stared at him. 'It's not in your interest.'

'It is in my interest, now, that nobody interferes with the jungle, especially up there. I started all this mess. I will do all I can to stop it.'

The priest nodded his head solemnly, understanding.

The Indian sat without a word, as if guarding Sylvia's body. Occasionally he swayed back and forth, mumbling something. Commending her spirit to the gods of the jungle, maybe. A kindred spirit. At least he was doing something.

'Excuse me, Father, but did this man,' Paul motioned towards the Indian, 'think of all that himself? I mean one has to know the mentality of people outside the forest. It needs, well, a lot of sophistication to know about publicity and the like.'

'It has been explained to him by somebody who was educated out there. Who knew what happens.'

'Where is he now?'

The priest raised his shoulders. 'Murdered, of course.'

'Just like that?' said Paul.

'Just like that.'

Paul thought for a while. 'I'll return the land back to the Indians,' he said.

'So that someone else may take it from them?' The priest shook his head in pity.

Paul was in despair. 'What else can I do?'

'Keep it so nobody else gets it and make sure it's not developed.'

'This isn't my country, you know,' said Paul impatiently. 'I was given permission to invest in this project, create jobs, produce an income for the country and yes, make a profit, but that's not their main preoccupation.'

The priest assumed a conspiratorial look. 'You are a rich man. People would listen. You can even persuade the government to do something. Offer some incentive. Let them declare it a national park. I don't know.'

'Stir the media and bribe somebody, you mean,' said Paul. 'Yes, yes, of course.'

'I am a doctor,' said Mark out of the blue, and Paul jumped to hear his voice after all this time.

The priest looked puzzled. 'Yes?'

'You said there was no doctor here.'

'Who would work here?' said the priest impatiently. 'There are no facilities. The Mission cannot afford a wage or medicines.'

'I don't need a wage,' said Mark. 'I will get medicines. I have a hospital in the States. I could sell it and use the money here.'

'Mark, wait until you had time to think,' Paul said gently. 'I can understand how you feel. I would do the same if I had any skill that would be of use here, but my skills would be appreciated elsewhere, it seems, and I am not going to lose both of you. I couldn't bear that.'

'I have thought enough,' said Mark. 'I am staying here with her.'

'She is dead, Mark,' Paul seemed to make a great effort not to cry.

'She is here,' Mark said. 'That Indian knows it. So do I.'

46

It was so clear to Mark, all of a sudden. So simple. 'She warned me,' he told Paul. 'She said she would not let me go.' He didn't want to go, either. 'That's what she must have meant.'

'She asked me to look after her kids, which means she wanted me to go,' said Paul. He gave a little smile. 'She is directing the whole show, as usual, and arranged everything just as she wanted it.'

Paul's employees popped their heads around the door.

'We have to start before dawn to get anywhere,' said MacIntyre, 'but if you think we would be of any use until the aircraft arrives . . .'

Mark couldn't be bothered with any of their solicitations right now and hoped that Paul felt the same. He did.

'No,' said Paul, 'there is nothing you could do. Get on with what you have to.' When they left he turned to Mark. 'Tomorrow they will be out of a job, but for the time being, their studies will keep them out of the way. Those morons too.'

They listened to engines roaring into life. The noise of one receded, the other approached. The priest stiffened. The Indian kept rocking. When a jeep screeched to a halt just outside, Mark caught the priest's apprehension. Paul shifted uncomfortably. The Indian stopped rocking. He had a satisfied smile on his face, as if he had achieved what he was after. He shook his head like someone who understood something said to him.

With the sun rising and the door closed, the atmosphere

in the church was stifling. The warmth, emanations of perspiring bodies, mould on the damp wooden roof – Mark prayed, not Sylvia, not yet, please not yet. It was more than anybody could have dared to hope already, but still he hoped.

The chapel door flew open to someone's kick and the two thugs burst in, guns at the ready. Mark, Paul and the priest came to their feet. The Indian carried on squatting by Sylvia's head.

'What the hell is going on?' Since there was no answer to Paul's question, he said even more sternly, 'What do you think you are doing?'

The thugs did not expect Mark and Paul to be there, obviously. They wavered. They must have known who Paul was by now.

'Where are the others?' Paul said.

It was a mistake. Paul was rusty. He ought to have capitalised on the element of surprise. One did not give an opponent a chance to recover. Advantage lies in the few seconds of confusion. One should not talk then, just act.

Paul glanced at Mark quickly, as if realising what had happened. It was too late for Mark to do anything. Where he stood, he was also covered when the two men turned to Paul.

'The plane will be here soon to take you away,' one of the hoods said. 'You do not need to worry about this,' and he pointed with the gun at the Indian, who seemed very unconcerned, compared to the priest, who was deathly pale. 'Vermin,' he spat. 'Standing in the way of progress.'

'He now works for me and he will come with us on the plane,' Paul said, trying to retain at least some authority since he had lost the element of surprise. 'Maybe, you should too.'

'You do not understand. He will ruin everything,' the gunman said.

'I own the company, I decide who ruins things,' said Paul.

The man considered things for a while, then a sly smile

spread over his swarthy features. 'But you are, er . . . dead, senhor. The other boss, he understands.'

He would, thought Mark, knowing Paul's father. He would sell his soul, if he had any, for profit. Maybe so would Paul a few aeons back, before the accident.

The other hood stared at the one who had just spoken, the wheels turning rustily in what passed for a brain, until he got the drift of the logic.

Paul had, too. 'A lot of people have seen us already,' he said.

The spokesman of the two gunmen laughed and the other followed, obviously without knowing why. 'The priest? Not even worth the bullet, and in the jungle people have accidents. Indians, rocks, waterfalls. Part of the job. Then others come. Life goes on.'

The whole thing was absurd. Things like that happened in films, and even then were too far-fetched. Surely they didn't mean to slaughter them all! But the two men were smiling insanely, and nothing could be more scary than two imbeciles with guns. Mark was out of ideas. The only comfort, if such it was, that they were taking their time. They were savouring their victims' fear, maybe. Sylvia had once said, death is ugly only if you fear it. He wasn't really afraid of it. It would be divine justice. Their lives for Sylvia's. But the priest was innocent and, most of all, the Indian.

Paul moved slowly away from Mark. As he moved, the muzzles followed him. Mark realised what Paul was up to. If they shot at him, Mark would have a fraction of a second to do something. It should be enough. He could do it, but he didn't necessarily want Paul as a bait. There had to be a better way.

Paul realised that he was near the Indian now, and kept moving away. The gunmen began talking to each other in Portuguese earnestly. Something was wrong. Then the talkative one spat something at the priest. The priest talked to the Indian, presumably in his language. The Indian remained silent, a smirking smile on his face.

'What the hell is going on?' Paul shouted.

'Shut up!' said the hood.

'The emerald. They want his emerald,' said the priest, deathly pale even under the sunburn. 'The Indian always has it around his neck. That's mainly why they want to kill him.'

One of the hoods moved the butt of his gun backwards sharply and the priest, standing behind him, keeled over.

This moment of confusion was what Mark was waiting for, but he glanced at Sylvia first as if to take his leave. He was fast but not faster than a bullet.

It had to be an illusion. Something to do with the slanting light from the door making green flames flicker on the emerald around her neck or his eyes watering at what would be, most probably, his last sight of her. Whatever! But why was everyone going crazy? Why did the hoods scream as if demented, why were Paul's eyes popping out of his head, why was the Indian chanting like a maniac?

If Mark was to do anything, this was the ideal moment. It was now or never. But he was paralysed by fear. He didn't want to do anything that would result in mayhem, bullets flying everywhere, hitting the guilty and the innocent.

One of the hoods stretched his hand towards Sylvia. He was about to grab her by the throat, and now Mark was left with no alternative.

47

Life came to Sylvia frame by frame, each brilliantly focused.

There was an El Greco painting of a Spanish grandee, down to the unearthly green tinge of the elongated face. Mournful eyes, black beard, caved-in cheeks. Except that it spoke. About emeralds, she thought, and then something smashed into it and it fell out of view.

It was replaced by a swarthy face as imbecilic as the Spanish grandee's had been intelligent. It grimaced horribly as if faced with a ghost before it recovered and was taken over by a look of greed, his hand stretching towards her to grab something. Her whole field of vision was taken up by that coarse fist.

She was startled by a noise out of sight, and as she turned she saw flames bursting out of a metallic tube and moved her head further at the grunt. Paul, in the most ridiculous clothes, crumbled up as if somebody had knocked his feet from under him.

She caught a swift movement with the corner of her eye, then a figure sprang into the frame, too big to be mistaken for anything but Mark, even in the comically small outfit. He was bent over in the fashion of American footballers, head tucked in, square shoulders forward. The fire-spitting gun was thrown in the air. Its bearer, another swarthy man but squatter and uglier than the Fist, followed, his head snapping back as if hit by a thunderbolt.

The Fist was now holding a gun, spitting fire. Mark's figure shuddered, but there was too much momentum for it to stop. It smashed into the Fist at chest level and the two bodies rocketed, locked together, towards the wall. There was a sickening crack and the Fist slowly slithered down the wall, leaving behind him a streak of clotted cream and strawberry jam, until he was in the sitting position. Mark followed him down to rest his head in his lap.

'What's going on?' she said, sitting up.

'We thought you were dead,' said Paul, still sitting down, but now his oversized trousers were scarlet with blood.

She couldn't find the connection between somebody mistaking her for dead and the incomprehensible happenings all around her. She looked at the spreadeagled figure in black robes; the ugly man with a jaw at a very unnatural angle; the Indian, her Indian, she noted, splattered with blood, sitting down, holding his bent knees, rocking back and forth, chanting something, his voice becoming stronger and stronger, adding an even chillier air to the atmosphere; Paul's bloody trousers and white face; the prone Mark in the dead man's lap by the wall.

Paul was trying to explain and not making much sense. What Mission, what scientists? And then he kept babbling about her looking dead. She had to think for a while.

'Oh, it happened before,' she said, when she realised what he was on about. 'Something in my genes. It skipped a few generations, that's all!'

'All? You should wear a disc around your neck to that effect, or somebody will bury you alive one of these days.' He shivered. 'We might have done,' he added. 'I thought Mark was trying to humour my flights of fancy by not denying that you could be in a coma or something.' Then he smiled. 'Well, I was right, sort of, wasn't I?'

'Now what?' she said, and then she realised that Mark was too quiet, and if he were dead . . . 'Oh God!'

She crawled towards him and turned him over. He was deathly pale but breathing. She looked at Paul. He was staring at her, too scared to ask.

'He is alive,' she said.

Paul relaxed. 'Thank God!'

Mark was bleeding from the chest and the hip. Probably

hit by one bullet that passed from one part of his anatomy to the other, both being at the same level, the way he tackled, bent forward. She didn't know how to stop the blood flow. With Paul it was easy. She removed his belt and fastened it tightly just above the wound in his smashed thigh.

Paul was able to joke. 'A couple of inches higher and my sex career would be over.'

'If we don't do anything for Mark,' she said desperately, 'he'll bleed to death.'

Paul sobered up and tried to think of something. At last he said, 'There is an airstrip down the track. It's some distance away, so you have to take their jeep.' He pointed at the two ex-gunmen. 'We are expecting an aeroplane, any moment now. We don't want them to sit there waiting while he bleeds to death. In case they are delayed for any reason, try and attract the notice of the workers in the bush somehow.' He was pushing her to get to her feet. 'You know how noise carries in the forest. Use the car's hooter, knock on a tree, make a fire, I don't know.' Now he was shooing her towards the door. 'Just use your imagination, but get some help.'

'I can't drive,' she said miserably.

Paul sighed. 'You are the only one that could.' He pointing out the slaughter all around.

She hesitated, and Paul got even more exasperated.

'You are not likely to encounter a traffic jam,' he said. 'Just point the car down the dirt track and go. It's as simple as that.'

If only it were as simple as that, but she only shrugged. There was nothing else she could do.

She got to the door, and for a moment or two she was blinded by the strong light. When her sight adjusted, she noticed that though the sky was so bright, it was almost colourless and everything up to eye level sparkled, low mist covered the deforested strip of earth that comprised the Mission, like a fluffy duvet. Only the tips of huts and tents pierced through it and the top of the metallic beast that crouched in it, feet from her. She walked to it, the Indian following her as if attached to her with an invisible string.

It was no ordinary car but a macho jeep, so high she had some difficulty getting into it, even with the Indian's help. When she sat in the driver's seat, her feet couldn't reach the pedals. Valuable time was lost trying to lower the seat, and then she could hardly look out of the car screen. Might as well. There was no road to look for. All she had to do was aim at a gap between the trees.

All the same, her palms were sweaty and she wiped them on her filthy shirt. Her legs were weak and shaky and only just reached the pedals. She turned the ignition on and the thing roared. She brought her foot up for the engine to catch but blood throbbed in her ears, preventing any detection of tone in the engine. The car kangarooed forward but she kept going, ploughing through the mist, either accelerating wildly or braking, trying to tame the beast.

So far, so good. If she could steady her legs and if she moved yet closer to the edge of the seat for her feet to have better contact with the pedals, she could do it. No need to speed. Just steady and slow.

She was getting the hang of the thing and felt rather proud of herself when she heard a very slight thump, felt it, rather. A little brown body sprung up from the mist, flipped over in front of her, limp and then sank back into the mist and dust.

She had seen it too many times before. Once in Africa, maybe for real, maybe not – nobody else seemed to have acknowledged that it had happened – and in her imagination every time she sat behind the wheel. But now, she was absolutely sure, it was no fantasy. This time, her destiny and the child's had collided.

She turned the wheel violently away from where she thought the child landed, tried to put her foot on the brake, missed and landed hard on the accelerator. The giant tree sprang out of nowhere at her and she let go of the wheel in terror, as if covering her eyes was a protection. By letting go of her only support, she fell off her precarious perch on the end of the seat and landed under the dashboard.

There was an enormous bang. The sort of noise that would carry well through the forest, she thought, suddenly detached from it all. She was aware of the wheel above her moving forward and heard the crunching of metal. The space around her shrank. She was being squeezed. The pain increased by the second. To the accompaniment of snapping bones, it became so intense, it went beyond agony into something almost exquisite.

48

Paul crawled out to Mark, ignoring the pain in his leg that cranked up a gear a minute. With the tourniquet Sylvia had applied, the bleeding had slowed down but not stopped altogether, and he felt weak.

Mark was shivering and trying to say something about Sylvia being alive, then gave up. Paul was scared. He was losing one friend just as fast as he gained another. The priest stirred. Paul called for help. He might have something, know of something that would help. In the meantime he tried to warm Mark up by rubbing his hands and slapping his face.

The priest came over. The middle of his face, where the nose should have been, was a bloody mess and his eyes were already swollen so much, there were only two slits left to look out of.

'We need help soon,' he said in the muffled voice of people that can't breathe through the nose and staggered towards the door, where curious heads of Indian children and adults were shyly looking round the door then bolting.

Why was he taking so long? Paul felt like screaming at him to shift his ass.

There was a screech of tyres and loud voices, then MacIntyre, Danny and Coogan ran in, passed the priest, still not at the door, and started talking all at once, adding to Paul's dizziness.

'What the fuck?' 'Oh my God! This is a bloodbath! Told you these motherfuckers weren't to be trusted.'

'You got the signal,' said Paul with relief.

'Signal! A fucking hundred-foot tree on fire. We thought the whole camp was up in flames. Might be soon if nobody does anything. We two carry them to the plane and you get the Indians to fetch water from the river. Hey, Padre, can you walk to the car? Shit, we need a stretcher to carry this one. Where are those guys? Waiting for a delivery? Why can't they come and help? Might be trying to stop the fire, if nobody told them there is more urgent business here.'

'A hundred-foot fire! Boy,' said Paul before passing out. She always did things in a big way.

A cool breeze touched Paul's face and he opened his eyes. He was in a small, white room, flooded in light. The silence was deafening. The bed he was lying in was too soft. He ran his hands over the crisp sheets.

What was happening? He had all the things he had been deprived of for so long: cleanliness, comfort, peace. Why did it all feel so unnerving?

He closed his eyes again and thought of the jungle gloom, noise, steam; Sylvia having a wash by the rocks, searching for sweet potatoes, arguing with him, her eyes on fire; Mark's golden eyes, the gazelle-like walk he shared with all very tall people, his remarkable ability to spring from lethargy to action; of himself climbing trees and laughing, laughing happily at the marvels of the canopy, at Sylvia's naïve idealism, at Mark's seriousness. None of this belonged here. This was foreign, too far removed from them. A white box. No. A white coffin. He shivered. Oh, God! Let Mark be safe!

Somebody entered the room. Paul was too scared to open his eyes. There would be bad news. He felt it in every particle of his body, and he couldn't handle it. Not yet. Not yet.

The door closed quietly and he was alone again. Had he ever told Mark what he meant to him? Yes. He had told them he loved them both. And he didn't want just one or the other. He wanted them both. But he couldn't quite have either of them completely. Sylvia because she was Sylvia and because she loved Mark, Mark because he was so very impenetrable physically and personality-wise and loved Sylvia. It didn't really matter, as long as he was there, solid, dependable, a friend. They looked so opposite yet shared so much, down to their love for the same woman. Maybe that was the nearest either of them could get to . . . But did either of them have her? *Three chiefs and no Indians.*

'I am mad,' he said out loud. 'They pumped me full of drugs or something.'

He had never, never in his wildest dreams, thought of Mark in these terms. He had said love before, of course, but not this kind. Why now? If, he corrected himself quickly, when, he saw Mark next, or Sylvia, he would be so self-conscious. 'Oh, shit!'

Where was Sylvia? Was she avoiding him because she did not want to break the bad news? Had she been reunited with her family? What were her plans? Surely she wouldn't leave without seeing him.

He spent a long time drifting in and out of sleep. Sometimes he heard hushed voices, felt pain. Sometimes he returned to the jungle. She was there, everywhere.

'He will be safe enough with me,' her disembodied voice said.

'When will I see you?'

'When you come back to the forest.'

The door opened. Her voice was still in his ears. He looked anxiously. No, it wasn't Sylvia. Just a nurse. She plumped the pillows, straightened the bed, talked cheerfully, too cheerfully, and he didn't understand a single word. She left and a man came. Officious. A doctor? He didn't look like it. Paul didn't know why a doctor should look different to any other person, but this one just didn't feel like a doctor.

'Ah, Mr Alexander. You look well. I will only ask few

questions.' He moved a chair near the bed and sat. All his movements slow, premeditated. 'Just routine.'

A fucking policeman. He should have recognised the demeanour. Was he to hear it from him?

The man kept talking. 'We have already talked to your compatriates and to the priest. We know what happened, or most of what happened. Ees just verification, you understand.'

'Self-defence,' said Paul. 'They opened fire and Mark had to do something.'

'Yes. Bad men. Good riddance. But about the lady. Such a mystery.'

'Where is the mystery?'

'The priest says, she alive. The Americans, she dead.' He spread his hands. 'But no body. No body, dead or alive.'

Paul started to feel cold. 'The other Americans thought she was dead at first, so did we, but they saw her later.'

With his bald head forward, bent a bit to the side and those beady eyes staring at Paul, the policeman gave the impression of a vulture. 'Later?'

'When she went to fetch them,' Paul said. 'She drew their attention by setting a tree on fire. A desperate measure, I grant you, but . . .'

'The fire,' said the policeman, nodding his head as if things fell into place. 'She started the fire. She in the car?'

'Yes. She went to fetch help in the car. But they must have told you that.'

'They saw the fire and came, but no lady.'

'I don't understand. She couldn't get lost. Not in a car. One would imagine there was nowhere to get to by car, except the airstrip. She couldn't have driven into the jungle.'

'No, she no go far. Sorry.' He took a notepad out of his pocket and flicked it open. 'Name, please.'

'Where is the fucking car, then?' Paul shouted.

'Hit a tree. Puff!' He spread his bunched fingers outwards. 'Tree gets fire too, and all they burn. We knew that, but not who is in the car. Not sure. Now it make sense.'

Paul just stared at him. It didn't make sense to *him*. 'There must be some mistake. If she . . .' he couldn't bring himself to say it. 'You would know from the . . . evidence.'

'The fire, too strong. Nothing left. Even the car almost all melt.'

Paul's stomach turned. He made a great effort not to actually be sick. The policeman looked away. 'Sorry. A good friend, yes?'

Paul didn't trust himself to open his mouth.

'I go,' said the policeman, but he didn't. 'Just one question. Name of the lady. For record. You know.'

For the record. 'Dr Peters.' That removed it a bit. Just a bit.

'She travel in the plane with you, yes? No record to say she in plane with you.'

'No. We met in the jungle. She was a survivor from another air crash. The jumbo jet.' It was all so unreal. He might as well be talking of a total stranger.

'Ah! And all survived all thees time in the jungle, and then . . . sorry. Really sorry!'

He might as well get all the bad news at once. And there would be. She had just confirmed it. She was taking Mark with her. 'My other friend. Mark, er . . . Dr Beckermann, he is . . . dead too?' and held his breath for the inevitable.

'No, no.' The man seemed pleased to have some good news.

Paul breathed again. A ray of sunshine in all the darkness. 'He knows about S . . ., about Dr Peters?'

'No. He not well enough to talk.' He patted Paul's hand. 'But no danger, the doctor said. He be well soon. I go now. Sorry.'

49

Nicol, his son, the press, television, all wanted to talk to him, but not Sylvia.

Mark could understand that her family would have come, that she would want to see the children. Maybe they didn't come here and she had to go to England. But shouldn't she have said goodbye? Did she come when he was unconscious? She would write or phone. She could reach him where she had left him. He was going nowhere.

He did not want to see Nicol, but how, with the eyes of the world on them? Husband comes back from the dead to say 'Sorry, honey, but I am leaving you'. Better see his son first. Then think.

The boy was almost a man. So much taller since Mark last saw him.

'Hey! Don't grow any taller or you'll turn into a freak like me,' he said, but he was brimming with pride.

Jo smiled shyly. 'You are not a freak, Dad, you are a hero.'

'What's with the Dad? You used to call me Mark.'

'You weren't a hero then. Paul told everyone how you rammed into those crooks like you used to tackle on the field.'

Mark grimaced. 'I am sorry about that. I never meant to use so much force.'

'But they would have killed everyone. They had guns.'

'Still. I am a doctor. I am not supposed to kill people.'

'Oh, Dad!' Jo waited for a bit and said hesitantly, 'Are you going to see . . . *her*?'

There was only one *her* spoken in that manner. 'Perhaps. Later. I have to talk to you, man to man.'

'She wasn't exactly the grieving widow, you know.' Jo was never fond of Nicol. None of Mark's friends or relatives were. 'Now she plays Penelope in front of the cameras for all it's worth.' He laughed. 'It's Paul who coined the name Penelope and told me who she was. I wouldn't have thought of it, but I was sick all the same.' The boy almost pleaded. 'Don't be fooled again, Dad.'

'That's what I wanted to talk to you about. I am not coming back.' He noted the boy's surprise. 'I am not running away, Jo. You will be able to come and see me whenever you want to. It would be fun. I'll show you how we have lived all these months. It was not that bad.' He smiled, already nostalgic. 'It was great after we were . . . well, shown how to accept the forest as a friend. We had some bad moments.' He passed a hand over his hair, almost shaved off now in the interest of hygiene. 'But one has those anywhere.'

'Paul told us about Sylvia. You must be very sorry. Paul is.'

So she had left, and what has Paul been saying, for Christ's sake. The woman had a family to think of. He spoke carefully. 'Yes, I suppose I am sorry to lose her company, after all this time.'

Jo, for some reason, became formal. 'Suppose, sir?'

'Well, it's her choice.'

'Choice?' Why was Jo so surprised? 'She chose to . . . I don't understand.'

Mark lost his temper. 'What is there to understand? That's how things are. I can't change them.'

A shadow fell over Jo's eyes. 'Right. I will see you later. Mustn't get agitated and open any wounds.'

As he was leaving, Mark shouted, 'How is Paul? How is the leg?'

Jo was subdued. 'The leg is in plaster, otherwise fine, but . . . *he* is devastated,' and left.

It took a while for Mark to recognise Paul. Clean-shaven, the extremely short hair emphasising his strong cheek-bones, smart clothes, except that a trouser leg had been torn to accommodate the plaster. Just like he used to look and hadn't for a while, only slimmer. It wasn't that Mark had got used to seeing him looking like a savage for ages. Paul was Paul, even with dirt and rags and beard and unkept hair down his back. But there was no Paul looking at Mark from behind those pale blue eyes. They were dead. Did she really mean that much to him? Had she seen him before leaving? Did he know something Mark didn't know? She couldn't just forget about everything that happened and cut off completely. Not Sylvia.

'All right. Tell me the worst,' he said. 'I guessed it anyway.'

'I suppose one would. It took me longer. I just didn't want to believe it.'

Mark was devastated. 'She really isn't coming back, is she?'

Paul's face was working. He looked away. 'Not this time, Mark.'

'You are absolutely sure?'

Paul was now looking at his hands. 'One has to have at least a body for any revival. There is nothing. Not even ashes. They are blown away, I hope into her beloved forest.'

'WHAT THE HELL ARE YOU TALKING ABOUT?'

Paul's head shot up, his eyes enormous with terror. 'Oh my God! You didn't know. You said you have guessed, and I thought . . . Sorry! I'm so sorry! I wanted to break it gently, but I just didn't realise.' He was openly crying now. 'I did it again, Mark. I sent her in the car after all she had said about it.'

Everything was restricting Mark. The stupid drip in his arm, the bandages around his chest, the cast on his leg to stop any movement of the hip. He couldn't breathe. He had to get rid of them.

Paul was fighting him. 'Please, Mark. I don't want to lose you both.'

People came in. People shouting. People trying to hold him down. People sticking needles in him.

How could any of it help?

50

Mark was sitting in bed, staring into mid-space, as he had been for ages. Paul touched his arm. 'You sure you will not come back home? At least until you get better.' He saw the stubborn look, and he shook him. 'No, listen. Then we will both come back.'

'You come and see me often, you hear?' But it sounded unenthusiastic.

'I can't leave you alone. Not like this.'

'I'll be out of bed later today, when they take the cast off.'

'I didn't mean that. You know.'

'I'll be fine,' said Mark, as if tired of saying the same thing over and over, yet it was the first time they had discussed the matter. 'The authorities granted a work permit, and the priest is spreading the word. He says the Indians took fright with all the goings on and the cameras, but when the circus is out of town they will be back. They will bring the sick they cannot cure with their own remedies. It might take a bit of time but they will come. By then, I will have all I need. I'll give you a list. You send everything here. I made contacts with a lot of doctors in this place. They will pass it on.'

Mark talked and talked, but not what Paul wanted him to talk about, what was necessary to talk of. He stared out of the window, feeling selfish. All he was thinking of was himself. How would *he* manage? He had already made all the noise he could with the eyes of the world focused here. All right, he had to keep the momentum. Was that enough?

He had to have something. There was not even a grave. Nobody to grieve with. After the first panic, Mark went into his unemotional mode, and now he got his monastic call at last. What of him?

'You are trying to get rid of me,' he said.

'Paul, I know how to use that medical equipment, but not how to purchase it, get the right people to install it, or even finance it. You have the machinery behind you. People who know people. You can get the job done. One of your firms can dispose of my assets, I'll sign any papers. I don't need to be there.'

'What about Nicol? Do I have to dispose of her as well?' said Paul, his eyes half-closed, a flicker of the old smile on his lips.

Mark sighed. 'Why bother? Tell her she can come and live in the jungle and eat rats and snakes if she so wishes. That should take care of it.'

'That and every dollar disposing of your assets would bring, you dummy,' Paul shouted, suppressed anger suddenly spilling over. 'Then what do you use for equipment, hah?'

'Oh shit!'

'OK' Paul resigned himself to the inevitable. 'I'll open a hospital fund. Put in some money myself and whatever you have, and register it as a charity. That would raise more money and she could not touch it.' He pointed at him. 'You, however, will be bankrupt.'

'I don't need anything.'

Paul threw his arms up in exasperation. 'Bullshit! You will need to be paid a wage from the fund.'

'What for?'

'Because even you will need something. If you spend your time looking after people, you can't go hunting, for instance, or grow your own food. You will need something brought in by plane, with renewed medical supplies and the like. And clothes. You can't go about completely naked. Be real, man!'

Mark tried to smile. 'There. You see how I need you?'

'Right.'

'And Paul, you have to give some money to Nicol, no matter what. It's only fair.'

'Oh boy! She has probably already lined up the next sucker, but if it would make you feel better, of course.'

'Thanks. When are you going?'

'I was thinking...' Paul began and saw Mark eye him warily, '... of going back to the mission. A short visit. Sort of take my leave. You know?'

'I'll come.'

'You are not strong enough yet.'

'I'll come!'

Paul stared at the skeleton of the car. It looked like a Salvador Dali clock. Even so, one could see that the steering column was pushed in so far that, even without the fire, no driver could have survived. The tree was a blackened stump. Rain and wind had polished both. Then a thought occurred to him and he stiffened.

'The rock, Mark,' he said.

Mark frowned at him. 'There is no rock.'

'Precisely. She was wearing it round her neck when she left. Rocks don't get incinerated.'

'What are you saying?' Mark's eyes glistened in that uncanny way of his just for a second. Then the light was extinguished. 'Somebody saw it and took it.'

'I hope not.'

Mark made a gesture of impatience with his hand. 'What use is it to us?'

'It's worth a million.'

'Paul, for Christ's sake!'

'No, listen.' Paul grabbed Mark by the arm. 'If somebody got it, it would be disastrous. If a rumour gets out that stones like that could be found around here, forget preservation. It would be impossible to stop the stampede.' He stared at Mark. 'Have you ever seen an emerald mine in

South America? A muddy great big enormous hell on Earth. No Indians, no hospital, no forest. We have to find it.'

'Suppose the Indians got it. It was theirs. They had it for generations, for all we know.'

'If they have it, fine. We have to find out who has been here straight after the accident. One of the geologists directed the Indians to put out the fire. The police did not come for a couple of days, at least. Nobody has mentioned a stone.' He thought for a while. 'But they wouldn't, would they?'

'It still leaves the Indians first on the list.'

'But we have to be sure. And anyway, not all Indians are like Sylvia's Indian. Some know of the world outside, of the worth of things like that stone. Whoever found it waits for things to quieten down and then tries to sell it.' He shook Mark. 'Somebody has to ask questions. Now. You see?'

Mark looked sceptical. 'And how do we find out?'

'Talk to everybody, starting with the priest. We can trust him. He already knew of the existence of the stone. Then piece together what happened immediately after the accident.'

'You talk to MacIntyre and the others, and I to the Indians with the help of the priest. But they would talk more if they could see some benefit. You go back and send what I have asked for.'

'But this is urgent.'

'Then send the things fast.'

Paul resented the abruptness and Mark's urgency to be rid of him, but this was no time for fighting each other.

The priest was glad to see them. His face was still a mess. Somebody had set the bones of his nose, but it was swollen into a purple blob and rainbow rings radiated from it to the rest of his face. The eyes were only slightly puffed now.

'I did as you have said,' he told Mark. 'They all know you will be here soon.'

'Any customers yet?' said Mark, with what passed for a

humorous voice now, that is, just a fraction more expressive than absolutely flat.

'Early days. They need some proof first. Maybe if you could do anything for that poor child.' He turned towards the shore and called out. 'Maria!' Then he turned to them. 'I call her Maria, I can't pronounce her given name.' And again, 'Maria!'

But Maria was hiding behind a boat, pulled out on the river shore.

'What's the problem?' asked Mark.

'Her arm,' the priest indicated his to show where it had broken. 'I was not here to do anything. I am no doctor, but I can do certain things.' He looked at Mark as if to apologise. 'I had to learn. Somebody made a dreadful job, and it heals badly. Maria!' He gave up. 'Well, you cannot do anything now. When you come next time with some instruments, you get a look at it. Otherwise she will be a cripple. Not a nice thing anywhere. But here . . .' The priest shook his head sadly.

Paul looked around. 'You need a generator. The one left by the geologists is too small for your needs. You have a radio. Where do you think you will keep the rest of the things Mark is talking about? Fridges and X-ray machines and the like. You need a building first.'

'A large tent. A kind of field hospital, to start with,' said Mark. 'And don't get too ambitious, Paul. We can't go about building enormous hospitals, or we might as well make roads and invite everybody to take over the place. If it's to be for the Indians, it has to be a structure that meets just their needs, something they would feel familiar with.'

'A wooden structure on stilts,' said the priest. 'For when the river rises.'

51

Back at the hotel in Manaus, Paul was still reluctant to leave, probably because he was denied the chance to play at detectives, Mark thought.

'I will not have all that much to do, other than ask questions,' Mark said. 'I will let you know anything I uncover, and then you can take over. You are better at persuading people to do what you want.'

Paul stared at him in this peculiar way he had of late. Mark knew that he expected him to show more feeling about her death. To discuss it. But he couldn't. What good would it do anybody?

'There is nothing I can do, Paul,' he said.

'There is.' Paul seemed to hesitate for a bit. 'Just, well . . . don't exclude me,' he whispered, looking away from Mark.

'I said, the moment I found out anything . . .'

'No, Mark.' Paul's eyes shone unnaturally. 'I mean from your grief. It's not just yours.' He pointed with both hands at his chest, almost violently. '*I* grieve and, unlike you, I can't survive bottling it up. I can't sublimate it by doing good or punishing myself with hardship. I need to express it. I need to share it. But only with somebody who knows.' He brushed his nonexistent fringe out of the way with both hands. 'I even tried to speak on the phone to her husband, for fuck's sake! Nothing doing. In his mind, he had buried her last year. He is getting on with his life now.' He let his arms fall by his side in despair. 'There is nobody else.'

It was unbearable looking at Paul like that, listening to

the anguish in his voice, and right now he couldn't run away. But if he let go, *he* would fall apart.

Paul came closer and then suddenly threw his arms around him.

Mark went rigid. What to do? His arms hung uselessly by his side for a long time then slowly, for nothing better to do, put them around the shaking shoulders and it didn't feel wrong. It didn't feel wrong, at all. Nor did the tears running down his own eyes.

He held Paul closer, tight enough to crush him.

Mark asked to see the little girl with the broken arm. All the children were orphans, it seemed. The adults left with their families after the trouble, leaving behind only the unwanted. There were one or two bad tummy upsets, more eye infections, some runny noses. All that was needed was some good food, vitamins and antibiotics.

'She is so frightened,' the priest said, offering him a chair set under a tree.

'I suppose,' said Mark, 'with all the trouble here, they are all nervous.'

'She, more than most,' sighed the priest. 'I said nothing, because it would make no difference to your poor friend. I only found out after the inquiry had finished.' He waved a hand. 'Why open wounds?'

Mark's heart skipped. 'My friend?'

'Well, yes. Maria thinks she caused the lady to have the accident. I say no, it was God's will.' The priest crossed himself.

'Why does she think that, Padre?' asked Mark lightly, but he knew what the answer would be. Sylvia had had nightmares about it.

'Maria was hit by the car. She must have been playing in the road. She was only just lifted off the ground, and she broke her arm on landing. The car couldn't have been going very fast.' He pulled a chair for himself but carried on standing, holding it by the rough wooden back. 'From what the child told me, I pieced it together. The lady veered off onto the tree and killed herself. Then the car caught fire.' He pointed over his shoulders, indicating the child. 'She told nobody but me. She trusts me.' He looked at Mark. 'Maybe I shouldn't have told you. You seem upset.'

'It's OK, Padre. It wasn't the child's fault. But would it be possible to talk with her?'

'There is nothing more, and she is so scared.'

Mark searched into his pockets for the sweets he kept for the children he treated at the Mission. 'Give her these. Tell her she has nothing to be afraid of.'

The priest went in search of the child. She came out of a hut shyly and then hid behind his cassock. The priest kept talking and walking slowly towards Mark. The child followed.

'What do you want to ask?' said the priest.

Mark remained sitting so as not to let his height intimidate the child even more. 'Was there anybody else near the car when it had the accident?' he said.

The priest stared. 'Do you have any reason to believe anybody else had something to do with it?'

'No, Padre. But Paul said the Indian followed Sylvia when she left the church. He might have seen what happened. He might have . . . I don't know.' But he could guess. The Indian saw the car catch fire. He knew Sylvia wore the stone. All he had to do was to wait and pick it up later. In that case all was well. No need to worry about it.

The priest bent down to question the child. 'Yes. The Indian was there,' he said, straightening up.

'Did he stay until they put out the fire?'

Some more questioning of the child. The priest became agitated. The child made to bolt. He prevented her. She started to whimper. He spoke reassuringly but held on to her.

Mark was getting impatient. What did the child say to upset the priest? What worst thing could have happened than Sylvia dying behind the wheel? Oh, God! Let it be that she was dead before the fire. It would be so awful if she had been burnt alive. Oh, please!

He spoke unsteadily. 'What did she say?'

The priest was pale. 'The Indian run away, but . . .'

'WHAT?' Mark couldn't stand the tension any more.

'With . . .'

'With what? The emerald?'

The priest crossed himself and brought his hand to his lips. 'The body.'

Absolute silence. Mark was hardly breathing.

'God forgive me,' said the priest. 'If I thought of asking properly before, we would have known. Found the body and give it a Christian burial. Now . . . after so many days.' He threw his arms up in despair. 'But if I saw the Indian again, he might tell me where the remains are. I recognise the importance of a grave. Somewhere to pray, somewhere . . .'

Mark interrupted. 'How can the child be sure she was dead?'

The priest was startled. 'I never thought of that, either.' He slapped his forehead. He turned to the child. She talked through tears, moving one thin arm limply to indicate lifelessness, her other arm, twisted pathetically, hung by her side.

'The child thinks she was dead. She said she was all . . . broken.' He thought for a while. 'Do you think it possible she is alive?'

Mark's heart was racing wildly. She must have caught the wheel in her chest. Anyone sitting in that seat would have. Could she live? It depended whether the broken ribs punctured the lungs or not. He dared not hope. With proper medical treatment, instantly undertaken, maybe. Out there, after so many days . . . 'I don't know.' After a little thought. 'Have you seen the Indian since the accident?'

The priest shook his head. 'No. He hides with his tribe for a long time. Then he appears. Nobody knows where to look for him. Never in the same place. They go where there is food, new game. One bit of the forest gets exhausted quickly. They move to another.'

Mark was thinking fast. 'If we asked help from the police or the army . . .'

The priest shook his head again. 'You'll never find him.'

'I thought so. I have to look by myself.'

'Look where?' said the priest.

'Where we came from,' said Mark. 'Beyond the falls. The Indian will find me, if he realises I am looking for him. He had always found us, when we needed him.'

First he should fly back to Manaus for medical supplies. No need to alert anyone. He would say he had patients and couldn't wait for his own to arrive from America. Then he would go back to the falls. He couldn't tell anyone else, or it would become some macho government thing and the Indians would get scared and hide deeper into the forest.

52

'But the Indian had potions,' said Paul into the mouthpiece, once he recovered from the shock of Mark's long-distance news.

'You can have potions for infections and all sorts of things,' explained Mark patiently, 'but not broken bones or punctured lungs.'

Paul wasn't letting go of hope. 'He cured your shoulder.'

'It was inflamed, not broken.'

'We can make it quicker and easier with mountaineering equipment,' said Paul.

'I can't wait for you, Paul. I have to set off right away.'

'I will be there, before you get your things together. You can't do this alone. I am coming. If you set off without me, I am still coming.'

'I'll meet you at the falls. The priest will get you there.'

As a rule Paul never received calls while in a board meeting, but since his return he had given instructions that any of Mark's calls should be put through to him whatever, whenever. Now everyone around the table stared as he got up.

'Sorry, ladies and gentlemen,' he said. 'I have some business to attend to right away.'

He could see his secretary becoming apoplectic. She'd sort it out, like she always did with all the messes he got her into. He left the boardroom before she could say anything and he could hear the clip, clop of her high heels as she gave chase down the corridor.

'I'll make it up to you one of these days Jessy, believe

me,' he said over his shoulder. Then he heard the thump. 'Oh, not again!' he said turning round.

She had thrown her file on the floor, just as he had guessed, and stood, arms folded under her ample bosom. 'That's it! I resign! NOW!'

She was encased in a mid-length dress-coat that fitted like a glove. Beneath the bosom she tapered to a narrow waist, to flare again but to a more restrained degree at the hips before the long, long descent down the legs to end in those ridiculously high sandals. Well, when one had taste, one extended it to everything, including a secretary. And this one had an awful lot of common sense under the deceptively bimbo-like blonde rinse.

'Can't it wait until I come back?' Paul said.

'And how do I know when that would be? Last time it took almost a year.'

Paul sobered. God knew what would happen and if he would make it back, at all. The Indians might not take kindly to white men taking potshots at them, and seek revenge on anyone. Sylvia would not be at hand to intercede this time.

'Jessy, I never needed you more in my life,' he said. 'Take care of this for me. If I don't make it back, the money goes into the fund. Not my fucking parents. Remember?'

Her blue eyes grew enormous. 'Mr Alexander, sir...'

'Please, Jessy, there is no time. Please?'

'Yes, sir!'

He blew her a kiss. 'That's my gal!'

Coming out of the building, he run into Jo, Mark's son. The boy had been laying in wait for him the last few days, asking about when Paul would be sending things to Mark, or going himself and could he come, too, he had promised his father and it was vacation and it would be just so cool if ... etc. etc.

'Not now, Jo,' Paul said. 'I'm leaving straight away.'

'Are you going to see Mark?'

'Yes, but I can't take you with me. Not this time.'
'Why?'
'We are not ready yet. There is nothing there, and there is something your father and I have to do, and you will only be in the way.' Paul kept walking towards his car while talking, and the boy skipped impatiently after him.

'I don't expect everything installed before I go. I want to help set things up. I can rough it. I camped with Dad many times.' Paul was now in the car and closing the door. Jo was hanging onto it. 'Please, Paul, I will be no trouble.'

Paul wavered, but just for a second. It would be too dangerous, and anyway Mark would murder him if anything befell the boy. 'No!'

Jo became defiant. 'If you two cripples could manage, why can't I? You might need somebody around the place to hold your crutches up.'

That was absolutely true. Mark was talking of scaling the falls, but they were both almost cripples, like Jo had said. Just out of plaster casts.

'He'll kill me,' he said.

Jo realised he was getting somewhere, and his eyes shone. 'You'll not regret it, Paul. You see.'

'Oh, get in!' And as Jo nearly fell over himself to do just that, Paul tried the last bit of insurance he could think of. 'What of your mother? What does she have to say about all this?'

Jo looked triumphant. 'She doesn't give a shit, as long as I am out of her way.'

'You drive?' Paul moved over for Jo to sit behind the wheel of the sports car.

'Yes sir! Mr Alexander Jr, sir!' He caressed the wheel. 'Gee!' He got in gear. The Jaguar shot forward. 'Wheee!'

'Can you keep it steady? I have to make some calls for equipment we need to take with us. I want to be alive to collect them.'

'I have my camping gear and Dad's.'
'Done any climbing?'
'What, trees? Like you did, you mean? No problem.'

'Yes problem, and keep your eye on the road. Those babies have no side branches for hundreds of feet, but I didn't mean that. I meant cliffs.'

Jo looked at him. 'I did some abseiling. Why?'

'Look out! How long have you been driving, did you say?'

'Oh, months. I drive Mark's car since he doesn't need it now . . .'

'Your Dad's car is sedate, like him. This is different. OK?'

'Yes, sir! Are we going climbing?'

'We are. I don't know about you.' Paul steadied the wheel himself. 'Up the waterfalls, and with any luck, down again.'

'Jeesus! I saw those guys. They are no joke. And all that water around. It would be fun, though!'

'That's the last thing it will be. You saw them with binoculars from downriver, right?' He didn't wait for a reply before ringing up his order. 'By the way,' he turned to Jo, 'what size boots does your father take?'

'I don't know. He has them made. Can't find the right size.'

'Oh, great! Do you think Nicol threw all his things out, or could we rescue some sport gear?'

'All that sort of thing I keep in the cabin. You know. Where Mark and I go fishing and sailing, that sort of thing. It's just ours. Nothing to do with Nicol and Mum.' He just missed climbing on the pavement and waited to steady the car before continuing. 'I even took all his football things there and everything else I thought of when . . . You know? They said that he was lost or dead.'

'Did you believe he was dead, Jo?'

'No, sir! I know Dad. He never gives up.'

'Well, he is not giving up now. He is going after her.'

'Who?'

'Sylvia. He found evidence that she might, well, just might, not be dead. He pretends he is going only to retrieve remains or find out for sure what happened, but he hopes, and so do I that she might be alive, somewhere out there. She doesn't give up easily, either.'

'I thought he said it was her fault and there was nothing he could do, last time we spoke.'

'What the hell are you talking about? Anyway, he doesn't like people to know how much he cares. Has he ever told you he loves you?'

'No. But he does things.'

'There you are.'

Jo seemed to be thinking for a while. 'How do you mean, he cares? More than you?'

'No.'

'Good. I don't want to get rid of one stepmother and get another. If she is alive, that is.'

'I couldn't guarantee that. If she is alive, that is.'

'You sure make no sense.'

'Well. She turned me down, but as far as I know, she hasn't turned down Mark yet.'

'Turned *you* down? You mean you are both interested in that way? What is she? Some kind of sex goddess?' He laughed. 'An Amazon?'

Paul chuckled. 'Not that you could tell, at first sight.'

'Like I know what you are talking about, hah?'

53

Mark thought Paul had overdone it. Nobody could call them unprepared now. Stout boots, the most sophisticated and up-to-date climbing gear, survival kits, machetes, hunting knives and guns, two-way radios, insect repellent, mosquito nets, even a hip flask of bourbon, in case. Who was to carry the darn stuff? It was hard enough unloading it off the boat at the base of the falls.

Mark had tried to persuade Jo to stay with the priest back in the boat and come to pick them up on their return. They would radio him and if, by any chance, they couldn't, he could come every so often to check that they had made it down.

'No,' said Jo. 'The priest can do that. You two need someone whole, in case of an accident.'

'It's no use getting angry,' said Paul. 'He is only taking after you in stubbornness.'

And here they were, on the spot where Sylvia had fallen.

'We might have buried her,' said Paul. 'Can you imagine that?'

'No,' said Mark. 'Not before decomposition began. I wouldn't have let her disintegrate in front of our eyes, but when nothing happened after the first day, I began to hope.'

'You bastard!' said Paul. 'You never said.'

'I was not sure. And if in a coma, she could have lasted only a little longer unless we got her to a life-support machine. Even then, one could not say when she would get out of it, if ever.'

Compared to the way they had climbed down, abseiling with the right equipment was a piece of cake, though Mark's hip troubled him and he was sure Paul was not too happy with his leg. Jo was having a great time.

The sun had set by the time they found a place to camp above the falls. No need for Mark to wrestle with caymans. Paul shot one. He could tell where the animal was from the yellow eyes shining at them in the darkness. If there were any Indians around, they would be in no doubt of their presence.

Mark sat by the fire, watching the insects swirling above it like she used to. He felt her all around him. In the air he breathed, in the gurgling of the water in the distance, in the sighs and groans of the forest, in the shadows. He heard her voice urging him to fly. He groaned with the need of her. *Where are you, my love?*

Before the sun rose, before he could see anything clearly, he knew they were not alone. There was no noise. Just a presence. He was tense but waited patiently. With the dawn light creeping on, a figure emerged from the swirling mist. It advanced towards him. Something caught a slanting ray from the rising sun. There was a green spark. Whoever was coming was wearing the emerald. He held his breath. The shadow resolved into the Indian he had met before. The one that spoke English.

He nudged Paul and Jo. They sat up.

'You come,' the Indian said. He pointed at Paul's gun, lying next to the extinct fire. 'That, good.' He bent down to pick it up.

The priest had told them that if they were to give

anything to the Indians, they had to ask for something in return, or they would be taken for fools. Mark put his hand on the gun.

'What will you give me?' he said.

The Indian motioned with his hands, and three more Indians came out of the mist. He said something to them. There was a bit of an argument, and one reluctantly put down an arrow with bright feathers worked into the tail. It looked very pretty. Jo was about to take it.

'Leave it,' said Mark. He turned to the first Indian. 'I want to know about the white woman.'

The Indian frowned. 'You don't like arrow?'

'It's very nice.'

'The arrow for the gun,' he said. 'My friend will be angry, you no like arrow. He made.' Then he pointed at the machete. 'Give me knife and you come.' He picked up the machete and started for the trees.

They all followed. No time to pick up all their belongings, but it was second nature for Mark to grab his medical kit. Jo took a rucksack that hadn't been unpacked, and Paul the remaining gun.

To keep up with the Indians they had to walk fast, even Mark with his long legs. They got deeper and deeper into the forest, away from the riverbank. No time for marking, to know how to return.

Mark lost count of how long they walked. Hours. Then they entered a clearing. There was a mount of freshly dug ground and a cross. The Indian pointed.

'I saw priest.' He pointed at himself proudly. 'I made.'

Mark was numb. He didn't know what he had expected. He had seen the steering wheel. There was no possibility of her coming from behind it alive.

Paul went very pale and sat down. 'No point in going any further,' he said when the Indian started to walk again.

Mark agreed and sat down too.

'Come! Come,' the Indian urged. His companions were already out of sight. He came up to Mark and pulled him by the sleeve. 'You doctor. You come.'

Mark got up. At least he could be of some use to somebody. Behind him Jo and Paul followed, like him at a slower rate. There was no urgency, anymore. But then they realised that they would be lost if they let the Indian out of their sights and started trotting again.

They heard the noise of people moving around and talking before they got to the next clearing. They came upon several huts made of palm leaves, scattered around any old how. A fire was blazing, and near it some people sat on a prostrate tree, drinking out of frothing gourds or eating. Some were lying in hammocks strung from a central pole under an umbrella made of wood and branches and poles forming the open walls of the hut. Women and children stood at the opening of more completed huts. Everyone stared at them.

Mark was out of breath. Jo and Paul had already collapsed by the fire. Somebody gave them something to drink. He accepted a gourd too. He didn't care what it was. It tasted sour and rather alcoholic. Not the best preparation for seeing a patient. A young woman with red facial markings and little pointed breasts gave him some manioc. He had it at the Mission. It was the local staple food. Bland but nutty and satisfying. But where was the patient or patients? Nobody seemed in any hurry.

The English-speaking Indian squatted by his side. He wanted to know if he mended bones. Mark told him about the little girl with the broken arm. Ah, yes. He had heard about that. He patted Mark on the shoulder. 'Good!' and went away.

Mark wished to do whatever he was fetched to do quickly and go, but he didn't want to show his frustration at the delay. They depended on the Indians to get back, and it wouldn't do to upset them. Anyway, it was too late to return now, and they probably had to spend the night here.

'What are we going to do about the grave?' Paul said when he rested.

'We can't very well dig her up,' Mark said.

'Why not?' said Paul. 'It has been done before.'

'The Indian was not likely to have used a box, and . . .'

'I get the picture,' said Paul, grimacing as if in pain. 'We can mark the place and come to visit it from time to time, until . . .' he balked.

Mark completed the sentense brutally. '. . . the bones are cleaned up.' But he too balked at being precise. It wouldn't be just a skeleton, but a pathetic pile of broken bones. He knew what a steering column could do when pushed that far with such force.

The Indian came back and was trying to get them into a hut. Mark gathered he wanted to show them their sleeping quarters.

It was very dark inside, but when his eyes adjusted he could make out hammocks radiating from a central pole. If he could get either Jo or Paul to take the opposite one to his, he wouldn't mind going to bed. He was tired. There was no hope he would actually sleep but he could rest his aching hip.

A parrot squawked and Mark turned to look at it. A child was standing at the back of the hut with the parrot perched on its shoulder. Mark was startled. He had seen him before, though he couldn't remember where. Something else stirred in the shadows, behind the boy. Some animal. Another pet.

Paul must have noticed it too because he squatted down and peeked into the darkness. Then Mark heard a scream, like a wild animal in pain, and saw Paul retreating on all fours, his face a mask of terror.

In spite of the crazy tattoo of his heart against his ribcage, Mark advanced. He first made out the pair of feverish eyes, then the taut yellow skin, and took a step or two backwards, in disbelief.

'Maybe I shouldn't enter a beauty competition just yet.' Her voice was just above a whisper. He could hear her breath in short shallow gasps, between groups of words.

Mark was on his knees now, like Paul, and made to put his arms around her but she raised a shaky hand. 'Don't! I am held together rather precariously. I'll fall apart.'

He didn't know what to say. 'Are you in pain?' he said, as if he needed to be told.

'Only when I breathe,' she said.

Mark just touched her hair gingerly, as if even that could cause her pain. 'Your ribs?'

'Mm!'

'I saw the wheel,' Mark said. 'It's a miracle it did not crush you completely.'

'I was not behind the wheel,' she said.

Paul found his voice. 'Who was driving the car, then?'

'I did,' she said. 'I fell off the seat. I was squeezed under it and broke a few ribs. No big deal. It just hurts a lot.'

Mark was unashamedly sobbing. 'All this time, my love. All this time.'

With two grown men crying all over her, she was getting embarrassed. She flicked a hand to show how unimportant it all was. 'Oh, most of it I was drunk or drugged.'

Mark fumbled in his bag and came out with a syringe. 'No more drugs, please!' she begged. 'I tell you what. I'll settle for whisky. I hope you did not come all this way without it. I'll never forgive you.'

Paul produced his hip flask. She smiled. 'What? No glass?' But she took a swig and wiped her mouth with the back of her hand. 'Ah! Nothing like the feel of it burning its way, all down the back of your throat. So sensuous. Pity it's not real whisky.'

'Bourbon, sorry,' said Paul.

'I'll forgive you, just this once,' she said. 'And remember the glass next time. Lead crystal cut into the shape of a thistle.'

Paul laughed.

She let Mark inject the painkiller in the end. It was the only way to move her. 'Brave girl,' Mark said.

'Nothing to do with bravery. I had to make it. I promised the children I'll go back.' She turned to Paul. 'Has anyone seen them?'

'I did,' said Paul. 'Happened to be passing by. You know?'

She gave a laugh that turned into a cough and gasped with pain.

'They are fine,' Paul said quickly, to stop her putting herself out to ask. 'They are going to a residential school. It's the only way Ian could manage. They said they didn't want to go when you were there, and that you had promised they never would. When you were gone, it didn't seem such a bad idea, and now they like it. They made lots of friends and might even come to America during vacation. Ian doesn't mind. I think he . . .' then he stopped.

'It's OK,' she said. 'He thought I was dead. He wouldn't have, otherwise,' and after a rest, 'I hope she suits him better,' she smiled mischievously, 'and that she wears jeans and sensible shoes and drinks beer. He tried for years to make me do it.'

'Unsuccessfully, I hope,' said Paul.

She swayed, and her eyelids were getting heavy. 'Bloody right,' she said.

Mark didn't put his trust in a simple pain killer. She was going under, but not before she noticed Jo.

'Somebody lend me a shirt,' she said. 'I wear nothing under all this hair. Don't want to shock the eaglet.'

54

Jo thought everything in this place was crazy.

He had expected nothing less than Zena the Warrior Princess and found a wizened, brokendown little thing that kept calling him 'the eaglet'. His father and even Paul, for Christ's sake, were fussing around her like mother hens. She had been patched up, bandaged into a parcel, and after a day of rest and a lot of drink all around, they carried her on a makeshift stretcher.

All right! His father was a doctor and wanted to be in charge of his patient. But Paul? Since when had he done things for himself rather than delegate? He wouldn't let the Indians help. He carried the stretcher with Mark. The kid with the parrot wouldn't leave her side, either. He jogged along beside the stretcher for hours.

When they stopped to camp in the afternoon, Mark and Paul acted in unison. Nobody said you do this, I'll do that. They just went and did it, as if through secret communication. Then Paul tied up a rope around himself and climbed up a tree. To brew beer? Mark went up another to gather fruit. What for? They had provisions.

The Indians had their own way of climbing. They tied their feet with vines and up they went. They raced Paul and Mark. Beat them to it. It all seemed so easy, and Jo was younger and fitter, so why not try? He couldn't get anywhere. Who was the cripple now?

The kid with the parrot was sitting next to Sylvia, and they both just stared at each other. When he came down, Mark said they were talking. Right! Neither had said a word.

The beer Paul made was absolutely disgusting. Jo had a tin of Coke from his rucksack while watching them make fools of themselves. The Indians had their own drink and they offered it freely around, but Jo had been told how it was made. He had no desire to drink anyone's spittle. He was amazed that neither Paul nor Mark bothered about it at all.

Mark and Paul were supposed to be different, right? Everyone said so. They didn't look it now. Somehow Paul was a little more serious, a little less talkative. Mark was more lighthearted and less quiet. They sort of met. She talked weird and they seemed to understand. Talked back the same. They had secret codes. Eagles, pumas, pacas, chiefs and Indians. Considering how old these guys were, it was downright embarrassing.

'Why didn't you let us know sooner?' Mark had asked the moment he thought she was strong enough to talk, after the ordeal of having her ribcage readjusted.

'They wanted to see if the puma and the hawk did all the things the shaman had promised they would do, before letting the paca go,' she said.

'Have you lost your powers of beaming?' asked Paul

'I beamed my head off,' she said. 'The reception must have been inadequate.'

'I was picking up something,' Paul said. 'Just not clear enough. How else would I keep hoping, in spite all the evidence to the contrary.'

'But the shaman is your friend,' said Mark. 'Why keep you as a hostage?'

'He is dead,' she said. It obviously pained her even more than her broken ribs. 'The others needed proof, before they respected his wishes.'

'The grave in the forest?' asked Mark.

She nodded. 'He was wounded in the church and didn't say a thing about it. He thought I had to be taken to safety first. It was too late by then.'

'We thought it was yours,' said Paul. 'The shaman was not a Christian, was he?'

'Of course not, but Chico saw the priest make graves like that, and he thought why not.'

'Chico is the Indian who speaks English, I suppose,' said Mark. 'Is he the new chief?' For someone who didn't like drinking, he was not doing badly with whatever the Indians were offering.

'No, I am,' she said.

Paul choked on his drink and Mark started giggling.

'That solves all our problems,' said Paul when he recovered. 'If you are officially the chief, then we must be Indians.'

She threw the drink all over him and he rolled around laughing.

Mark said between hiccups, 'If you are the chief, where is your seal of office? I'm not becoming an Indian without some proof.'

'I gave the stone to Chico,' she said. 'He is deputy chief until I get better.'

Paul sobered. 'Are you coming back?'

'Of course. Until Chico's son grows up, at least' and she pointed at the boy with the parrot.

Paul started to laugh again. 'You will be a missionary?'

'Don't be silly. The only interest I have in their souls is that they have bodies to keep them in.'

'I thought that was Mark's job,' said Paul. 'You heard he is the Mission doctor now?'

'Ah, well,' she said, not surprised in the least. 'I will supervise him too. And the priest. I am sure he does a lot of good and means well, but like my Father Confessor told me when I was a child, it's the same God everywhere, whatever you call it. I wish missionaries saw it that way.' She became excited. The drink, maybe. 'Why should the Indians become Christians? What does a Jew on a cross have to do with them?' She held a small gourd with drink in one hand, but the other came into a life of its own.

Mark was trying to restrain her. 'Keep still,' he kept saying, 'you will undo all my hard work.'

She was not to be quietened. 'God made us in his own image?' she asked Mark and then went on and answered it herself. 'What a lot of bull! We make God in our image. Vengeful people have a vengeful god, bloodthirsty ones a bloodthirsty god, and so forth. The Indians have the forest spirits. Why not? I am sure God couldn't care less.'

'You seem sure there is a God,' said Paul.

'Not what most people mean by it. Energy, maybe. It's constant throughout the universe, everything comes from it and goes back into it. As far as I remember the description of God – everpresent, alpha and omega – is not all that different. Most people like to give it anthropomorphic qualities. If it helps them, who am I to deny them their comfort?'

Now that they had reached the bottom of the falls and everybody was busy setting up camp, Jo thought maybe he should thank her for saving his father's life, and Paul's, of course. Looking at her and them, it didn't seem very likely, but Paul had insisted it was so.

'If I had passed them by and didn't help, I would be bad,' she said. 'If I helped, I am great. Under what circumstances would I be normal?'

She had a point. 'All the same . . .'

'Now you are all saving my life, should I be grateful?'

'I suppose it would be up to you.'

'Well, I am not!' She moved her head in a way one associates with tossing hair. Habit, Jo supposed, for now she was bald as an egg. Mark shaved her hair off. He said he had no choice. It was full of creepy crawlies. 'You should all be grateful to me,' she continued, 'for giving you the chance to play heroes. Do you think an opportunity like this comes easy in a pedestrian, modern world?'

She was teasing, of course, but Jo had no quick answer.

She patted him on the hand. 'I will tell you a secret you

have probably guessed at. I didn't save them.' Jo wished he never blushed so easily, but she just winked at him. 'The Indians did,' she continued. 'They saved me too, of course, but that was not the main object. I am the proverbial mosquito on a bull's horn. Whether I am in or out of the forest, dead or alive, it's neither here nor there.' She must have noticed his surprise and explained patiently, as if he were an idiot, 'Paul could protect this part of the forest if he was made to hang around long enough to get to appreciate it, and your father could save the lives of the Indians. If the Indians helped me, it was to bring that about.'

'But they must like you. They made you a chief.'

'That would keep me here for some time. Paul and Mark, still grateful to me, would hang around too. Otherwise, they might have done their bit and gone home, and everything would go back to where it was. On a knife edge. Far-reaching policy for savages, don't you think?'

'Do you believe they have actually worked it all out like this?'

'Maybe not, but their instinctive behaviour had the same effect. They didn't kill us, and here we are: all working for them.'

Jo thought for a while. 'I don't know whether to do Medicine like Dad, or Biology, but I want to work here too,' he said and hoped she wouldn't laugh at him.

'Of course, you do,' she said, as if it was the most natural thing on earth.

Paul and Mark were back.

'The priest will be here by tomorrow,' said Mark.

Paul sat next to Sylvia. 'So you will not stay in America after you recover?'

'America?' Sylvia said, amazed. 'What do I need to go to America for, in the first place?'

'This is only a temporary job,' said Mark. 'You need X-rays and a lot of care. I would be able to look after you better over there.'

'I thought you work here now,' she said.

343

'Paul would let me have leave of absence,' Mark said, winking at Paul. 'He finances the operation, after all.'

'But I have to see my children,' she said.

'I will bring the kids to you,' said Paul.

'I still have to come back here,' she said. 'There will be so much to do. I have it all planned out.' Paul rolled his eyes, and she ignored him. 'Besides the welfare of the Indians,' she continued,' there are all these plants to collect, illustrate, identify, find out what the Indians use them for. Before the forest disappears.' For a moment she became sad. Mark took her hand. 'We are not going to hold back what they call progress for ever,' she said. 'We have to be realistic. We can delay it, that's all.' She cheered up. 'I will write a book about herbal medicine in the Amazon and illustrate it myself.'

'I thought you were ready for a bit of luxury. You stay here with him, and you say goodbye to all that,' said Paul.

'Oh, no,' she said. 'I will appreciate it even more when I visit you. I will let you spoil me rotten. Anyway, I am led to believe you move about a lot. No matter where we are, you would be coming and going.' She shook a finger at him. 'And don't forget you have promised me dinner in Paris sometime.' She placed a hand on her bandaged chest. 'And I promise to show you paradise.'

'I thought you already had,' said Paul.

'The Aegean,' she said, ignoring his smirk, and spread her arms around to encompass an imaginary landscape, though wincing with pain. 'The whole of the Mediterranean, in fact, and Mark will have to find some young doctor in search of adventure before he settles down, to act as a locum, from time to time. He says he has never visited Siena or Florence or Athens . . .'